SPARK CITY

BOOK ONE OF THE SPARK CITY CYCLE

ROBERT J POWER

DEPAOR PRESS

SPARK CITY
First published in Ireland by DePaor Press in 2018.
ISBN 978-1-9999994-0-7

Available in eBook, Audiobook, Paperback and Large Print Paperback

www.RobertJPower.com

For Rights and Permissions contact:
Hello@DePaorPress.com

CONTENTS

For Jan.

Without you, I could never have written a line, and without you, I never would have wanted to.
You are my muse, you always have been.

Samara
Spark City, City of Light

The Great Mother

Mer and Jeroen
Danger Abord

Dead Town

Rock of Erroh

Raxt's Nest

There's No River Here

Raven Rock

Just a Strain Not a Town

Cathbar

Sands of Adawan

Beginning of the Skyroad

And Erroh's

SIGI'S MAP
This is as accurate a representation as you'll find in these wastes

1

ERROH

"My friends call me Erroh." He grinned.

"I'm not your friend." Wrek pointed his sword menacingly in the smoky air. This was going wonderfully.

Cards were always a weakness for Erroh. He loved the slow tantalising progression of a great hand played out perfectly, the unknown outcome of the game as the first card was dealt and the mystery of players and their participation. What they brought to the table and what absence was felt when they left the game. Accomplished card players never revealed any obvious details until the game reached its epic conclusion. Sometimes it was not about winning the hand. Sometimes it was about the journey itself.

Erroh's head was spinning from the smoke billowing out from a scorched fireplace in the corner of the dimly lit tavern. He could smell the matured odour of a thousand former clients and the sweetness of fresh sawdust concealing unwelcome wastes under his feet, but mostly he could smell the liquor that stood at attention in a clear goblet in front of him. He knew he must be on his fifth glass already, or maybe his ninth. His heart was beating out of rhythm, and he was feeling right at home.

"You dealt from the bottom and I've had enough!" cried the behemoth with the sword whose tip remained steady, lingering menacingly close to his forehead. The world had slowed down, and Erroh's stronger arm began to itch. His sword lay snugly in its scabbard, hanging on his chair behind him. It may as well have been a mile from his reach. He liked when the world slowed down. It gave him a few moments to formulate plans, simple plans, which never worked.

Across from the gambling table, the outburst had disturbed the innkeeper Sigi from his stirring.

"Don't deny it or I'll have your pelt. Maybe I'll have it anyway." Blood was in the air.

Far off in the distance thunder began to rumble through the forest-covered valleys. The last of the sun's rays disappeared under the horizon and the final flickers of natural light escaped through the one grubby, cracked window of "The Rats Nest Tavern". Broken picture frames adorned the walls, the art they once held lost a lifetime ago. Perhaps several lifetimes. Who was counting?

Erroh hated thunder. He had discovered that loud noises brought very bad things. He hated bad things. In truth, he hated a great many things, such as drunken wretches, swords in his face and accusations of cheating. Most of all he hated being caught cheating.

Erroh offered a smile, raising both his hands in the most neutral gesture he could muster. "A mere misunderstanding between comrades of the road." He wondered if his opponent wandered the wastes like himself, or was the tall warrior weighed down by a mate and a life of boredom. Erroh didn't want a mate. He reminded himself of this almost every day. He was far too young, having been born in the last year of the

2

"Faction Wars," almost two decades ago. To many, he had just come of age. To some, he still had a great deal to learn. The weapon's tip came a little closer and grabbed his attention.

Two farmers dressed in their finest work clothes sat at the table in stony silence watching the events unfold. They were not part of this fight. They held their cards close to their chests, eager to live through the oncoming storm. The volatile atmosphere was about to explode and they wanted little part in the fireworks.

Besides, it wasn't their bet.

"I suppose I owe you an apology," admitted Erroh, slowly lowering his trembling hands and letting them lie on the dark brown table.

"You owe me more than that!" Wrek roared. The weapon shifted menacingly with every word.

"Let me buy you a drink and we'll be square," he countered, smiling his best "don't stab me" smile. Many females would swoon at his disarming charms, sharp, attractive features with eyes that dazzled. Wrek was unmoved.

A flash lit up the night sky and for a moment, the room was illuminated.

"My apologies. I offer a drink in reparation." Erroh spoke as if speaking with a dear friend while reaching under the table and flipping open his trouser pocket in one fluid motion.

"What are you doing?" snarled Wrek.

Erroh was scared, but that offered advantages according to his father. Adrenaline could gift a warrior further speed or strength. Not a great deal but sometimes enough to be the difference in battle. His father was always willing to offer advice on such matters. Adrenaline also helped when running away. Erroh had learned that trick all by himself. Unfortunately, Wrek stood between him and the door.

"I'll plead with no man for my life," begged Erroh. With his free hand, he rolled a coin across the old cracked playing table.

"Have a drink," he whispered, disguising the fear in his voice. This was just another way to play a hand. When he played cards, he gave very little away. When faced with a sharp blade, he gave even less away. This moment was taking an eternity. It was all in the lap of the gods. Erroh wasn't quite sure how he felt about the gods. He wondered if they played cards.

The moment ended.

The large figure of Wrek suddenly struck downwards. It sounded like thunder. Cards flew, mugs spilled and goblets shattered. Wonderfully cheated coins took flight as the sword struck the old wooden table leaving a fresh scar upon its surface. One solitary coin spun its last and came to a stop and then silence.

"I will have a drink!" boomed Wrek magnificently.

Erroh breathed a sigh of relief. The night wasn't a complete ruin after all. His glass was lost to him forever but that was a small matter.

Wrek reached across the table. "For my troubles." He grabbed what remained of the little pot of pieces in front of Erroh. They chinked beautifully as he dragged them back through the carnage into his loving embrace where they belonged.

Finally sitting down Wrek adjusted his seat with little grace and stretched out his arm. With one grubby hand, he lifted his chalice and motioned to the barman for his volatile sine. He was a rich man again.

"Don't splash the pot," quipped one of the farmers,

testing the waters and shuffling a fresh hand. Wrek picked up the sword from the centre of the table and sheathed it.

Erroh relaxed. He inhaled softly and calmed himself but his hand remained under the table. He leaned back and stared into the eyes of the big man. Was he wise enough to learn from this? He certainly hoped not. How rewarding could life be if he took the same steps as his father Magnus? His father's steps had been great strides, while his own were far less impressive. He pulled an object from his pocket and threw it violently at the richest man at the table. It flew gracefully like a dagger in the harsh light. Wrek had just enough time to close his eyes before the projectile struck him.

It was no dagger. It was something else entirely.

It was the ace of Queens, the primary card of the deck and it ruled above all others. A card that could guarantee victory if used shrewdly, but catastrophic if lost in a fool's gambit, and a fine card to call upon when all other attacks have failed.

"Will we play again?" asked Erroh, grinning as he returned a second hidden card to the deck. For now, he would play fairly.

"Aye, we will, Erroh." Wrek laughed, taking delight in the younger man's boldness.

This was living on the road. Everything was different out on the road.

———

Erroh opened the doorway and stepped through, into the night. The glorious fresh air brushed up against his face, he took a deep long breath and closed his throbbing, blood shot eyes. After a few seconds, he started to feel human again. He braved a few tentative steps away from the sounds of merriment. His body struggled with simple orders and his mouth was dry, abused from the evening's festivities of beverages and conversations and narrow escapes. He looked around the yard. It was nothing more than a dilapidated wall doing its best to hold off the thick growth of wilderness that spread across all corners of the Four Factions. At the far end of the enclosure, there was a sign that hung from an old wooden post. "Welcome to the Rat's Nest" it said. A welcoming place indeed.

He reached down to his pack and took out a battered metal hipflask. It had been a few days since he had last come upon a stream, but he opened the lid and drank deeply. Immediate relief poured its way down. Draining the contents, he closed his eyes and enjoyed the breeze against his clean-shaven face.

"Where you headed, friend?" Sigi said as he stepped through the doorway carrying a bucket of sawdust. He tossed the waste casually over the wall nearest.

"A little further up the road." The shattered moon's light caught the leaves of the one tree hanging over the perimeter wall. It swayed in the breeze sending eerie, skulking shadows across the courtyard like giant roving fingers. At least the rain had cleared. Erroh never liked sharing sleeping quarters with anyone else. He preferred his solitude out on the silent peaceful road where it was safer.

"Count the stars in the sky, they say," said Sigi, tossing the bucket back through the doorway before walking to an outhouse beside the tavern. With a grunt, he pulled the rusty bolt and the door creaked open.

"Aye, they do." Erroh glanced above and absently counting the little bright dots. It was a habit most wanderers were afflicted with when sleeping out under their gaze. He needed to bathe. He needed to sooth away the aches of the last few day's miles and despite his misgivings, it might be a fine idea not to appear a complete wretch once he reached the city of light.

Erroh began stretching for the walk ahead, a daily routine that he had followed for two lonely years. No longer could he find ways to delay his last march and the dreadful fate about to befall him. Soon he would reach journeys end. Spark City was calling.

Sigi was busy sorting through his treasures. He lit a candle and shined it over the shelves that hung across the wall. He loved the art of trade. His little brewery afforded him the luxury of accepting over-inflated offers. Hidden a half mile from his tavern, only he knew of its existence, a secret he kept wisely. He loved his place in the world. Many people loved his place in the world also, until the following morning.

Sigi was very generous with his sine in dealings. Alcohol was the blood of this world and brewing great yielding alcohol was a fine way to make money. Making money was all he had learned, it was all he had ever needed to learn.

"Are you going to the city?" Sigi asked wiping the dust from the bottle. Breathing over the glass and wiping it a second time, he held it up above his head and looked at it in the moonlight. Satisfied that the fluid was clear and at its most enticing, he walked under the old oak and waited for the opportunity to engage in some trade. He watched patiently as Erroh limbered up.

"I'm headed to The Spark all right," Erroh grunted, touching his toes.

"It's a long way to the city."

"I've come a long way."

"Where have you come from?" Sigi asked, readying himself for the pitch.

"East."

This transaction is going splendidly, thought the tavern owner. Low murmurs from within the Nest interrupted the quiet as the clients dispersed for the night. One of the two farmers stumbled out the door and staggered towards the faded grey stables alongside the tavern, uttering only a muffled profanity after stepping on something unsavoury behind the wall nearest. Nothing more was heard save for the familiar thump sound of a drunken body falling into a mound of hay. That will be an extra few pieces for lodging and some breakfast, thought Sigi cheerfully. He would make eggs.

Wrek would take his usual bed in the sawdust, or behind a wall, anywhere he felt like falling unconscious really. For now, the sound of Wrek singing to one of the picture frames filled the night.

Sigi folded his arms taking the young man in. "Bit of a walk to go. A good sleep will help you on your way. Better to travel in the light as well."

"If it's all the same, the road calls," Erroh replied and bent down to his rucksack, flipped the top button then untied a knot that held the contents. "I suppose I could use some salt." Salt was a staple ingredient in even the blandest meals while walking the road. It also had many other qualities, to those in the know, and it was very expensive.

Sigi produced the small cloth pouch. He handed it to Erroh and allowed him inspect it for rocks.

"What else are you willing to part with?" Erroh asked as he dug into his bag. He pulled out a small purse and unbuttoned the seal.

He presented a small capsule to the innkeeper. A light metal case, two fingers in length, a smooth surface that, when twisted and opened, revealed the most precious commodity in the world.

8

They were ancient words from before.

Sigi stared at the little slip of paper inside. His fingers trembled slightly. He had never seen a lost capsule before, let alone been this close to any scroll of history. Most people hadn't; though they spoke of the great mysteries that each one revealed.

"What else are you willing to part with?" enquired Erroh again.

"I have sine. Plenty of sine," uttered Sigi excitedly. The little sheet of paper had only a few sentences, some words smudged from age and wear but it did not matter. The beautiful letters would likely find a caring home in the Nest.

"I have a map too, a reliable one." Counter-offer made.

Erroh raised an eyebrow. It was amazing the improved quality in merchandise offered when a capsule was involved. His last map had ceased to bear any relevance to his path at least a hundred miles back. The last few weeks he had simply followed the sun, but this close to the end, a map would serve him well. Knowing his luck, he could miss the city by a handful of miles and keep walking north. Would that really be so bad?

"Have you any soaps?" Erroh still had a fair amount of credit to spend.

"I do." Sigi rushed towards the doorway and disappeared inside. It was a generous trade, but Erroh was satisfied enough. From experience, a map was only as good as its locality.

The eager barman returned after a few moments leaving the door swinging behind him. In his hand were some finely bartered goods. Erroh accepted the soaps, the bottle of sine, and the map. His eyes scanned the creased parchment and tried to decipher the crudely drawn lines and oddly marked points. It would suffice, though barely.

"It'll serve you well, as accurate as you'll ever get out here. I made it myself," Sigi whispered knowingly.

"Going to the city, going to get me a family," sang Wrek from inside the tavern. Erroh knew that song; it was not one of his favourites.

He donned his leather vest and tied the buckles tightly. He hated this armour. The weight was restricting and his movement was never as fluid. There was also a flaw along the shoulder. An interior strip of thin metal had fallen away, leaving a fine chink for any wandering arrow to devastate. At the city it would cost a fortune to repair, he would need to hone his skills at cards. He buckled his sword around his waist and picked his pack up.

"At least don't gamble with an Alpha when you reach the gates. Most are bigger and meaner than Wrek," warned Sigi. "More beast than man when angered."

Ah yes, the old glorified fear of Alphalines. Bigger? They were exactly the same size as anyone else. Erroh wasn't going to delay his departure by sharing his thoughts on the matter. Better to agree and perhaps throw in a jest at their expense.

"I've heard they practise on horses before they mate with their own kind," Erroh said grinning and walked from the tavern, his feet silent upon a threadbare muddy path. Somewhere a little farther it led to hollow darkness and an almost endless forest.

"I'd keep those particular jests to myself," called Sigi before returning into the warmth of his tavern to close up for the night. However, not before he joined Wrek in a fine duet, a song about the mysterious trials for those entitled few who made the long walk to Spark City.

2

ROCK

The dawn's rays glinted down through the branches above his head – his tired, spinning head. The leaves rustled softly as each bough rocked gently in the breeze. Throughout the night, he had slipped further from any sign of civilisation, but Erroh was more at ease in this quiet forest than in his own place of birth. There was a serenity to walking in such solitude, embracing the natural world, enjoying the morning air after the musky tavern. He even found a smile forming on his lips until he cracked his left knee against a fallen log.

Pain.

And tearing.

Some stumbling as well.

He fell in a heap and shockwaves coursed through him. They started somewhere around the kneecap and erupted spitefully through his body. Pulsing wet surges of agony with potentially dire consequences. Who would leave a jagged log out here in the middle of "The Wastes" anyway? He had always thought it a curious name for eternal forests of green that covered most Four Factions of the world. It was a title from a different era still used to this day. The Road was the path taken with a taste of civilisation but the Wastes were the glorious freedom of silence and wilderness. Moreover, The Wastes had torn his fuken knee apart.

He instinctively blamed the absent gods, even if he struggled to believe in anything other than his own actions. The absent gods however had quite the faith in him but rarely did they let him know and when they did whisper thoughts in his head, he was disinclined to hear them.

He crawled beneath the branches of an ageless tree to escape the morning heat and rested his head upon one of its gnarled roots. It was a fine place to lament in the quiet and gather his miserable thoughts. When the first wave of pain had passed, he dared an inspection of the wound. A crow above him sat on one of the branches and peered down. He imagined it mocking his clumsiness, a fair criticism, for his knee was a mess.

Blood seeped out through a deep slit in his skin in a steady flow that could lead to unfortunate things if not treated swiftly. The crow had its own opinions on the matter. It began heckling him. Erroh wasn't sure it knew the finer points of a healer's touch. He took a clean rag from his rucksack and poured a few drops of sine into the centre before placing it across the wound. He tied a knot tightly and carefully bent his knee. It would do for the time being, but he knew there would be a cost for such gracelessness.

As the day drew on, the morning breeze dissipated. The sky became a radiant blue; it stretched out magnificently with no blemishes to mar its beauty, and Erroh hobbled slowly through the wilderness in search of a suitable site to camp. Leaning on a sturdy fallen branch, each step he took was painful, but he followed the scribblings of the innkeeper's map and finally he heard the most welcome sound to any wanderer, the beautiful and babbling sound of a stream.

The brook's cool water flowed seductively through the clearing, untainted by the sun's heat, meandering with each crease in the land. Erroh was in love. It expanded into a slow moving pool, and Erroh had his place to recover. Reeds and long grasses grew along the sides, a large willow tree hung out over the water providing wonderful shade. He left his belongings in the long grass within easy reach and carefully he dropped into the water.

Dipping under the surface, he drank deeply. He hadn't realised the thirst he had earned. Lost in pleasure, he let himself float across the still surface, enjoying the gentle drag of the current easing him towards the nearest bank. This was it; this little sanctuary was his new home. He was done. It would be a grand life to live, floating along the banks of this little oasis without unwanted responsibilities. This was a life better suited to him than any Spark City promised. He was happy alone, was he not?

Erroh stripped off his clothes and threw them under the trunk of the tree. Gliding to the edge, he pulled himself out into the scorching dry grass. The water on his body began to evaporate in the heat immediately. He reached down apprehensively to the discoloured tourniquet. Crimson fluid had begun to leak out steadily.

He opened up the little tin and sighed dejectedly. Taking out the needle and thread and some dressing, he poured a few drops of sine into the deep hole, then he poured a few more down his throat. Both caused a great deal of stinging. His arms began to shake as he held the threaded needle. He closed his eyes and took a few deep calming breaths. The first few seconds were the worst. It took him two attempts to break through the skin.

He sat in silence for a while, performing the operation. His resolve was pushed to the edge of madness, and he battled the urge to fall unconscious every few moments or so. He did his best. He never screamed out and his hands stayed firm. Finishing the last disordered stitch, he cut the thread and fell back in the grass. His short black hair was drenched in sweat and involuntary tears sneaked out of his eyes. They did so in silence as he curled up in a ball and held himself until the shivering stopped. He never saw the sleep steal up behind him.

The first drops of rain woke him from his slumber. He opened his eyes, and tentatively got to his feet. The sky had turned from vibrant blue to something far less agreeable. The shattered moon was barely visible in the gloomy night and a deep cold had covered the land where once there had been burning warmth. Retrieving his cloak to stave off the chill he grabbed his pack and damp clothing and shuffled around the clearing searching for shelter. The rising wind blew on his hood and caught the rain as it began to fall heavily. He thought about seeking cover among the trees, but he didn't trust his senses in this light, and besides, they would offer little reprieve from a cutting wind. He cursed his stupidity for not making a camp. The cold crept into his bones and took hold. He pushed on from his wonderful pool into complete darkness, dreaming of finding sanctuary in a little shack or a mossy cave.

What he found was a rock.

It was a very nice rock because it was the only object that could provide any type of cover. He burrowed his frame into the long grass at the foot of the grey boulder, which stood as high as a southern steed, and placed his pack under his head while pulling the heavy cloak over his trembling body. Droplets of rain struck from above, they rolled down his covering and were lost in the grass. There were worse places than under a cloak, protected by rock, to spend a night. He closed his eyes and rubbed his hands. It was something his mother had taught him. Soon enough, there was less a chill running through his body. The sounds of the storm calmed him and after a little time he surrendered to fatigue and fell into a more natural sleep.

At first light, he stuck his head from out under the makeshift cover and tasked himself with assembling his bow. It was a stunning, and useless, bow. In truth, it was useless in his hands alone. To anyone else with the slightest skill at archery, it was quite a treasure. His stomach rumbled as he attached the top arm to the centrepiece, patiently screwing the bolts tightly with its accompanying tool-key. He flipped it upside down and did the same again with the bottom limb. He hated this weapon, and he really hated this process. Grunting, he attached the thick cord securely to each end. Testing the draw and stability, he reached for his quiver. A bow was not a blade. It was a weapon for hunting and little more. Some would agree while others less so.

He hobbled cautiously towards the trees using the grand weapon as little more than a walking staff. As usual, it took a few shots before he downed a bird. He imagined his father's sarcastic comment as he finally made the kill. It would likely involve something about a barn door. It was a fair jest. He felt a pang of regret as he retrieved his meal. A little for the pigeon's life he had taken, more so for the lost arrows. He knew he should practise more, but he just couldn't bring himself to care enough. He was simply no archer.

He gathered some damp twigs and after stripping them of their bark, placed a few in a small triangle. The rest he stripped into delicate strips of kindling. Unlike his skills with a bow, fire-lighting was a natural ability. Such a morning was no test of his skill, but he was not complaining. After a few moments, a spark ignited the tinder beside the miniature tower of twigs and a comforting crackle filled his ear. It helped his racing mind find peace. In the far distance, he saw a thin stream of smoke emanating from behind one of the countless tree-filled rises that shaped the land. He watched the smoke disappear into the blue above. Looking down at his own miniature flames, he turned the little handmade spit expertly. His fire was just as impressive in its own way.

Erroh was stuck here. A prisoner in this beautiful haven until he was certain there was no sign of infection. However if he did spot the first warning signs, he knew that tainted things could be cleansed by fire. He had learned that from his father. Salvaging fallen logs from the forest, he was able to dig a few holes around his rock and wedge them in tightly. With some rope, he tied a long slender branch across both logs. He stripped a few large branches and spread them across the roof of his shelter. It took hours with his injury but by day's end, he had made a perfect little life for himself at "Rock."

Every day was the same, predictable and peaceful. Each morning he would crawl out from beneath his castle, check the stitching for infection, and then bathe in the water. After stretching his muscular body, he would step tentatively into the woods and attempt to hunt a few birds.

In the afternoon he would sit, lost in useless thoughts staring out over the hills watching the smoke in the distance.

The innkeeper's map had a distinctive blotch in that vicinity. Big enough to be a place of interest, yet like every other scribble barring the one, it had no name. Perhaps it was just a stain.

Eventually, restlessness pushed him to unsheathe his sword. In truth, his father would not allow such a thing as a simple wound around the knee to come between his studies of warring. They were fine stitches, they would hold.

He always held "Mercy" in his left hand. Unlike most perfectly adequate swords found out in the wastes, the weapon was a marvel and put many others to shame. Forged many years before the Faction Wars, its steel was near flawless. Its hilt suggested nobility, baring a crest of goat's horns wearing a crown. Its guard was sturdy and bore suggestions of many failed strikes and its body was strong and thick. Erroh kept the edge sharp and well oiled. When held in the sun its finish was capable of blinding.

Aye, a marvellous weapon indeed but in truth, its leathered grip felt wrong in his hand.

Perhaps that was the point.

Careful not to tear his knee apart Erroh always began by spinning the deadly blade in an arc above his head, faster and faster until it was a blur. Without stopping, he dragged the blade to his side. It always looked impressive, extravagant but it was little more than childish bravado. Few however would dare such reckless manoeuvres themselves. His father considered it as little more than a habit. However, not all habits were necessarily bad things.

As days blurred into one, so did the nights. He exhausted his mind with solitary card games. More often than not, when unable to solve a game out, he would cast the little grubby cards aside in annoyance, convinced they plotted against him. A few breaths later he would pick them all back up and deal himself a hand once again. To finish most nights, his thoughts would return to "the Cull" in Spark City. The fuken Cull, the event he knew little about but was destined to attend. An event he had waited his entire life for, and still the only knowledge he had were whispered embellishments. Some said it was life or death to attend. Some said that those who failed were castrated and bled to death. Some said it was simply a test of prowess as a male. Others merely suggested it was a divine meeting of the minds where wits were tested and the winner was gifted a female Alphaline to mate with and spend a life.

Such a treasure was terrifying.

Only a select few were chosen to attend, and Erroh was one such individual. It was not through luck either. His fate was sealed, and he felt his doom nearing as each day passed. They were wonderful thoughts to have as sleep took hold.

———

It started as a low rumbling noise.

Sprawled out under his cloak, he woke and reached for his blade instinctively. The wind was still, the night was clear and something was coming. The shattered moon was full and it lit up the lands. Crawling out of his camp quickly, he shook his head to wake his senses and listened for the threat. It was approaching from a path on the far side of the clearing. He slid the leather armour over his head, desperately trying to regain his composure, as his fingers became numb tools. He struggled with the buckles and his arm began to itch. Wishing the absent gods had delivered a cave in which to hide, he stood alone in the centre of the clearing, sword outstretched.

Onwards came the ominous rumble, building in intensity. It owned the darkness. Erroh saw birds scatter from their nests in terror; they flapped confusingly in the dim light. Their crying protests were lost in the disturbance.

It was louder than thunder.

Vibrations stirred the tall grass, they danced in unison with every thump from beyond the trees, and he waited for certain death. The first of the many sounds began to emerge from the wall of noise. He expected to see some terrible beast break though the tree line and crash into his world, some loud beast that could probably fly. That made no sense, he knew this world, and he knew her creatures.

He heard incomprehensible voices in the air, vulgar throaty tones of indistinguishable words, horribly foreign to his ear. The thunder surrounded him. It caught in the valley's walls and reverberated right back at him deep down to where all his fears and instincts lay. He had walked the road and never truly felt fear before. His father would have urged him to gather the fear and use it to strike harder.

After the many days spent in the glade, he knew he could make his way through the forests if needs be. Aye, the stitches would tear but anything was better than facing whatever lay a few trees away from him.

"Pass by," he whispered to the gods who he did not believe in. In the noise, who would hear him anyway?

His mind raced. If it was not some mythical monster, than perhaps it was an army. He had heard many marches in his young life though he himself had never donned a uniform nor waved a flag of allegiance. Moreover, what army could march anyway? There were no armies in this region anymore. The world was at peace. Only the brutes from the frozen lands of the southern territories bore grudges, and though much of the world was uninhabited he found it difficult to imagine they would ever venture this far north unnoticed. Whatever the southerners were up to, it was keeping them busy. Maybe it was a convoy of Alphalines, alluring, uninterested, and returning home to their tower in the city. None of these thoughts helped.

Hooves beat the ground and long grass danced merrily in time with the cacophony of noise all around him. Closer still.

Then something happened.

The thunder began to pass by. He saw a few flickers of burning light through the dark, their brightness making little impact against the thick shroud of leaves, which covered the camp. It was the leading voices of riders. Yelling their mounts onwards, Erroh listened as the wave marched further on down the valley. Howls, barks, and squeals from a thousand beasts met his ears and a deadly curiosity came upon Erroh, but he ignored any instinct to seek out the noise. Instead, he took uneasy breaths and listened for the noise to fade.

Only when the last of the torches reached the bottom of the valley did his nerves begin to settle. They headed towards Spark, but there were many miles between here and there.

Aware that hunting packs frequently left one or two scouts a mile or two behind, to catch any creatures foolish enough to come above the ground too soon after they passed, Erroh waited.

A calm breeze played across the dell, leaves took flight playing soothing songs. It was glorious after the deafening symphony. With the distant rumble finally lost in the noises of the forest, he took his place by the side of Rock. Opening the plug on the bottle, he leaned back and drank in the angry liquid. Keeping one ear on the road, he downed another healthy swig, corked it, and lay back in the grass. After counting the little specks in the sky for a while, he closed his eyes and slept lightly.

———

He wanted bread. Bread and cheese. Melted cheese with some bread. All of the bread. He would love some boar as well. All he wanted was boar. Huddled around the tiny fire under his shelter he turned the pigeon-laden spit. The smoke stung his eyes but it couldn't be helped. The soothing tapping sounds from the rain, now grated his head. He was eating pigeon again. A slimy bit of grey meat fell from the body and dropped into the centre of the flames. A little black cloud rose up from the oily piece and into Erroh's face. A few drops of water fell onto his forehead, through a gap in the shelter above his head. It just added to his misery.

He wiped the drips away and sighed. He did not bother adding salt to the horrible meal. It brought little flavour, so why bother waste any? The first bite of the oily meat was the worst but then again, swallowing was almost as bad. Every day the meal became less appetising. He grimaced as it slid down his throat. He cast his gaze out through the downpour. The smoke behind the hills had not appeared today. He imagined it was because of the heavy rainfall. Distracting himself from the taste, he set about picking at the stitching with his knife. Each thread snapped apart satisfyingly as his wrist flicked the tip gently. An uneven scar ran across his knee as he tugged the remaining stitches free. He had been here long enough. Time flew when you were hiding from your fate. The city was calling and beneath his immature longings of freedom where he kept safe his loneliness, hope and warmth, something was beginning to stir, as his father had suggested it would.

Stretching his knee, it felt good enough to face the road, and good enough to step into the Alphas' domain.

He knew most of the lore surrounding them and enjoyed

hearing the ridiculous tales in every tavern along the road. The reverence with which all "lowerlines" treated Alphalines was mythical. Some thought them wild brutes, often whispering they were less man and more animal, capable of incredible deeds, should they feel the whim: wild, like fire in the night.

Magnus insisted that Alphas were no different to any supposed lowerline male or female. They were human but they were dangerous. Every one of them was considered an elite warrior. Every one of them had endured a demanding life of education and training. Every one of them was a master in the art of war. Erroh liked to think he was good with a blade himself.

Meeting Alphas was not the only reason to be in the city. His little sister lived there now. Would she even remember him? Sent there a decade ago, apart from a few exchanged letters a season they were strangers. When he'd begun his walk, the letters had stopped. Maybe she would have word of his parents. That would be nice.

He stretched his knee and stood out in the downpour. Dressed in only his black leather trousers, he spread his arms out and stood on his toes. Favouring his stronger side these past weeks would not serve him well. Leaning his head back and closing his eyes, he stood as still as possible. He had always struggled to master his balance but it was a battle he would win eventually. This, he was certain of.

Erroh reached for the steel and fought the pommel's weight ever so much. It trembled in his hand and the rain splashed down upon the metal. The driving wind delivered another harsh gust against his cold body. He took his stance. Muscles screeched with the strain as he began the first slash. The cold bit into him, and he felt involuntary shakes throughout his body as he performed the second manoeuvre.

His body knew the sword form instinctively. By the third move, his body flowed smoothly and his knee offered little complaint. He followed the strikes with a few slight feints and then he thrust, slashed, and killed invisible opponents with great violence. Throughout the storm, he trained. His mind clear and his body warming, he found a peace. He twisted, spun, and let the beauty of swordplay overwhelm him completely. He performed his tricks and he did so with proficient violence and speed. He pushed himself through all his routines completely and his knee held firm.

The following morning, once dawn had broken, Erroh took a little blade and brought it to the surface of his rock. He scraped at the massive stone and eventually dust fell away. It would be wrong not to leave some mark upon his sanctuary. Standing back, he surveyed his mark for time, allowing himself the slightest bit of pride. "Rock of Erroh." It was a fine name. It had been a fine rock.

He considered tearing down his shack but thought better of it. Perhaps it would be a welcome port of call to another lonely traveller along the way, some windswept night having prayed to the gods of shelters for grace. Perhaps time would simply cover it up in a thick canopy of green as it did the rest of the world.

After gathering his belongings, he disassembled the great stringed bow and stored it back in his pack. As the first warm rays of the sun began to warm the road, Erroh stretched his limbs for the walk. He did so with the skill of a young man that had walked many miles already. He picked up his pack, left the parting of the trees, looking forward. There was no need to look back.

3

LEATHER AND STEEL

He would never eat pigeon again. Fuk pigeon. He thought about that boar he had promised himself instead, and then the melted cheese. They were fine thoughts to occupy his mind, as he stepped further into the wood. The ground underneath him was soft and broken. Never being a terribly skilled tracker, he struggled to make sense of the many marks from the mysterious noise, save for them being fresh, varied, and plentiful. In the light of the day, they seemed far less terrifying. He headed towards the smoke following the route a pigeon might take, desperate to flee inaccurate arrows. His eyes were thin slits of concentration and each step was as careful as the last, wary of subtle obstacles like gnarled roots, greasy mossy patches and fallen jagged logs.

The warm rays shone down through the leaves of the ancient trees. Their massive trunks, sturdy and aged like mountains. They probably stood grandly before the birth of this world. They had seen things he had only read about. They survived such things and now they swayed in the wind almost soundlessly.

"This is freedom," he muttered, wiping a bead of sweat from his brow. He had been alone so long he sometimes forgot his own voice. It was a strange thing to hear his quiet words in this eternal green, a single voice with lonely words. Thoughts of the city, and his few days of freedom left, returned to him. He still had miles to walk. Alone.

Eventually the heat caught up with his determination, and he forced himself to take rest at the bottom of a pine-covered valley.

He sat in the grass under a break in the trees and let the sun shine down on his face. It was only here that he finally noticed the difference. The smoke was black, a dark bruise on the radiant blue, and an affront to the beauty of the day. He stared up at the ominous sign and felt a chill run down his spine. The monstrous black clouds looked like death. Something terrible lay ahead. He considered changing course. "They might have boar," he whispered.

A few hours later, he reached the top of a valley edge and looked down to the settlement below. It was little more than a few decrepit buildings clustered together, slowly losing the battle to the certainty of time. A faded road ran through them, cracked, grey, and ancient. It turned to nothing but mud and grass beyond the town's boundaries. It was a glimmer of the old world and all was deathly still. There was no sound in the air but the flapping of the flames. There would be no boar tonight.

Various pieces of cloth hung across the windows of some of the ruins, acting as braces against the harsh winds but there was no one left for them to protect. In the centre, a fire rose into the evening sky and it was terrible. The flames would never stop burning in his mind, and he would not let them either. Cattle and swine ran freely throughout the devastated town, their pens knocked down during the attack. They were oblivious to the horrors that surrounded them, happy to graze in their newly obtained freedom. Chickens pecked at grain that had spilt messily onto the ground from torn open bags. Some grains were lost from the chickens grasp and carried to the bottom of the street in a steady little stream of red.

Terrified.

Touching his sword along his waist as if a comfort, Erroh walked cautiously into the village to search for anyone left alive. Even he was able to recognise a cavalry's tracks in the soft muddy ground as he drew nearer. The path turned from mud to hard stone as he neared the town and each step he took became louder. They echoed in the stony silence and each step nearer seemed to steal his hope and replace it with an awful despair. It is no small thing to walk among the dead, no matter what bards, poets and storytellers declare.

The nearest body still held a pike in its hand and a hole in its chest. The strike had gone through cheap armour and downed the defender where the road met the town. The body lay in a heap, it would never move again. Its eyes unfocused, staring into the heavens, the wind ruffled its hair. Erroh moved on from the dead man towards the rest of the devastation.

Slowly he stepped between each structure, his eyes darting each and every way, his sword still sheathed, peering into the ground floor windows where he could. His heart dropped like a heavy weight with every grisly corpse he discovered. He found quite a few. He discovered an old man still asleep in a little dark room in the last building. He looked so peaceful with a warm blanket covering his body; Erroh almost went as far as checking for a pulse when he saw the slit across his neck. The blood had soaked up in the straw underneath.

It was too much. He had seen death before, though

nothing like this. He ran from the building, his sadness and horror giving way to an anger he had never known himself capable of.

"Face me you animals!" he roared, pulling the blade from its scabbard, challenging the world to a duel. He charged through the town, his mind a furnace of rage. He could not see sense. He could only see the injustice of the world. It was all he could do. He wanted to destroy. To tear these brutes apart, whoever they were. He wanted vengeance for those whom he had never known.

When he had calmed himself he returned to the centre of the town where most of the bodies were strewn like discarded delicacies for feasting carrion birds. Their shields and bodies were splintered and split alike, and their masculine limbs still gripped swords, flails and battle-axes. Of all the horrors, when he came upon the smallest fighter of them all it was the image of the broken pale boy which stayed with him longest.

And then he braved the females burning in the pyre. They had been chained to each other and set alight and now the flames rose as high as a killer seated atop a great horse. He hoped their throats were slit before the end. Through his weeping eyes, he could still make out their shapes.

There was nobody left but the dead. The fire would run its course, the sun would set, the ashes would scatter and the world would carry on. All he could do was remember and hate. A hate far deeper than the simmering revulsion his father held for those who ruled this world now. He wished his father were with him now.

Scavenging was shameful work but there was a fortune in this place. Each edge was as sharp as the day they were forged. All the blades would find a strong price in Samara, he thought grimly. Only a couple of the finest pieces would end up in his sack though. He knew it was wrong to take the weapons of any fallen warrior but steel was steel, and he hadn't a piece to his name since the card game.

The spot he chose was beyond the meeting of road and stone. It was soft ground and easy to dig. It would catch most of the sun of the day. In truth, he had few places from which to choose. It was a fine place to rest peacefully. Had he the will, he would have gifted each dead warrior a solitary grave but as it was, he could only do what he could. They were dead. He recovered a spade and dug into the soft ground. To his relief, the ground gave way without much difficulty.

When many hours had passed and the day turned to night, Erroh finally dropped the shovel in frustration. Not even half way through the first foot across, he was too exhausted and heartbroken to continue. His grand thoughts of a deep grave were now all but a sober wish. He could do no more than cover the bodies deep enough to deter the carrion birds. It was regretful but it was a task greater than his capability. Worse than that, a part of him wanted to take up his belongings and leave this nightmare behind but somehow he didn't. Instead, he found a place just outside the town and beneath one of the many surrounding trees lay down with some bread. Trying not to think of the baker's likely fate, he wrapped his cloak around him and watched the shattered moon spit her shards of light across the sky. He thought it a fitting display in honour of the fallen. He did not sleep well.

The following morning, he found himself at the fire. The flames had burned away but whoever had lit this terrible pyre had been greatly skilled at such things. What remained were glowing embers and the heat was almost soothing. It would smoulder for the day. To kill a male in this world was a great sin but there was no greater crime than taking a female's life. The thoughts of their brutal end once again tore through him anew. This close to the city it was no mere barbaric crime, it had to be an intended affront to the "Primary." It was a venomous warning, or else an unsettling declaration. His eyes broke from the dying fire to the painted words scrawled messily on a building at the far end of the town.

"The Woodin Man walks. The tainted must burn."

He would bear the message in its fullest. Erroh answered to the Primary like so many others. Her wrath would be greater than anything he could imagine.

The two fiends entered the town wearing heavy armour. The smaller of the men wore leather with matching helm; the other covered himself in thick steel. Their movements echoed loudly in the dead silence. "Leather" moved like a hunter, watching for prey. His head shot to either side, searching for any stirrings in the quiet buildings or the surrounding greenery. In his grasp, he held a thin short sword.

His companion, "Steel", rested a massive war hammer on his shoulder as he walked confidently. He took the lead and they moved through the village. They stopped by the flames and exchanged low cautious words. Leather stalked around the fire while Steel propped himself up against a cart filled with vegetables at the edge of the road. He removed his helm and rummaged through the produce absently. Chewing on a fresh carrot, he stared into the fire. The bodies had almost burned to nothing. Almost but not quite. Leather eyed something of interest behind one of the buildings. He hopped a long wooden log fence and disappeared while Steel took another bite of the vegetable and tossed it carelessly into the fire. They talked more, but Erroh could make out very little from behind the trunk of a large oak where he slept the night before. Steel stepped towards the enclosure and after a few seconds received the heavy load from his companion. They carried the slaughtered swine across the road easily enough. Their feet splashed uncaringly in the pools of crimson and they sat down by the warmth. Steel lit up some weed tobacco from an old wooden pipe while leather stripped the fresh swine. He attacked this task with relish.

The smell hit the air, and Erroh was disgusted. What type of men could pick up battle spears from the dead and use them to cook meat in the embers of dead females? But his mouth salivated. It had been weeks since he'd eaten well. The two figures remained undisturbed, and Erroh finally found the courage to move from the safety of the tree. He had a task to finish after all. He resented the strangers and their disrespect, but the last thing he wanted was to engage them aggressively. There were two of them; it was hardly a fair fight. He left his armour behind, intending there to be no further bloodshed. The town had tasted its fair share already. It was unlikely they lived an honest life but they were not responsible for such atrocities. Their crime was only disrespect, was it not? He took a calming breath and slipped from his hiding place out onto the main pathway. They never heard him coming. It probably didn't help matters.

"May I join you?" he called out. They were fine words. He'd taken quite a time to form them. He held his hands apart and smiled, which usually served him well. Some of the carrion birds viewed the events with intrigue. Maybe they found his choice of words merely adequate.

"Who the fuk are you?" roared Steel, climbing to his feet and grabbing his hammer with both hands.

Leather hopped up quicker and immediately began to flank Erroh. His eyes darted from side to side searching for a second or third attacker. "Answer him." He passed his sword from hand to hand smoothly. He had skill, and he was probably a bandit. Erroh could see a black sash at his elbow and doubted it was decorative. Perhaps it was something else. He took three quick steps wide of Erroh.

"I'm here for the dead and nothing more," Erroh said, leaning to the side, just enough that the pommel of Mercy became visible to the fighters. It hung loosely at his waist.

"It's all that I carry," he assured them, allowing just enough fear to enter his voice. In truth, he was indeed terrified.

"Are you alone?" Leather circled Erroh, his sword favouring the right hand. It was low and ready to strike. It was all going to end in the next few breaths. Erroh undid the buckle on the scabbard, let it drop loudly to the ground, and stepped away from their reach.

"I'm alone." He retreated a few steps more. He dared a "let's be friends" smile.

"That's probably a mistake," hissed Leather, getting into striking distance. He moved like a viper. No longer hunting, he had his prey. His eyes no longer searched for Erroh's hidden companions. This one was quite alone.

"Ah, leave him," said Steel dropping the massive weapon.

Erroh glanced from the bull with the hammer to the viper with the blade. Slowly, the leather foe lowered his sword. His eyes remained focused on his quarry though. He licked his dry lips and sighed in frustration. There would be no blood for now. "Now stop that running away shit."

Leather flicked his greasy hair out of his eyes and returned to cooking his own piece of meat, muttering a few curses under his breath. The birds were disappointed but there was something in the air.

The smell was intoxicating. Steel was quite the chef apparently. Lanced on a pike over the flames was a half onion and a slab of swine meat. He poured a thick golden liquid onto the slab of meat and sat back contentedly. A few drips of honey slipped through and found their way onto the onion underneath. Erroh smelled the sizzling flavours, licked his lips, and hated himself greatly for it. Leather ripped his own half-cooked slice from his own spit. Content that not all the blood had been burned away, he chewed noisily. His eyes never left Erroh as he took a seat on an old overturned wooden barrel. He pointed to the carcass of the swine beast.

"Tear yourself a piece," he grunted between bites. It was almost a challenge. Erroh was quickly sensing the mistake he'd made in revealing himself. He also wanted to try the recipe. Who wouldn't? He could almost taste the succulent honey-soaked meat, and he very nearly accepted the offer, but he remembered the burning. There would be other fine meals to look forward to down the road. He shook his head limply.

"Thank you, friend. I have eaten," Erroh said, seating himself on a slight kerb of the road, as far from Leather's eerie gaze as possible. Steel sat between them, seemingly lost in his culinary concentration. Erroh could not fail to notice the subtle exchange of smiles between both men. Perhaps they were just glad of the company.

Steel flipped the meat onto its other side. Red droplets of juice seeped down into the onion; a few met their fate in the flames. It was a small sacrifice. "What happened here, boy?"

"I saw smoke and came upon this," Erroh said shrugging. They seemed satisfied with his answer. His appearance suggested him incapable of such brutal deeds. They didn't know him at all.

"Was everyone dead?" Steel asked.

"The males were slain, and the women…" Erroh gestured to the fire. They nodded. They'd noticed the lack of females among the dead. They'd noticed the unusual mounds of ashes.

"Very strange." Steel twisted the meat again. He was no Alpha. An Alpha would be horrified.

Silence but for the crackle of swine beast.

"Your family?" asked Steel as if it were no small matter.

Erroh shook his head deferentially. "I'm just passing through, sir." As long as he was not a threat, they would leave him be.

"Yet, you attempt to bury them in a mass grave?" Steel sneered, motioning the spade still stuck in the ground. The grave itself was taking shape. It would hold a dozen but it would be shallow. It was better than being gorged upon by beasts, he told himself.

"Aye."

Leather began to snigger, then went on eating. Smears of grease dribbled down his face. He did not bother to wipe them away. It was so easy to hate this man. Perhaps that was his intention. "I like the flavour," he said letting food pop out of his mouth with every word. He stared intently at the half-cooked flesh. "The way the meat was smoked," he muttered. He watched Erroh hopefully. He wanted blood. His fingers played at the pommel of his weapon. Erroh refused to react. Show them you are not worth it, he thought to himself. He sensed they too were eager to know what had occurred here. Until they were certain he had little information to offer there would be a decision to make on their part. To slit the throat of a young man in a dead town would be easy enough. To let him live would be easy enough too. Steel took the chunk of meat off the fire. He tore it free and threw the fallen warrior's spear aside.

"Females always make the best meals," he joked, biting into his perfectly prepared meal. His eyes watched for perilous insult to be taken, and Erroh felt a shiver run down his spine. Perhaps he hadn't played these bandits well enough at all.

"I need to finish the task," Erroh muttered, climbing to his feet and walking off towards the grave. There was bile in his mouth but that may have just been the bitter retort he'd swallowed. This was no tavern, where charm and cheek were appreciated, or at least tolerated. He thought about the last brute he'd met in that tavern. What had his name been? It was a small matter now. That brute had shown warmth in his eyes. These two, however, had the look of killers.

As the hours passed, Erroh found the going even tougher. His body was ravenous and his hands slipped on the handle while digging. He dug into the soft soil without slowing though his body ached. Dig, hoist, and repeat. It was a miserable mantra of movement and as darkness drew near, the mounds of dirt became plentiful and terrible. By nightfall, the bandits had procured for themselves a wandering cow, sturdy enough to pull an emptied vegetable cart. With the produce cast aside, all of the weapons from the blacksmiths now lay neatly in rows. They would fetch a fine price in the Spark, or some other settlement out in the wastes and the scavengers were delighted with their spoils. They stripped the pieces from the dead as well. They wouldn't catch as fine a price, showing the signs of combat in their finish, but some diligent cleaning would clear most of the blood. They did not take all blades though.

Erroh leaned over the little broken body of the boy. There was a fine sword still clutched in his blood soaked hand. There wasn't a blemish on the steel, despite the many wounds dealt to its former owner. The bone pommel was simple, yet carved out with great care, and with a leather grip that felt comfortable to the touch. He held the piece in the air and its balance was excellent. The edge was as sharp as Mercy's even though it lacked the decoration and age of his father's blade. It was new to this world without any heavy history, and perhaps this is the reason he liked it so.

"Thank you," he whispered into the little ear, which would never hear again.

The child's armour was not a fit. All it had accomplished was prolonging the little one's torture. The tiny frame had been unable to move properly under the weight and his attackers had known this. The fear he must have felt. The scuffs in the dirt told Erroh the tale of this battle. All of the town's defenders were slain swiftly in a fierce charge, but the boy had endured a worse fate. Erroh could see the embedded footmarks in a circle around him. He imagined the show; he could almost hear their bloodthirsty cries.

He closed his eyes, but he could see it all. Another set of far larger footprints had faced the boy. He must have fought so very bravely with the beautiful sword. He had no training. He had just swung wildly. The child's killer had dodged and counter attacked with a flick of a blade across his face. Erroh wanted to wipe away the little tear stains, which ran down the young warrior's cheeks; mixed with dried blood. Erroh placed the blade into its covering and strapped it around his waist. Then he picked up the boy and brought him to a bed where he could rest as a hero.

"Work of Alphas, no fuken doubt," Leather suggested, sitting down for the evening. He dropped a dried log onto the embers to keep them smouldering a little longer.

"Don't think any Alpha is capable of such an act," Steel argued, sitting opposite the fire. One of his newly acquired axes lay resting in his lap. He teased the edge with a whetstone. Erroh sat at his kerb eating a scavenged piece of bread. He said nothing though he had quite a few opinions.

"Aye but a pack of them, driven demented by their whores in mating season."

Both of them laughed. Erroh just chewed. All conversations came back to Alphas no matter the company. If the wind blew too hard, it was an Alpha's fault no doubt. If he told them the truth of all he knew about Alphas, they would just laugh and slit his throat. Or they would argue his points and then slit his throat. Erroh swallowed his bread. He liked his throat.

"I reckon I could play with an Alpha whore," said Leather. He twisted his sharpened blade and caressed it gently with oily twitching fingers. He was smiling to himself, lost in thought. "It would be fine times." This time Erroh did laugh as he climbed to his tired feet.

"You came into town with a fine looking sword," Leather muttered, rising effortlessly with him. So began the end.

"Aye." Erroh's eyes flashed to Mercy still in its scabbard in the centre of the town. He'd left it there to make a point. From behind him, he heard Steel rise.

"A boy like you has no need for such a weapon nor the new treasure at your waist." Leather's meaning was clear. Surrender his weapons to them and they would leave him be. Steel grabbed his hammer.

"I think it suits me," Erroh said coldly. He backed away from both men. Around his waist, the child's sword bumped awkwardly against the cart full of weapons. Leather drew out his sword and circled Erroh while Steel moved into range.

"Don't do this," Erroh pleaded as both menaces closed in around him.

"Close your eyes, little one," hissed Leather. Erroh bit

back a witty retort. It was too late for charm to find a resolution. Leather leapt forward.

He slashed his blade across the undefended chest of the young gravedigger who called himself Erroh. Instead of a kill, there was a blur of movement. His sword missed its target and the parry sent the blade down into the ground. He tried to swing a second time but his opponent stepped in and ducked under his attack. Erroh thrust forward violently, and he felt his body twist as if he was nothing more than a plaything. The sword punctured through his leather suit and into his chest and suddenly he was unable to support his weight. The moving blur pulled the blade free, and he fell to his knees. His vision darkened, his bladder released, and he watched a fetching blade swiftly embed itself deep in the face of his attacking comrade. Somewhere a hammer fell to the ground and a wet scream fell silent with it. Then something heavy crashed among some barrels a few feet from him. His mind couldn't hold any thoughts beyond these last few breaths.

Blood tasted in his mouth, and he lay by the fire dying. He tried to breathe but his lungs felt heavy. They were filling up, but he was not near a river. His killer leaned down beside him, and he tried to speak. To explain that whatever had just happened, was not how things were supposed to be. His voice left him and all that remained was terrible pain. He could barely feel the presence of the young man leaning over him, helping him on his way with a quick slice across his throat.

4

HUNTED

Erroh managed a handful of steps before his body betrayed him. Somewhere between the grave and the freshly killed, he fell to his knees and began to retch violently. He replayed the fight in his head again. He had offered them a chance, had he not? This was not his fault. He held that thought, he held it tightly and then he locked it away. He wiped the bile from his lips and shook miserable thoughts from his mind.

Though to sit in melancholy would suit his mood, he made a fresh fire for himself at the far end of the town and sliced some swine meat and set it to cook. Adding some onion and honey to the meal, he ate a second portion. His body ached from the day but soon the fire's warmth comforted him with whispered suggestions of sleep. Instead of succumbing to necessity, he stripped his shirt off and scratched at the three little scars upon his sword arm. There was one for each regretful memory. Now there were two more to add. Steel had been a clean kill but Leather had left behind a spray of crimson across his shirt. Whatever would the female Alphas think of him if he presented himself in the city, drenched in blood? Perhaps they would clap, cheer, and demand to know of his prowess. There would be questions. He wiped his sword clean and placed the blade's tip into the blaze and sat back patiently. When it was hot enough, he wrapped the middle of the blade in cloth leaving the exposed tip just below the third scar.

"Steel," he whispered and placed the sword down on his bare skin. The sizzling was unbearable. The pain wasn't pleasant either. After a few agonising breaths, he lifted it back up.

"Leather," he whispered through clenched teeth. After a moment's hesitation, he pressed the sword down and fought the scream growing in his throat. He knew the searing pain would pass. It was all about controlling it until it did.

He pulled the blade away and muttered a curse under his breath. Staring at the cooling tip he took a few relieving breaths. The pain began to subside a little, leaving behind two perfectly acceptable welts. He held the sword out and studied it in the flickering light. He had taken two lives with it and felt a bond. He made a foolish oath of revenge on the perpetrators and then he christened it "Vengeance." He thought it would make him feel better but it really didn't.

The following morning Erroh pulled the last body into the large shallow grave and covered up the twelve fallen warriors, sleeping now in the darkness beyond. He left the bodies of Leather and Steel where he'd struck them down. Let them serve as a meal for the carrion birds.

He gathered himself, his belongings and prepared to depart. He left the cart of fine weaponry behind. The thoughts of profiteering from those he'd buried now disgusted him. The embers had finally burned down to nothing and the dust had already begun to take flight. In a few weeks, nothing would remain but the scorch marks on the ground. Strapping both blades behind his back, he gathered his belongings and left the town. The riders' tracks accompanied him for a few miles until they followed a river west while he needed to walk north. After agonising over the decision, he followed his own path. The oath could wait until he settled matters in the city.

———

The boar was fast. Most boars were but this one appeared to enjoy the thrill of the chase. Erroh enjoyed a good hunt himself. He crashed through the thicket in pursuit of the wild beast with bow in hand and all thoughts of the dead town were far from his mind. The boar had turned towards the sun and now charged effortlessly through the endless green. Clever little boar. It was harder to see through the cluster of leaves and branches with the sun in your eyes. Deeper and deeper into the quiet woods Erroh ran, eager not to taste defeat. He hated to lose. It went against everything he'd ever been taught. Sometimes winning was more important than attaining what the heart desired. He sprinted through heavy shrubbery with its sharp briars and rough animal trails and he'd never felt more at peace. His knee was strong, he was sure footed, and the Hunt was a fine way to spend one of his last ever days alone. Alas, the quarry took another sudden turn, and Erroh lost it in the greenery. Slowing to a jog, he heard its hooves thunder off into the distance. He tried to be magnanimous in defeat. He still cursed the boar quite colourfully for a few seconds until he fell against a tree and took in as much air as possible. His entire body was drenched in sweat. His breathing a desperate panting, he dropped the bow and unused arrow. It had been a good run and a great chase for miles. He imagined the great boar would become a legend among its clan for surviving a battle with the great Erroh, line of Magnus. It would have its choice of many mates despite one tusk being slightly smaller than most. He opened his water tankard and drank the disappointment of the chase away. He should have taken the shot earlier. It was a small matter. He wasted some water by pouring it through his hair. He felt he deserved it. Cool and re-energised, he found a path and returned to his wanderings.

From her hiding place, a tall female with hunter's eyes watched him. She made no stir and simply waited to see what route he would take beyond his failed hunt. She had already loaded a thin bolt onto her crossbow. She checked the sights and watched the leaves for wind. She moved gracefully, at one with the canopy of green all around her. She thought him quite good looking, and she thought him prey. Her eyes were blue and beautiful. She was wise and strong like most Alphas. She thought he had a strong walk, he was proud and from the way he carried two blades upon his back, she sensed his threat.

Wonderful.

She slipped between the trees, close enough to strike, but her padded feet were silent in each step for she knew the art of the hunt. He was completely oblivious to her. Silly boy. She enjoyed the chase for a few hours until he found a campsite, and she seethed silently. Why couldn't he have just walked a little further? It was not the first time she had stalked careless travellers. Her family would fret for her, though no more than usual, as this was the only real hunting she could do these days. She climbed into a tree and nestled herself in. Relaxing her head on her slim powerful arms, she sat and waited. He could take two obvious routes. One was a worn path, which would lead him to the edge of the forest and from there he could follow a road that led to the glow of Spark City. If he followed the stream, he would be walking on her territory. As he slept, she leaned back in her branch, whittling a thin strip of wood into something a little more deadly.

The following morning, she watched him stretch, strip, and practice with his sword for a short time. He was skilled after all. This pleased her. Then he bathed in the stream. This pleased her more. Then he set off on his travels, following the stream. This did not please her greatly but sensing an opportunity, she dropped down from her branch and followed. She did not reload her crossbow. Maybe when she spoke with him, and looked into his eyes, she would know.

"Little Cub," a female voice called gently from behind, and Erroh spun around and lost balance. He flailed his arms wildly and tripped on a root and ended up in a puddle of mud.

"Cub," the female repeated, ducking elegantly beneath the branches. He looked up and met her blue eyes and decided she was stifling a laugh. He remained in the mud and willed it to swallow him up. There were probably finer ways to meet a pretty lady. No, not pretty. She was more than that. She was beautiful. Her long dark hair was dishevelled and wild but it shone in the morning light. Her mocking grin from a shapely jawline was appealing. Her ears, well, they were nice too.

"You're talented with the blade." She made a show of loading a bolt and letting the crossbow hang carelessly down her shapely waist. All parts of her were shapely. She wore snugly fitted leather trousers with a simple blouse that complemented her perfectly. She was regal, as though her bloodline was stronger than most. He could sense such things. Then she smiled a smile that could flatten any male. Fortunately, he'd already knocked himself to the ground.

"If you try to unleash either sword, this bolt goes through your teeth," she said smiling.

Such a lovely smile.

"What a waste of teeth," Erroh agreed. She was older than he was by at least a decade and the absence of fear on her face was disconcerting. She looked through him into his soul, if he believed in such things, and he recognised her for what she was immediately.

"Am I on your land?" he asked and bowed his head. It seemed like the thing to do. He knew his place in the world and in that moment, it was in the mud.

"Aye."

"I'm sorry."

"What's your name, little cub?"

"My friends call me Erroh." He didn't grin.

"That's an interesting name, Erroh."

The Alpha turned from him and strode down along the stream as if their meeting was no great matter. Before disappearing from view, she turned and waited. Her eyes were burning in excitement. He scrambled to his feet and followed.

It was incredibly rare for any Alpha to live so close to the city, and the forest seemed to fall silent in her magnificent wake. She wore her lineage proudly. Birds stopped their busy conversations, as she floated across the rough terrain. Especially the cooing of the pigeons, but that could have been the presence of Erroh. His fame may have spread in avian folklore. They walked a few miles through thick brambles and dense woodland. Wherever she had settled was not a journey easy to take.

"I'm Mea," she said suddenly. He thought it a fine name

but said nothing. Alphas were careful in the company they kept. They took mates to create a stronger line for this new world. To make little attractive Alphas that would come of age and mate with other attractive little Alphas and so on. This one would have a mate no doubt. From her age, she may have had young cubs of her own. Erroh had never properly met a female Alpha of the city, and for once, he understood the mystique. She was refined, but she was very much the same as he.

"You have some interesting routines. Your speed is something to behold," she said slowing her pace, and he walked beside her.

"You saw my routine?"

"Aye,"

"Oh."

He thought about the stream. He wanted to argue that the water was coldest in the morning.

Eventually they reached a plateau and from there, Mea proudly presented her home to Erroh. It was impressive. The land was lush and green with many rows of varying crop patches. The house itself was long and wide though not terribly high. Its wooden walls only hinted at a few years age. He imagined them thick enough to endure the north's unpredictable weather. Strong oak would last a lifetime and the thatched roof was impeccable. She obviously took great pride in its upkeep. Was this the type of house he should build? The only other structure was a two-storey barn, though there were foundations for a third smaller shack between both buildings. A large wooden fence encircled the farm and the only entrance was a barely worn roadway no bigger than the width of a cart. Thick clusters of trees concealed the rest. It was quite the Alphaline sanctuary. Erroh followed her through the trees, wondering if he may very well have walked past without noticing.

"Jeroen will want to meet the young male, who kept his mate away for an entire night. You had best behave," she said, appearing to take great delight in his sudden fear. "Don't worry at all. He's a gentle little soul."

"Why am I here?" It was a fine question; he'd worked on it for hours.

Before she could answer, two magnificent hounds came bounding from an open doorway, they barked excitedly as they raced towards the Alpha. They were delirious in their welcome and when they stood on their hind legs, they were almost as tall as she was. Satisfied with their licks, they turned to him and growled in primal "Rip your fuken throat out," growls. Despite himself and his love for hounds, he took a nervous backwards step.

"Whisht," hissed the female, and both dogs ceased their threats immediately. Erroh relaxed for a few breaths until an impressive male appeared from the house and stopped in his tracks. His brown beard and matching hair were immaculately cut. His shoulders were broad and sturdy, and he matched her age. His fists were clenched, and he wondered if they were capable of shattering bone in one swing. Erroh clenched his own rather small hands. It was simple instinct.

"You look tired, Mea," he called. "And I see no fruits from the hunt."

"He chased my kill away," she argued pointing to Erroh, smiling a smile that could topple mountains. Luckily, she directed it at her powerful mate and not at Erroh, who shuffled from foot to foot uncomfortably as the taller figure looked through him.

"He's good with a sword. I'm going to sleep for a while," she said and strolled in through the doorway, the hounds followed.

"Kept her out all night did you?" he asked scrutinising Erroh's ragged appearance with his brown eyes. He crossed his large muscled arms and waited for the proper reply.

"I had no idea, sir." It was the right answer, and the bearded man laughed.

"Aye, Mea is light on her feet. My name is Jeroen." He offered his hand which Erroh gladly took.

"My friends call me Erroh."

Silence.

"Your name is Erroh, and you are going to the city?"

"Aye,"

"That's quite interesting."

He presented himself as a farmer but Jeroen emitted raw strength in every movement, like a subdued warrior taking joy in creating, while patiently awaiting the next great war. He gave a fine tour of his farm pointing out every vegetable patch, each head of livestock, their value and the next extension or two they were planning. Erroh found he immediately liked the man. It was hard not to.

"There is a bed here for you tonight," he said when their feet touched the chippings of a crude sparring circle. He gestured to the barn, and Erroh was wise enough to accept his offer graciously. This was no rustic tavern out in the wastes.

"If you're going to stay, you best make yourself useful." His tone was less that of a farmer and more of a master.

5

JUST ERROH, OF THE ROAD

"When you meet my son, Tye, you can spar with him," Jeroen said, hammering the thin post into the ground. Erroh nodded, holding the offending piece of wood as steadily as he could. He'd suspected the reason he was asked to stay was not for simple labour; they required him to be a challenge for their offspring. A young Alpha's education was constant testing and they obviously saw something in Erroh. Jeroen swung the large gate of the sty. It creaked loudly and halted after a foot. He cursed and pulled at the post until the gate swung freely. "You don't speak much do you?" he muttered, though not unkindly.

"I know my place," replied Erroh. He really did and until he was certain there was safety in this place then he dared not speak too freely. They moved up along the enclosure, quietly fixing any unstable posts and as the hours passed, the land darkened and the air grew cooler.

Announcing himself with a careless leap over the farm's boundary wall, Tye graced everyone with his presence. He was a few years younger than Erroh but old enough to wield a blade. Sharing the same bloodline as his parents, Erroh suspected he was quite proficient a swordsman already.

No problem friends, I'd be delighted to fight your Alpha kin.

"Who's the lowerline?" Tye hissed. He did not meet the eyes of Erroh. Such things were apparently beneath him. He did however, look him up and down, and if he was impressed with what he saw, he said nothing. Erroh remembered his father warning him of the disrespect some younger Alphas held. A harsh life learning the way of the sword was likely to give any wild youth certain delusions of grandeur. Still though, most grew out of it. Tye was delighted to learn of his new sparring partner, if only for one bout. His hair was wild like his mother's, but Erroh could clearly see both his parents' good looks in the child. He would break hearts in the city no doubt. Or at least claim his reward. He sported a thin line of hair above his lips. It was a youthful and endearing attempt at adulthood. His eyes burned with excitement and passion. He had little fear for Erroh.

Both combatants followed Jeroen to the wood-chipped arena. Throughout the back of the homestead were crude dummies, straw targets, and racks of swords and shields. This was the territory of warring Alphas. Any wandering fool was certain to see this and it was here that Tye would have received his education.

"Apparently, our wandering friend from the road is quite capable with weapons," said Jeroen, lighting a few torches carefully around the sparring ground. It added wonderfully to the atmosphere. As if there were two gods about to enter the fray.

"Apparently, the road is dirty," teased Tye. It was more than passion behind those eyes. It was a burning sun of rage and aggression. He needed to work on some of his jests

48

though. This was certainly something Erroh was willing to pass on.

"Show respect," growled Jeroen, recovering two sets of wooden sparring blades from the rack. His eyes gleamed with excitement. Apparently, there was nothing like some violence with your firstborn and a stranger to get the juices flowing.

"I'm merely stating fact." Tye's eyes caught Erroh's, and he grinned. Knowing you are capable of great things could be a curse, Erroh thought. Having children was probably a curse as well.

"Did you practise today?" asked Jeroen.

"Not yet," hissed the young Alpha, limbering up. Erroh did the same though with a little less vigour.

A sleepy eyed Mea appeared from their home, bearing a cup of steaming liquid. Offering none to anyone present, she merely stood watching both her son and guest stretch. She was still as radiant as before.

Erroh watched the child warm up and wondered how far the teachings between master and son had reached. Certainly, the child would best any man even at this young age already. It was a small matter, Erroh was quietly confident in his own ability. He knew the measure of his opponent, regardless of blood or standing in the world. This was exactly why his parents had invited him into their home. They could evidently see what so few others could. Perhaps if he didn't bathe as frequently, he wouldn't stand out as much.

The younger one cast aside his armour and under shirt. Despite his youth, his upper body had developed well under a heavy routine of physical training. His father must have pushed him to the limit, as was the way.

"I'll only hurt him a little, Mother." His demeanour was outlandish and crude, but Erroh could see the concentration forming on his face. All fun and games aside, an Alpha wanted to win. Always. In everything they did. A simple instinct to be the best, for their masters demanded it of them. In truth, a life dragged towards perfection was difficult to cast aside once away from a master's watching eye. Erroh was not against a little friendly competition himself.

Tye had nearly come of age, but he was not ready for the road. To send him out into a broken new world just yet was irresponsible. Not for him, but for his victims, and there would be plenty. Perhaps in a few more seasons he could begin his march and the road would finish his education. It would show him respect. It would show him humility. It would show him how to bluff. It would show him how to win.

"Never underestimate your enemy, Tye," warned Mea taking a seat near the arena. The hounds sat obediently by her side, she patted them gently, but her eyes never left the combatants' preparations.

"He only uses one," she called to her mate.

"He carries two blades on his back, though," muttered Jeroen, holding two sturdy wooden swords in each hand. His shoulders dropped a little bit. "I thought he dual wielded." He sounded deeply disappointed. He tossed one of the sparring swords to Erroh and dropped the other aside. Tye reached for his own wooden piece and after checking the balance, began a quick warm up routine.

"You really don't fight with two blades?" Jeroen asked once more. His tone was both hopeful and pleading.

Erroh's father fought with two "Clieve", but he himself chose only one sword. He wasn't strong enough to wield two weapons as menacing as those. He wasn't against using a shield in his other hand though. He'd been quick to learn that he didn't like being hit in combat. He shook his head and started to strip his shirt off. Mea leaned up against her mate and whispered loudly, "I really like this part." She smiled that smile of hers, and Jeroen replied with some incomprehensible primal growl. She looked into his eyes and gave him a quick wink. Tye prepared himself for battle by impressing the world with deadly blows to countless invisible enemies. His speed was incredible. His body was a blur of movement and grace. What speed and agility he would have when he came of age. A sobering thought.

They stepped into the ring to face each other. The crunchy feel of the ground underneath and the fresh aroma from the chipping was almost homely.

"We appreciate you doing this, Erroh," Mea said quietly from behind. Jeroen nodded in agreement. Aye, they knew all right.

"Do you need a shield, shitpants?" called the excited youth. It still wasn't the finest jest but at least he was consistent. Erroh caught the irritation in Jeroen's face. Underneath the beard, he may have been covering a prophetic smile.

"Please ignore the manners of my darling. Hurt him, but not too much," Mea whispered so only Erroh could hear. She was lovely. For a moment, he feared the Cull a little less.

"No shield, Tye, but thank you for the offer," said Erroh. Certain he would need no shield. He was but a child after all.

"Go furrow with the swine," Tye sneered. The jest was crude and swift. *Much better, little one.*

"Best of luck to you too," Erroh offered anyway. This battle was not life or death. Merely pride and a lesson were at stake.

It was likely this was not Tye's first skirmish with a wanderer. It was even likelier that he had bested them all comfortably as well. This natural confidence had given him a dangerous belief in himself. It was not the fault of his parents;

it was their duty to arm him with the abilities to survive in this world, to achieve great things, to be the best little Alpha he could be. It was probably hard to learn restraint when everyone except your parents were terrified of you. The other reason could be that Tye was just a little shit.

"Erroh, what do you see before you?" Jeroen asked.

"I see a talented young Alphaline. Raw, overconfident, but still a dangerous foe." This pleased both parents. Erroh knew his place. He wasn't above complimenting two fierce warriors about their offspring.

"And need I ask you, oh great pride of mine?" Jeroen asked.

"I see another smelly barbarian of the road, Father."

Jeroen shrugged and stepped away from both fighters.

Tye didn't hesitate. He charged at Erroh from the very start. His strikes were fierce and each crack of clashing wood echoed loudly throughout the farm. Onwards he slashed and lunged with terrifying speed. His father had instructed him well. The young one was relentless in his pursuit of a hit, and Erroh blocked the strikes as they landed. Left then right, then a feint, then a right again. He was swift, smooth, and controlled, childish enthusiasm at its finest.

Erroh retreated under the barrages to the edge of the sparring ring, Tye pushed his attack on, and the fight quickly burst out into the courtyard. What were boundaries in war anyway? Erroh took it all in his stride. He had spent many years under the tutelage of his father studying many forms of swordsmanship, and he could avoid the attacks before they hit. That said, Tye's attacking form was very different to those he studied. It felt awkward, incomplete, yet wonderfully devastating. He never countered. He was happy to defend and learn.

Faster and faster the young Alpha moved, throwing

everything into his attack, and it was exhausting to defend against. A bead of sweat rolled down Erroh's forehead and Tye, believing his opponent was tiring, pushed once more. He charged forward and lashed out repeatedly, eagerly awaiting the blow that would strip down Erroh's defences. He was exceptional, and Erroh retreated further from the never-ending onslaught. The child would be elite. There was no mistaking that.

Just like Erroh.

"Enough, Tye!" Erroh shouted, spinning away from an attack, holding his guard. His arms burned from the constant blocking and his pride stung from resisting the urge to counter. "You're a fine swordsman but you have no chance of breaking my defence." Their skirmish had brought them closer to the warm glow of the house, and Erroh could smell warm food cooking. Enough violence. Time for supper. He could see his opponent's parents watching him closely, and he relaxed his stance. He lowered his weapon and stabbed the wooden tip into the ground.

"Take the draw," he offered. He even bowed. The child would have been wise to accept the offer. He would have been wiser to recognise a superior swordsman too.

"He's exquisite, for his age," Erroh said, to the watching parents. His eyes, however, never left the figure of the beaten Alpha. No, not beaten. It had been a draw after all. Erroh hated draws as well.

Tye's stance remained. "This was no fight. You're a fuken snake, slipping and ducking from every blow." He spat in the dirt. "A coward's form."

Erroh shrugged. He had hoped the child would see what was in front of him but alas, the youth was still lost in the moment. The red mist clouded his vision. Erroh knew that red mist well. It sometimes stole good sense from young Alphas, and the older ones as well. Sometimes an Alpha couldn't win. Sometimes that truth was difficult to take.

"Know your place," warned Jeroen, stepping towards his thunderstorm of a son, but Mea laid a hand gently on his shoulder. "Leave him be. Tye's just not as good as he believes himself to be," she suggested.

Moreover, sometimes a mother just wants to see some manners put on her child.

Thank you for that, Mea. Erroh gripped his sword and waited for the inevitable attack. The young Alpha did not disappoint.

"You are good, despite being from the blood of a whore," Tye growled. It was a fine jest, and it served its purpose. What did Tye know about his mother anyway? A flash of anger filled Erroh's mind. Tye leapt forward with blade raised. Erroh met the slash with such power, that the young Alpha stumbled backwards, arms flailing with a dumbstruck look upon his face. He managed to last a few more seconds, defending wildly as Erroh struck back with a force he had not shown before. In one fluid movement, Erroh disarmed the little shit, by means of smashing his sword in half. Wood broke a lot easier than most metals, especially expensive ones. The follow through was a swift satisfying punch into the face of the juvenile. He probably shouldn't have done that. Tye fell to the ground stunned, blood already seeping down his nose. Erroh stepped back, waiting for the outbursts from the child's parents.

"Well fought, Tye," Mea mocked in delight. Jeroen stood over him and offered a rag to stem the flow.

"Doesn't look broken. Go, and accept the defeat like a man." He reached down and pulled his dazed apprentice to his feet. Tye nodded and the blood began to cease its steady drip. Holding the reddening rag to his face, Tye muffled some words of congratulations. In one fell swoop, his confidence was tapered nicely. He should have taken the draw.

"What do you see now, darling?" asked Mea, looking at her wounded kin.

"I see another Alpha."

"Aye, you do," said Erroh quietly passing the sparring sword back to Jeroen who in turn returned the weapon to its rack. Mea succumbed to mothering ways and checked her child's nose. Satisfied that he needed no medical treatment, she let him pick up his shattered weapon.

It wasn't Mea's night to cook, but her usual lessons with her son and crossbow were overlooked for the evening. A young cub could only learn so much in a day. Instead, she had poured a great deal of energy into creating quite the spread. Upon a long mahogany table, fine chunks of peppered steaks lay on a wooden platter, piled high with roasted salty potatoes. Surrounding the meat were various bowls of buttered vegetables still steaming from the pot. In front of each placemat sat a goblet filled with an expensive looking red wine. Aye, it was a fine meal indeed. Fit for a king. Above the meal, a crude wooden candelabra emitted a warm light encouraging comfort, and Erroh felt very welcome. Mea raised her glass and toasted their guest while Tye, bested, took a few pieces on a plate and retired to his room to stare at his new broken souvenir.

Mea sat at the head of the table. Gesturing to Erroh to eat merrily, she cut up a few pieces and ate daintily herself while Jeroen attacked the vegetables with relish. Throughout the meal, they spoke of trivial things like the turn of the crop, the brew of decent wine, and the suggestion that the city's economy was weaker these last few seasons.

Eventually, Mea just came out and asked.

"Why give the appearance of just a wanderer?"

"It's quite difficult to get a card game going, when every opponent believes you can spit fire from your mouth at will," Erroh replied between wonderful bites of buttered sprouts.

Jeroen laughed loudly. It was a great noise. "Don't they know that only happens when we get truly enraged?"

Erroh smiled and began to relax.

"The old lies serve us well," Mea agreed.

"In the first days walking, I wore my pride a little too openly, but I quickly discovered it brought more trouble than it was worth. So I decided to fit in like everyone else." It was a half-truth. "I am line of Magnus." That was the rest of the truth.

Mea stopped chewing. Her eyes flashed with excitement.

Jeroen was quite vocal in his approval of this revelation. "We're in the company of some right royalty here," he said toasting Erroh and his apparent royal ancestry. Erroh smiled, taking the jest on the chin. Most people, Alphas and lower, considered Magnus to be nothing more than a fierce barbarian from the Savage Isles, a brutal and violent warrior who'd stormed through the Faction Wars leaving ruin behind. To his vanquished enemies, this was probably a fair criticism. Erroh still thought him a good man, all savagery aside.

"I heard he had a son named Erroh," said Mea. After a moment she added, "I'm sorry about Tye's behaviour." She hesitated as if she were to say something else, perhaps an apology about his mother Elise. There was no need.

"Let us hope Tye can learn some humility from today," Jeroen said. "We hoped if any Alpha showed up on our land, we could let him thrash some sense into the boy."

"And you did," quipped Mea. "It was fortunate that you

played the hapless wanderer perfectly. You had me fooled for quite a time in truth."

"I shouldn't have punched him."

"No, you really should have," said Jeroen.

"It's true, he's a little shit sometimes," agreed Mea.

"It's good to see a young Alpha. There haven't been any at the city for quite a time. You will have quite the choice," Jeroen said. He smiled but there was a little worry behind his warm eyes. Erroh wasn't sure if this was a good or bad thing. What choice?

"He'll have no choice in the matter," hissed Mea. She held her glass out and dropped some pieces of steak onto the ground for her hounds and Jeroen took the apparent hint. Don't say anything of the Cull. Apparently, there was a choice. Or there wasn't. He knew so little. It was so fuken frustrating.

"You are here for the Cull, are you not?" she asked, just to be certain.

Everything in life led to the Cull.

"The Cull was great. Then again, it usually is for females," she said as helpfully as possible. Jeroen snorted a laugh that could have been disgust.

"It's not great for Alpha males," she admitted. "But you will do fine. It's not nearly as bad as it sounds. You will not die within. Like I said, the lies have served us well." She went to say more, but her eyes lit up, and she changed the subject. "What word is there from the road?"

Erroh thought himself comfortable enough to reveal his last few days. He began where most good stories should have begun, the night he awoke to some thundering noise. His voice broke gently describing the horrors he'd seen. Terror, revulsion, and self-pity were simply not poetic enough for a good tale. A skilled bard or storyteller would shamelessly omit gritty truths in the telling, but Erroh included them all. Taking lives was no casual task either and Mea placed a comforting hand on his. It was a small maternal gesture but it was welcomed.

Cheer finally returned to the table, as the night turned to morning. Finishing the last of the wine and safe in the knowledge that the city would likely offer answers to the mysterious attack, Mea and Jeroen regaled the younger Alpha with their own stories from the road, wonderful humorous tales from when they were young themselves. Erroh sat silently watching them. Still in love, still mated and deep down, he desired something similar.

The following morning, Erroh became acquainted with a new beverage. He sloshed the contents of the cup around in his hands, its soft aroma in the steam catching his nose as he studied it.

"It's cofe," Mea said. "It will become your best friend." It was terrible. He ventured a second sip. It tasted just as terrible.

"What is it made from?"

"Not really sure. It comes from beans, but beyond picking it up at the city market, I've never seen a plant," Jeroen said. His eyes glanced longingly towards the varying patches of crops. Perhaps a cofe farm lay somewhere in his future if no war was to break out.

"We've been buying it for a few seasons now. Since it first appeared," Mea said. "It costs a fortune. There's a lot of money to be made in exotic beverages."

"A man could rule Samara's economy with the right exotic beverage," Jeroen muttered to himself and Mea nodded absently. Maybe they had ideas above simple farming.

Whatever the reason, the cofe was disgusting.

"I hate it," he said, drinking it down.

6

THE MASTER

They suggested he wait a few more days before walking the last few miles. Without his journal, he had miscounted how early it was in the year. The Cull began in the last week of every third season. It was either their hospitality or the overpriced beds in a ramshackle tavern. He chose their offer of friendship, but he was loath to sit around idly waiting for boredom to sink in.

"My attack will come from both sides at any time, Erroh," Jeroen said grinning from across the sparring arena. He was strong despite his holding back. Erroh parried his next attack but still received another sharp hit in the stomach. He countered and hit nothing but fresh air as Jeroen danced away. I asked for this lesson, Erroh thought bitterly, looking at both swords in his hand. The two figures clashed for hours. A tangle of wood and limbs, and Erroh struggled terribly. At least he showed the watching Tye how to behave when being outclassed. Every time Erroh found himself sprawling in the dirt spitting blood and chippings from his mouth, he offered no complaint. Instead, he caught his breath, thought about what mistake he'd made, and invited the next attack. This offer Jeroen was happy to accept.

"My right hand just doesn't want to help me at all," Erroh said between bouts. It was not a complaint or an excuse. It was a request for an answer. They had sparred lightly with one sword at the beginning, and Erroh had easily defeated the taller man, but when Jeroen picked up a second, he had struggled to land cleanly. In any attack, Jeroen's blades acted as both a shield and an attack. It was most impressive.

"Your father is an able swordsman. I expected he would have taught you how to handle a second sword," Jeroen said.

"I chose a shield as my second." Erroh's father had pushed him towards duel wielding, but he knew that once he mastered that skill, Magnus would have pushed him towards the Clieve. His love was for the blade. The Clieve were something else entirely. It was the only thing both master and apprentice could never agree on. In the end, Elise had swayed her mate's mind and it was something Erroh was eternally grateful for. You had to be a certain type of brute to wear such vicious weapons. Not to mention the need for shield bearers on either side at all times. Erroh was happier alone.

"A shield is fine against arrows but a skilled swordsman can use a second sword just as defensively, but with far more efficiency. All you need is practice," Jeroen suggested with a twinkle in his eye. "About a year of sparring should do the trick."

The painful lessons continued for the rest of the day. Tye was an excellent partner as Erroh strived to learn how to fight a new way. The child attacked with his usual vigour, driving his opponent back. This time however, Erroh was not controlling the fight and Jeroen watched on, quick to offer advice where needed.

For a few wonderful days, Erroh found himself in

routines that he enjoyed. Wake up, work the farm with Tye, and then train brutally under the watchful eye of Jeroen. After dinner, sometimes armed with nothing more than a glass of wine and a deck of cards, he would laugh and mock the night away with the family of Alphas. Before sleep, he would venture to the far end of the farm, look north to the strange glow beyond the horizon and think about how fine a life he could have, were he to meet a female like Mea. Perhaps, it would be someone strong and passionate to compliment him. Then fearful thoughts would take his mood, and he would slink away and find solace in dreamless sleep.

On the last night, she joined him at the wall.

"You should smile more," she suggested. She startled him, but he returned his gaze to the city.

"I find that when I smile, all females swoon, so I keep that weapon to myself." Perhaps she made a point. He'd fallen out of the habit of smiling. He was very good at it, he recalled. A wolf howled from nearby. Its call was lonely, primal, and threatening. Somewhere beyond, a second howl filled the peaceful night.

"We're the dominant pack here, they will soon pass us by." Mea's eyes watched the darkness, just in case. It was the hunter in her.

"Wolves can't be trusted," muttered Erroh, and another howl echoed from far away. The wolves were moving on as quickly as they arrived.

"It's alright to be afraid of the Cull," she whispered.

"Aye," he agreed, feigning bravery and failing spectacularly.

"You are a fine catch, Erroh."

"I certainly am," he lied.

"You will have no problem attaining a mate."

"I'm sure too," he lied, and she laughed.

He was terrified at any thought of spending an entire life with a stranger. No matter how appealing she could be. They would have to share food out on the road. And other things. He'd taken a life, but he'd never actually attempted to create a life.

"Did your parents tell you anything of their Cull?"

"They told me nothing," he muttered, shaking his head in frustration. If she wanted to hold him and say all the most reassuring things she could imagine, she made no attempt. Not that he needed such comforting. He was an Alpha after all.

"I just can't imagine walking the road, hand in hand with another," he said.

"I'm sure she's just as nervous," Mea said. He hadn't thought of that. That this fabled mate he was destined to meet had real thoughts and real worries of her own. He had just seen her as nothing more than an ominous eventuality.

"Tell me something about the Cull," he whispered. Something, anything.

"Do not lie." Though they were alone, miles from eager ears, her eyes danced from side to side as if speaking of the Cull would bring doom upon her household and line.

"As long as you are honest, you will find success," she said. It sounded like a warning but then her face brightened. "I expect the highest of the lines will try to fight it out for you. It will be quite bloody." Her eyes ceased their frantic searching for eager ears and stared at him with delight. "Words will be spoken."

He didn't understand, but he wasn't going to interrupt.

"What do you really understand of the females of the city?" she asked. He knew about bloodlines, he knew about Alphalines, and he knew about a Culling. He shook his head, fearing that to speak aloud might stem the flow of her words.

And she did not stop speaking. She spoke to him as though he were a child or an enthusiastic apprentice, the way his own mother had when teaching him the ways of the world. And, like his mother, she used the same careful tones, which endeared and educated at the same time, a skill they had both learned in Samara, no doubt. Oh, how he missed Elise terribly.

"Though there is nothing as obvious as a class system between the females, there is still an unspoken divide. All females are bound to earn an education within the great walls, but there are a select few who carry higher standing above all others. A privileged position within the city is a fine place to be, but such a place is not simply bought or earned through small deeds. It is earned in blood. In lineage to be exact," she said in that wonderful, familiar tone.

He knew most of this already.

"The finer the heritage, the richer the bloodline. Such things are very important in a prospective mate. Such things are very important for the bloodline to continue and grow stronger. For our children to outdo us. This is why we Cull. This is why we are called Alpha," she said. The wind began to blow and the trees above them began to rustle their leaves. It was a haunting call of loneliness only sounded when the world was darkest. The horizon appeared to grow brighter in reply. So close.

"When the son of Magnus and Elise walks into the Cull, it is likely you will attract some attention. Though remember, it isn't a name which will win her heart." Her words sounded a little hollow.

"I was under the impression that a name like mine would not serve me terribly well among some quarters," he said trying to disguise the irritation in his voice.

She nodded sadly. It was all she could do.

"What if I rejected this honour?" he asked. "What if I just go find a mate somewhere out in the wastes?" It sounded like a plan, and an ill-conceived one at that. Her sigh certainly suggested as much. Perhaps the Cull really wasn't at all as bad as they made out. Perhaps a life of wondering what it could be had led him to a paranoia. Perhaps he really was a coward who favoured the simple life of solitude. Then again, was his life not perfectly acceptable as it was? Certainly, he had urges and bouts of loneliness, but there were ways to deal with such things. This close to the city, was he ready for a mate for life? And when it all came down to it, there was always the fear that he would fail. He didn't know in what way he could fail, only that he could.

"You'll find whatever you seek, little one."

———

There were no tears the following morning though he felt a loss. Tye walked him to the edge of the farm, the younger Alphaline even offered a deferential bow as they parted ways, and Erroh began the last stretch of his great march.

By late afternoon, he broke through the deep trees and came upon a well-worn road. Anxiousness and perhaps a little excitement drove him forward. He followed the road through mile after mile of dense forest and never realised how tired he was even when the ground at his feet turned from mud to rock. A few miles further and the trees opened up at the crest of a hill revealing the great walls of Spark City in the valley below.

They were ancient, like every remnant of the times before, but these massive stone walls were greater than any he'd ever seen or even read in his young life. They stood hundreds of feet high, reaching deep into the sky above. A lone beast of grey rising up above an ocean of green, and Erroh felt insignificant in their magnificence and in their terrible ugliness as well. Hidden somewhere behind them was Samara, the fabled city of light, home of the divine Primary and her daughters, in every sense but blood. He felt elated and terrified. His prize was so very near.

"It's a big wall," he muttered to the wind and continued walking down through the valley, which opened out into wide fields of crops. The many farmers working the fields of wheat or caring over the countless mounds of potatoes ignored the lone wanderer as he passed. They only cared about their field. Perhaps they were not impressed by a solitary wanderer of the road; perhaps they did not care if he was an Alphaline coming to claim a prize.

There was more than one path leading to the city. Erroh imagined it was symbolic that all were welcome from each faction of the world. Or else it was just an overzealous road builder, eager to earn a few extra pieces for a job excessively done. As it were, he took a fine cobbled path down alongside the "Great Mother," where she flowed at her wildest, passing the city, and meeting a vast lake beyond before streaming out into a thousand channels, sating the thirst of the lands beyond. He'd heard many people suggest that from the city's harbour, it was possible to sail a galleon to the edges of the world. If one knew the right route that is. He suspected this too was just another old lie. He'd seen few rivers on his travels capable of holding anything larger than a dozen handed barge. Nevertheless, the massive river did serve a purpose. Elise had explained the use of cylinders in the water, and a wonderfully sounding word called electricity, and he had nodded along with her, smiling his complete understanding and concealing utter bewilderment. She'd smiled knowingly; he was only able to fool her for so many breaths. She'd told him the river was a beast to be controlled and left it at that. Even now, watching a long line of massive wooden cylinders digging into the heavy flow, he felt just as lost. Their low humming noise suggested he could be no further from the reassuring silence of the wilderness. All suggestion of solitude was lost as the paths converged into one fine road at the front of the city where Erroh encountered many other travellers, who congregated loudly at the gates where guards dressed in black armour sorted them into wanderers, farmers and general traders with calm efficiency. Not that it was an easy task. Erroh listened to fine compelling arguments between soldier and lowerline as they challenged their value to the city. Curses, mocking and suggestions of greasing wheels filled the air. Erroh couldn't help but notice they all shared the same desperate ambition of gaining entry to the city. Luckily, the guards in black were eager to help them on their way. At a fair cost of course. In truth, most were granted access, once coins were gifted. It was quite a profitable station. Those wretched few without a strong enough argument or the riches to gain access were denied the shifting metal scream of the city gate opening. Instead of returning to the wastes, they moved down along the side of Samara where a few other similar wretches scattered out between great wall and water. Erroh could see crudely erected tents and shacks lined up unsteadily, and he felt a sense of sympathy for these unwanted exiles. For whatever reason they had walked to the city, they now found themselves unwanted. Worse than that, they were simply unnecessary. Regardless, nothing could be done for them, so he fell in line and waited for entrance.

7

SPARK CITY

"You here to trade?" asked the guard, leaning out from a jutting wooden platform in the wall above Erroh's head. Four similarly dressed guards covering the city gate watched him uneasily. Perhaps they sensed his bloodline. They were the Black Guard, the grand protectors of Samara, the "Wolves of the Spark", and they were never to be trusted, according to his father.

"I'm here for the Cull," Erroh replied, though it made him feel uncomfortable. Spoken aloud it brought the event to life, did it not? No longer was it a carefree few miles down the road. He swallowed and feigned confidence.

"You had best not be lying about such a thing, little cub," the guard growled in a way that suggested the last thing Erroh should ever do was lie. He looked Erroh up and down, searching for deceit or confirmation. Somewhere behind the massive gate, Erroh could hear a low rumble of noise. Thoughts flickered back to a night out in the forest.

"It is my right," he said, when the guard made no movement to allow him through. Surely, an Alpha wouldn't be stopped at the door. How embarrassing to be unable to pay his way at the last few steps. In truth he had things to barter, but not with this brute.

"Not many would claim such a thing." The guard's eyes fell to the pommel of Erroh's sword. He thought he saw a flicker of recognition on the man's face. Or perhaps it was an assumption that a lowerline would never have the wealth to afford such a piece? Whatever the guard's thoughts, it was enough.

"Go to the office of the Primary. If you fail to present yourself there, the city isn't big enough to hide you," he warned and pulled at a heavy winch. His eyes never left Erroh as he spun the winch furiously. They hinted that they would remember him. The scream of steel startled Erroh as the gates creaked opened just enough for a single Alphaline to squeeze through, upon which the low hum of civilisation he'd previously heard became a disarming roar of twenty thousand inhabitants.

This was the famed City of Light. He hated it immediately. Everywhere he looked, wave after wave of dreary colours moulded together as one. There was a haze of grey, brown, and black in the people, in the buildings, in almost everything. He could taste it in the air too, an affront to his quiet life walking the road. All around him was a cacophony of unnatural noise, a tempest of activity, and he was overcome. He'd never expected to see so many buildings towering over him: grey stone structures sturdy, aged, and filling the city from wall to wall. Running between them were narrow streets with smooth cobbles, and people flowed through like swelling gushing currents in the Great Mother's drift.

Panic.

He gripped his chest as it tightened. So many people. His eyes couldn't focus on one for more than a few seconds. So much motion. The citizens thought it a small matter that so many could be crammed in behind these massive walls, while he thought it a simple matter of suffocation. They moved as one, and Erroh stepped in against the main gate to collect himself. He could hear their talking, shouting, laughing, crying, wailing, screaming, and cursing but most of all, he could hear their bartering, and he began to calm himself. He could see beyond the masses, gaps in the ocean of bodies. It was only at the main gate where many paths met that the crowds seemed to be at their worst. There was more than enough room for all, he told himself. This was a massive city. It was at least a mile in width and thrice as long. There would be no crush, he just needed to find a route and move with the right current. He would treat it as though crossing a precarious stretch of rapids. No problem.

He noticed something else. Hanging loosely on the nearest walls were thin lines of cord no wider than his finger. Attached to some cords every few feet were delicate looking glass balls, perfectly lined up resting against the stone wall. They never seemed to end, with each cord covering the length of the wall and beyond. The nearest string of balls hung just above his reach, but he could almost swear they were glowing. Not enough to affect the drawing darkness of the day but they were pleasant to gaze upon. Perhaps it was just his imagination. His mother had insisted that there was great beauty in the city. Little glowing balls were not the worst. He ignored the fresh scent of flowers and followed the glowing balls along their route. They seemed to flicker slightly and become a constant glimmer. He wiped his eyes and watched again. Then he looked away, deciding it was a trick of the light. Then he looked once more.

. . .

A young female walked by carrying a blade and scabbard in her hands, it did not match her yellow dress in any way, but she didn't seem to mind. She glanced at him with startlingly disarming eyes while he stared blankly around, completely oblivious to her. After a few seconds waiting for him to notice her and perhaps answer a question she had to ask, she shrugged her shoulders and disappeared back into the crowd. Her mind was on other things.

Aye, they definitely were glowing and to watch a tiny light burning without kindling or oil was a wonder to him. They were eerily beautiful. He blinked and his eyes stung. This he didn't like as much. Eventually he ceased his staring and stepped into the crowd cautiously. It took him longer than he thought to manoeuver the streets confidently. Two years of walking at his own pace hadn't prepared him for the tight surge of people and their unpredictable march. Bumping and grinding, he fought the tide and his balance. The warmth, the stench, and the unpronounced aggression. He fought his rising anxiety once more as sweaty bodies surrounded him. They all appeared to stare blankly straight ahead, and Erroh was unable to do anything but match their collective charge, lest he stumble, fall, and probably die under their crush. However, he did not fall in the end, instead he slipped between their swell and found his feet and before he knew it, he'd ventured deep into the city in search of his prize and getting completely lost at the same time. When the crowded streets became little more than steady streams he finally swallowed his pride and asked a passer-by for directions. As darkness began to appear in the sky above, he found himself standing in front of the offices, knocking on their oak doors. To his surprise, and despite the late hour, they opened.

A man named Seth greeted him and swiftly led him down a thin corridor to a gloomy windowless room where he gestured for Erroh to sit on a cushioned stool. A solitary ball of light hung from the ceiling above and swung gently in Seth's wake as he closed the door behind them. He was old like Erroh's father but his hair was thinning at the centre and his skin was meticulously shaved clean. He wore delicate glasses with eyes that suggested kindness in them. Perhaps it was just the light.

"You're the first this year," Seth muttered. Rooting through his desk, his hands flashed over numerous scripts and books. As he did, his hands brushed a half full mug of dark liquid hidden among many sheets of parchments which he instinctively lifted it to his nose. After a breath, he dared a sip, grimaced, and slid the mug away from where it came.

"My name is Erroh."

"Aye, you're the son of Elise and Magnus," agreed Seth. "I know you have a sister here too. She will be along, but not today." He looked at Erroh as if he'd forgotten his manners and smiled. "You are here to Cull?"

Erroh nodded, his stomach turned.

Seth scribbled a few important looking notes down on paper. The swinging light above them sent shadows across his aged face like fingers reaching out, unnerving Erroh more than it should have. This room felt wrong. He missed fresh air and light. How could any man sit in a room like this all day and not go a little mad?

"She will be interested to meet you," Seth said, reaching up and steadying the little light above him.

Who would? His sister? His mate? Someone else? His stomach turned again.

This wasn't the arrival to Spark he had imagined at all. He had expected at least a little grandness. A few trumpets maybe. Instead he sat in a little room with a man he was not sure if he liked or not.

"Place your belongings in here please." Seth slid a chest across with his foot. He ran his finger along an old ledger, its pages dry and yellow from age. He muttered a few more times and finally found what he desired. "Sign here," he said tapping the page and gesturing to a black quill among the official looking debris. But Erroh didn't want to sign anything. He just wanted to know what was to become of him. Questions burned in his mind, desperate pleading questions about the Cull. He opened his mouth to reveal his ignorance but instead he sighed and picked up the quill like a good little cub and scribed his name. He wasn't supposed to know anything about the Cull. What chance would he have of learning something new, sitting here in the beast's lair?

"I have some worrying news from the road," Erroh said, returning the quill to its inkwell. Seth blew at the ink and looked up with curious grey eyes. Go on, they suggested. So he did. He made it as far as describing the message on the wall before a dismissive finger silenced him.

"It's late in the day, and the Cull must take precedence," Seth said, leaning across the table. "All of the females have been waiting their entire lives for your arrival. We shouldn't make them wait any longer, should we? Rest assured, you will be allowed to deliver your worrying news at an appropriate time."

What type of wretched wanton female spent her entire life waiting for a mate, Erroh thought despondently? Then again, what type of male walked a few thousand miles just to meet her?

Seth brightened. "On to the formalities. May I see the proof, for the right to attend?" He glanced helpfully behind

Erroh's shoulder. He removed his father's sword and slowly presented it to the enquirer.

"It's a fine blade," he said running his fingers along the edge and caressing its crest.

"Mercy."

"I know its name," Seth said, placing it carefully into the chest. "Will this blade also be proof, for your future line?"

It was such a simple question with too many connotations. Erroh imagined a young cub, sitting in this very room, two decades from now, nervous and anxious, hoping to follow in his father's footsteps. What strides would his own son have to take to match his own? What type of father would he be? Was he even ready to be a father yet? Oh fuk. He thought about bolting as panic overcame him. He coughed, it was all he could do, and a word appeared in his mind. Beautiful and obvious. Like father like son. Instead of fleeing, he quietly removed the other sword from his back and presented his token. He thought about the foolish oath.

"Vengeance," he whispered.

This pleased his inquisitor; it was hastily scribbled down. It allowed Erroh a moment to dispel his worries somewhat. This was only ritual. He might not even be chosen. Or he would not choose. Or there may in fact be no choice at all. All he knew was that "words would be spoken," according to Mea. He shook the unhelpful thoughts away. He was in this event now; best he could do was keep his calm. How bad could things get anyway?

Seth placed the second weapon into the chest and locked it, before leading Erroh from the room, down the end of the thin corridor to one final door. A thousand coats of varnish hinted at its care but age had still cracked its finish in numerous places. In the fading light, he could make out decorations of battles carved into its oak frame. Aye, it was a fine old door and it looked as sturdy as a jail gate.

"This could take a time," Seth said before disappearing back to his office. There was a distant slam, and Erroh felt very alone in the building, thinking disconcerting thoughts about the future.

It did take quite a time. Erroh paced up and down the corridor too many times to count. He stretched his routine fully, which proved less distracting than he had hoped. So he did it again. He hummed songs from the road, some of defiant brigands, some of visiting cities and some of great death marches through the desert, but time passed slower than the darkness in the little window above his head and soon enough he found himself fighting exhaustion. Soon after that, he fell asleep outside the grand oak door with the finely crafted finish.

"She will see you now," a voice whispered in his ear, and Erroh shot awake, his hand reaching for a weapon. Any weapon. Seth was kneeling in front of him and approved of his reflexes. He stepped away, gesturing to the open door beside them.

Erroh wiped his eyes and stifled a yawn before it overtook him, the hallway had turned to complete darkness but there was a slight glow from the open door, and he stepped through into a chamber, which unsettlingly reminded him of an arena.

There were more of the unusual glowing lights in the floor at his feet. They spread out along the bottom of the wall matching its circular shape. The only other object within was a similar door opposite to where he entered. The room was no more than forty steps across, but he couldn't see the ceiling. The floor and wall was the same black metal worn by the city's guards and his feet echoed loudly as he stepped into the centre of the room and waited. The lights at his feet blinded him to anything more than a few feet above his head. He tried to remember how high this building had been from the outside, but he cursed his memory. He felt like he was gazing upon a starless sky and someone watched from above. After a few breaths, he heard a creaking, like a foot on a badly maintained staircase. He spun on his heels for any clue but nothing revealed itself. He stepped up to the second door and tried to push it but it stood firm.

"Of course," he hissed loudly as the door behind him slammed shut, and he heard the predictable click of a lock. In that moment, he decided he did in fact not like Seth at all.

Another creak in the rafters above distracted him and immediately Erroh fell silent and stared up into the nothingness. "Who's there?" he called. No one answered, and why would they? They were too busy hiding in the dark making their choice about him, or something along those lines.

He heard another noise at the far side of the room and again he searched with little joy. He was not alone, this he was quite certain of. His body shook though not from anxiety. In the dim light, he caught his breath, and he realised just how cold this cell was. No, it wasn't a cell. It really was more like an arena and a place to view a fine ambush.

A few more noises came from high up above. He did not bother to look this time. It was his attempt at defiance. "I can hear you," he muttered under his breath and then he looked up again anyway. They sounded like padded footsteps; delicate like a feline at hunt. "I can hear you." The phantom sounds replied and became an incessant moan all around him. It felt as though the building itself was alive, slowly waking from a slumber, and he was stuck within.

It's a test, you fool.

Of course. That made sense. This city harnessed sunlight in a ball. What else could it do in the dark? The noise grew to a roar, and Erroh almost believed some beast would drop from above with talon and venom. The room's noise reached its zenith and fell unnaturally silent, and Erroh found himself staring into the stillness of darkness once more. He could feel eyes upon him. His father had told him to trust his instincts. If you can't see, then listen. So he did. But his imagination betrayed him. He heard a hundred sets of blinking eyelids, a thousand carefully taken breaths and lastly he heard ten thousand skipped heartbeats. But really, his ears heard nothing. And then after a few moments of nothing much happening, something happened.

Four men dressed in the city's armour crashed through the far door and attempted to surround him. They carried crude heavy clubs in their gloved hands and they moved with murderous intent. He leapt back before they could surround him fully, reaching for his sword he cursed loudly. It was a fine curse with just enough crudeness to merit the situation. Four against one was a different kind of beast altogether.

Well, at least there weren't five, whispered the absent gods in his mind.

Retreating to the wall, he kept his hands up. This was a test. It had to be a test. The nearest Wolf leapt forward and swung viciously at his head. He ducked under the blow and stumbled away. Not a test. They meant to kill him. Magnus was right. He spun away from another strike and the wooden club cracked against the wall behind him. A loud metallic echo filled the room and disappeared in the rafters above. He swung instinctively, punched the attacker across the black helm, and regretted it immediately. He stifled a scream and rolled under a third and fourth attack nursing his aching hand before crashing against the far wall and stumbling to his knees. The room was far too small. He cursed loudly again and felt a lot better. Ducking and dodging was no battle plan, neither was striking out at metal. He leapt to his feet as the guards tried to form around him and waited to strike. His first victim broke the flanking formation by swinging wildly in the hope of a killing blow. Erroh sidestepped and grabbed the man's helm while stamping viciously down on his knee. It lacked grace but there was a satisfying pop followed by wild screaming. Wrenching the club free and shoving the injured man to the ground, he turned to face the other three. Despite the adrenaline and the fear, Erroh was still. Everything around him seemed to slow down, and he could feel the turning of the tide. This battle was already over. He just needed to trust himself and move with the moment. This he did, with very little difficulty.

They circled him barking new strategies and after a few breaths, they attacked as one. The loud crack of heavy wood clashing filled the room, and Erroh held them off at the expense of one glancing blow across his ribs. A fair trade. Pain screamed through his body, but he countered the offending attacker with a strike across his chest, which knocked him to the ground, Erroh's follow up across the faceguard knocked him out. Grabbing the man's club as he fell, Erroh charged the remaining two and struck with combinations of his own. In the end, it wasn't a fair fight at all. He battered their defences and easily struck them to the ground. They were adequately skilled but simply no match for him. Their armoured hands covered what blows they could as he fell upon them, like a rabid dog unleashed and crazed, when suddenly a voice pierced through the melee.

"Enough, Erroh." A light above him came to life, and Erroh, kneeling on one of the Black Guard, stopped mid-strike. He looked up and recognised her immediately even if he'd never had the pleasure. Her name was Dia, she was twice the age of his father, and she was to be served without question, for she was the ruler of the world. A light illuminated her regal shape, and she stood grandly on a podium on the balcony above. The room that had known such thunder now fell quiet. Even the sobbing moans of the first attacker were barely audible. The Primary had spoken; it was wise to listen.

"Those that can walk, leave," she hissed. Erroh watched in silence as those that could walk, dragged their broken comrades away from whence they came. A tinge of guilt for his brutality stung him. It mattered little that they'd started it. It had been a test.

"Your father taught you well, and you share his taste for violence," she said coldly. He placed his weapons on the ground.

"Thank you, Mydame." He accepted the compliment for what it was, and dropped to one knee in reverence. She was dressed in a deep red gown, long, tightly fitted and incandescent in the simple light behind her. He didn't know if he should feel honoured or if this was simply protocol for a young Alphaline to meet the leader of the pack. He had never expected to speak with someone so grand. Who needed trumpets anyway?

"You may rise, son of Magnus," she said, gesturing slightly with frail fingers. "You have come far. However, it took quite a time to get here. Perhaps you are a slow walker or perhaps you were not ready?" It sounded like an accusation.

"I am ready now," he answered, and she sighed. It was worth more than a thousand mocking words. His hands shook from the adrenaline of war, and he held them behind his back.

"I also hear you have news of the road. I would imagine

you have quite a lot after so many years walking," she said, almost but not entirely hiding the derision in her tones. This is how a politician mocks you, he thought miserably. "Go on then, Erroh. Tell me of the news."

He did.

He spoke quietly of the smoke and the dead town, the message and the pyre. He left out the details of Leather and Steel. Speaking of the other horrors was strangely comforting, for knowing she could act on such matters was reassuring.

When he finished, she gave it little thought. "The bandits responsible will be hunted down and punished." He almost argued that it couldn't be so simple but, with a heavy heart, he accepted the bitter truth. It would appear that such an attack was a common enough occurrence. How hard must any person's skin be, to learn of such horrors and brush it off? The podium creaked as the old female straightened her back and stood a little taller.

"Will you take the pledge?" she asked, her voice laced with formality and unexpected excitement. All depressing talk of burned females, broken towns, and shallow graves forgotten, they were lost in the dark rafters above.

What pledge?

"Aye, Mydame." He hoped his face didn't show his confusion.

She spoke loudly and distinctively and gestured for him to repeat her words. She'd done this before, he could tell.

"I shall never reveal what occurs within these walls. I shall answer in only truth, like my father before. If I am chosen, I will never leave her side. Nor shall she step from me. On my name, on my legacy, and on my child's birth-right," Erroh repeated, and she seemed happy enough with his words. She offered a few of her own. It was more information than he'd garnered in a decade of asking.

"We have seen you tested and worthy to present yourself. There is nothing else to face but the questions. Tomorrow, at first light, return here so we may know the measure of you as a man. You are forbidden to leave this city until a female chooses you," she spoke as if addressing a large crowd. He offered a deep bow. His thoughts now consumed by choices, questions, and mates.

"Thank you, Mydame." The world exploded into brightness all around him. A thousand electrical lights roared into life like a cruel uninvited dawn, and Erroh could only stifle a scream from the shock of blindness. He shielded his eyes until the burning passed, and he could make out shapes again. He looked back up to where the Primary stood and was not disappointed with what his bleary eyes met. Dia had gifted him a glimpse of something wonderful, intimidating, and teasing. If truth be told, he was suitably impressed. Standing side by side in a circle above him along the same balcony were the fabled females he'd heard so much about. A hundred or so but who was really counting. He suddenly felt like a prize bull at a market. They were expressionless and they were beautiful. As still as delicate porcelain statues, they looked down at him with piercing lovely eyes. So deliciously alluring that he ignored just how much they stared right through him. He'd seen females of beauty through his great walk. He'd even dared a few shared words with them, but never had he seen such goddesses. Many wore wild colours in their long flowing hair, while others expressed their beauty in lavish gowns of silk and lace. And he desperately tried to drink each one in and commit them to memory. He spun around, unable to focus on any particular beauty until his gaze returned to the Primary. She was grinning cruelly.

Beside her, a female with startlingly red hair whispered in her ear before the terrible darkness returned and once again, Erroh was blinded for a few breaths. Fine trumpets indeed.

"Each of the females in the room are of age but at most, only four may step forward to win you." To win him? Would somebody please explain this entire event once and for all? He bit the frustration down. He had an audience after all. They'd seen everything. They'd heard everything.

"You are the first Alpha to arrive this season, and my girls are patient. Do not presume you will taste success." She bowed before disappearing into the darkness theatrically leaving Erroh alone with a hundred hidden females. Unsure of what to do and no stir above, Erroh bowed in turn to the darkness and retreated to the doorway swiftly. To his eternal relief, the door creaked open, and he slipped away from prying eyes. His retreat carried him quietly down the dark hall to the offices of Seth where in uncomfortable silence he accepted his belongings and scribbled directions to his lodgings. He made to ask the older man further questions of the Cull but thought better of it. Soon enough he found himself out on the streets of Samara, staring up at the strange bulbs alight.

His mother was right about the beauty of Spark City.

Night had fallen completely and the lights had answered in turn. The shadows cast from the little glass bulbs danced everywhere, and he watched them in amazement. They were like frozen fireflies, suspended in the moment for eternity, their will bent to the hand of human so that darkness could never prevail. Unprepared for such a sight, he found himself strolling through the streets wearing a stupid grin of astonishment on his face and though the air still felt thinner than out in the wastes, in the darkest hours the city felt vibrant and alive. This was their race's symbol of progression. Spark City was the future of this fledgling civilisation.

He followed the lights through archways and stone pathways without too much trouble. Few people walked the streets since the markets had shut down and the only noises filling the night were drunken revellers in the busy taverns he passed. Eagerly reading the name above each inn but meeting little success, Erroh followed the instructions until he finally came to a less impressive tavern than those before. A low murmur of subdued chatter slipped out of the unvarnished front door. He could see a few shadowy figures through the cracked and grimy windows, and he felt right at home as he stepped through the creaking door of the "Pig in the Hole" and immediately made a stupid decision. He ordered a drink.

8

FIRST IMPRESSIONS

E rroh stumbled into his quarters long after midnight. Fine quarters indeed. Below the main floor of the tavern, deep in a musky basement, it resembled a single-bedded jail cell. It was about the same size as well. Only the best for the son of Magnus, it would appear. He stripped his clothes, draped them carelessly on the back of the only chair, and waited for the room to stop spinning. Removing the key from the bedside, he locked the door and felt the claustrophobic atmosphere immediately. It had only been a handful of beverages. He shouldn't be drunk or at least this drunk. He tasted the sediment from his last glass of sine on his lips and shook his head foolishly. A bad tavern, a bad brew. Fuk it anyway. He'd only had enough coin for a drink and a few hands but the absent gods had seen to it that his hand had stayed steady enough to earn an extra little bit of wealth. It was only a little cheating on his part anyway, enough to pay for a few extra celebratory glasses and a few more hands. His thoughts were on honey bread when he fell against the door loudly and reaching out in the dark to steady himself, he found a switch pleading silently to be flicked.

This he did with relish and the room immediately turned to bright. Wonderful. He flicked the switch again and found himself in darkness once more. This too was wonderful. After repeating the process a few more times, with a childish grin on his face he turned to the bed. It had looked more appealing in the dark. The pillow was worryingly heavy with an aroma of sour milk on one side and a seeping, damp stain on the other. The mattress was a suspiciously coloured brown sheet, covering some straw. The tattered blanket was reasonable enough, apart from the long forgotten chunk of meat clinging to its surface and the small nest of grubs that had made their home within. He ripped the bedding away and flung it at the door. After clicking the switch a few times, he fell into the straw and closed his eyes.

The beast ran at him. He could not move. His feet were stuck to the ground. He could feel the thunder of its hooves on the sandy ground. It sounded like hammering. He lifted one foot up. He tried to step forward. The great beast just thundered nearer. It was behind him, hunting him, shouting at him. Screaming profanities. So terribly loud. Then everything settled. This was nice. He was back home. He was walking for a few days across his land. It was his father's land. And he had boar. He had also learned to fly. It had been a lot easier to accomplish than he had ever imagined. The land began to shake again. He fell out of the sky. Then a birch tree started shouting profanities. Then it was all dark. He had fallen from the sky, and he was dead. He lay there, being completely dead while the darkness called him a "useless tyke."

.   .   .

"I called you an hour ago," the tavern keeper spat. He stood over Erroh, his fingers flicking the wonderful switch up and down. It had the desired effect, and Erroh rose drowsily from his bed. "It's not my fault if you're late!" he shouted, returning the spare key to his pocket. "It's not my fault you would sleep through a storm," he added before disappearing up the stairs to the inn above leaving Erroh with his bleary thoughts.

He was late.

Stumbling over to the bucket of waste in the corner, he lifted the lid and retched violently. Cursing the brew, he wiped his mouth and lamented his decisions. The room spun again, and he steadied himself against the doorframe. Wearily he dressed and splashed some fresh water from a basin in the corner and dared a glance in the mirror. A scruffy city urchin looked right back at him and grinned maniacally. It was his attempt at an endearing smile. He splashed more cold water on his face and pulled himself away from the mirror. The sun had come up, the city was coming to life, and he was really fuken late.

By the time, he'd made it upstairs his stomach had begun to settle. He was even beginning to feel like himself but for the poisonous smell on his breath. The unimpressed innkeeper was at the bar, cleaning up from the night before. He looked as tired as Erroh felt. He looked like a man who didn't want to be up this early in the morning (or indeed this late). Perhaps it explained the tainted alcohol he'd served.

"Do you have any oranges?" Erroh croaked in his most hung over voice. Without a stick of eucalyptus or a few fresh leaves of mint at hand, he was desperate.

"No," growled the innkeeper.

"Do you have any fruit at all?"

"No,"

Erroh sighed.

The innkeeper sighed as well.

"Do you have anything for my breath?" Erroh asked desperately. He couldn't help notice how bright the morning sun was. He rubbed his eyes and lamented his foolishness.

"I have some orange mead."

———

Erroh watched the last flight of his breath in the dimly lit room. It left his mouth in little puffs, hung in the air and disappeared forever. He tried to slow his gasps but the run had exhausted him. He'd only taken one wrong turn through the winding streets before reaching the offices and being shepherded back into the arena of the Cull by Seth. He shivered and glanced back up at the illuminated balcony. There were no secret females today. There were no females at all. He kept an uneasy eye on the door opposite lest they felt the need to challenge him once more. It was something to do while he waited. And oh, he was waiting here quite a time. So late. He tried not to imagine that attending so long after dawn would have consequences. The mead churned in his stomach, and he fought the burning sting of bile and citrus until he heard footsteps.

She was small. That was his first impression, and he immediately straightened up as she walked along the edge of the balcony above. Her dark hair was tied in an intricate bun with delicate strands flowing out behind her. Her painted lips were an unnatural red, and he immediately wanted to kiss them. Calm yourself Erroh. He decided to stare at her neck as she walked around to the podium. It was easier than leering crudely at her enthralling shape barely hidden beneath her bright gown of silk. She had a fine walk and when she reached the podium and faced him with her stunning dark eyes, he was quite certain it was love at first sight. At least on his part. He soon realised her eyes were narrow slits of annoyance.

He was late. Sorry about that.

She spoke gently with a little quiver in her voice; it was reassuring to see someone else uncomfortable. Such a pretty voice too.

"My name is Lea. As lowest standing, I will lead this choosing," she announced as bravely as she could from the podium.

He nodded again. What did the lowest standing mean?

"Four have found you of interest," she said. "All of whom you may choose to accept as potential mates."

Excellent.

"Do you have questions?"

Did he have questions? Aye, he had a few. So many that his head was likely to shatter if he held them in a moment longer. So many that unless he was careful, he was likely to betray his complete ignorance.

In a sense, my dear Lea, I have a fuk load of questions.

"What happens?" he asked.

"We talk," she said, as if it was no matter.

Go on.

"About?" he asked when she didn't go on.

"Anything we feel like."

She frowned as if trying to explain to a child. "We ask questions and you answer."

"And what if I answer incorrectly?"

She almost smiled. "There are no incorrect answers, Erroh. There is only the truth."

He didn't really understand this at all. He was here to participate in the Cull. The actual Cull. Wasn't this where they sorted the finest of the bloodlines through feats of strength or daring or some such? He hadn't come here to talk. He had come here to claim his birth-right.

"Are there any more tests?" he asked.

"No more tests, just talk,"

"So when does the Cull begin?"

"It began the moment you bested the Black Guard. Your skill is not in question. Your participation is no longer in question either. The city and the Primary deem you worthy to be a mate, but it remains to be seen what type of a man you are," she explained rigidly as if reciting from memory, as if this was etiquette for this youthful age. As if this separated the weak from the strongest lines: as if this was how it was done. He always considered the Cull as barbaric, in a way, but this was something entirely different.

"And then what happens, after the talking?"

She raised an eyebrow, and he thought he sensed a smile, though not a terribly warm one.

"One of us may choose you as a mate for life."

He said nothing. He merely weighed up her words. He was here to attend, and he was here to win a mate. Hearing her say what he already knew did unsettle him somewhat. All thoughts of freedom were now lost. It was simply too late. Staring at this beautiful female above him should have settled any lingering trepidations, but he felt no better.

"Each day ends when I decide there is nothing more to be learned. It may be after a thousand questions, it may be after one. It is at this time that one of us may choose you. If none step forward, we reconvene the following dawn." She had a lovely voice. She glanced to something in the darkness beyond. Maybe it was another female. Maybe it was three, eagerly waiting to present themselves to him.

"How long does the Cull usually last?" he asked, trying and failing to hide his anxiousness and unexpected excitement. He heard a creak in the rafters above somewhere behind him.

"Traditionally, a female has made her choice by the second day. Many step away from the event completely by the third," she warned, though her eyes suggested it would not come to that. At least that's what he told himself.

"Do many choose on the first day?" He dared a charming smile and stopped immediately, remembering the mirror's unsettling gaze. He should have shaved.

"That is a rarity." He heard steps behind him, and a beautiful figure glided across the level above.

The second female moved as though she owned the room, nay the entire city. Her stunning red hair caught the light in each bulb, and she glowed. It flowed out behind her like a wave of fire and when she stepped up beside the smaller figure of Lea, it came to rest on her shoulder. She couldn't have appeared more graceful if she tried. Her dress was as black as the darkness around her and it fit snugly to her frame. She exuded confidence unlike any female he'd met before, and Erroh was drawn to her. It wasn't just beauty in her face; it was strength. She looked him up and down quickly and pursed her lips thoughtfully. He hoped she found him pleasing. He also felt like prey.

"This is Roja."

He bowed but his eyes lingered on her figure for a moment too long. It was the male in him and he'd been walking the road for so very long. They locked eyes, and Erroh was sure he had irritated her. Instead, she raised an eyebrow and bowed deeply.

Then a third entered.

She passed by Roja with barely a glance and took her place alongside Lea. Her straight hair was an unnaturally painted blue and it hung down her long sharp face wonderfully. Like the other girls, she was beautiful, though she didn't attempt to win his favour with elaborate gowns and overly painted features. That didn't make her appear any less enchanting. She wore a leather dress and a silver blouse. She exchanged a few whispered words with the host and both exchanged a warm smile. She directed that smile to Erroh, and he felt a little light headed.

"This is Lillium,"

She is a goddess, he thought.

He bowed to her and a few improper thoughts crossed his mind. He averted his eyes back to the first deity he had met today, who was busy introducing the fourth girl.

Her name was Silvia, and she practically fell into the room in her finest white gown. She bounced up beside Roja, evidently far happier to be participating in the event than the rest. Her big eyes glimmered in the light and her beaming smile was contagious. She was small like Lea, and she flicked her flawless blonde hair from her face adorably. He wondered if this was a skill she'd perfected, while garnering the attentions of many watching males. She needed no such trick; her beauty was more than enough to hold his attention.

"Hi, Erroh," she said in a northern accent, before smiling at each girl in turn. There would be worse things in the world to wake up to than that smile every morning, he thought. Though waking up beside any of these creatures every morning was likely a blessing from the gods who he didn't really believe in.

Who needed freedom anyway?

"Erroh, line of Magnus, do you find Roja acceptable?"

asked Lea formally when all four girls stood at attention above him. Then something bad happened. The room began to spin slightly. His eyes met Roja's. The stunning redhead did not blink. "Aye, I do." That was it. He'd cast his vote. Made his choice as it were. If they accepted him, he would leave this city with a mate.

"And Lillium?" Lea gestured to the blue-haired girl beside her.

"Aye." If she was happy about it, she wasn't eager to show it. The room increased its spinning and his stomach spun with it. Stupid cheap alcohol, he thought bitterly and tasted citrus on his breath.

"Silvia?" Lea asked and pointed across to the glorious little blonde.

"Aye." He returned the contagious smile she offered. It was all he could do as he hoped for the moment to pass. The lights at his feet appeared to glare accusingly at him. He wiped his brow, closed his eyes, and wondered how bad it would be if he was to collapse in a wretched heap or worse, throw up all over this shiny black metallic floor.

Lea looked through him though and spoke "And do you find me, Lea, of appealing taste?"

He fought the dizzy spell with all his will.

Do not collapse, he roared in his mind

A few seconds of silence passed, and he felt himself settle. The battle was turning.

He did not faint. So he looked back up.

In his defence, it was only a few moments pause.

The three girls looked nervously in Lea's direction. The petite girl held herself proudly, the only appearance of embarrassment, was a few seconds of uncomfortable blinking.

"Aye, very pleasing," he answered awkwardly, shaking

the haze from his mind. It was a trivial calamity on his part. He learned in that moment the precariousness of this event. It was an expensive lesson. Though she never said it, he had destroyed any chance of a coupling with her. Her eyes become narrow slits, and the old advice his mother once passed on about a "female scorned" came to mind. If looks could kill, he supposed. He thought about apologising for his hesitation, but he just couldn't find words that wouldn't make the matter even worse. He couldn't exactly tell her he felt like throwing up instead of saying she was the most beautiful creature he'd ever seen.

"I'm glad we are to your liking, Erroh of line Magnus," she said. The echo in the room enhanced the disdain in her voice. One female lost, three to go.

"Let's begin."

The blue-haired goddess named Lillium brushed her hand against the shoulder of Lea and met Erroh's eyes with a dangerous stare. She didn't approve of his hesitation either. It was her question to begin.

"Have you killed a man?"

He swallowed deeply to conceal his surprise. Memories of blood and violence and horror sprang to mind. This was no simple question to ask of any man or woman, yet it was a simple answer. And he did answer reluctantly.

"Aye, I have." He was a killer. It was something unspoken of, yet she had little difficulty breaking the taboo open for all to see.

"How many have you slain?" she asked. Lea turned to her. If she gestured anything, Erroh didn't see. Regardless, Lillium stared unblinkingly at him and waited.

"Five," he said, just above a whisper, scratching his arm nervously. Five men had died at his hands. Five horrific deeds he locked deep down in his mind with the rest of his most terrible things. He didn't know which of the females gasped the loudest. He did hear a whispered curse from somewhere above, but he had looked away in shame, sorrow, or regret. Perhaps all three. There were some things people shouldn't ask. There were other things people shouldn't answer. And there were things people shouldn't speak of at all.

"Were they deserved, son of Magnus?" asked Silvia the blonde, without the hint of a smile. This was probably for the better, already an uneasy atmosphere had fallen upon the room, and the event had only begun. Nevertheless, it was a fair question and granted him the opportunity to suggest he wasn't a complete barbarian.

Like his father?

"They were bandits, and on each occasion I had no other choice." Silvia waited for him to continue. "Though death is never justified, they fell upon me. They struck first, I struck last." Justified or not, it was near impossible to explain such gruesome things. He had taken lives; it was not something to be thrown around casually with words.

"You nearly doubled that tally when you first set foot in these chambers," muttered Lea, casually picking at a splinter of wood on the podium. He remained silent lest he make it worse.

"Would you have killed them had our Primary not hushed your aggression?" Roja the redhead asked. Her voice was commanding and it disguised any shock.

"Aye."

Silvia couldn't contain herself. "Why would you think such an action necessary?"

Four voices, attacking at once. Slow down, ladies, this was difficult to follow.

"It was necessary not to get killed," he admitted.

"They would not have killed you," Lea said.

"I was not aware at the time." His head was spinning. It wasn't from the tainted alcohol. Speaking aloud was an underappreciated art form, and he was out of practice. He was not used to questions thrown his way like this.

Lillium shook her head in dismay. "You somehow expected no show of force? No exhibition to show your prowess?"

"I honestly had no idea what to expect." He was outnumbered. Like beasts of the Hunt, they were stalking their prey. It was all going to end terribly.

Lea sighed as well. It was a terrible empty sound that appeared to echo around the room. "We expect all of your answers to be honest, Erroh." You were right, Mea. The Cull is great.

Silence hung in the air. The first barrage of words dissipated, and Erroh waited cautiously.

The redhead spoke next. "Have you ever hit a female in anger?" What was her name again? Roja. That was it. It was a fine name.

"Never, nor would I." That should have been enough. It was black and white.

Lillium had beautiful eyes, they looked at Erroh with murderous intent. "What if she deserved it?" She might have taken Lea's embarrassment to heart. Relax, lady; it was but a momentary hesitation.

"She would not deserve it," he answered as confidently as he could. Barbaric as they may see him and his lineage, he would not strike out at a female under any circumstances.

"What if she misbehaved?" the blue-haired female added. He sensed a trap. He was clever like that.

"Such as?" This was deadlier than walking the road.

Lea took over. "Met with another man?"

"I would not strike her," he said. It was a good answer in his mind.

"He has no balls," whispered Lillium loudly for the rest of the pack. This was going well.

"I'm sure his balls are just fine," hissed Roja, glaring at the blue-haired accuser. Lillium returned the expression with equal venom. Interesting. A strange thought occurred to him. What if at the end of the day, more than one female wanted to claim him? He stole a quick glance at each female and wondered a little more. What if they were battling each other for the right to mate for life? Perhaps great games were afoot, and he was indeed the prize. He felt a little better about himself.

Then it got worse.

Lea smelled the air and asked a question of her own. It was a simple question.

"Have you been drinking today?"

He thought about lying. It probably would have helped. A thousand excuses popped into his mind, but instead he nodded apologetically. It was my breath, you see, from the previous night's poisons and the matter of throwing up a short time before. These things happen, my beautiful friends.

Neither female commented on the question. Their disappointed faces were enough. They'd waited their entire lives to compete in this event, and he'd presented himself as a barbaric killer with a fondness for heavy drinking. He felt a terrible sinking feeling all around him and in these chambers; he doubted there was any rope on offer. He waited for the next onslaught.

"What do you plan to do after the Cull?" asked Lillium.

"Return home."

"That's a long walk," she insisted.

"I'll capture a mount," he said.

"It's still a distance!" she snapped.

"Aye, it is." He missed walking the road alone.

She grabbed the rail of the balcony tightly. "What if your mate doesn't want to move that far?" she hissed. Beside her Lea winced.

"So you do not want to move that far, Lillium?" he asked before he could stop himself. Was that even her name? He took a breath and reassured himself that it was. She didn't answer, and the room's silence became uncomfortable. Lea turned to speak but the blonde interrupted her.

Silvia sniggered. "Come on, Lillium, we are all waiting?" Beside her Roja laughed lightly, and Erroh thought it a delicious sound. For a few breaths, it was no longer four against one. There were issues here between the females. He thought about Mea's suggestion of entitlements in the city.

Lea stepped in. "Stop stirring a brew of trouble. Let's move along." She sounded more confident than before. Perhaps she was growing into her role. Whatever her role in the Cull was, it certainly wasn't going to be finding a mate. Erroh had seen to that.

"I'll ask whatever I choose to," muttered Silvia, folding her arms. It was a fine tactic after receiving a reprimand and though it was a petulant pose, she had very shapely arms. "Lowerline witch," she added under her breath.

The room felt much colder all of a sudden and Lea's face changed from confident to anger and then to embarrassment. She tightened her kissable lips and fought what Erroh guessed was a vicious retort. The moment passed, and she said nothing.

Lillium wouldn't let it go however. "Know your place." To Erroh's surprise, Silvia's veneer of petulance cracked. She stood away from the balcony as if an extra foot of distance could save her from the burning stare of the blue-haired female.

"And what place is that?" Roja the redhead whispered from beside her. Though he could barely hear them, there was no denying the challenge she offered. He didn't understand the hierarchy of this city, but he suspected Roja's status was quite high.

"Apparently it's by your side," spat Lillium. Despite her casual appearance, Lillium hinted entitlement as well. Or else she was not easily intimidated. Regardless, Lea was certainly intimidated, and she tugged at the blue-haired girl's sleeve gently, just enough to drag her from the brink of argument. Had they forgotten a perfectly foolish Alpha male standing below them?

Lea tried to steer the ship back towards port. "Do you surpass the skill of Magnus with a blade?" Both females glared at each other once more before turning back to their potential mate.

"He passed on his talents as best he could," Erroh offered, a little too weakly for his taste. What type of brazen fool would suggest that they surpassed the greatest living warrior in warfare? He knew he was good but Magnus, well, Magnus was something else entirely.

Silvia leaned forward "Fine words from an apprentice."

He tried to sound humble. "I can hold myself in battle."

"We are all well aware of your brutality," Lea said.

"Like father like son," muttered Silvia finding common ground with Lea. Their argument lost in the wind.

"I believe Magnus had killed far more by his age," Roja said. Erroh didn't like her tone or her suggestion. Not one little bit. "Erroh is most certainly not his father."

Lillium nodded. "No, he certainly is not." Their disagreement forgotten as well.

"Perhaps you fight more like your mother?" Lea suggested. Her eyes were narrow again. Perhaps he should have apologised.

"That's no bad thing. Elise is a divine goddess of war," muttered Lillium.

"She was a divine goddess of many other things as well," said Silvia.

Silence.

He held his tongue and wondered if bolting for the door was still an option.

Then Roja offered him a reprieve. She hissed Silvia to silence as if insulting his mother had insulted her. "Do you enjoy besting a man with a blade, Erroh?" Her natural qualities would stir any man. She bit her upper lip subconsciously and tilted her head and looked into his soul.

"I do." He waited for the explosion of words. He was quickly learning this game of words.

"A humble answer," said Lillium.

"But I do not care for fighting," he admitted. Was that true?

"Why do you not care for fighting?" asked Lea. As she spoke, she placed her hand gently across Lillium's own. It was a fine gesture of calming between only the closest of friends. Erroh had embarrassed her and Lillium was fighting her fight magnificently. It was only a matter of time before the blue-haired female threw something heavy at him. Maybe Silvia.

Why did he not care to fight? Good question.

He knew the proper reply. Something about hating to spill blood, or preferring the skill of words above violence, and though these were certainly influences, he said something far more truthful and foolish and regretted it straight away.

"It scares me."

Like the uncomfortable moments before, this seemed worse than the last. Lillium turned to speak but caught herself lest it become even more unbearable. Lea found great interest in the splinter once more. Silvia clicked her tongue a few times and fell silent, caught in a great many deep thoughts no doubt.

Eventually Roja said it.

"Are you a coward?"

He hid the awkwardness with a defiant smile.

"I may very well be."

She tried to hide her amusement. "What type of man admits he's a coward to prospective females?"

"A brave man?" joked Erroh. At least he was still swinging. His father would always have a place for him in his army though he'd still have to earn it. Maybe he'd be given an elite group of fighters to wage war upon twenty thousand faceless foes. That campaign would probably have more success than this event. His eyes fell upon each of the females. They didn't appear terribly impressed with his wit.

Ah well, next question.

"I think we're done for the day," announced Lea. Beside her, the females nodded in agreement. They had heard enough from the legend's son.

Perhaps he should have lied.

"Thank you for your honesty, Erroh. Has any girl made her choice?" she asked formally, and the world went quieter than ever. He suddenly felt dizzy. They glanced quickly at each other soundlessly, all waiting for either of them to make a terrible mistake or a beautiful choice. Seconds slowed to nothing but the count of breaths in the light, and Erroh felt the crushing weight of disappointment. None had chosen.

And then something happened; she stepped forward having waited for every other girl to reject him. She was an angel, and he was terrified. Each girl looked at him, then to her and back to him again. Countless emotions surged through him. Mostly fear and excitement. Perhaps it was love. Lea leaned over the balcony, her hands laying on the dark mahogany surface. They locked eyes, and he listened to the concerto that was her voice as it resonated through the dark chamber. "None have chosen you, Erroh. Come back tomorrow."

Each girl quietly left the battlefield without looking back. They were eager to escape this miserable battle of wits. He heard a heavy door close far away in the distance and then all the lights dimmed to nothing leaving him standing alone in the dark, where he belonged.

9

NEXT QUESTION

Tomorrow would be better but for now though; he felt like shit. Seth had obviously seen a few bad first days in his time and refrained from any comment. Leaving the claustrophobic office, he made his way through the morning crowds and found himself at the marketplace where he spent a few pieces on fresh cofe and some heavily floured bread.

When he tired of the endless bustle and cry of sellers and buyers, he ventured deep into Samara's heart. This was the great city of light after all, and he was keen to know her a little better, if nothing else so he could dislike her that little more. This city stood the test of time; he wondered what stories it could tell. He wondered what battles it had seen, and he wondered what battles it would see, for this was peacetime but all things changed.

Sturdy inner walls with wooden archways at various sections separated each district of the city. The poorer areas were simple wooden shacks at the edges of the walls while deeper in some of the richer homes had a second floor. He imagined the more successful merchants owned these. He wondered was there some skilled merchant shrewd enough to have earned himself a third floor tall enough to rival the chambers of the Alphalines or the tower of the Wolves? It was unlikely.

At various parts of the walls there were a few flights of steps leading skywards, and Erroh felt lightheaded watching a lone Black Guard make the trek high into the searing blue to patrol along the top. What would become of him if a strong wind just grabbed him? What thoughts and fears had driven the ancient beings to create something so monstrous? If their intention had been to lock themselves behind their stone and survive the great fires, they had succeeded. However, it hadn't been the fires alone which ravaged the world. Like time they too had passed, but their legacy lived on. This city could never fall. It would never burn. It was eternal. The first Primary had desired a place for her Alphas to learn and live. She had chosen well. Three hundred years and counting.

The librarian was thrilled with the new treasures. She had all seven capsules open in front of her like little soldiers waiting for millennium old orders. She inspected each perfect piece from the past closely, stopping every few seconds to remind him how amazing they were, how thankful she was and it felt good each time she did. He gently insisted that it was a small matter. It was wonderful to bring such childish glee, to one so old. Her name was "Massey," and he liked her immediately. She was the perfect example to the uninformed; there was little or no difference between bloodlines. They were all of the same race. Though her tanned skin was aged and her body tired, she carried herself as regally as any female he had met, and she spoke as though she had walked the road longer than most. He imagined her spending her youth eagerly searching in tombs, caves or forgotten wells for any sign of those precious metal tins from the past. A fine life he imagined but this world was vast and a thousand such lifetimes would still never be enough to assist this world's advancement. Rarely the scrolls dated from the same era. Many spanned across hundreds of years. Usually around the time of some cataclysmic event, for there were many. Some of them were words of hope and joy scribed onto little crisp pieces of paper for those that would come much later, but in most cases, it was their last few terrified words gifted to the future. If only they had thought beyond their fate. If only they'd thought of those who would follow. Instead, they'd dug them deep into the ground, desperate to keep a record of their useless life; never thinking the next world would need a little help in its advancement. The bulb of electricity above their heads flickered but stayed lit. Thank the absent gods that at least some had scribed words of importance. That some dug holes deep enough for some printed books to stay shielded from the great fires. Sometimes it hurt to think of what had been lost, but seeing any attempt at creating libraries was a fine reminder that life survived.

This library in particular was as small as the building suggested. Nestled between two of the richer houses, he'd almost walked past before spotting the little plaque over the doorway. The capsules belonged in a better place than his pack. She would not accept his donation so they had agreed upon a small exchange. The few pieces he now carried in his little pouch were barely the value of one scroll but it is what his parents would have wanted. So therefore, it was what he wanted. A man with all the knowledge of what was lost was a man that could rule the world. Or woman.

There was a fine selection of scrolls hanging from frames on all four walls but the true wealth to this building was the humble collection of books at hand. Despite most of the ancient relics too scorched or water damaged to read from first page to last, Massey's enthusiasm wasn't diminished in any way. Regardless of their condition, she'd stacked most of them on shelves around the room in alphabetical order. Moreover, those in their most legible state, she kept locked in a large glass cabinet beneath a curtain out of the sun's light. It wasn't just expensive treasures of old, which lined the lesser shelves of this fine room though. There were newer books, little more than crudely penned stories, poems, or even political rhetoric, scribed by those with a better education than the common lowerlines. They were still just as beautiful despite the grammar spelling and artistry. Her words warmed him with the thought that books would rise again, and perhaps when this world found its feet and put down their swords forever, they would.

At the far end of Samara were heavy sturdy gates almost as big as the wall itself. They protected the harbour. When opened over the deep settled water, vessels from the river could sail through and dock. If there was a weakness to the city, perhaps a naval assault was the smart attack. The small dock itself was awash with traders and seafarers, loading and unloading cargo, under the watchful eye of the Black Guard. On a few occasions Erroh was almost trampled by horse driven carts streaming from the barges, laden with fresh supplies to those who'd bid the highest. The last leg of his tour of the city brought him beneath the massive frame of the city arena. He hated it from first sight. Maybe it was the darker shadow it cast across the streets that set him at unease, or the thoughts of so many bloodthirsty people screaming for entertainment as combatants battered each other to a glorious pulp. The grandeur of sport was alive and well in Samara.

One side of the arena was built into the great wall, and like most of the buildings, it was sturdy and destined to last forever. He imagined the number of people that it would seat on a glorious day of a tournament but in truth, hearing the roar of the crowd would be something else. He dropped his head in disgust. That was just the Alphaline in him, he supposed.

As he ended his tour, the city lights sparked to life. The little glowing embers slowly began to blaze into life all around. It was unnatural but beautiful. He wondered would he ever get bored of the sight. He watched the city light up the night for a little while before gently turning the handle of the dented old door and stepping back into the Pig in the Hole.

He had a plan. It was a simple plan and it worked. He had some food brought to the shithole, cleverly disguised as his chambers. It was a mash of potatoes, sweetcorn with butter. All a higher line needed to build up the stamina to impress the waiting deities come the morning. He washed it down with a glass of warm milk and for the first time all day, no longer felt the delicate suggestion of nausea. He then prepared stage two of his plan. There were really only a few stages, at most two. They involved eating and preparing for the second day properly.

He washed the stains from his clothes in the cold water and rubbed sweet smelling liquid into the fabrics. He laid them out for the night and reassured himself they would be dry by dawn. As long as there were no wet patches in embarrassing places, he would be fine. He spent a fair part of the evening meticulously shaving his wild bristle into something he hoped was respectable. After staring at himself for a little too long in the mirror, he shaved himself clean completely. Finally lowering himself into a bath of tepid water, he scrubbed all sign of the road from his body. Laying down for the night after flicking the lights on and off a couple times, he left the door unlocked and closed his eyes, pledging that he would face his unstable adversaries with renewed vigour. He would face their questions and charm them. He would be clever and careful and in the end, he would win. Whether or not he was ready to win was another matter and what he would do with his prize was something else entirely.

———

"Are you serious?" cried Lillium. "Nothing built?"

"No, nothing built yet," he replied, trying and failing to win her over with his most hopeful smile.

All four girls had returned for round two. It should have been a good thing, but the very first question had exploded in his face, though not in a literal sense. That would have been a lot less painful, figuratively speaking. No, this was a portent of the day to come. It was a fine question. He should have answered with a little more of an explanation or with a little bit of that Erroh charm he thought he had. Instead, he had answered like a wanderer of the road, disinclined to give much away.

"So, you have no home for your mate," confirmed Lillium. He opened his mouth to answer but Lea spoke first. She didn't wear as much red on her lips today but looked even finer than the day before.

"Why don't you have a home built?" she asked and tightened her still very kissable lips. He thought about Jeroen and Mea building their farm together, and he could think of worse things.

"I thought she and I could build it together." It sounded smooth. He dipped his head humbly.

Perfect.

"Together?" one of the girls muttered. Roja it was. Was that her name? He was sure it was. Roja with the red hair. Lillium of the blue and Silvia of the blonde. And Lea with black hair who justifiably hated him.

"Aye, together."

"Not very prepared for this were you?" said Lillium. Perhaps she was no fan of manual labour, which was a pity because she had fine arms. Long, slender and perfect for sawing logs into building materials. She tapped her finger loudly against the balcony rail and wore her prowess a little more obviously than the other girls. She was a hunter. Perhaps all of them were, and he was little more than a field mouse, scurrying through their talons, desperately trying to avoid the inevitable snatch.

Was he prepared for any of this?

"I suppose not." All three glared at him. Perhaps this wasn't the most charming answer.

"Do you at least have land to your name?" asked Roja.

He nodded his head, which was something.

"Is it in the territory of your father's land?" Lea asked a little more nastily than needed. She wore a darker dress today. He imagined she would take to the hammer and nails. That was fine. He had never been skilled at such things, and she could vent some anger.

"Aye, there is suitable land around his territory." In Erroh's defence, Magnus's hold was in the east. There were worse parts of the world to rear a family. He held his tongue though, next question please.

"Good thing your father did all the work," said Lillium. He wondered what he would look like with blue hair. He would probably look stupid. She carried the look well though. It matched her eyes. Still though, fuk off woman.

Silvia tried to help, and he loved her a little bit for it.

"Is the land good and fertile?"

"Aye, it's rich land."

"Do you intend to farm?"

"Aye."

"Have you ever farmed?"

"No."

"How will you support yourself and your mate?" she asked. Smaller and more fragile than the rest, he wondered what she could bring to their joint venture. Of all the females, she appeared less prepared for a life of toil. Still though, that smile could warm any male's weary heart. He would work twice as hard to earn her praise and more. Aye, when it came down to it, he was not above the primal urges of a pubescent cub.

"His father will help him. Next question," Roja jested.

"I believe that's Lea's decision to make," Silvia said, staring ahead to avoid the glaring look from her closest friend.

Roja bowed with as little respect as she could. "My apologies. I don't know what I was thinking." She would demand a castle, thought Erroh. A castle, an army, and probably a throne. A highest-lined female like her was used to such things. Like Silvia, she would probably not build it with him either, though she was more than capable. Her skills were likely found elsewhere. Perhaps she would be suited to bartering for the finest materials. Fine materials were needed in the creation of castles and thrones. She would be a stunning queen.

What wonderful thoughts to have while staring up at their shared disappointed expression. When they had walked into the arena the day before there had been the unmistakable flash of excitement in their eyes but now that spark had turned to a dull ember. An unsettling thought occurred to him, what if they all rejected him? Surely, that couldn't happen, could it?

It could.

Lillium decided to drag up an old question, which had been bothering her. Thanks Lillium. It wasn't even your question, you blue-haired bitch.

"Why would you drag your new mate all the way across the wastes?"

He tried to be witty.

"It's a nice walk." He met a terrible silence. So much for wit. On to the next plan.

"Could be a lonely one," Lea muttered.

A few of the girls laughed.

All of the girls laughed.

Though the road had done little to improve his communication skills, he lost none of his talents in reading people's behaviour. Much of this skill he learned through healthy bouts of gambling, but in this uncomfortable game with these deities, no matter what cards he held, the odds were slipping further and further away. He wondered if he could ask for a fresh deal.

"What of our children, Erroh?" asked Roja. "If we are so far away, what of our children?"

"I don't understand."

"Of course you don't," sighed Lillium. She leaned across the balcony, supporting her head in both her hands perfectly portraying her disinterest.

"If one of us gave birth to a girl, Samara is a far walk just to visit her," explained Silvia in her own tone of mild irritation. The air felt thinner, and Erroh found his chest tighten slightly.

"My mother found a way," he said.

"Oh, yes, Elise the queen of the four kings," Silvia mocked and Roja gasped.

"How dare you?" the redhead hissed, taking the words right out of his mouth. Even Lillium shook her head in dismay, and Lea? Well Lea hid her head. He thought he saw a smile on her lips before she did. A fine trait to laugh at suggested innuendo.

"I am sorry for saying such a thing, Erroh," Silvia said quickly, though she did not direct the apology towards him. Her eyes locked with Roja's venomous glare. Twice Silvia had mocked his mother, and twice now, Roja had been angered.

"Elise is a legend. I meant no disrespect," she said, finally looking away to Erroh below. She smiled sadly, as if it was he who had uttered the slur. He accepted her ignorance; she was from a defeated faction, was she not? Nevertheless, wars were not forgotten, nor were their reasons for declaration.

"No need to apologise, my dear," he said, hiding his own anger. He even bowed, it was a nice touch, and she rewarded him with her most devastatingly grateful smile. It was almost a nice moment in the day, before Lea attacked one last time.

"Now that we have spoken with you, Erroh, do you still think you are ready for a mate?" It was a great question, though it should never have been asked.

Each girl knew it.

Each girl held her breath.

"I am not at all ready for a mate. I never was." He had more to say. Oh yes, he had a great deal more to say but the rock had been cast. Why bother adding to his trouble? If he lied and declared himself ready for such responsibility, there would be uproar. They were waiting for him to fuk up; he could see it in their eyes. If he tried to scurry away with a tissue of lies, any one of their talons would tear him apart.

"This is just wonderful," growled Lea.

"This is a disaster," agreed Lillium.

"This is a nightmare," spat Roja.

"This is a fine waste of time," said Silvia shaking her head.

"Do you even want to mate with us?" Roja said after a few uncomfortable breaths.

"You are the most beautiful females I've ever seen," he offered.

"Some of us less so," Silvia mocked, staring across to Lea, who shrunk visibly at the reminder. The room exploded with heated words, a hurricane of venom between four stunning females he thought more than appealing. Lillium screamed profanities at Silvia and her suggested sleeping habits, while Roja with pointed finger hissed her disappointment, displeasure, and disgust with the line of questions. Lea took umbrage and met the challenge wonderfully, accusing all in attendance as farcical, petty, and exceedingly nasty. Lillium grew tired of Silvia's weak retorts and took to threatening any who met her eyes, apart from Erroh who remained quiet throughout. The last words spoken were Silvia's suggestion that one of the other girls leap into the Great Mother, but before the accused female could retort, Roja suddenly turned on Erroh.

"What are you doing here, Erroh?" she screamed. Her voice echoed around the dark room. It was enough to cease the arguing.

"Winning you over?" he countered.

Oh, Erroh.

This time Lea laughed, a delightful melody sung at the most awkward of times when all hope is lost.

"Show some respect, Erroh," growled Lillium from beside her.

"I have been shown little!" he snapped back. It was petulant but fuk it, he had tried his best all morning. He had washed his clothes and everything.

"I believe we have learned enough for today," declared Lea, wiping her eyes. All girls agreed. They really had learned enough.

"Thank you for your honesty, Erroh. Has any girl made her choice?" she asked. Erroh thought he heard a little break in her voice. It was evident she wanted the Cull to finish as soon as possible.

The silence was deafening.

Lea and Lillium both stared over at the other two girls carefully for any sign. Roja would not make eye contact with anyone. She found a spot in the floor to stare upon with as much hatred as she could fathom. Her fingers gripped the balcony like claws. Seconds passed, and Lea stepped forward. She looked incredibly disappointed.

He knew how she felt.

"None have chosen. Come back tomorrow," she said.

Roja nodded and walked from the balcony, Silvia followed quickly behind while Lillium merely stared down at him as though his appearance suddenly pleased her. She did not smile; she merely tilted her head thoughtfully and stepped into the darkness, leaving only one beautiful girl in the room with him.

"Wait there, Erroh, I'm coming down," she said, the bitterness that laced most of her words no longer present.

10

IF HE'S AN IMPOSTOR, PUNISH HIM

His body shook gently. It was just the cold, he told himself rubbing his arms briskly. Fearing another test, he watched the wooden door. After a short time, she stepped through without weapon or malice, but she did catch her sleeve on the handle of the doorway, ripping it slightly. It was only a slight tear, but she cursed loudly. End of a perfect day? He knew the feeling.

She stood a step away from him, but up close she was extraordinary. He almost forgot their history. Almost, but not quite.

Her face was porcelain. Flawless and delicate and fuk it, she smelled like sweet flowers. His heart began to beat a little faster despite himself. Alone at last. "More of your kind arrived since yesterday,"

"And?"

"They need to be tested." She smiled, flashing her perfect teeth like a predator. "By you." She let the words hang in the air for a few moments. Her warm expression was about as appealing as the room's temperature.

"Why not use Wolves?"

"Because we have you." She took a deep breath and the smile returned. She was playing him, and he was fine sport.

"What if I refuse?"

Fear flashed across her face, or perhaps anger. He decided she would likely be a terrible card player and such things were important if mated to Erroh.

"This is no simple request, Erroh. You have little choice in the matter," she said stepping closer with her wonderful velvet dress hanging loosely in all the right places. How could he possibly be annoyed with this creature? He resisted the primal urge to reach out and touch her hair, caress her cheek and perhaps make a desperate grab for her chest. His attempt to suggest it a compliment would fall on deaf ears, her striking porcelain deaf ears.

"How many arrived?" he asked taking a step to the side. A fine manoeuvre indeed.

"We are fortunate. Two during the night and one this morning," she said. He decided not to be terribly offended at her obvious delight. The real Alpha males had arrived, it would appear. Still though, he had never fought another mature Alphaline outside of his bloodline. The taste for competition was appealing. He knew he was good. But could he be great?

"I can't fight all three," he said concealing his trepidation, excitement, and bloodlust. He was the son of the greatest warmonger to ever live, after all. Best not leap headfirst into their expectations.

She patted his hand. "That would be too much for you." He liked her touch despite the mocking. Like his own they were freezing. They had been in this cold room far too long. She obviously thought the same and beckoned him to follow through the doorway, down an ill lit corridor with a solitary glass ball lighting the way. His feet touched dreary stone, tiled thousands of years ago. It probably hadn't been polished since. This route was probably only used a few times every year, when the season was right for young Alphalines to fall in love. At the end of the passageway was an old wooden staircase that travelled up into the upper echelons, but she directed him onto into a small dark cell as big as his bedchambers and just as luxurious. She flicked a switch with the skill of a girl who had illuminated rooms most of her life. He resisted the urge to flip the light a few times, as he walked in after her. The room was the same grey stone as the city. Most of the glass bulbs were shattered leaving a solitary flicking light above their heads. A long stone bench jutted out from the wall that was cold to the touch and just about wide enough to sit. The closest thing to water was a pipe that dripped some peculiar, discoloured fluid into a metal bucket in the corner. Various pieces of black armour hung on the wall while some sparring clubs lay discarded in a small wooden chest in the corner. Lea took a seat and waited for him. "It could be a while, Erroh. You should check your armour," she said while examining the rip in her dress's sleeve. He thought about sitting across from her, sitting down right beside her, sitting as far away from her as possible but instead he settled with inspecting the armour. He pulled the heavy body of metal from the wall and grunted under its weight. Its perfect glossy finish held a strange beauty to it; he looked into the jet-black steel and ran his fingers along the edging. Not to be trusted.

"This will never do," he hissed. "I won't be able to move."

She rolled her eyes. "You have to fight in the armour. It is protocol."

He knew not to argue, so he simply nodded his head. His father would not approve.

There was a flicker of movement at the door, and Lea stood up suddenly. Erroh turned to see the Primary standing before him. Face to face without the grandeur and excellent lighting, she appeared less than exceptional, as though a beast had drained the essence from her body, leaving a thin layer of bone and membrane behind. Aye, she was delicate, but there was still fire in her eyes. He bowed deeply, and Lea greeted her graciously. She did not return the gesture, as if she knew how poorly the Cull was going, and though she may have blamed Lea, her suspicious eyes focused on him. It was an unnerving feeling to have someone stare into your soul and find little within.

"So he agreed to help us then?" she asked.

"Aye, Mydame, he is honoured to fight," said Lea. She did not meet Erroh's eyes lest she give anything away. Erroh was too shocked to say anything.

"That is pleasing. Get him anything he needs. There is no great hurry just yet. The Alpha males can wait," the Primary said before turning from the doorway leaving an uncomfortable silence behind her. Thankfully this was quickly replaced by the terrible sound of at least a hundred wanton females filled with excitement and uncontrolled giggling, as they began their judgemental march from their chambers to the arena of the Cull. Some passed the doorway, as they made their way somewhere up to the darkened rafters above, eager to catch a glimpse of their possible mate. All but one that is. Lea sat back down and tended to her ripped cuff. She looked a little ashamed. He took a breath to calm his anger. What point would it be to lose his head with her now? He might have agreed to the duel; if nothing else, than to vent the frustration from his weary mind, and who wasn't a fan of breaking from endless conversation and breaking into some wonderful violence. Still though, it was the principle of the matter.

He was also quite certain she was a bitch.

"Why did you tell me I had no choice?"

She bit the side of her lip as if caught thieving a sweet cake. A forbidden sweet cake with some cream and sugared almonds on top. He really wanted that cake, and he certainly wouldn't offer her a slice.

She did not attempt to answer.

Perhaps he would offer a slice and shove it in her wonderfully painted face.

"Answer me," he demanded. All around them the noise began to grow as more and more females gathered like a hunting pack. He only noticed the female sitting in the corner of the room.

Her eyes narrowed. "It made you look good in front of the Primary did it not? Stop acting like a whelp and try on the armour." She covered her face in her hands and stifled a scream. It was an effective counter on her part, and he returned to the armour. He thought about the little boy in the dead town. No matter how many times he inspected the armour, it never seemed to improve. It looked fine but it was far too heavy for his frame and there was no protection on each side.

"Why do I have to wear this armour anyway?" he asked after a time when he could no longer take the awkward silence.

"It won't hurt if word were to emerge that a humble Black Guard could handle a fine young Alpha male in battle."

Admittedly, it was a sound tactic.

"What of the four I fought?"

"They were just humble Black Guard," she replied brightly. Her eyes implied she didn't feel he had been all that impressive. "This time he will be armed when you enter." She pointed to a crude set of clubs hanging on the wall. He thought again of the black armour and worried aloud.

"I will break a rib," he said sliding the chest piece over his head.

She watched him struggle with the armour in silence before disappearing out the door. Off to steal a glance at her potential mate, good riddance, he thought reaching for the helm. Menacing and black like the rest of his suit, he slipped it onto his head but a little protruding shard of metal scraped sharply against his brow. Though it looked fine, there had been a lazy touch in its creation. He took it off and inspected the damage, cursing the blacksmith as he did. One direct blow and it would tear his face right open. When Lea returned a little while later carrying a tray with some provisions, she placed it down beside him and returned to her seat. Somehow, she managed this simple task with wonderful disdain.

"This pretty piece is not suitable," he said picking at the metal jutting out above the eye. "Can you get me another one?"

She shook her head.

Of course she did.

"You should eat," she said, just cold enough to discourage any suggestion of conversation. That was fine with him; he'd spoken far more in the past two days than in the last few seasons combined. Even if he wanted to speak, it was likelier that he would just make matters worse between them and there was probably a rule against engaging in secret conversations anyway. Still though, he had words he needed to say to her.

He broke the hard bread in half and bit into the smaller piece, leaving one slice on the plate. Chewing slowly he reached for the carafe and poured some clear liquid into the goblet provided.

"It isn't mead," she muttered under her breath. Touché my dear. He drank the water and chewed on the bread, stopping only to break a creamy piece of cheese from the wedge and smear it on top. A few freshly picked grapes finished off the meal. He popped one into his mouth and found himself pleasantly surprised with the combined flavours of the juices clashing. It was much better than pigeon.

"I'm sorry for the first day," he said.

She looked at him in surprise, with beautiful eyes wide open.

"I don't want to talk about it, Erroh," she said glancing at the doorway, lest there be listeners. The noise of a wave of excited females still echoed through the building. Nobody would be listening. It is just you and me.

"It had nothing to do with you. I was nervous, and my mind was elsewhere," he whispered, shrugging and daring an apologetic smile. She slid up beside him. So close, far too close. Her perfume struck his senses again, like wild flowers from somewhere far away. Somewhere exotic. He inhaled deeply.

"Fuk you, Erroh. It's easy to apologise when it's just the two of us alone with no one else around," she whispered in his ear and it might as well have been a screech. Her beautiful lips were inches from his. They were wonderful and enthralling and lush and incredible and so many more things. He could feel the warmth in her breath, and he felt an overwhelming urge to kiss her.

He did not however. He listened to her harsh truths instead and felt her shame, felt just how deep the embarrassment was, that his misstep had caused.

"You should have just rejected me outright instead of

fumbling your words so spectacularly. Now I have to sit through this disaster with my head held high pretending I belong here. Pretending it was no great matter. Pretending I don't hear the jests at every meal. Pretending about any feelings I have for you, Erroh." She shuddered for the slightest of moments as if she fought a tear, and won the day. This was a good thing. He couldn't see her cry. That would have been too much.

"Would you like something to eat?" he asked. It was all he could say. How could he ever put into words how ashamed of himself he was? And even now, he had attempted a pathetic apology and made matters worse.

She remained silent, folding her arms but at least she faced him once more. Perhaps he should tell her he thought her most beautiful of all. Would that help? Perhaps in the next day of questioning, he would share this revelation with them all.

"Why don't you back out, Lea?"

"Oh, I want this Cull to be concluded as soon as possible. Maybe if you weren't such an idiot, you would have won a mate by now. I'm certainly not going to add more fuel by being the first to step away. Oh no, my dear Erroh, I will stay and see this one through."

"I don't understand," he said.

She looked at him. Of course, he didn't understand.

"In easy to understand terms, Erroh. If I stepped away from you before any girl chooses you, it would be confirming how little character I possess."

"I'm sure you have character," he said.

"Can you please stop talking to me?"

"As you wish." He took a grape and swallowed it. It was frustrating being unable to form any meaningful sentences with his words. How poets and bards composed such epics was beyond him. He offered the food again; it seemed like the thing to do. This time, she accepted and broke a bit of bread and took a small bite. It was the best part of his day. Eventually the footsteps began to slow and finally they came to a silent halt.

"It will be soon enough," she whispered looking out through the doorway. Erroh rose to his feet as quietly as he could. It needed to be said.

"You are incredible, Lea. I am truly sorry for my stupidity. You deserve someone far greater than me." It was a better apology. For a moment, her beautiful sharp features cracked, and she almost smiled. Instead, she nodded acceptance and finished her meal. This was just as good.

"If you happen to take a few bruises in this bout; that will be fine by me," she said, and he finally understood his penance for her shame. It was only fair. A young girl appeared at the doorway, timid in the presence of Lea. She whispered something to the most beautiful girl in the world and fled from the room as quick as she had arrived.

"It's time, Erroh." A strange tone had entered her voice. It was colder, capable, and just a little unnerving. "I'll come back and collect you whenever you're finished," she added in that same tone as if there were other things on her mind. Darker things. And then she flashed him a look that may have been concern. Or regret. Or a little shame of her own? He couldn't tell.

"If he's an impostor, punish him," she said and disappeared out the door.

He did not hesitate at the door to the arena. Why keep his opponent any longer than was needed. War was in the air, and Erroh felt alive despite the burden of armour. His heart pumped rapidly in anticipation with each pulse sending him deeper and deeper into a wonderful frenzy of competitiveness. He needed to win and he'd do whatever was needed to win. Maybe it was true what the females thought of him and his bloodlust.

It was a small matter. Did he really care what they thought of him?

He did.

He opened the door and attacked.

Erroh's opponent was ready. Perhaps it was the club on the ground that warned him. He was taller than Erroh, his long unkempt hair swept out behind him as he countered Erroh's opening strikes, and with each counter, he displayed fierce strength. He hid his youthful face behind a beard but there was no mistaking a grimace of anger and unnerving composure. He was no impostor, and he too was intent on victory. It only took a few moments for Erroh to realise that the weight of his armour was a bigger problem than he had initially thought. With the piercing scream of metal joints clashing in his ear, he wondered how clumsy he must look to the silent females above. Clumsy but still deadly. His opponent thought so too and slipped away from their engagement. He weaved a few times and began circling Erroh like a hunter would a vicious animal caught in a snare. Erroh knew he was beaten. He could hear it in his laboured breath. He could see it in the misty air too. On a fair day with proper weapons and lighter armour, he might best this man but as it was, the fight was over and both of them knew it. It was only a matter of time before a heavy blow came. Erroh changed his stance; he held his right hand out in front of him and held the second tight against his chest. The world slowed, and Erroh heard nothing but the beat of his heart and the stalking footsteps of his vanquisher.

All the girls were watching.

And then the counter attack came. He leapt in, his single

club, barbaric and brutal hammered loudly against Erroh's, and they struggled for ground. Not for very long though. Erroh was beaten back, and the larger man pushed home the advantage. The grunts and growls replaced the clatter of wood and steel and it was Erroh's own groans which were loudest. Through the thin slits in his helm, he somehow met each strike, blocking and parrying and pushing himself until sweat drenched his brow, his arms and then his back, but still they charged back and forth like a pendulum counting the world's moments, impossible to separate. Just when Erroh felt he couldn't take any more violent strikes, his opponent began to weaken. Just enough that each blow did not steal his breath. Just enough that Erroh could move a little easier. Just enough that he began to believe again. This fight was not done. He had a chance after all. The women would see his prowess once more.

In ill-fitting armour as well.

And then a glancing blow, no more than a desperate counter, grazed Erroh's helmet and shifted the heavy piece just enough to tear his skin open. It only felt like a scrape and Erroh struck out, striking his opponent across the knuckles. It wasn't enough to break, just enough to neutralise. The taller Alpha screamed and retreated, holding his hand. The club clattered loudly on the ground, but Erroh did not attempt to attack. He was distracted by a mild case of blindness. Warm fluid streamed down the inside of his helmet, and Erroh wiped uselessly at his face. It was no scrape after all.

Seeing Erroh's hesitation, the Alpha leapt forward and struck. Perhaps he could smell blood. Erroh attempted to deflect but the damage was done, the dye had been cast, and bones had been broken. Or at least fractured.

He heard the terrible blow across his ribs before he felt it. It sounded like a crack. And when he did feel the devastating strike, he was already collapsing in a terrible suffocating heap. He couldn't think, couldn't scream, couldn't do anything, but gasp pathetically as the pain tore him apart from the inside.

But it did not end.

His opponent reached down and gripped him in a powerful fist and if he spoke words, Erroh didn't hear; he was lost in his own pain. At least he didn't cry out. At least they did not hear his agony. His vision darkened and more blood streamed into his eyes. He felt a massive injured hand lock behind his neck. It held him, kept him in place. And then he felt a second terrible blow to the same area of his ribs and this time he did cry out. It sounded like tears. Erroh swung madly with his fists, knowing the attempts were futile. He struck bone but there was nothing behind it. He gasped and sucked in what cold air he could, and he waited to die. For this was the Cull and it was likely such things occurred in the Cull. Just nobody spoke of it. If the Alpha ended his life, he could do nothing. That sudden thought stirred him, and he tried to rise again. He was broken but still he tried desperately to crawl. Away from his vanquisher or towards him, he couldn't tell. Lea had quite the justice gifted to her. They would make quite the couple, he thought bitterly.

"Enough, Aymon!" roared Dia and the room blazed to brightness.

He saw the Alpha now, standing at the far side of the room, breathing in deeply and staring up at the leader of the world with dull worship. With the fight done, and Erroh having failed to cover himself in glory, he gave up. He lay in a ruined heap, gasping for air. He couldn't hear anything but mumblings between Alpha and Primary. He simply lay there wondering if any helpful Wolves, eager to take away unwanted waste, would come along and remove him from the arena.

And someone did.

With little care, two guards carried him to the backroom and placed him sitting up against the wall. He attempted gratitude but neither man was interested to engage in conversation. They remembered his brutality. He was certain to be the butt of many jests this evening. He removed the helmet and enjoyed the warm sensation of blood running down his face. It was showing little sign of slowing. A fine flow altogether. Lea was not waiting, but he wasn't terribly bothered. What bothered him was trying to catch his breath. An underrated task on the best of days, he mused bitterly. Eventually when he did catch it, what remained was the searing pain along his side and it did not subside in the least. What a disastrous showing.

Magnus would not have lost that way.

His father would have found a way to attain victory, and Erroh cursed loudly and then felt a pang of homesickness. Aye his father was brutal and feared by many, but he was also kinder than most and some of his kindness would be welcome. Perhaps just a quick reassuring jest, as he pulled him to his feet. When such childish thoughts offered little comfort, Erroh stripped some fabric from his shirt and placed it across his brow. It was something to do while he waited for the scorned female Lea to return to him, as she said she would.

11

PUNISHED

H e waited for quite a time but Lea never returned. Of course she didn't. It was so predictable.

He cast his chest plate aside in disgust. It would take a week to recover from this hiding, perhaps two. He poked at the damage and his body responded by jerking violently. Perhaps three. Time flows differently when alone, aggrieved and melancholic, but after what felt like an hour a diminutive young girl appeared at the doorway.

"The next testing will be in half an hour or so," she whispered formally and spun on anxious heels back towards the corridor.

"What do you mean?" he shouted before she made her escape. She glanced longingly at the exit before turning back to face him. Some blood dripped down from his eyebrow again. He swiped it away irritably. Her eyes followed the drips as they took flight and her face turned a little pale.

"The next test will be in around a half hour, sir," she repeated slowly while edging ever so subtly out the doorway, and Erroh could only stare at her in astonishment. Well played, Lea, well played indeed. You witch.

He almost delivered a fine whirlwind of profanity and opinions at the young girl, an outburst of such an injustice that even the gods themselves would take note, but instead he dropped his head in grim acceptance and nodded a few times.

"Get back your pride, little cub," whispered an imaginary voice in his head.

Ah, pride. It was such a dangerous thing at the best of times, and Erroh suffered greatly from it. With pride came strength of will. They came hand in painful hand, and were always desperate to drag the greatest men and women down to the depths of wretchedness. He swallowed deeply and the pain almost sent him to the ground.

"Can you get me some bandages and anything to help with my little scrape?"

She nodded and ran from the room.

"Thank you!" he called after her and leaned back against the wall. He never saw her again. A different young girl arrived and handed him a long metal box before disappearing. The small rusty hinges creaked when he opened the medical case. It contained nothing more than a few old bandages and a small capsule. He placed a piece of fabric against the cut and dabbed the deep hole before popping the cork and pouring in some brown liquid. He assumed it was disinfectant. He hoped it was disinfectant. Painful tears streamed down from his eyes, so it was probably disinfectant. He finished off the repairs by cleaning away the dried blood with a little water. He felt like a new man.

Until he set foot back in the arena.

The bald brute matched Erroh in height but slower in movement. With arms the size of tree trunks and probably as sturdy, every attack that Erroh blocked, sent him crashing from one side of the room to the next. He tried in his ill-fitting armour, he really did, but early in the skirmish, his fierce opponent discovered his weakness. Perhaps it was the wheezing panting in every break; perhaps it was the feeble squeals every time he defended his ribs. Whatever it was, his opponent soon hunted him down as though he were a chess player terrified to step away from protecting his king. With the last of his energy, Erroh turned to flight. It wasn't the noblest form of warfare but it was all he had left. He slowed the pace as best he could and kept clear of strikes. It simply added to the boredom of the contest and the silent audience knew it.

As with great things and some not so great, things must end. After a handful of dull moments, Erroh finally let fatigue get the better of him. He halted his pathetic retreat and met an attack as both clubs clattered loudly in the dark. His attack was mistimed and his Alpha opponent broke through his guard and knocked him to the ground with a blow across his shoulder. It was hardly a glorious killing blow, but Erroh fell to his knees gasping in front of the girls letting his weapons roll free of his grip.

"Enough, Doran," the Primary ordered in her great booming voice.

The lights blazed to life and then Erroh lost sight of his opponent. He gasped for air and thought about rising when suddenly something grabbed him from behind and the world went painfully dark.

———

Darkness.

Movement.

Scraping.

The ceiling was moving and scraping at the same time. There was pain, and he was dimly aware that he was not having a good day. He was struggling to breathe and his arms were outstretched. He could definitely hear a scraping sound. Something seemed terribly wrong. He could feel his senses returning slowly. Something told him that this confused state, was a finer place to be than in the cold light of awareness. It was his fingers making the scraping sound. That didn't seem to make any sense at all. He tried to focus his vision, and he suspected he was bleeding. It certainly tasted like it. He tried to remember and it hurt. He stopped trying to remember. Everything seemed dark grey and painful. Like the grey of the city. There was a flicker of recollection. Something about the city, had he reached it already? He still couldn't quite grasp it, but he was close. So close, if only the scraping sound would cease. Then he felt something new. It was a pulling sensation at the legs. He looked down and saw two black demons dragging him to his doom. That wasn't a great omen at all. Had he lived a good life? Had he died a believer in the gods? Did it matter? He felt his conscious mind knocking at the door of this terrible daze. He tried to kick out, but he was dragged into darkness. Then his eyes burned as somebody ignited the sun in front of his eyes. And then he remembered. The two Black Guards left him lying in the middle of the floor and stepped noisily into the hallway. The sound of a heavy door slamming signalled their departure. They were getting quite skilled at removing him from the arena. It was an underrated skill, he imagined. Struggling to his feet, he shook his head and regretted it immediately. He gripped the wall behind him like a demented living scarecrow and waited for the world to stop spinning. When this failed, he crumpled to his seat and threw up all over himself. This was no simple task with shattered ribs. Between each horrific retch, he allowed himself a brief moan. When his body was satisfied that it could betray him no further, he crumpled to the floor and hated the city and every nasty female living in it. He saved a special little piece of bitterness for Lea. There would be reparation and such a thought granted him comfort. Maybe he would throw her in a river.

Enjoying wonderful thoughts in his mind, he pulled the armour free of his body. The clamour echoed around the halls and throughout the silent building. Good, he hoped the noise broke into the Primary's speech. She could fuk right off as well.

His head continued to spin and his stomach began to churn once more. He managed to make it to the bucket of waste this time though and took full advantage of it. Spitting out the last of his stomach contents, he leant against the wall and contented himself with waiting for death. Fuk the Cull. Fuk the city. Fuk everybody.

He missed home, his family, and it wasn't too long before he thought of the one female in the city who did care about him. Was his younger sister available yet to meet with him? Was it not a peculiar thing to come this far to see kin, and she had not yet appeared? So many things about this place were so unsettling. He wanted to leave this very day, to escape back into the green of the wastes and walk the road as a fierce predator. Such childish thoughts. He shook his head in frustration and felt pulsating stabs of burning pain. He reached behind and felt a wound. Aye it was small and already the blood had stopped but it was volatile to the touch, as if some fiend had struck him from behind when the lights had come on. So much for honour in battle.

Eventually he heard the familiar sound of a hundred female feet shuffling around once again. He heard a door open and bursts of giddy excitable laughter and conversation.

They really were having a great time. It was at this moment that a prophetic and expected thought occurred to him. He was not built for these people, he was not built for the city, and he would find no mate. He would leave the Cull a failure. Such liberating thoughts brought him little comfort, and he felt a loss unlike anything he'd ever experienced before. He felt tears but kept them at bay. He was not broken yet; he was only beaten. That is, until he heard the delicate footsteps of another young female not old enough to torment any young men. He already knew what she would say before she said it.

"The final testing will commence whenever you desire," the young girl said from the doorway. She lingered, taking him in. He could see concern. He thought her a good actor.

"Is there anything you need?" She had an eastern accent familiar to his own. He growled something inaudible, and she took the hint. Charming Erroh.

He tore the last of the armour from his tenderised body and threw it into the corner, vowing never to don the black ever again. The one consolation was that Dia would probably shout at Lea over the matter of him fighting in plain clothing.

He knew he had a concussion, but he didn't care anymore. Let them see what they did to him. He grabbed his weapons and shuffled to the doorway one final time. He would fall, and he would fall terribly, but it would be magnificent.

———

Wynn rubbed his arms in the cold air and stretched them out. An attack was coming. It wasn't just the club at his feet; it was the sage bit of advice gifted to him from his father upon leaving his wing. Although Marvel may have lied about that as well. He wasn't above such things. Wynn sighed loudly in the darkness and wondered how the females above him kept so quiet. Maybe that was another lie. He could feel the adrenaline gathering within him. It urged him to move, to tap his foot, to call out, to do anything at all. He was never able to sit in silence for too long yet here he was, standing in the dark for quite a time behaving as though his future was at stake. At least the complimentary bottle of wine they'd left for him in his lavish quarters was fine for settling his nerves. He'd drunk just about enough to relax but not enough to sway his judgement or ability. It was a decent vintage as well; perhaps he would indulge once the test was completed. His father had told him he would be treated like royalty despite their family ties to the east, and so far the city was living up to his expectations. He heard footsteps from beyond and reached for the club just as the door opened and a ruin of a young man charged through in search of blood.

Excellent, Wynn thought. Movement, at last.

Erroh didn't care just how much of a wretch he presented himself as. It was only a little blood, sweat, and bile after all. What mattered was the weight lifted. His body ached and struggled but at least he could move without hindrance. His opponent gave off the appearance of a god, if Erroh believed in such things. Dressed in brown leather garments from head to toe, he gripped the club like a master of the blade. His blazing dark eyes stared in pure concentration, studying Erroh for a weakness, a confident grin upon his face. His neat ponytail whipped out behind him as he struck, and he struck quicker than either man before. Within moments, it was evident for all hidden eyes to see that Erroh was meeting his third Alphaline of the day and they had saved the finest until last. Wonderful news.

They clashed loudly in the dark, each club hammering loudly as they met, parried, blocked, countered and withdrew and begun the cycle again. He did not share Erroh's aggression but his style was graceful, accomplished, and pleasing to the eye. Erroh could imagine the females swooning over his chiselled features as he grinned with every feint and strike. Erroh didn't like that grin, he didn't like that grin at all. It was far too confident and assured.

They struck back and forth and the silent room watched and held excitable breaths.

"You are completely fuked," Wynn uttered between scuffles. It wasn't a threat and it wasn't mocking, it was just simple observation.

"Aye," Erroh wittily replied, charging forward, tasting fresh blood in his mouth, and hoping it was not from his lungs. Erroh swung loosely and a swiping counterblow caught the bandaging above his eyebrow, not tearing it free but pulling it across his vision, ending any chance of victory. But the final blow did not come; instead, his opponent lowered his blade and stepped back.

"No way to win," Wynn said. He was putting on quite the show, and Erroh nodded in appreciation. It was an honourable move. He tore the bandage free and wiped away the fresh stream of blood. He had plenty to spare.

Once again, the two figures charged each other in a brutal storm of barbaric weapons but it was Erroh who faltered first. The pain had crippled his mind and no amount of lightened burden could compensate. He was weary. Weary and ready to lose. Finally, after one last fine display of violence, he could take no more. Erroh's hand dropped too low and the ponytailed Alpha leapt in, only to meet a fist to the chin. Perhaps had Erroh been stronger he may have done more damage than a slight welt but as it was, the strike did little more than daze his opponent. Off balance, Erroh tried to strike once more but his body simply collapsed forward and his opponent calmly stepped out of the way, as he crumpled on the floor.

The females probably loved that.

He tried to rise, but a heavy boot kept him in place.

"Stay down, friend." It was a fine suggestion, and Erroh finally admitted defeat with a gasp. The lights erupted to life, and Erroh knew his task was done. All three tested, all found to be worthy. This one was probably worthier than most and as for himself? Well he had been as disappointing as expected. At least he was consistent.

On cue, the magnificent Primary made her appearance and his opponent fell back to one knee and bowed in respect. Erroh rolled away from the light and climbed to his knees. He didn't bother to bow. It would just hurt more. He was content to wait for permission to leave the arena with his tail between his aching legs and leave the females to ogle a proper Alpha male.

"Well fought, Wynn," Dia said. She tapped the edge of her podium irritably. "Line of Magnus, you may leave."

———

Nobody came for him. He didn't know why he expected them to. His mind was little more than misery and loathing. Better that than concentrate on every single ache in his body.

After an hour of waiting, the excited noises of a hundred females filled the tower, wilder than before, and Erroh suspected why. Who would pair with this god of a man? A fresh Cull was in the air, and Erroh was simply nothing special. Ancient heavy doors opened and closed far above, little feminine footsteps hurried up and down stairs. Some sounded as though they passed by his doorway but no spiteful little witch looked in. He thought about the four females and wondered if they'd witnessed his destruction. It was likely they would have enjoyed it. Good for them.

Bitches.

When the last footstep disappeared into the silence, he was still alone. A terrible empty silence surrounded him and all he could hear was his laboured breathing. Moments passed and the silence became unnerving. His waves of anger left him, replaced by droplets of sorrow instead. The droplets formed into a stream and so on. In the lonely silence, he lamented. He did not belong here in the great city of Samara, the fabled City of Light, the fuken Spark. He belonged at the far end of the world, the place he used to call home. He wanted to go home. A fresh trickle of blood broke through his bandaging. It flowed down his grubby, bruised face, and he ignored it. His thoughts were on the silence.

Still he waited and nobody came. When the lights went out all around him, the first tear slipped from his eye. He could have blamed other things, like the pit of acid in his stomach, the concussion, or the broken ribs. All were dignified reasons to cry, but it was the loneliness he felt, and the desire to feel kindness again. They'd forgotten to come for him. Erroh made no noise as the tears fell freely from his cheeks. He cried in silence so no one would hear, at least that was something.

When enough time had passed that he was ready to face the harsh world once more, he dragged himself to his feet. This monumental task took more out of him than he would have cared for and sliding along the wall; he slowly reached the doorway before blindly tripping on the step and collapsing backwards back into the cold cell. Fortunately the bucket of waste broke some of his fall. It was still warm. He didn't know how, and he didn't want to know either. It covered his chest in a warm blanket of hideousness, and he cursed loudly. He may have cursed a few of the females while he was at it. When that failed to solve his miserable predicament, he pulled himself to his feet. Aiming for the doorway, he once more began his treacherous journey from this cursed place. He managed three steps. It started as a stumble, continued into another fall and finished with complete and devastating unconsciousness. As he fell, he had a last little depressing thought about how lonely he was going to be in life. He dropped heavily against one of the walls and then to the floor where he lay like discarded wreckage, invisible in the dark.

Only one person in the entire city noticed his absence.

12

WORRYING NEWS FROM THE WASTES

The old healer produced a small bottle from his satchel and held it open a few inches from Erroh's face. Nothing happened, so he shoved it right up his nose. Something happened. His eyes shot open and his body jerked violently, trying to escape the horrific odour. A female held him down, calmly whispering in an accent he recognised, and he relaxed.

"Hi, Lexi," he groaned, looking at his younger sister in the dim light. She had grown so much, her hair was a darker brown than he remembered, but her face was the same apart from one or two blemishes, which accompanied youth. It was something she would grow out of, and she was becoming quite the little lady. She looked like Elise. How many years since she had left? It was eight at least. He coughed and tasted blood and terrible pain all over. An old man dressed in a fine suit of satin with a long sash of leather hanging down his chest, kneeled above him and stared into his eyes irritably.

The healer, shook his head as if standing over a dying body without recovery. "I cannot treat him here."

Lexi disagreed. "He will walk. He will not be carried,"

She was far younger than Erroh, but she was giving the orders. That was how it was, he supposed. A master healer had little to argue with a female Alpha of the city.

"And if he can't walk, you will treat him here until he can walk," she added and sat back against the far wall. "No one will see him in this way," she warned. The healer sighed and began with the ribs. His bony fingers dug deeply into Erroh's side and explored painfully. He mumbled a few times under his breath, Erroh thought he heard him mutter that the "break was not bad" or else he "needed a break badly." Something along those lines. At some point, like a weasel, Seth appeared and exchanged a few heated words with Lexi. She sounded like Elise as well, apart from the cough. By the time the healer had treated him there was more bandaging covering his body than skin. Not that he dared complain, his healer was not gentle, but he was thorough. The prodding and cleaning hurt just as much as the injuring.

"I'll get him a day's rest for the blood loss and the ribs," the healer muttered as he left.

"You need a wash, Roro," Lexi said, helping him to his feet. She still had a way to grow, but already he could feel her tremendous strength. She would be strong like Elise. He took his cloak and shuffled from the dismal building through the city as it began its changing of the light. With his cloak to cover most of the damage, and leaning on her when the pace was too much, they made it back to his decrepit chambers without drawing too much attention. Evidently, it was quite important to keep up appearances in the city.

———

Lexi paced back and forth radiating a perfect fury from her petite frame. She kept her hair in a simple ponytail; her green eyes were untouched by complementary paints. She was not of age, so she cared little for beautification. At least for now. Soon enough she would break hearts. Perhaps she would someday cause wars with her appeal. Perhaps she would end them too with her brutality. Just like their mother.

"You took your time," she growled, turning the anger of his treatment right back at him.

"Aye, they told me to take my time."

"They were here only two seasons back," she said running her finger along the edge of a shelf and was not surprised with what she found.

"They've both been here since I left?"

"Twice."

"All is well?" he asked. He didn't think they would make the journey again.

"Aye, Erroh, all is well." She blew the dust from her fingers. If she was sad, she hid it well. If she was concerned about her mother's health, she hid that too. If she was happy living in this city with her countless sisters, she hid that as well.

"That's good to know." He wondered how worried they might have been when they learned he had not arrived. When Magnus and Elise journeyed to the city, they didn't spare the mount's charge. It was a big world with more than one path and his path taken was the longer way round. Perhaps he would consider attaining a mount when he returned home. Was he that excited about telling them of his failures?

"I heard about the town, Roro," she said when there was nothing else to say.

"Let's not worry about such things." He braved a smile.

"How was the road before that?" she asked instead and it was a fine question.

"It would not have made much of a tale," he admitted.

The gods watching him may have disagreed.

"Do you miss home?" he asked, and wondered how much she even remembered of their parents' stronghold. Oh well, sacrifices needed to be made for the rebuilding of a race.

"Not at all. Do you?" she lied openly.

"Not at all," he lied in that same tone.

"I'm no great fan of this city," he said after a moment's pause. He didn't want to insult her, and he certainly didn't want to add salt to her life if it was a deeply hidden wound. She was free to leave the city if ever she decided. Aye, there were repercussions and not just the taint on the glorious family name. There was less chance of finding a fine mate with a good bloodline out in the wastes, and was that not the entire point of their lives?

"I love it here." She had more to say but fell silent.

"It is an impressive thing," admitted Erroh, realising he may very well have insulted her home without thinking. "It's a marvel of our civilisation." His words sounded hollow and they both knew it.

"No it isn't, Roro, it's a collection of bricks overly protected by an ignorant wall, built by the ancients to compensate for manhood issues." Aye, he had insulted her home. She'd obviously been working on that little speech as well. "It's not about the city. It's about the ideals of the city," she said as if explaining to a child. Of all the unpleasant tone of voices he'd heard that day, this he liked the least. "We rule the world, and we do a fine job of it as well," she said, sitting at the edge of the bed.

"Alphalines?" he suggested.

"The females of this city." She flicked her head dismissively. "Males had their chance," she said grinning.

"The four kings?" he suggested.

Silence.

"You're speaking like one of the wretched who were beaten in the Faction Wars," he said.

"There were five kings, Roro, and nobody won the war."

He pushed her away in mock irritation, groaning in pain as he did. "Ah whisht, you're sounding like Elise," he hissed. It was quite the compliment, and she smiled wonderfully.

"I'm sure Dad would agree with you," she jested.

"We certainly share the same distaste for the city and its ways. Fuk this place," he said grinning. For just the briefest of moments, it felt as though they were back at home, arguing as siblings did.

"The world has known peace for decades since Dia accepted rule. It is the longest peace there has ever been." Her voice was serious. She was Alpha female; hear her roar.

"Aye, but there is always something in the wind. Peace will diminish and armies will clash. It's why we train," he argued.

"Spoken like a true male, Erroh. And when the wars do come, will you seek to protect us? Do you think the females of Samara could never be your equal in battle? Do you think we haven't spent hours honing our skills in battle or learning to survive out in the wilderness? Do you think we have spent an entire lifetime knitting, giggling and waiting for a strong male to plant a seed in us? Do you think this is all we are?" she countered.

"I didn't say that, but it's probably true." He took silent delight in the flash of anger in her face. "We are physically stronger, and we are to protect you, are we not?" he declared pompously. Was it not in his pledge to protect his mate?

"If Elise faced Magnus in battle, who would be left standing at the end?" she asked.

Well played.

"That would never happen, but I see your point." It was

good to see her. It was even better getting a rise from her but what pleased him most was seeing how happy she was here. This was no place for him but it certainly was for her. He stretched out on his bed. The warmth was making him drowsy and made him forget the aches in his body. She pulled the blanket up to his neck, lest there be a chill.

"You should sleep, I'll see you before you leave," she promised.

"This Cull will never end. I'll be here a while," he muttered pulling the blankets tight. Warm was good, warm make all pain fuk right off.

"I think your Cull has gone on a little too long already." Her eyes betrayed her worry.

"I'm not making a strong impression on the females."

"Oh, I've heard you are," she said.

"What have you heard?"

"Enough."

"From who?"

"Does it really matter?"

"I suppose not," he said yawning.

She stood up and walked to the door. "In truth, Erroh, no Cull should last more than three days. If you don't win them over by the next day I believe it will end."

"Would that be so bad?" He had liked his lonely life before, had he not?

"It would be shameful."

"I can live with a bit of shame after this," he said gesturing to his broken body.

She nodded sadly. "I suppose that is where we differ. You wouldn't be the first not to attain a mate, but you are the son of Magnus and Elise. To waste that bloodline would be a terrible loss."

"I'm no prize mount out to stud. I'm sure the city will

survive."

"There have been fewer Culls than ever," she said. "This one matters."

Maybe it mattered because it was her brother participating.

"Do you know the girls I Cull with?" He sat up painfully. What do they like, what should he say?

She looked around guiltily, as if the walls were listening. After a few breaths of struggle, she nodded.

"Lea is fine, I suppose. A little unremarkable, and her status in Samara is low, but she is quite attractive, and I'm sure she would get along with you, though from what I heard you aren't terribly interested in her anyway. Beggars can't be choosers, Roro."

And she's not to be trusted, he silently suggested.

Lexi continued.

"Lillium is a strong choice, but she's not easy to get along with. She is highest lined, like you and I. We have never been friends but we could be sisters, I suppose. I don't know, her hair is fuken crazy." He could see the guilt in her face of speaking these things aloud. Still, what is a little sister spy for anyway.

"Roja carries the world on her shoulders; but don't let that get in the way. She behaves differently to most females, but that is the price of becoming future Primary."

Erroh's eyes widened.

"She is Dia's granddaughter. She is strong and wise and loyal, she is kinder than most, and a female I care for deeply," Lexi whispered.

"She hasn't shown me this kindness you speak of."

"Perhaps she was not ready. Perhaps you should try convincing her," Lexi said in all her childish glory. If only things were that simple.

"And Silvia?"

Her face darkened. "She smiles a lot," Lexi growled. "Don't try to win her over, it won't make a difference either way."

So not Silvia then?

"I've said more than I should, Roro. Please try harder," she pleaded and disappeared out the doorway. He thought miserably of the females for a few moments more before falling into a deep, unsatisfying sleep.

————

He never fully awoke the following day. His lucid dreams were laced in wonder, fear, sadness and joy. He remembered nothing but the dull ache of his entire body every time he woke up with fists clenched and his body covered in sweat. At some point the master healer returned to apply a warm menthol balm across his chest, and administer a spoonful of dark green medicine supposedly assisting with the pain. In truth he wasn't entirely sure if that too was a dream, but the room's scent had unquestionably improved. It was only the sound of heavy knocking in the late evening that pulled him fully from his stupor and the continual knocking, which pulled him from his bed.

"This is a shithole," his visitor declared, thrusting a bottle of sine into Erroh's hand and slipping through the doorway before he could bar him entry. The tall Alpha with the annoyingly perfect ponytail took a seat without invitation and made himself right at home by gesturing to the bottle and smiling devilishly. There would be no drinking alone tonight.

"I have a view and everything in my room," the ponytailed Alpha said, and Erroh disliked him immediately.

"My name is Wynn, it's a pleasure to meet the son of

Magnus." Erroh took two glasses and poured small measures into each. Just enough for a mouthful. Just enough to be courteous. Just enough to display his irritation at Wynn's presence. He made a point of grimacing with each movement.

"My friends call me Erroh." He handed the glass to Wynn who drained it immediately and handed it right back before Erroh could sit down.

Outmanoeuvred once more.

"Another?"

"Aye, Erroh, that would be grand."

Erroh refilled generously and took a seat at the bed.

"A fine vintage," Erroh lied, grimacing at the poisonous taste. "Thank you for the gift." He swallowed and coughed as he did.

"It was the least I could do to make myself feel better after easily beating the son of Magnus," Wynn said, sipping carefully on his volatile beverage.

"It's a kind gesture." Erroh did not rise to the jest. He sipped the sine right back at the arrogant cur.

"You look like shit. It matches the room," Wynn said, and Erroh nodded patiently. It was all he could do. That and count the breaths until he could politely ask the Alpha to leave.

"I want a rematch, Erroh." For the briefest of moments, Wynn dropped the veneer of confidence. Sincerity such as craving a fair fight irritated Erroh even further.

"I don't need to be battered again." Erroh poured the Alphaline a top-up. Wynn nodded disappointedly. Wonderful.

They sat in uncomfortable silence for a few more breaths until Erroh was about to ask him to leave when the Alpha's face darkened.

"I heard about the town of the dead. I heard they burned the females. I can't believe such a thing."

"It's all true," Erroh whispered placing his unfinished

glass on the bedside, his taste was bitter enough without the taints of under-brewed liquor.

Wynn coughed nervously, and Erroh hoped he'd finally realised that his company was unwanted.

"The Primary met with me alone today. There have been similar attacks throughout the factions. She said there could be panic if word is spread," he said.

"Of course she did," growled Erroh. At least it explained her dismissal of the attack as simple lawlessness.

"When the Cull is completed I have to ride east and speak with Magnus."

Erroh eyed his companion coldly. "What do you want with him?"

"I must seek proof that he's warmongering again," Wynn said looking away.

Magnus had taught Erroh a fine skill when enraged, a simple trick that any hot-headed lowerline could learn as well: counting to ten as the red mist descends.

One, two, three.

"My father is not marching, and he is certainly not butchering innocents," hissed Erroh, and Wynn had the sense to nod in agreement.

Four, five, six.

"I'm sorry if I offended you, Erroh, but I had to tell you."

Seven, eight, nine.

"Mydame has ordered me east, so I go east," he said, and Erroh begrudgingly accepted it as his apology. It was their station in life. When the Primary called, it was every person's burden to answer. It could have been different. There could have been a king but that would have ended in tears. His father had certainly seen to that.

Neither Alpha said anything and the wonder of silence allowed the volatile moment to pass by. Admittedly, Erroh thought it a brave act on Wynn's part, seeking him out and suggesting the victory skewed. It was an even braver act that he'd broken the Primary's confidence and spoken of her request, not to mention chancing the wrath of Erroh in the process. It galled him to say it but Wynn wasn't quite as annoying as he'd originally presented himself to be.

"When I first entered the ring to battle you, Wynn, I thought it was a young girl I was facing. I didn't really want to be seen slapping a female around. But far be it from me to suggest you cut your hair," Erroh mocked.

Wynn laughed and met the jest admirably. "I win most fights in that way, but for the trickier bouts, I have a lovely dress."

Fuker was witty as well. There were worse things in the world to base a friendship on.

"When I heal, we will talk about a rematch," Erroh conceded and it appeased his new friend greatly.

"I spoke with your other combatants, Erroh. Three fights in a day?" said Wynn grimacing.

Erroh's face darkened at the same notion and the unwanted record. Three costly defeats, and it was likely that if Wynn knew, then the rest of the city did as well. His name would be ridiculed, no doubt. Perhaps he should have kept the helmet on.

"Nice heroes those two, they'll make their mates very happy," Wynn said grinning.

"I'm sure I did my part to rise their stock," Erroh hissed.

"I had the misfortune of sharing a meal with them earlier this evening. The food was splendid, but not all Alphas play well together. They both got on just fine with each other. A fine female by the name of Roja hosted us. Wonderful red hair," he said stretching.

"Perhaps she will be in your Cull," Erroh muttered. It

appeared that everybody else was invited to the table of entitlements.

"I have met my lovely females, and she is not one of them, and I doubt a fine goddess like that would enter a Cull for little old me anyway. Did you know she is to rule the city someday? A terrific sense of humour as well," he said.

"Probably at my expense no doubt," spat Erroh and was annoyed at himself for it. It shouldn't have hurt but it really did.

Wynn looked at him and frowned. "Your name didn't really come up."

Of course it didn't. He was just an afterthought wasn't he?

"They mentioned a skilled Black Guard testing them and when Dia mentioned your lineage after our bout, it wasn't hard to discern what happened. I'm smart like that," Wynn, said grinning. "I imagine the heavy armour got the better of you. If that ass Aymon got the better of you in a fair fight, and I could barely beat you as you are now, I would imagine our masters would be terribly disappointed in the pair of us. Perhaps when you are healed we could settle it in a fair contest?"

"If I agree to fight you, will you stop asking?"

"Absolutely, friend,"

"I'll keep that in mind so."

The night moved on and neither mentioned the reason all little Alpha males journeyed to the city, but it was ever present in the air, like a crushing boulder hinged delicately upon a precipice, and it was Wynn who tipped it.

"How's your choosing going?" he asked late in the night when Erroh had once again begun to falter.

"I hate them all, and I think they hate me right back." He could have said more, but he left it as it was. He wasn't particularly interested to know exactly how well Wynn was charming his potentials on his first day.

"It sounds as bad as mine," Wynn admitted. Wonderful news. It wasn't going terribly well for his perfect comrade after all. It should have made him feel better, and it did. It really, really did.

"It only gets worse, my friend," Erroh said. It seemed far easier to break the rules this late in the night but still, speaking of the secret event with another went against his upbringing.

One simply does not speak of the Cull.

"I have them all, right where I want them," Wynn laughed.

"I have them a step from the door," whispered Erroh and began laughing with him. With it came a wonderful surge of relief. For the first time since he'd arrived in the Spark, he didn't feel quite as alone.

"They are as tough as stone but they are beautiful," Wynn admitted wiping his wistful eyes.

"They really are," agreed Erroh, thinking back when each stunning girl entered the arena.

"There is one I like in particular," Wynn admitted and stood up to leave. The hour was late and the Cull was calling.

"Same time tomorrow?"

"A bit earlier, around noon."

"Splendid, we'll meet in the tavern upstairs, win us a few pieces in cards."

"You speak my language."

Wynn stepped from the room and flicked the light switch a few times with undisguised glee. It was always good to make a new friend on the road.

13

NOT GOING HOME YET

S he wore dark blue today. It was regal and fetching, but he thought better than to compliment her. Dia tapped her finger on the high podium as she spoke, each word accompanied by an irritated drumbeat. He had expected to meet four vindictive females, instead he faced just one, and the orders she was giving him were disappointing.

"You want me to travel all the way to Conlon to deliver a letter?" Erroh asked again. The snow-covered region of Conlon was deep in the south, inhabited by barbarians who barely answered Samara's call. There was no region more hostile to Magnus and his kin than the south, and Dia was sending him regardless of his protestations.

"Mydame, with all due respect, I intend to return home after this," he pleaded, but Dia was not listening.

"There is a tavern in Conlon named "Little Rose." Enquire after a man named Gemmil. For two decades he has been my eyes, my ears and voice in the south, and he is a trusted friend."

"Please, Mydame," he interrupted. It was too far. At least two seasons walk or two or three months on a charging mount. She was sending him to the bottom of the world on a whim. It was called the Southern Faction, but it was like the other three in name alone. For most seasons, it was covered in snow and many a wanderer had disappeared attempting to walk its inhospitable roads. The cold or one of the many aggressive tribes who inhabited the region likely took them. Regardless, few people dared to enter the territory, and Erroh thought no differently.

She raised a finger, and he fell silent. Her eyes didn't burn with anger, but she was irritated, and she spoke as if addressing a child. "You are as petulant as I had heard. You think it a small matter to question the Primary as if your bloodline demands it. Your father is a legend and I'm sure following in his footsteps is a terrible cross to bear, but the arrogance to walk into this city and behave with such disdain is reprehensible. My girls deserve more than that."

His face reddened, but he held his tongue. He even managed a subservient nod.

"A seal from Spark City should guarantee you safe passage, but I cannot trust a simple lowerline with a task as precarious as this. I trust you because of your name and what horrors you have already seen. There have been more attacks and if such deeds are happening in the south, Gemmil will have answers. If the attacks have originated from the southerners, Gemmil will know the perpetrators. You wanted justice, this is where justice is born," she said, and Erroh finally saw the pain in her face. For the briefest of moments, she appeared less the politician and more human. Perhaps it was the blue dress.

"Should we not spread word, Mydame?"

Whispered words of the road travelled as fast as the wind.

"I have no interest in creating a phantom terror across the land and having every lowerline and his whore camping at the city's gate," she said, and Erroh flinched at her prejudice. She seemed to notice. "They would flock like moths to the city's light and with them would follow an eclipse that burns the world to the ground."

Was she suggesting the city wasn't safe from attack? Again, he thought to argue, but her suggestion of his arrogance had shaken him. He thought he had been quite a courteous little cub since he'd walked into Samara, but the city thought differently.

"I can't allow that to happen. Nobody will be told until we know our enemy. Until we know what army is marching." He understood perfectly now. She was indeed accusing his father of warmongering, and she was sending Erroh as far south as possible. Who knew what misery father and son could evoke if they marched together? It was painfully obvious that she was mad. After twenty years at the seat, she had lost her senses. It was time for another to take her position. Surely, someone else was up to challenging her.

Elise would have been a fine choice.

"If the people come, we haven't enough resources. These walls will protect us and only us," Dia declared as though he was nothing more than a scared citizen clinging to survival, and she the brave leader standing against the storm. Aye, she was mad but there was little he could do but drop to a painful knee submissively. Somehow, he doubted his father would have pledged himself so easily.

"I will travel south after the Cull," he pledged. The Primary nodded before stepping away from her podium, back into the darkness. Good little cub.

It wasn't long before the females returned to do battle with him. When they had settled in and enough time had passed to address the awkwardness, Erroh spoke first.

"Is she late?"

Lea shook her head. She loved the uncomfortable moment. He could see it in her misty cruel eyes. They were sharp, beautiful like glimmering diamonds cutting into his soul, tearing him apart, leaving him for dead.

"So Lillium found more interesting things to occupy her time?"

"She didn't want you to be her mate," Silvia said helpfully. Of course she did.

"She obviously doesn't understand what a catch you are," muttered Roja, and Lea smiled beside her. He had never thought his skin was so thin but the rejection hurt. It didn't matter for a moment she had never looked or spoken to him with any warmth. What mattered was that she had been the first to step away. He had never liked her anyway, had he?

Had he?

Silvia spoke first. "We should talk about why Erroh missed yesterday." Her smile was no longer warm or inviting. It was quite the wonderful sneer. Lea dipped her head in shame. She suddenly found something interesting to stare at instead of the battered wretch below her.

Roja toyed with her wonderful red hair. "We should talk about sex."

"Oh, that's a much better idea," agreed Silvia. Erroh didn't like that tone. He didn't like it at all. The blonde smiled at her redheaded companion nastily but said nothing. Lea refused to look at Erroh or indeed open the questions. Instead, she waited patiently for Roja to begin the battering. She didn't have to wait long.

"Have you ever had a female, Erroh?" Roja asked biting

her lower lip unconsciously. A fine technique to trap unsuspecting victims, he imagined. She raised an eyebrow and continued to play with her hair. It was another lure, no doubt. Wonderful hair, wonderful lips. He wasn't certain what the correct answer was. As usual, he chose truth. It was the wrong answer.

"I have had no such pleasure."

Roja was taken aback "Why? Is there something wrong with you?" Beside her, Silvia sniggered, and she hissed her to silence.

Was there something wrong with him? In truth, it was both a fair and ridiculous question. There were countless things wrong with him, many of which had only occurred in the last few days and some things a little before that. Instead of allowing his demons to surface, he shrugged pathetically.

"Do you even want to furrow one of us?" Roja snapped, foregoing the alluring pose. It was a crude question and there was no safe reply without sounding like a craven beast. Silly redheaded female with fantastic body. He very much wanted to furrow with all of them. Even at the same time, if they were up to such misdeeds. He wanted to kiss, touch, writhe, thrash, and hold any and all for they were still so very beautiful.

All four were goddesses. No, three.

He searched for a witty reply to appease her. Clever words worthy of a confident well-endowed man.

"Aye, I would." He hung his head. He could not be himself here. Maybe if they walked with him out on the road, they would see his prowess, they would hear his charm, they may even laugh at his jokes. But in this room he was a failure in everything. What if the Primary was right and his arrogance had brought this upon him? This made him feel even worse. He wasn't built for battling wits in the Cull.

"Well, that's something," Roja said. Perhaps she noticed his torment and thought it less fun striking at an injured animal. Perhaps she was as tired as he was. Perhaps they all were. Perhaps the day off had taken its toll or else there was something in the air he hadn't noticed.

"May I ask if there was any particular reason you haven't been with a girl?" asked Lea. She didn't bother concealing the cruel smile around her kissable lips. If Roja had shown a breath of mercy, Lea did not intend to join her.

"I wasn't interested. I thought it would be better to wait for a worthy mate." It had sounded a lot nicer in his mind. Looking around at the three remaining girls, it was obvious they were unmoved by this sentiment. Like most answers, he regretted it immediately. Still, why break from tradition?

Silvia struck the next sarcastic blow.

"Well that's very noble of you, but it's a little disappointing to hear that you have no experience in pleasuring a female." Lexi had warned him of her. There was cruelty hidden beneath her smile, albeit a very attractive smile. At least Lea wore her nastiness openly.

So very tired.

"I know where things are supposed to go," he said trying to hide the humiliation and failing. Nobody said anything for a few long moments as each female silently judged him for his lack of prowess upon bedding and straw. Of course they did, because they were all whores.

Tired and beyond caring.

"I assume all of you are skilled at pleasuring males then?" Erroh said before he could catch himself.

"Some of us have talents," snapped Roja without missing a beat.

"Some more than others," Silvia muttered under her breath and both females exchanged venomous glances.

Something in the room changed, as if two best friends had recently had a falling out over some unknown matter. Perhaps over a male? Perhaps two?

"I know what I like, Silvia." Roja shrugged casually, but her eyes cut through the diminutive blonde. Erroh watched with grim amusement. It was all going to end in tears but for now, it was nice to see a little disharmony between the goddesses.

"I'm sure you like many things," hissed the blonde. She picked a loose strand of hair from her shoulder and dropped it over the side of the balcony as irritably as she could. It was something to do instead of glaring at her friend in unrivalled disgust.

"I'm sure you like anything you can get," hissed Roja dropping any pretence of cordiality. What marvellous event occurred on their day off to cause such hostility, wondered Erroh. Please ladies, do go on.

"Well, at least I'm not a whore!" shouted Silvia.

"You're a little bit of a whore," countered Roja.

"Any whore is a little whore in comparison to you, Roja."

"Oh go fuk yourself," Roja muttered eyeing the doorway from whence they came. He knew she was done with this event. They all were. All they had left was bitterness and aggression. Lillium would light the way for the rest to follow. There would be no females come tomorrow. Was this even a bad thing?

It was. It really, really was.

Lea finally found her voice. Louder than usual. "Shut up, both of you." It suited her. It was the closest thing he could get to actually complimenting the little witch. "Can we please continue with the Cull?" she said and both females fell to an uneasy silence. Before Lea could steer the questions to safer shores, Silvia took the helm and ruined it for everyone.

"Which of us do you find most appealing?"

"Don't answer that," warned Lea.

It was a good warning, and Erroh nodded at her.

He answered the question.

He favoured one girl above the rest. A girl on the very first day he could have imagined spending a little time with. He looked at her. Looked right into her beautiful eyes, but he just couldn't bring himself to speak her name, so he lied and ruined his chances with all of the girls.

"Lillium."

"Oh," said Roja. She hid her disappointment well. Or else she didn't seem to care.

"I see," whispered Silvia, smiling sadly, and Erroh almost felt hurt for her. She was quite the piece of work.

"I think we would have all been happier had you held your tongue," muttered Lea. Her face was pale, and she was glaring at Silvia who knew well the misstep she had taken. In a moment of rage, she had asked a terrible question and now there was no coming back from this.

"I think it would have been better had you lied," said Roja coldly. She was up to something.

"I think we've spoken enough for today," said Lea. All strength lost from her voice. He'd winded her with his words and felt elated about it. It was petty but it was the little things.

Before she could wade through the formalities of his rejection, Roja interrupted her. "I have a question and it is my right to ask," the redhead said quietly.

Lea gestured to continue.

"I would very much like to see your body, Alphaline," purred Roja seductively. Erroh wasn't fooled though. The anger flared from her, and she had him in her sights. The bow was taut, the arrow certain. He had sinned against her and now he was to be burned.

"Remove your shirt," she said biting her lip, feigning arousal.

"Oh, that's a fine idea," agreed Silvia.

Lea didn't bother to dissuade him. She merely sighed and waited for him to do as he was told, like a good little cub.

"Remove your shirt!" she roared a second time, and Erroh jumped despite himself.

It was this moment that the city crushed him. It wasn't the brutality of the arena or the questions ridiculing his life. It was the simple order by a female to demean himself for their pleasure. It was their right apparently, and he was in their world.

Painfully and slowly, he unbuttoned each clasp. The gods that seemed to enjoy scripting his misery, showed little sign of ceasing the relentless harassment. He took a breath, removed the garment, and dropped it on the floor. He tried to stand proudly and display the mosaic of purple and black with pride, but he was beaten. He couldn't meet their eyes. He wanted to flee. He wanted the Cull to end. He wanted so many things.

Roja was impressed. "He's quite well built under those rags."

Lea nodded in agreement.

"Hard to see with all the bruising though. You got a terrible kicking, did you not?" Silvia said. He had hurt their feelings and this was his penance.

Silvia was not yet satisfied.

"I would like to see a little more though. It is our right to see what he has hidden beneath his waist." He hated her. Maybe he hated them all; it was hard to decide while suffering such humiliation. He slumped his shoulders and his arms fell to his belt. He couldn't be made do this, could he?

"No one here has any serious interest in seeing his manhood," said Lea.

"I agree," hissed Roja.

"I do not think any of us are quite in the right frame of mind to question. I think we're done for the day," Lea said. "Thank you for your honesty, Erroh line of Magnus." She looked across to the other two. "Has any girl made her choice?"

It was a stupid question.

Neither girl made the remotest effort to move. Roja shrugged away any disappointment and stood back from the balcony. He reached down and picked up his shirt, already leaving the room as Lea pronounced that none had chosen him. He stepped out of the door before she finished asking him to come back tomorrow.

14

FEMALES

"Maybe they really do hate you?" suggested Wynn once Erroh had regaled him with his tale of woe. Little Alphalines were not supposed to speak about the Cull but after what had occurred, Erroh told him everything. It was his petty little act of defiance. The one little enjoyment was seeing his friend's reaction upon hearing that Roja had found him pleasing enough to put herself forward. All morning they sat in the corner of the tavern away from prying eyes and griped on about their lot in life. Erroh chewed on some honey bread and washed each crusty bite down with a generous mouthful of ale. By his third gulp he'd come upon a little line of sediment at the bottom of his glass. Gesturing for the next round, he sloshed the last few drops and downed the awful brew in one bitter swallow. Ale was ale, and he was not feeling terribly content with being sober.

"It isn't even noon," said Wynn as Erroh gestured more obviously for another glass. He sipped at a cup of steaming black cofe sitting in the little ceramic mug. Wynn's endearing bravado was somewhat subdued and tapped his foot underneath the varnished table subconsciously. He was nervous about his second day Culling.

"I'll only have one more," Erroh lied.

"Did you really like Lillium most?" Wynn asked, from the worry on his face it was evident he was thinking deeply on Erroh's mistake.

"No. It just seemed like the thing to say. I was just weary with everything." Erroh accepted the fresh tankard and attacked it mercilessly. This seemed to put Wynn at ease.

"Who actually appeals to you most?" Wynn asked, daring a hopeful grin.

"I liked Lea at first but maybe only Roja now. I don't know."

"I haven't seen Lea. I'll be sure to keep an eye out. It would have been nice if Roja had been in my Cull, she's quite the lady," admitted the ponytailed Alphaline.

"A good match can be made on the second day," said Erroh, returning to his drink.

"Aye."

"You'll be fine. It could never be as bad as mine," Erroh said.

"I believe your Cull will be written in the annals of time," laughed Wynn. They both knew Erroh had stirred quite a brew of trouble. They both knew he was leaving without a mate. But good friends don't need to say such things aloud. Good friends make jests to ease the sadness.

"Well yeah, I like to be memorable," laughed Erroh.

"When I'm done, I'll come join you for a few fine beverages. We'll have a fine old time of it," Wynn said getting up from the table. He spent a nervous moment fixing his irritatingly perfect hair in a nearby mirror before disappearing out the door into the crowds of Spark City's streets.

———

The afternoon heat turned into an uncomfortably sweltering evening. With no cool breeze to breech the walls, the bitter stench of a thousand grubby bodies began to mature nicely, and Erroh with them. He didn't notice though, he sat in the Pig in the Hole and slowly pocketed another cluster of tiny pieces. They chinked happily, as they met their new master, and Erroh became a rich man. The final player stepped from the table and stormed off in anger towards the nearest friendly face to beg the price of a drink.

Eventually the busy tavern's door opened and a beaten young Alphaline appeared through and sought out his drunken friend. Erroh waved wildly and matched the smile on his friend's face without noticing the terrified skip in his step. When he traversed the crowd, Wynn took a seat and ordered a drink. He closed his eyes and leaned his head back against the wall and waited patiently for it to arrive. When it did, he drank heartily. His hands shook and his feet tapped loudly under the table. It had been a rough Cull apparently.

"Tough session?" Erroh chinked mugs with Wynn.

"Long and interesting," Wynn said. Something had happened. The fear was evident as was the table shaking from his feet.

"Would you kindly stop spilling my drink?" muttered Erroh, lifting his goblet before the contents spilled out. As he did, his companion kicked hard at the table. It was a narrow escape.

"I was chosen."

"Oh."

"Yeah."

It took Erroh a few seconds to rise above the sudden melancholy, to rise above the anger and the jealousy, but he did. He sighed theatrically and raised an unsteady glass to his friend's good fortune.

"Congratulations and fuk you," he cried out.

"I knew you'd be thrilled."

"The poor girl. I fear for her happiness," Erroh said and gripped his own mug as if it were the only thing keeping him afloat. Perhaps he was destined for other things. Perhaps he could live a solitary drunken life, happy in taverns such as this, listening to word from the road. He looked around the bar and tried not to be put off by how stained the old brown walls were.

"I make every female happy, she will be no different," Wynn declared pompously, but he was still shaken.

"Was it the girl you favoured?" Erroh asked and signalled for many more rounds with the skill of a man that planned to spend the rest of his life a drunkard.

He smiled guiltily. "Aye. She will join us presently. Afterwards, I thought I would walk with her along the wall." He looked at Erroh for reassurance.

"You have the rest of your lives to get it right, Wynn. A walk sounds perfect for now."

Lillium glided gracefully through the tables of the bar and sat on the last remaining seat beside her man. She was dressed extravagantly in a deep green gown of silk, which made her stand out even more in a place like this. Erroh blinked rapidly and his stomach turned, but he concealed his dismay almost perfectly by looking down at the table. He caught a faint aroma of sweet flowers and his hands began to shake, so he put them to good use by ordering a round for the happy couple and for himself.

"Hi, Erroh," she mumbled, playing with her perfect blue

hair and sneaking brief glances at her mate. It was better than staring at the male she had so gloriously rejected. He suddenly didn't want to be at this table anymore, and he ignored his anger of Wynn never telling him. In truth, could he have said or done anything differently were the roles reversed? Their shared Cull had been a disaster. Why should he punish either one?

"You know, he'll never let me live this down," declared Erroh, feigning a smile. It was his way of giving his blessing. It was all he could do and though his jest was hollow, her sad smile illuminated the table. Easy come, easy go.

"Just remind Wynn he isn't nearly as good a fighter as you," she said before looking down at the table herself. He wanted the embarrassment to pass. He also wanted the ale in his stomach to settle. Throwing up in front of them both would just add credence to her decision to slip from his ungrateful grasp into another. I could have had her first Wynn, remember that.

"That's why I want a rematch!" Wynn slammed his fist down on the table a little too loudly trying to emphasise the point. He was excited; he had a female.

A few patrons looked up from their cards and drinks at the sudden outbursts. The innkeeper carried a worried expression. Alphalines with alcohol were always an accident waiting to happen. They were laughing now but the atmosphere always turned nasty. Such nastiness often brought bruising. He thought about packing it all in. He thought about a wonderful retirement, away from Alphalines, away from Dia, and away from her exorbitant taxes. He watched the group in the corner and poured himself a glass of sine. There was a long night ahead.

. . .

"Wynn beat me. He's the finer fighter." Making him look good somehow made Erroh feel better. Maybe it was the grateful smile on his friend's face.

"No, Erroh, you almost bested him despite a broken rib and a concussion. I know who I favour," she said. Her eyes were sad, but there was another smile growing on her lips. Her rather nice lips. Perhaps had she smiled more, things could have been different.

Let it go, Erroh.

"It's easier to speak comfortably in this place," Erroh said, receiving the drinks and paying with a few coins from his ill-gotten winnings. He raised his glass. "To friends."

He had presumed it would be one of the more uncomfortable nights in his life, but he was wrong, and much of it was down to the company. He thought he had the measure of Lillium but outside of the Cull, she was a different type of beast altogether. She was warmer now and not just in her radiant smile. Her words were laced with a delicate kindness he'd not heard since he'd begun battle with her. Perhaps in another life, they could have been friends. Perhaps they would still be. But love? Well, she had made her choice, had she not? And as the hours passed and the conversations came easier, a wonderful cheer filled their table. He almost felt like himself, charming, witty, and confident. And he made her laugh. He thought it a wonderful sound, which couldn't but bring a levity to the dreariest of moods. But that wasn't all. He quickly learned that she was equally witty and more than once caused both Wynn and himself to spill their drinks from laughter as she regaled them both with ridiculous tales of the city, seen through the eyes of the entitled. She was wonderful. She was a goddess. She was spoken for and the victor was quite taken with her. From the nervous glances she stole, Erroh suspected that she too was quite besotted herself. They would be a fine pairing and such thoughts offered a little comfort. When he felt Wynn had used him as a mediator for a long enough period, Erroh suggested they leave him for the night, early as it was for young lovers. The unease immediately returned to them both, but Erroh cast them aside by calling out to the innkeeper for "just one drink." Perhaps Wynn could bring her for a walk down by the river.

Before they left, Lillium turned and took Erroh's hand. It was warm and it gripped tightly. A fine hand in truth, Wynn had done well.

"I'm sorry, Erroh," she whispered in his ear. They were a few simple words that cut through him. "You are a fine man, you will be chosen, and you will make her happy." She sounded as though she regretted how things had been. It's a little fuken late to say such things, he thought and anger suddenly blazed in his stomach. Biting retorts almost surfaced to wreak a great and terrible revenge. Instead of screaming, he smiled weakly. He did it for Wynn but in truth, he also did it for her.

"Everyone kept telling me that I would be chosen, but there is no coming back from these last few days," Erroh said. He tried not to sound as feeble as he felt, but she still looked away in shame. "I'm sure they'll soon share the same sense as you," he added, sipping at his drink as if its bitterness was an ambrosia required for happiness. For tonight, it was. He took a second swig and drained the glass. He hoped the innkeeper was already on the way.

She had more words to offer, but she could probably read his stubbornness and possibly the anger so instead of arguing any further Lillium leant down and kissed Erroh on the lips.

A fine kiss and it was all she could offer. He fought the shock of her being so close. He also fought the glorious pleasure of her taste. Drawing away after a wonderful moment too long, her smile had turned from sadness to tragedy.

What might have been, dear Erroh?

"A last kiss, I hope?" muttered Wynn from behind. Erroh grinned, and she looked deeply into his eyes one more time, before her chosen mate took her hand gently and led her from the tavern into the clear night. Erroh allowed her taste to remain on his lips for a few breaths more, before deciding to forget about her forever. Besides, he had alcohol to consume and dark hateful thoughts to consume him. To his dismay the innkeeper was distracted, delayed, and finally defeated by an argument between two city farmers along the way. Not to be undone, Erroh downed what remained of his companions' beverages and gave up on himself completely. Without his companions at his side declaring their silent love for each other, he found it far easier to mutter curses under his breath and think distasteful thoughts about the Cull, the females and the city as a whole. It was far easier to blame the entire world for his woe instead of looking to his own shortcomings. He struggled to his feet and gracelessly thundered passed each table, stumbling and tripping over every possible obstruction that his awkward feet could find. No one argued. They knew their place. He'd lost count the hours he'd spent drinking but his body remembered. He reached the edge of the bar and spilled a large handful of coins loudly cross its surface. A few pieces rolled off the top and bounced happily on the floor. The crowds of revellers around him fell silent though none dared to pick up the Alpha's fallen riches, and Erroh didn't bother to pick them up either. He was busy gripping the counter for support while the room ceased its spinning. He was no stranger to alcohol, but he suspected he might have taken more than he could handle. Not that it worried him in the slightest though. In fact, he liked a challenge.

"What's the most I can leave the city with?" Erroh called to the innkeeper, gesturing at the pile of pieces strewn messily across the counter. Lillium had confirmed how unstable the city's economy was these past few months. Pieces were in short supply and every time a trader left with bulging pockets of coin, it became less stable. It was only a matter of time before straight out bartering returned to fashion. Such a thing could not be allowed to occur in Samara. It wouldn't affect Erroh, so he didn't really care about consequences. At that moment, he didn't care if the city became bankrupt, besieged, or burned to the ground.

"You can carry out around a hundred, I think. A man like you could probably smuggle a bit more," the innkeeper said grinning. "Who would dare check you, eh?" He eyed the fortune of cheated coins.

"I don't need a hundred," declared Erroh, hearing how drunk his voice sounded, and deciding it sounded marvellous. "I just need another drink. And some bread. And a bottle of sine. In fact, make it two." He pushed the pieces across the bar. "And buy a round of drinks on me. I'm never getting to leave this city so I think I need to make newer friends," he said and giggled stupidly at his wit. His new friend Wynn had a mate who was wonderful and come the morning they would be departing the city, leaving him behind. It almost made a young Alpha want to drink himself into a deranged stupor and say all the things on his mind to any who would listen. So that's exactly what he was going to do. It was a terrible plan and it worked perfectly.

"There's more here than what you are asking for," the innkeeper said carefully. A drunk Alpha was a dangerous Alpha. A drunk Alpha with delusions of generosity was a very dangerous Alpha come morning when sobriety reared its ugly head.

"It's alright," explained Erroh in his wonderfully drunk voice. "I'll just win more tomorrow," he said before covering his mouth and burping loudly. "Don't forget my wakeup call!" he shouted, stumbling down the stairs three at a time, away from the roar of the crowd. "Or do. I don't really care anymore," he muttered to nobody, as he fell in through the doorway of his chambers.

He forgot to sleep or at least he forgot falling asleep. He might have slept. He couldn't remember. He didn't stop drinking, even after throwing up a few times. At some point, he'd attempted a few songs himself. Great songs, not about the city at all. When dawn broke the innkeeper appeared at the open doorway, brandishing a fresh black eye.

"Are you up yet, cub?"

"Aye," replied Erroh. He was sitting on the floor in a corner of his room holding his half-consumed bottle of sine in his lap. His head was resting on the bedside locker. He wasn't sure why he brought it over to this side of the room either, but it had seemed like a good idea at the time. He looked back up at the figure in the door and pointed to his eye. "Was it me?"

The man shook his head. "Different one of your sort."

"The one with the ponytail?"

Again, the man shook his head. "You should clean yourself up," he said turning away and walking slowly back upstairs. It was fine advice, and Erroh knew he probably looked as bad as he felt. He splashed his face and tried unsuccessfully to wipe most of the crust from his face before chewing on some glorious honey bread and washing it down with some water. He freshened up his breath by taking a few mouthfuls of sine. Never one to take any unnecessary risks, he pocketed the bottle for the long walk to the arena.

Above in the bar a manmade hurricane had struck the interior and left complete devastation in its wake. The floor was littered with debris with overturned chairs and cracked tables and there were hints of bloodstains to be found by the keener eye. Among the ruin of the inn sat the innkeeper who was busying himself with screwing the leg back on an old wooden bench. He did so with the resigned look of a man who'd tasted many mornings as unpleasant as this. Erroh took another swallow and fought the reflex to throw up. He could have offered to help and perhaps on another day, he may have, but instead he walked past without saying a word, out into the blazing morning sun for the final day of the Cull. Aye, the last fuken day. He would make sure of it.

It was a short walk but it took him longer than normal because he really didn't care anymore. His loneliness and sense of rejection had changed during the night. What started as a trickle of anger with the Alphaline witches; was now a tidal wave of fury. He had tried to win their favour with honesty and they had punished and beaten him for little more than cruelty's sake. Sitting at a table with Lillium had been the final straw, and he intended to set alight the entire field.

―――――

"I really hate this place," he said when the three witches took their place above him. He rubbed his eyes clumsily and hiccupped as quietly as he could. He cleverly held the bottle behind his back as he had little intention of sharing it with them. After a moment, he decided it would be rude not to, so he held it out for all to see.

"Thank you for telling us that, Erroh," Lea said. Beside

her Roja was pale. Silvia less so.

"Maybe we should postpone until tomorrow. It's quite obvious he's still suffering from his injuries," Lea said. She could recognise a dangerous and wounded animal and rightly so, for she would be the first one attacked.

"No, this could be entertaining," Silvia said. Of course she did. Roja however shook her head. She could see they'd pushed him too far.

"He's completely drunk," added Silvia helpfully.

She had not pushed him far enough at all.

"Yes, I am." Erroh waved the bottle for any takers. There were no takers, so he shrugged and drank deeply.

"This Cull is done for the day, he's not in his right mind at all," said Lea once more. How many days had they lasted, one more would hardly make a difference.

"I'm not staying another fuken day with any of you whores!" he shouted.

"You have to stay until it's finished," Lea warned, but Erroh could see the fear in her face and oh, how he hated her the most.

"And you have to fuk off," he suggested.

Roja was not troubled; she spoke like a leader. "You should listen to her." Maybe she should have led this Cull. He thought about suggesting as much. He took another drink instead.

"Honour your blood line, Erroh," Lea said.

He stared at her in unrivalled hatred, and she looked away in fear. Maybe it was shame. She certainly wore the same expression as Lillium.

"He has no honour," said Silvia, finally seeing the turn of events for what they were but refusing to cease poking at his anger.

Erroh shrugged. "I don't want a mate who takes this long

to choose me. That's why I'm happy for Lillium. She saw Wynn, she appreciated him and chose him, but I want none of you."

"Maybe he was a finer choice," Roja said. She would make a fine card player. Or else she was emotionless.

"Oh, I think we can all agree he's a finer choice than me," he laughed desperately. "To the happy couple." He raised his bottle and drank. It didn't matter that it offered little comfort to him. It just made him hurt a little less.

"There are rules in the Cull," Lea squeaked. She mumbled something about "entitlement" before her voice disappeared into uncomfortable stillness.

Nobody was really listening anyway.

"I like this version of Erroh," decided Silvia.

"Oh shut up, Silvia," he suggested. That wiped the stupid look from her face.

"You shut up," replied the witty little blonde.

"This little runt needs to be taken away and put out of his misery, he's no Magnus," Roja said.

He didn't mean to do it, it just happened. The bottle was in one hand, perhaps his left and then it wasn't. It was somewhere in the air. And it was moving with great velocity. It met the wall at their feet and did what any self-respecting glass bottle would do, given the same circumstances. It died a good death. The shards scattered everywhere and the females jumped back.

Erroh spoke to Lea one more time and it was a fine address in an attempt to end proceedings.

"I'm deeply sorry for my behaviour on the first day; I will forever regret my lack of respect. It was careless and I hope you find a mate worthy of you in the end." He should have stopped there.

But he didn't.

He had one more thing to say.

"May he never see you as the cruel manipulative bitch that I do." He bowed theatrically. He saw a tear form in her eye just as he turned away and left the three remaining Alpha females behind him.

———

Word spread throughout the city of his performance, or it felt as much. He could never be certain as he spent the rest of the day hidden away in his bedroom like the brave Alpha he was. When the last of the alcohol had left his body, so began the crushing feeling that only the most obnoxious drunks are gifted to, come the first breath of sobriety. He pledged never to drink again. A lie he knew but a lie that served to alleviate his guilt. His heart hammered wildly, just like Lillium's angry rap upon his doorway to which he never answered. She spoke through wood and steel and begged for entrance, but he turned away in his bedding and dug his head into the pillows. On the third attempt, she cursed loudly and disappeared away with Wynn following quickly behind. Only Lexi was allowed enter but conversation was uneasy. She was distraught about his behaviour but said little more once he'd insisted gruffly that her questions would be unanswered. When neither one of them could take another uncomfortable silence, she slipped away and left him to his miserable pondering.

That last night in Samara, he slept better than ever.

He woke up to the feel of a long pike prodding at his chest. Opening his eyes, he snatched the shaft of the pike and thrust it aside swiftly. He was halfway out of bed with fists swinging before he realised there was no second attack coming and his wake up call was not an assault, but two anxious Black Guards standing their ground in the doorway with lowered weapons.

"She ordered us to retrieve you," ordered the nearest guard. "It's almost noon. We shook you a few times and you didn't stir." He gestured weakly to the pike's tip. He wore an "it seemed like a good idea at the time" expression. Erroh nodded and dressed quietly.

"What is this about?" Erroh asked, splashing cold water on his face. His stomach had settled but the headache remained. It was well deserved. "I can't be under arrest for shouting."

The two Black Guards did not march him through the city or attempt to chain him. This was a good thing in his mind. Thoughts of being chained up or jailed were worse than losing an eye. His heart sank a little when they left him at the doors of the Cull. It was likely the Primary was going to give him his marching orders. She would probably have a few words to offer on the matter of the last day of the Cull. He couldn't hide under the pillow for this particular attack.

However, the leader of the world wasn't there to meet him. Lea entered from above and walked quietly. She appeared nervous and it almost felt like the very first day all over again. She wore a bright yellow dress. It really suited her. She smelled of flowers.

"Are you in control, Erroh?" she asked.

"Aye."

"I thought you were going to attack one of us," she said, and he dropped his head in mild shame. He would never hit a female. Not even if she deserved it. Had they not spoken of this matter? Still though, what did it matter now? "I would never strike a female in anger."

"You said that before," she said.

"And I would say it again, many times." Even at this moment, she could not let matters go. He felt the anger rise again.

"I need to record the ending of this Cull," she said.

"So it's done?" He could already taste the clear air of freedom.

"Aye, Erroh, it's finished," she said smiling in relief.

"And all girls rejected me?"

She looked across to where each had stood and nodded knowingly. Her face was smug. It didn't need to be so smug. Stop being smug, you witch.

"All girls rejected you," she said wistfully. Her smile grew but there was still fear, lest he leap up and drag her down to his level.

She leaned against the balcony rail. "Before you leave, can I ask why you behaved like that?"

How could she not know? He could have answered her, allowed her closure on this miserable event but instead he shrugged.

"It seemed like the thing to do," he muttered. To this, she nodded and accepted it as truth.

"A fair answer after everything that has happened," she admitted, but he wasn't really listening. He was already thinking about the road ahead. First a few months ride down south through snow and storm. No problem. Trying to locate one patron in one solitary inn in an entire region? Not a problem either. And then he would face the long road home to his disappointed family and a place in the army. Bit of a problem.

"Perhaps someday you might see that I'm not as nasty as you think," she said, tilting her head and letting her cruel eyes stare deep into his soul. "And I, Lea, choose you as my mate."

15

NEW CUSTOMERS

T he noise. The terrible noise. It was everywhere and it
pulled Sigi from his sleep. It came from beyond the
stained walls, on which hung his precious decorations.
Somewhere far away. The rumbling shook the sawdust
covered floor and up through his body. He heard Wrek
emerge from his cave behind the bar. He had never seen the
behemoth show fear. Now he saw terror.

"That's not thunder," hissed Wrek dressing himself
frantically. This consisted of little more than putting his boots
on. The sound was growing, the sound was nearing, and the
sound was familiar. It was a great march but there was no
army in this part of the world, unless Magnus had had enough
of peacetime.

"Soldiers," he muttered and crashed through the main
door out into the courtyard to catch the sound in the air.

.   .   .

"Excellent," replied Sigi rubbing his eyes and slowly stepping behind the counter. He opened a cool press and took out some bread. He hoped he had time for a quick meal before business took a wonderful turn. Soldiers meant coin. Wrek hated change but Sigi always saw opportunity and business had been bad. Few wanderers had passed through in search of fortune at Samara these last few weeks. Eerily so.

This was bad and Wrek knew it deep in his soul. He needed to get up high to find the source. The Rat's Nest was the only freestanding structure for miles in any direction and a natural area to make camp. So it made a perfect spot to run a tavern.

Sigi stepped out into the sweet morning air. He could see it would be a fine day. The sun would blaze and there would be many mouths with a thirst to quench. He watched Wrek pull himself onto the roughly patched roof and keep climbing. Sigi listened to the noise a little more and bit into the slice of bread and chewing contently as one does, in the knowing that a few tough weeks of business were about to end.

"While you are up there, there's still a leak by the chimney to be patched!" he shouted to the climbing man before walking back inside.

Wrek staggered across the roof and looked out across the plain. He could see them through a gap in the hills. Their flags worried him most. They were deathly black with crude slashes of crimson symbols at the centre. They travelled in tight formation. He counted fifty brutish cavalry leading a few hundred foot soldiers. It was a small army, but an army nonetheless. They were dressed in leather skins with fur lining underneath and unpolished metal plating on the outside, crudely tailored by unskilled hands and far too warm for this part of the world. Both men and women marched together as equals but it was evident they were no Alphas, nor were they from Magnus's army either.

"We have to go."

They moved through the pass alongside, no more than a couple hundred steps across and the noise grew louder. However, it wasn't the cavalry or the hundreds of soldiers causing this thunder. The noise emanated from four large carts of wood and steel with wheels the size of a mount. They rolled slowly and tore the ground up underneath them. What did they carry?

"We have to go." Maybe they'll pass us by, he thought as he hid himself behind the damaged chimney. "Maybe they'll think we're a ruin among the overgrowth," he whispered aloud. It was a suggestive prayer to the gods above who'd cursed him to a life as miserable as this one, with all ill decisions leading him to this very moment. A bead of sweat dripped down into his eye and instinctively he wiped it away with a grubby hand. A few of the horsemen caught the movement but only glanced towards the building just as the last rider entered the pass. He held himself still and after a few breaths, they continued on their way. They never even bothered to send a scouting party and cruelly enough, Wrek began to believe.

It was always a little nippy, first thing in the morning despite the sun. The early breezes normally left a chill in his bones so

Sigi bend down and lit the fire. A moment and a few coughs later, there was a fine glowing flame. He threw some tinder down and warmed his hands.

Lovely.

Wrek smelled smoke and a terrifying realisation struck him. By the time it did there was delicate puffs of white cloud soaring majestically into the air calling out "over here," in their own little language. A few of the Riders gathered and Wrek began to pray a little louder. "Maybe Sigi is right. Maybe all they crave is a drink." But there hadn't been any business these last few weeks, had there? Many of the wanderers of the road had simply vanished. As if hunted down to extinction. The tall bouncer dropped the last few feet from his perch just as the piercing cry of war horns filled the air. The low rumble of the wheels ceased and the horns blew again.

Sigi heard the call of death through the walls and immediately realised his error. Sometimes, he had to admit, his tall companion saw things others did not. He stood at the doorway frozen in thought, but no answer came. The horns fell silent only to be replaced by the roar of charging mounts. Panic overcame him and then a giant arm reached through the doorway and pulled him into the fresh morning air.

"We have to go!" Wrek shouted. He dragged Sigi through the courtyard out into the nearest line of trees. It wasn't a great plan but it was all he had. Get to the thin line of trees; figure something out from there. Behind them, the first rider appeared at the tavern's outer wall.

"We're fuked," Wrek hissed through gritted teeth ducking under branches. He still held Sigi's arm roughly. "They'll catch us here," he hissed, falling up against a tree. He took a deep breath and spun around looking for salvation. He couldn't remember belting his scabbard, but he was grateful that he had. He looked at the tavern keeper gasping for air against another tree, and he wondered if leaving him behind was the smarter move. It probably was but it wasn't in Wrek to do such a thing. "Not enough cover," he whispered, searching and failing for the next part of the plan. Any moment now, the attackers would discover the inn was near empty and the tracks they left behind would be easy to track.

Wrek unsheathed his sword for the last time in his miserable life. He kissed the blade for luck. May it take many of the fukers out before he fell. "When they come, you have to run for it." He heard the first troubling movements from the tavern behind them; loud voices with a foreign tongue and then a wet scream of pain before falling silent. The last few weeks had been bad for business but one traveller had arrived at the door the previous night. He'd been a nice enough wanderer, but not much of a drinker. He'd slept in the barn like most guests.

Sigi grasped Wrek's shirt. "I have an idea. I have a place they won't ever find." They heard the crack of branches breaking as some of the Riders turned from the tavern and into the trees. They found fresh tracks and so began their hunt.

Fresh fear brought wings to their feet and they sprinted through the green. They tore their clothes on brambles, scraped their faces with stubborn branches until finally a quarter of a mile from the tavern Sigi came to a sudden stop near a cluster of trees.

"We made it. We can hide here," he gasped falling to his knees.

It was a bush.

It wasn't a particularly impressive bush and Wrek, deciding that the innkeeper had lost his mind, reached for his sword again.

Sigi dug his hands deep into its leaves and pulled. The difficulty was in keeping the roots of the shrub alive and attached to the metal opening of the trapdoor. He hated farming bushes to cover the entrance to his brewery. An exhausting and usually a futile task but these roots were particularly strong and the bush had taken nicely. The hinges creaked and the trapdoor revealed its safe haven.

Sigi slipped down into pitch-black, his feet silent on the steps cut roughly into the hard soil. Their every blind step led them deeper into the ground and Wrek followed without question. He could hear one of the searching hunters only a few branches away. He pulled the trapdoor shut. "Lock it behind you and don't take a step," whispered Sigi from the nothingness. Wrek kept his hand on the handle of the trapdoor. Above him, it sounded like the end of the world. Thunderous hooves passed above them, and he held that handle as tightly as he could. It was one hopeful piece of shrubbery against an entire army. For the love of all the absent gods, stay strong little shrub.

A spark was struck, illuminating the little cavern and Wrek saw the dim figure of Sigi bringing a second candle to life, and then another. He saw two little bolts at the hatch, and he slid them across carefully.

"It's my little distillery," Sigi said from the bottom of the steps. It was rather impressive. It was at least half the size of the tavern and each of the walls were lined with sturdy red brick. Built to last. There were a few barrels lining the walls and the faint smell of sine was in the air. In the centre of the room was a large wooden table that held the distillery itself. Wrek tried and failed to make sense of the milliard of funnels, wires, tubing, and beakers.

"Sorry about the darkness, can't light too many with the trapdoor sealed," Sigi said offering Wrek a seat at the table. There was still a breeze, and Wrek spotted a small chimney at the far end of the room which led up to the surface. Its mouth was hidden in a tree trunk, no doubt.

He sat down on the offered stool and sighed deeply. Above them vibrations could still be heard but it sounded as though their hunters had already given up the chase. In their defence, who would consider searching for two men under a bush?

The innkeeper, ever fulfilling his sacred duties, took two small decanters from a shelf, unscrewed both corks, and sniffed the contents. Unhappy with one, he resealed it tightly. The second however he approved of and handed it across to Wrek. Wrek took a swig and passed it back. Breaking from tradition, Sigi joined him. His mind raced but the fear was already leaving him. They would ransack the "Nest" but the distillery was still secure and with it, the means to rebuild or indeed relocate. He took a second mouthful and grimaced at its almost but not quite perfect fermentation. Still though, he was alive. War was coming and war was good for business. He looked carefully at the giant who'd offered to sacrifice his life while giving him a chance to survive and nodded thoughtfully to himself. A strong ally to have for the places they would need to go.

"What next?" Wrek asked, his eyes distant, his attention on a little flickering flame doing battle with the breeze. He didn't want the candle to blow out.

16

ESCAPING THE CITY

"You look a mess," Erroh muttered, checking his pockets for some cloth to clean the mud and blood away from her.

"I heal well," Lexi replied trying to deter him. She was a mess. Excursions outside the city were apparently tough. So was the way of the young Alphaline in training. He wondered just how fierce the lessons were. Were they tougher than a life under Magnus's eye? He wondered how many bones she'd broken already.

"You're still limping, Roro." She took the rag he offered, daubing it against one of the scrapes. It did little good, as there were too many. It did little good to draw out a long goodbye as well.

"A few days out in the fresh air will do me the world of good," he muttered. His hands shook and he pulled them behind his back. It could be years before he would see her again. That was just how things were, he supposed. He reached over and hugged his sister warmly.

She rested against the city wall. "So you tricked a poor girl into keeping you?"

"Aye."

"You have to protect her, Roro. You have to let her protect you as well."

"Aye."

"I have to get back," she said. The parting of ways was hurting her as much as it was he. They barely knew each other but that didn't matter.

"You're not staying to meet her?"

Lexi shook her head.

"I've met her before. And what type of idiot shares their first few moments alone with anyone else?" He could see the regret in her face. Lea was fine, but it was Roja she had always favoured.

"Is she a good match?" he asked.

"Only time will tell," Lexi said and suddenly grabbed Erroh and hugged him once more tightly. She did not weep, though she shuddered a few times and let him go. He felt the tears threaten, but he too held firm. He was Alphaline after all.

"I need to go before I fall to pieces."

"May the wind be at your back," he said.

"May the road rise to meet you," she replied and then she was gone. Would he ever see her again? Deep down where sorrow found a home, he had his doubts.

As usual, Lea kept him waiting. There had been no trumpets announcing their coupling, merely a signature upon an ancient parchment with Seth as witness. He recalled her hand shaking just as much as his own. Her sweet smell of flowers and then with the drying of ink, he was mated for life. Even now, he was still in shock. At least Wynn and Lillium had spent an evening together before leaving the city together but

Lea had gently insisted they meet the following morning to depart.

He closed his eyes against the morning sun and thought about his new mate. She was beautiful. She was the most beautiful creature he had ever seen, and she was his. It didn't matter that she was a nasty piece of work. What if she only mated with him out of necessity? Her standing was lower in the city than the rest of the females, and he was the son of Magnus and Elise. A cold shiver ran up his back. Could she be that deceitful?

Could she?

When she did arrive, it was awkward from the start. She did not smile. Of course she didn't. A smile would have helped but instead she glared at the ground as if it was an enemy to be defeated, while noticeably struggling with her pack strapped on her back. At least she was dressed for the road in simple leather garments, looking less extravagant but still annoyingly enthralling nonetheless. He was sure there were customs or etiquette upon meeting under the shade of the wall, but nothing came to mind. He thought of saying something reassuring, warm words to melt the ice and make them both feel better. He searched for something, anything. He noticed her hair. It was magnificent, with each strand pinned and styled to perfection. How many hours had she spent making herself pretty for the wilderness?

Far too many hours.

"I've been waiting for an age," he muttered when she stopped in front of him.

"I've lived here a while," she countered and adjusted the backpack. "It took me a while to pack what I needed." She looked sad. She also looked irritated. He couldn't decide.

"We're walking?" she asked. She sounded irritated. He decided she was irritated. That was fine. He had a lifetime to learn her mannerisms. He imagined there were warmer ones deep down beneath that spitefulness.

"I thought it might be best to walk the first few miles. We can pick up a few mounts along the way." Maybe this princess was too good for walking. And perhaps for now, riding a horse with damaged ribs sounded about as enticing as a diet of pigeon and tree bark.

"You know best," she muttered quietly, and he did not rise to the bait. This wasn't the Cull anymore. Out here, he was king and she; well, she was to be his queen. He sighed dejectedly and strapped his own pack around his shoulders before leading his glorious mate from the fabled City of Light.

She walked beside him from the start. She studied the ground as though dirt and brush was new to her. Her laboured breathing in the burning heat soon began to grate on his nerves, but he said nothing until they reached the crest above the city. She stood beside him and stared back at the city. She wasn't to know that life on the road was far better. He was sure she'd learn swiftly. It would only take a few bruises.

She knew it would be awkward once they were alone, and she was right. This was probably a good thing, she reassured herself. She wasn't sure her voice would hold up under the torrents of emotions coursing through her so she remained silent. She took deep breaths and tried not to think how monumental this day was. This was how it was. Her life had led to this day. She wondered why it hurt so much. The last few days had taken its toll and standing looking at Samara and saying goodbye was almost too much to take. She sighed loudly and shook thoughts from her head. It had all worked out, had it not?

It had all gone to plan.

It was a fine plan.

"Do you need help with the bag, Lea?"

"I won't slow us down."

"You know best," he said before turning his back and walking away.

They travelled in silence for a few hours. Relative silence. She stumbled a few times under the weight and exhaustion. It wasn't that she was unfit or unprepared for uneven trekking; she was simply out of practice. After a few hours when she was weary of the march and her breath struggled to catch in her lungs, he turned around suddenly and suggested they rest. As exhausted as she was, she saw there was barely a bead of sweat upon his brow. He looked irritated, and she declined straight away out of principle. She was tougher than she looked.

Erroh shrugged his shoulders and sat under the welcoming shade of a tree regardless. He left his pack to his side and enjoyed the relief in his feet. He closed his eyes and stretched his legs out gloriously. She could do whatever she wanted, he was going to sit and rest from the heat. He heard her move back towards him and felt her presence as she sat down beside him. She smelled of a sweet aroma that enamoured his senses. It was wonderful. Still though, harder to hunt, smelling nice. He would have to say it, when they were hungry. For now though, he kept his eyes closed. It was safer that way. He knew he was being a coward, sitting under a tree with eyes closed, hiding in plain sight from his mate, but he was afraid to talk. Walking in silence was much easier. Brave

Erroh, afraid of little Lea and her shapely figure. He listened to the forest, the chattering of birds, the sway of leaves and the gentle hum of insects. He didn't miss the city's drone in any way.

Eventually after a time, he grew bold. He opened his eyes, to start a conversation. Wasn't that the sort of thing mates were supposed to do? She had her head resting against her massive rucksack. Her cruel eyes tightly shut. She was playing the same game as well. That was fine. Small talk could wait a little while longer. How long would he be like this? Would he ever look at her the way Wynn had looked upon his Lillium? He reached for the metal flask and unscrewed the top. She stirred a little at the movement and opened her dark eyes. She was so beautiful, and there were moments when he forgot such things. She reached out for the flask casually. He passed it over in silence, and she drank too much before handing it back.

She let down her hair, then began tying it back up in a less extravagant ponytail. She'd spent an hour tying it up perfectly. She'd done it for him, but he wasn't ready to see anything beyond the events of the Cull. Was she ready to? Not at all, but it was a small matter. They had the rest of their lives to sort out their issues.

"Your rucksack is too heavy," he muttered, stretching his body. His ribs were beginning to hurt and they were only a few hours walk from the city.

"I can manage it," she replied lifting the overfilled bag onto her back. She shrunk under its weight, and Erroh decided to make life easier on both of them. She wouldn't last a hundred miles before burning out to nothing. He pulled the bag from her and dropped it on the ground.

Enough was enough.

"Your rucksack is too heavy," he repeated hoping she could take his hint. Instead, she stood with irritated arms on hips. She was quite slow on the uptake. She also had wonderful hips.

"I said I'm fine, Erroh."

"You need to lose something in here." He reached in to pull out the contents.

"Don't ever touch my pack!" she screamed. It was an effective tactic. He dropped the bag and raised his hands away.

"You never touch a girl's bag!" she roared again, grabbing it up as if it were a little defenceless cub. He started to argue, but she moved to the other side of the tree and began slowly removing the contents while cursing quietly to herself. He didn't understand what the problem was.

Females.

She removed the carefully folded yellow dress first and placed it on the grass, smoothing it out as she did. Then she removed a little metal box and put it beside the dress. He waited at least five seconds.

"What's in the box?"

"My things."

"Nice things?"

She sighed irritably and flipped the lid. Inside were little capsules of oils, sweet scents, and small colourful boxes of different makeups. It was everything essential for a pretty young Alpha female, to remain pretty and young.

"We'll be keeping these," he noted.

She pulled out the book and ink and put them aside.

Instinctively he reached for it, and she snapped it from his grasp.

"My journal," she muttered.

"I lost mine a while back," he said, and thought about his own little writings, sunk in the bottom of a river somewhere.

"I'm sure it would have been an interesting read," she said. This was good. This was easy small talk. She pulled out two pairs of shoes and placed them by the dress.

"You only need one pair," he said.

She pulled out a third pair guiltily. After a painful internal debate, she tossed one pair into the grass.

"And you can't bring the dress either." He lifted the silk piece up for closer inspection. It was bright, yellow, and completely unsuitable for life on the road.

She started to scream. To be precise, she started screaming at him. Wonderful colourful curses fit for any true wanderer of the road. Unprepared for the tirade, he took a step back lest sharp words turn to violent actions. He knew he'd said the wrong thing and it certainly involved the dress, but beyond that, he was mystified. Whatever the reason, she was insistent they keep the yellow dress, and he quickly agreed. He was clever like that. He tried to offer a helpful suggestion for the walk forward.

"You should wear the sword against your back," he said carefully, pointing to the ungainly scabbard strapped at her perfectly shaped waist. "It won't trip you the farther into the wastes we travel. This is a fine path here, but there are plenty miles ahead over uneven ground."

She nodded but made no move to undo the strap. Instead, she pulled out a metal chest plate that was thick and sturdy. Even an axe would find it difficult to penetrate its body. In truth a fine piece, perfect for warfare, but like the dress, completely unsuitable for the road ahead. It was far too heavy. He shook his head, and her face flushed in embarrassment or annoyance.

"Does this have sentimental value?" He kicked the heavy steel with his foot.

"It was all I could afford after the sword. They came as a set."

"You bought your own sword?" he asked in surprise.

"I didn't have a chance to plunder any towns recently, and I certainly don't have a father generous enough to gift a sword like Mercy," she growled. "All of these things I earned myself. And the yellow dress, most of all," she added, just in case he'd forgotten.

He felt his anger rising again but realised the flush in her face was embarrassment after all. She could not afford many things; she was a lower caste Alphaline, was she not?

"I'm keeping them," she muttered. Maybe she had over-packed somewhat but that was not the point. Fuk him. That was the point. After a few breaths, she left a few bright shirts, one pair of shoes, and a heavy piece of armour behind. As irritably as she could, she strapped the sword down her back and felt much better moving. This annoyed her even more. Not just for his suggestion but for her own stupidity. She was better than this. She had always excelled out in the wastes in training. The city had softened her. She would do better, if only to get the better of him.

"Come on, Lea," he said sighing.

After a few more hours walking the path, he slowed and gestured her to follow him as he stepped through the treeline. They walked deep into the forest silently. He seemed to know where he was going which was fine for her. She watched the ground for sign of track or footstep but saw little, so she listened instead. Within the deep forest, there was an aching silence and despite herself, she thought it beautiful but after a time, she heard something else. It was something delicate, graceful, and indicative of hunting.

"Something is out there," she whispered suddenly, peering into the deep green. The sun was fading but there was still enough eerie light to spot movement.

"I hear nothing, Lea, we're on safe ground here anyway."

"How do you know?"

"We're miles from the nearest path, and few people would travel this far in," he offered, ducking under some branches and holding them for her as she passed.

"Well, we've travelled this far in," she countered, removing a blade from her back and felt a lot better about herself. She'd handled a sword many times; her technique was quite accomplished, but she'd never struck out in anger. That will change, a voice in her head whispered.

Erroh just stood and watched. If he had jumped every time he sensed watching eyes, he'd never have walked many miles in the road. "What are you doing?" he asked, looking around and again, still seeing nothing.

"I think you should take out your weapon?" she suggested. He resisted the crass joke that formed in his mind. It was too obvious, and they weren't ready for his childish jests just yet.

"Come on, Lea, it's not far," he whispered, touching her shoulder and gently tugging her on to move.

"Can we run?" she asked hopefully.

"There is no need."

Silly Alpha girl, there is nothing to worry about.

Then he heard the twig snap. He grabbed her in close and

stepped forward unsheathing both his blades. His speed took her off guard. She stood behind with her own sword ready. Watching him turn from docile wanderer to deadly threat in less than a breath was admittedly impressive.

"Is that you, Mea?" he roared but there was no answer. He spun his blades absently, gripping them tightly as he did.

"Tye?" The forest took little notice. It could have been any manner of beast that broke the twig. "Let's go," he whispered after a few moments. Better to get to safer ground and let it come to them. If it was her infectious paranoia affecting him, that was all right. There was nothing wrong with paranoia in the woods.

Whatever it was, they left it far behind. Moving quicker through the deep forest was difficult with his injuries, but he led the charge and finally relaxed when his feet touched a familiar path. He had promised to return and his word was good.

They followed the path until they met the wooden perimeter fence of the homestead. He called out over the farm and waited until a very excited Mea exited the door. Her hair was dishevelled for once, but she was glowing. A few seconds later an almost equally happy Jeroen followed Mea through the doorway. He was buttoning up his shirt.

"Couldn't show up an hour from now?" he bellowed with a smile across his face.

17

ONE FOR THE ROAD

S he accepted the hug from Mea because she had little choice in the matter.

"You took your time," said Jeroen looking Lea up and down. From his stare, he considered her a fine catch.

"Mea and Jeroen, this is Lea, my mate," Erroh said. Lea nodded apprehensively until Mea took her warmly by the arm and declared there were "female discussions to be had," before whisking her away from the awkwardness. Erroh couldn't help but notice the look of gratitude in his young mate's eyes. Anything was better than spending another moment with him, apparently.

Jeroen lit the torches on the patio outside their home and stoked the burning pit from where a few strips of meat were slowly cooking. He poured some rich wine and toasted to young love. The breeze brushed against Erroh's face and his hair waved gently in the wind. It was nearing the end of the warm season but the night was clear and refreshing. He sipped the wine and remembered what relaxation felt like.

"You were so loud crashing through the forest, you were

an easy kill," Tye declared from behind them. He dropped his crossbow at his feet loudly and sat down with a hopeful look upon his young face.

"So it was you, hunting us?" Erroh said, and the smaller Alpha nodded enthusiastically. "You move well," Erroh said, making father and son's day in the process. A third glass appeared and a small measure was poured. Just enough to tell him he had done a good job. Just enough that when he swiftly finished, he would disappear so the male folk could talk of manly things like females and secretive events of the city.

Jeroen pushed gently, and Erroh revealed the past few days of his life. For most of it, he listened without comment, merely laughing and shaking his head in bewilderment, and the more the tale was told, the better Erroh felt.

"Don't tell Mea you had to fight three times," Jeroen warned when Erroh told him of the trials.

"It's a small matter now."

"It only takes a small matter to get her riled up if the city messes with any of her family," he warned.

Family.

Kind words, and he was humbled. This refuge reminded him of what a strong coupling could become. Of what a strong family was. It reaffirmed his decision to return.

"I know why you are here, little cub."

"For the drink," Erroh laughed, sipping the wine.

Jeroen smiled. "It's easier sitting among friends drinking in this sanctuary than spending an awkward first night attempting and failing to mount her."

"I am in no mood to mount her." This time Jeroen laughed.

"Of course not, and why would you want to bed that girl anyway, she's positively repulsive."

"I told you what happened. I told you of her cruelty," Erroh hissed, letting his anger surface.

"I'm sure many men would find that a reasonable trade. Besides, you were no respectful gentleman to her. You embarrassed her terribly. It will take a fine while to walk that one off," Jeroen said grinning.

"She is the most beautiful girl I have ever seen," admitted Erroh. He went to say more but stopped. He caught a glimpse of the two female forms on the far side of the farm talking. Plotting, no doubt. They walked side by side. She had a fine walk, she was beautiful, and he was terrified of what was to be.

"Was there another girl you wanted?"

"They were all horrible," Erroh said shaking his head.

"But Lea was a little less horrible to you?"

"No, she hated me the most."

"So why did she choose you?"

"I think she liked it, when I cursed at her. I think she's that type of female." Erroh smiled half-heartedly.

"You need to talk to her about it down the road. For now, leave things as they are," Jeroen whispered, lest his voice carry in the evening breeze.

Erroh shrugged and sipped some more wine. There were no real answers found in conversation. In time, he and the stunning Lea would have to find their own way. Maybe they would, and maybe they would do it hand in hand, but in truth, he had his doubts.

Mated for life. The thought kept returning to him. He looked over at the girl again. The girl he was stuck with until he took his last breath. He looked over at her and drank his wine a little faster. He wished it was something stronger.

Jeroen patted Erroh's shoulder. "Mea and I had our own

problems. We still struggle to this day, but we find a way and you will too."

"Aye," was all Erroh could manage before the two females finished their circuit and appeared at the patio. Mea leaned down and kissed her man before hugging him tightly. It didn't matter to her how uncomfortable the newly mated couple were. What mattered was that love was in the air. Erroh watched Lea stare into the sky in wonder. She'd probably never counted the stars in the city's glow. Her eyes were weary and the paint was running a little. He'd seen his mother cry enough through the years to recognise clever and quick concealment. She normally cried for weeks after a visit to the city. Sometimes Erroh questioned the purpose of the city. He knew his father certainly did. Maybe he could ask Lea about it someday. Maybe she cried because she missed the place. Maybe she cried for her choice.

"To the happy couple," toasted their hosts. Lea raised her glass and looked nervously towards him.

To the happy us?

"To us," announced Erroh indifferently and clinked glasses with the girl. They both sipped. Mea and Jeroen followed suit. Their eyes met. The young couple had been through a rough Cull.

The tougher the Cull, the weaker the choosing.

"Our first night was not quite as comfortable," said Jeroen smiling at his beloved. She laughed and played with a sliver of meat on her plate. The hounds at her feet sat patiently.

"What happened?" asked Lea, leaning one arm across the table and resting her head against it. The events of the day were knocking her out, yet the night was young.

"We were quite far from the city, it was raining and Jeroen hadn't even mastered the art of fire." Mea sliced the piece into two and flicked them under the table. There was a slight commotion but at the end, both hounds were sated.

"We were so in love we didn't need a fire," joked Jeroen.

"It was very cold, and there was no food, so he tried his finest moves on me."

"I was smooth. You loved my advances," he argued and poured some wine into their glasses. Lea tried to decline the top-up, but he would not be denied. She'd never been the greatest drinker but tonight called for a certain amount of numbness.

"Oh, yes, darling, you won my heart that night in the freezing rain. It's a terrible shame I caught a chill and had a headache for at least a year." She laughed and kissed him. "We've made up for lost time since." In that moment, she was a newly mated Alpha with her prize male and all guests were forgotten. Her eyes were only for him, and Lea sighed delicately. Erroh shrugged and sipped his drink.

After a time Lea excused herself and when she was out of earshot, Mea leaned in towards Erroh.

"She made a good choice, Erroh," whispered Mea.

"What do you mean?"

"I won't betray her trust, Erroh." She smiled that disarming smile and patted his cheek gently.

"I'm sure she has spun you a fine tale. In truth, I made an error on the first day, but I said I was sorry," he said quiet enough that his mate wouldn't hear him. "I don't understand females."

Jeroen laughed.

"We are a rare breed," she agreed. "You both made mistakes, Erroh, but does it matter now?"

"I suppose not," he lied.

"One more thing, little cub," Mea said in a tone which suggested she had an insightful point to make. "She's going to look extremely appealing some night out on the road." Her voice dropped to a near inaudible murmur.

"That's possible, she does have a nice walk," he whispered.

"Ignore your urge to tear every stitching of clothing off her. Wait until you're both ready."

He was more than happy to wait. He could think of nothing more awkward than lying atop her, looking into her cruel eyes as they moved with each other. What if she was critical?

"You were able to alleviate such urges out on the road alone. Let nothing change," Mea whispered, winking mischievously. "There is love to be found from the Cull." She squeezed Erroh's hand as Lea returned to the table.

It was Jeroen alone who attempted to silence Mea's fury, once she heard Dia's insistence they journey to the Southern Faction.

"Her word is law," Jeroen argued playing the voice of reason to her venom.

"Fuk her laws." Lea shuffled in her seat hearing this.

"This is not the moment to pick another fight with her," Jeroen said, and the sleeping hounds bravely got up and disappeared indoors. There was a storm brewing even though the night was clear.

"I'll pick any fight that I can win!" Mea shouted. Her eyes were locked on the faint glow beyond the horizon.

"I'm sorry, I shouldn't have said anything," Erroh said.

"Not at all," Jeroen promised. He scratched his beard "Besides, Mea is right. She's normally right, but this is no time to speak of revolution." He took Mea's hand gently. He was a man skilled in taming tempests.

"Aye, not the time," agreed Mea bitterly after a few moments. She took a breath as though she'd been counting and pulled her eyes from the city.

The table fell to uncomfortable silence, and Lea broke it.

"This is still better than sitting in the rain somewhere, fighting off the advances of an excited little cub," she said, and dared a smile. Mea began to laugh under her breath, as did Jeroen. It was just enough for the tension to lift. Well played, Lea.

When conversations returned to less precarious topics, the night passed on far too quickly. There were jests, there were even laughs and in delicate moments, he even noticed Lea smile, though not at him. As a group of friends, they wasted the night away wonderfully, finding comfort in each other's company, as if it were the last night they could ignore the awful feeling that a terrible storm was forming just beyond the horizon.

———

They sat on opposite sides in the loft drinking water spitefully at each other. Both were too exhausted to endure awkward conversations or anything beyond, so they enjoyed the silence. Eventually she lay back in her own bed of straw and when sleep took hold, her goblet of water slipped to the floor. Erroh leaned back in the straw and enjoyed a little time all to himself. He sipped his own water in preparation for the morning's hangover. He looked at the little river from his mate's fallen glass. She would regret that come the dawn. It wasn't his problem. It was easier staying angry. The die had been cast, and she was his prize. He had walked for two years to claim her, and she had waited for him. He felt the weariness overcoming him and let it take him. He shifted himself in the straw to ease the strain on his ribs. Draining the last of the water and placing the goblet down, Erroh stretched out in the softness. He took one last look at the girl he thought most beautiful in the world, and he muttered a curse before falling into a deep sleep.

18

I CALL HIM DAD

S he moved gracefully around the room, she moved
everywhere gracefully. The first rays of the dawn were
shining through the cracks in the walls. Little spots of light lit
up the floor, just enough light to prepare her belongings,
which could be packed up efficiently into one small rucksack.
She thought of her room and her bed in the city. Erroh stirred
and stretched out in the straw. His eyes fluttered in deep
sleep. One of his hands had strayed from the warmth of the
bed. It was hanging down the side, his fingernails were black
from rubbing against the dirty ground. She sighed and
thought about the city again. She drank more water, freshly
drawn from the well; she knew it would help with the
headache.

The farm was peaceful. She liked peaceful. Peaceful was
safe. The silence also afforded her a few precious moments
all to herself. He stirred again, and she knew he'd wake soon
and the terrible, uncomfortable conversations would continue.
She began brushing her hair and applied a little paint to her
lips while stealing glances at her beautiful mate. She still hurt
deeply from his words and his actions but still he took her

breath away. He always had. Ever since she had first seen him, staring like an idiot at the city sights, enthralled with the world. He had shone brightly like the city. He hadn't noticed her then. He still didn't now.

They ate a fine breakfast and after some persuasion, Lea tasted some cofe and hated it. Erroh finished her cup for her. He considered it a kindness on his part. Conversation was light as the long walk was on all their minds. For Mea, Jeroen, and Tye it was the sadness of departure. For the young couple it was the terror of walking alone for a time.

"Your line will always be welcome here," Mea whispered in his ear, hugging him tightly. "Protect her." It was a fine warning and it stuck in his mind. She turned to Lea and kissed her on the cheek.

Jeroen handed Erroh the gifts and embraced the younger Alpha. "Make use of them, Erroh. Safe travels to both of you," he said, and Erroh felt the sadness of their kindness overcome him. Instead of dwelling on it, he led his mate from the sanctuary into the deep unending green of the wastes.

———

She wore his armour. It brought out the colour in her eyes.

"I'm supposed to protect you, after all," he jested, as he helped with the clasps. It was only a gesture. It wasn't even a grand piece either; the shoulder was still unprotected. Ah well, it's the thought that counts.

"And I am quite the damsel." It may have been a mocking reply, but he wasn't certain. Regardless, she still wore the armour and like most items of clothing, she wore it well. They walked the first few miles in silence, through thick undergrowth and unforgiving terrain. He marched carefully while she managed to kick every possible loose rock and snap every innocent twig along their path. After a time he could take no more.

"Can you walk quieter, Lea?" The afternoon heat was now beating down through the broken canopy of greenery. It shone directly into his eyes. He reached for his canteen and drank a little water. Such heat wouldn't be a problem further south.

"Sorry," she said.

She knew she was far clumsier than normal. Her mind was preoccupied, what with trying to stifle thoughts of misery and misjudgement. He passed her the canister, and she drank deeply. "I'm out of practice." It was the truth. She wasn't used to speaking truthfully to him. He took the canister back and shook it. Of course he did. She wasn't even able to drink water without him having issue.

"We need to get you one of these," he said resealing the cap. He rubbed his ribs, and she saw the strain in his features.

"How's the pain?" she asked carefully.

"It's fine."

"We could take a break if it hurts too much. We've walked for hours."

"I can take a lot of pain but you've seen that already," he said, shrugging and wincing despite himself.

"It should only have been one fight," she said quietly.

He raised an eyebrow.

"I'm sorry it was more," she said. Her mouth was dry again. She wanted more water.

"Ha," he cried out, shaking his head before turning away

and walking on. "I apologised in the Cull and you didn't accept it, so allow me the same courtesy."

"I said I was sorry," she growled. It was the opportune moment to clear the air, but he said nothing. To ignore her seemed like the finer tactic.

"Don't ignore me," she said.

He was in no mood to speak aloud, so he skilfully ignored her a little more and felt grand about it until she ruined everything a few miles later.

"Being the son of Magnus doesn't mean you can have everything handed to you on a silver dish, Erroh."

"I never had anything handed to me on a silver dish," he said.

"Oh, I'm sorry. I meant to say gold platter," she countered.

"That's fine; apology accepted," he growled.

"See, that was easy," she said, stopping by a tree and leaning against it. Sweat poured down her brow. The going had been tough, but she'd matched his step. Just a little out of practice was all. "I'm also sorry the son of Magnus hated every moment in the Spark."

"I didn't hate the leaving part," he muttered.

She smiled slightly. "That's because it was with me." It was a weak jest.

"Aye, that was the reason," he said and her smile faded.

He discovered that walking was good because walking was better than fighting. Time passed and their hatred cooled to mere loathing and the world began to return to normal, whatever normal was anymore. He watched the sky and wondered how many silent miles could be travelled before the sun set. They could have a nice fight, once they made camp. It would be better than awkward conversations anyway. He cast a glance back at her and met a hostile glare, so he looked forward again. He didn't suggest any rests, and she didn't either. Her footing improved as fewer and fewer steps made loud noises with every mile taken. Soon enough while taking the lead it was easier to pretend he was still alone out here.

Eventually he slowed and came to a halt by a moss-covered trunk. He reached into his pack and pulled out the innkeeper's map. It was still true enough for a few hundred miles more, he imagined. She leaned against the log. Perspiration dripped down her forehead, her lipstick had faded, her hair was tangled, but she still looked stunning. Erroh on the other hand looked a ruin. His face was a smear of wilderness, dust, and grime. Worse than that, he felt a ruin as well. The sharp pain in his side had spiralled into complete agony. Erroh was no stranger to this type of anguish. It builds character, his father would have whispered. As was the sound of dislocating bones.

"We're aiming for this little spot on the map," he said studying her face as he pointed his grubby finger at a blot on the tattered paper.

She rubbed her shoulder absently. "It looks like a stain."

He didn't like her tone. Of course, it looked like a stain, but she didn't have to say it like that, even if it did look like a stain. It was a fine map; it had cost him a fortune. "It might be a stain, but at least it's a direction to go in."

"What's the scale?" she asked.

"It might take us a few more days," he said. He absolutely did not like her tone at all.

She placed her bag on the ground. "Long walk for a stain."

That fuken tone. She took his canteen and drank a little too much water again. He didn't rise to the bait.

"It could be a town," he muttered, checking the water again. He was thirsty but not enough that he would drink any. It was the point of the matter.

"It's south, and there's a water line nearby should we run dry. Bad thing to run dry out on the road," he said.

"We're walking to the stain then," she said and reached over and took his flask again. She poured some of the precious liquid into her tangled hair. It felt wonderfully refreshing. The water trickled down her back, and she felt even better.

"Are you completely stupid?" he snapped, ripping the water from her grasp. He screwed the cap on as loudly as he could. Her eyes narrowed to cruel slits. "We can't waste any water."

"Don't call me stupid," she growled, staring at him while still appearing fierce from her sitting position.

"Don't drink all the fuken water," he stated slowly in terms that she could understand.

She fingered her long damp hair. "I didn't drink all of the water." In the heat, steam had begun to rise from her hot skin. She flicked her hair back and a few precious drips flew to a beautiful death in the long dry grass. "You're a fuken ass, Erroh."

"What's your problem, Lea?" he growled, dropping down onto the ground beside his pack.

She faced him, radiant, perfect, and full of malevolence. She resonated a power in her small frame, something he hadn't really noticed before. She wasn't defenceless. He could still take her in a fight though. He shook the unhelpful thoughts away. It was the world's oldest law, never to strike a female. Before meeting her, he would have thought there was no grey area.

"My problem is my not being Lillium."

"Oh, that."

She grabbed her pack in one smooth motion and started walking. Her point was made, and he watched her disappear through the canopy of green. So much for the break. He struggled painfully to his feet and picking up his own bag, followed her.

She walked well despite the terrain but more than that, he found her walk incredibly pleasing. He thought about her last statement and felt a pang of guilt, but then thoughts of the arena and her betrayal sprang to mind, and any guilt swiftly dissipated like drying water on warm porcelain skin. He didn't think she had the right to be as hurt as she was, while he on the other hand was completely justified. Was he even willing to work it out with her just yet? If she fell to her knees and begged forgiveness for her behaviour, would it even make a difference? Aye, it would. Until the next fight.

A few miles later, she returned from the bushes demanding the canteen to wash up. Erroh refused and began walking away. Another argument ensued. He gave his reason that she was "wasteful with the water", and she referred to him as "a complete waste of a man." Eventually they decided that completely ignoring each other was the best thing to do. It was fortunate they were gifted in this particular art.

As the frustrating day drew to a close, they began to search for suitable places to set a camp. She spotted the little dip in the ground, an excellent place to camp he had to admit. His inaudible grunt was enough of an accolade. There was no stream or river nearby but if Lea improved her water consumption, all would be fine. As she settled herself, he hid the canister in the bottom of his pack subtly. It was one of his finer plans.

He did his thing with the fire, and she was suitably impressed. He set the kindling alight and caught the spark. She watched curiously, as he dropped the first of the pieces of wood onto the growing flame and the smoke sailed carelessly into the darkening sky. He blew at the little fire and satisfied that it would not die out, sat back, and began the process of making the little spit. She looked around, unsure of what to do next. It would take her a time to remember all she'd learned of the road but watching him would certainly help. She'd never seen anyone light a fire that easily.

"I'm sorry I called you stupid. It's just we've got to keep an eye on our water," he said, bravely avoiding eye contact.

"I forgive you," she replied. "Can I help?" She gestured towards the spit.

He shook his head removing a chunk of raw meat from his pack. Mea had been kind enough to part with some onions and a little honey too. As if suddenly remembering he was cooking for two, he took another cut, speared both pieces, and set the meal over the fire. The reassuring crackle of a tiny fire relaxed him immediately.

"What's it like being the son of the great and unvanquished Magnus?"

"I call him Dad."

She sat down and crossed her legs opposite. Her eyes watched the little dancing flames. They certainly weren't watching him.

"What's he like as a father then?"

"He's a father," Erroh said shrugging. "A good man I suppose." He leaned in closer to inspect the meat. It was a small fire and the spit was a little high. Slow cooking was a pleasant way to idle away the evening though. Better that than concentrating on mending bridges with his beo.

"I suppose it would be hard to see him as anything but a good man," she said, watching his face.

"What do you mean?" He felt like a bluffing player asking what the latest bet was. He never liked to reveal his feelings for his father to strangers.

She saw him clench his teeth, but she didn't care that she had insulted him again. How had it come to saying cruel things for the sake of it? She just couldn't help herself.

"I meant no disrespect," she lied, but he said nothing.

Why talk, when one can brood? He just went back to working the meat. The fire was a little small, she noticed. Or else the spit was holding the meat a little high. She wasn't sure how much more she could take. She wanted to grab him and scream in his face. This was not how it was supposed to be. Destiny was supposed to have brought a great and caring giant of a man into her life: a man she could love and a man who would love her back. Erroh's beauty had blinded her. He had such an effect on her while she had little or no effect on him. It was heart-breaking to feel like this. Maybe she had seen a spark in him that wasn't there. Lea held back a tear. If she cried and he didn't react she would die. Destined love was for young ones with no idea of the world. It was a few years since she'd come of age, and she should have known better. Maybe this was what she deserved. Despite her best efforts, a tear formed in her eye, it filled up and in all its melancholy slid down her face silently. Not to be beaten, her other stunning eye unleashed a tear of its own. Would he ever forgive her for the unfair treatment he received in the city? Could she ever forgive him for his own indiscretions as well?

The doubts, the terrible doubts had played in her mind all day. They had danced through her subconscious ever since she had made the choice. Perhaps she should have left Erroh on the final day of the Cull, and now things had gradually deteriorated. She knew what was next. He would try to take her to his bed soon. This she was certain of and though Mea had reassured her that there was something more to those pretty features, she still feared. There were flashes of his warmth on their first night together. Mea and Jeroen were an amazing couple and they brought out the human in him. She wiped the tears from her face, rubbed her eyes, but couldn't stop thoughts about her home. Was she going to follow in the footsteps of her own parents? She felt her chest tighten as though about to break. Her father's hatred for her mother had never stopped him from mounting her, for they bred a fine family. Neither had told her of their own Cull because neither had visited all her life. She was the forgotten child. She was the lowest ladder in entitlements, and Erroh was to be her first proper family.

She stared into the flickering flames and listened to the sounds of the crackling. It brought a comfort long thought lost, but the worries remained. Would Erroh turn into a beast like her father? Some said Wiidenn was a good man, but she could only remember the fighting. Would she turn into her mother? She watched him turn the meat on the spit and fought the emptiness. What was she doing here?

Erroh was master of the cooking. The spit was only a minor flaw in his plan. She sat opposite in silence, which was no terrible thing for her words were a distraction. It allowed him more time to concentrate on the fine art of cuisine and if nothing else went right, Lea would enjoy the meal. He would make sure of it. When the onion was nearly finished, he tilted the meat to let the greasy juices flow into it. Perfect. He sat back and stared at the meat as it began to sizzle. It would need a turning soon but there was no need for salt. Her words still played on his mind. He placed a small piece of wood onto the fire and the sparks exploded into the night. Far above he watched a shard of the moon tear through the peaceful sky burning away to nothing. It was a fine night indeed, but he dared not spend too long enjoying it. Reaching over he picked up the little jar of honey, glazed each piece of steak, and dripped a little honey into the onion. He inhaled the sweet flavour but his mind began to sour. They always wanted to talk about his father, whoever they were. Many in the world believed Magnus a barbaric and cruel man. She probably viewed him no differently either. The Primary and the city wrote history any way they wanted. Magnus and Elise saved the world from itself. There were no great records written of that though, were there? Speaking ill of his line wasn't the best way to endear herself to him.

Two beautiful Alphas sat opposite each other on the outskirts of the unforgiving wastes. They were completely alone in each other's company. Erroh glanced at his mate and watched a tear run down her cheek. He felt the urge to let go of his anger. To comfort her just like his father and mother would have wanted him to. He watched another tear fall and his heart broke a little for her. All he had to do was swallow whatever pride he had and reach out to her. She looked from the fire into his eyes. He could read the pain in her perfect and cruel face. Erroh looked away and turned the meat.

She watched him and felt like dying inside.

19

MILES TO WALK

I t was a fine evening without the sound of thunder nor the touch of a cold wind. The sounds of the forest against the crackling flames played a gentle lullaby, but Erroh resisted the urge to sleep. He had probably gone overboard with the meal but when she accepted her third helping, he knew he'd done at least one thing right the entire miserable day. Climbing to his feet, he removed his shirt and stood across from her. She barely noticed him, her eyes lost in the flames but there were no fresh tears to be seen.

"I think we should work off that meal," he said stretching gingerly. He was still in pain after the day's walk but pain could be tolerated, especially in the name of some fun.

Her stomach turned, and she stiffened in fear at his words. Was this how it was to be? It wouldn't be rape for they were mated for life after all. Like mother like daughter in choices, and he was just another charming brute with ill-timed desires on his mind. Her fear quickly turned to disgust, and she formed a fist.

It was a natural reaction. The last naïve belief in love, honour, and hope began to fade away forever, and she whispered to the absent gods above "Please don't." She knew that furrowing with him was an inevitability. She knew this and embraced it, but such acts were reserved for a few miles down the road, when warmth could be shared between them. Perhaps love? Or at least the sharing of primal urges. Please, not like this. Not with venom and bile, still fresh on both their lips. She looked up at his naked chest warily and his arrogance infused her with hatred. A swift strike to his ribs would halt things for the evening but what of the following night? Perhaps it was best to allow events to occur and overcome this misery as soon as possible. She wondered would he be gentle? Would it be quick? She also wondered why he was walking away.

Ignoring his injuries, Erroh reached into his pack and retrieved the two sets of wooden sparring blades gifted by Jeroen. He tossed her a set. As they clattered down on the ground in front of her, she stared in both bewilderment and relief. She exhaled slowly, and he thought he almost saw her smile. Almost but not quite.

"Don't worry, you can leave your shirt on," he said lightly. He held the two wooden pieces in his hands and patted their tips against his naked chest. "It hurts more when struck," he explained. He didn't understand women, but he could grasp a little retribution. She was angry. Let her vent her fury. It was his gift to her.

"I can't beat you," she said and climbed to her feet. He began stretching once more, and she followed suit. Her own stretches matching his.

"We have a long walk ahead of us. Who knows exactly

how good you may be when we arrive?" he said, shaking himself loose.

When she was limber, she also took off her outer shirt revealing a wonderfully fitting blouse underneath. Their eyes met, and he read her thoughts. She wanted no special treatment, and she too was willing to accept a few sharp strikes of wood on skin. Albeit a little less skin.

"You're going to hit me really hard along my side, aren't you?" he said, daring a smile. The taste of war was in the air. He felt the reassuring surge of adrenaline that only comes before battle. Perhaps she felt the same. He'd never fought another female with similar training to him before. She held only one sword in her right hand. It was not raised yet and it did not quiver. It hung ready at her leg ready to strike. It was a fine fighting form but his eyes dropped down at her shapely blouse again. She saw this and her arms closed over her guard ever so slightly. That's okay my dear, we have all the time in the world.

But until we do.

The loud crack of both swords erupted in the darkness. She blocked his strikes easily enough but never tried to push home any advantage. She knew that would be a mistake. Any fool could see he was testing her. He moved gracefully, striking out with both swords while studying her movement. He took her in, and she fell back and let him attack though not entirely of her own volition. His speed was something to behold. Walking he carried a slight limp but fighting he was divine. But for his arrogance, she could see the pain he endured with every strike. Back and forth in their first dance they swayed, spinning, thrashing, and awaiting the killing blow. Searching and finding a fine distraction from awkward thoughts and words.

For the briefest moment amid the storm of their swirling bodies, it was Lea who spotted a weakness first. It was something barely noticeable beyond his careful defence of injured ribs. When he struck he led with his left every time. A stronger strike followed by a less impressive right. A simple weakness and nothing more than a bad habit from a young Alpha who'd spent many years training with one blade. Keen to take advantage, she met his next attack and countered with a clean strike across his chest before receiving a nasty blow against her own shoulder. She dropped her guard, and he swung again. An instinctive regretful strike and it snapped loudly against her wrist, and she shrieked in shock and pain. The blade fell clear, and he spun away rubbing his chest irritably. She held up her aching wrist and bit down a curse as she examined the welt forming across her skin. At least it was better than forcing himself upon her, she mused bitterly. Still though, the night was young.

"Well, you asked what it's like being the son of Magnus."

She picked up the blade and attacked. He countered a little too carelessly and his arm slipped from defending his ribcage. He hit her across the arm once again but at the cost of receiving a fierce blow against his injury. It was a satisfyingly dull sound and his accompanying yelp was the cherry atop the cake. She did not follow through as he stumbled backwards. She allowed him a few strained breaths between clenched teeth. She was kind like that.

"Good shot," he wheezed in agony falling to a knee. She ignored the suggested whisper of guiltiness in her mind easily enough. Had he not challenged her to fight instead of talking matters through? Still, there were far poorer ways to waste away the hours. Battle was ingrained in her. It always had been and she'd savoured the taste of pretend battle with her sisters of Samara where victory was met with polite applause and fatal loss with jesting and ridicule. After a few more breaths, he climbed to his feet and resumed his stance as if crippling pain was no matter. She didn't hesitate and leapt forward with deadly intent and met his blades once more.

Above them, the shattered moon passed further on across the sky casting deadly shooting stars here and there, as it did. In the distance dull echoes of ancient thunder rose above the dull clatter of wooden blows as shiny shards of stone struck the land. Some scarred areas of the world were common with such events. Some areas were well known for such things, as well. The young Alphas paid little attention to any of this as they sparred until Erroh's recovering body could take no more. With a truce called, both figures collapsed down on either side of the fire's dying embers, panting. They were exhausted, drenched in sweat, and exhilarated. It was a grand workout indeed. They were to be sparring partners for life.

"So being the son of Magnus is painful and demanding," she said when her own breath had settled, continuing the conversation from before. There was no mocking tone to her words, and he had no need to bite back a retort. It was almost courteous and quite the improvement in civility. Perhaps hitting each other with sticks for half the night was the right way to go about things.

"He pushes hard and it hurts," he said and a thousand bruises came to mind. Just as many cuts quickly followed and bones breaking too. Oh yes, few Alphalines forgot the taste of their first broken bone at the hands of their master. "Training was tough, brutal even, and I'm eternally grateful for it." He rubbed at one of his fingers.

"That was certainly tough," she agreed flexing her own fingers over the warm fire. Their eyes met and they shared a grin. At least they could bond over violence. That was something.

"Your technique is smooth but fierce," he said leaning over and taking out the canteen. After a sparing mouthful, he threw it over. She drank deeply. Far more than she needed to in fact and it was he who looked away first. Point made.

"Thank you," she said. "Give me a week and I'll take you." She lay down beside the warm embers of the fire.

"So I only have to wait a week before you'll take me?" he asked playfully, lying down as far from her as the fire's warmth would allow.

"You'll be waiting." Her meaning was clear and definite. Nevertheless, with his mood lifted and no shrewd thoughts to let matters be, he jested once more. He did this because he was an idiot.

"This little wanton cub will happily wait for amazing treasures," he quipped, daring not just a smile but also a suggestive wink. His meaning was clear and definite. You have nothing to worry about, my dear.

"Oh fuk off, Erroh."

"I was only making a joke, Lea. Guess you can't take a joke either?" he muttered, hoping she'd retaliate. Hoping she'd put him in his place with some fine mock of her own. Was that not what people did? He waited, and she did not reply. Instead, the most beautiful girl he'd ever seen turned her back to him and immediately killed his mood. He sighed and closed his own eyes. Tomorrow would be a better day.

"You're not going to make me cry again," he heard her say with such revealing sorrow that it stung him. He raised himself up from his makeshift bed, but she did not stir. He searched for the right words.

"Lea?"

"You're a highest lined brute," she hissed turning.

"Aye," he agreed, sensing she had more to say. Sensing it would be wise to keep her talking.

"You never wanted me," she said just above a whisper though it may as well have been a roar. He reached out and touched her shoulder. He didn't know why he did it. Her skin was warm, and she recoiled from his touch. Of course she did. Thoughts of the Cull flooded back, and he instantly felt the rush of blood.

"She's my best friend, and you want her more. And now, I have to live with that." Finally, he saw her true torment. Shame enveloped him. It wasn't simply his hesitation upon meeting. It was the false words spoken in anger that cut her deeply and for the first time in days, Erroh thought beyond the pain of the Cull. He thought beyond his own misfortune and realised the part he had played in their miserable dalliance. Why did she deserve his revulsion more than the others did anyway? All the girls had been spiteful from the first breath and all the girls had attacked relentlessly. It had just hurt more from Lea.

"From the moment I saw you I thought you were most pleasing of them all," he said.

She glared at him and took his words as lies.

"The first time you saw me, you looked right through me. Don't patronise me, Erroh, don't you fuken dare."

He had that coming. Mere words couldn't pull him from the hole he'd dug for himself. He hated digging holes.

"I beg your forgiveness, Lea."

"No."

"For everything,"

"No."

"Thank you," he whispered.

After a few breaths, she bit. "For what?"

"For choosing me," he said and part of him meant it.

"You're welcome, brute."

"I'm your brute," he said and something inside him stirred. A warmth he hadn't felt before. Perhaps it was just tiredness. That was likely it. "Are we okay?"

"Not really. Not yet." Her face darkened.

"It's okay; we have plenty of miles to walk, plenty more words to share," he said and began adjusting his blanket to form an adequate pillow, a fine technique his father had shown him when out on the march, where a good night's sleep was worth its weight in reinforcements.

"Don't rape me," she said. Her voice was steady and controlled.

"I didn't do anything!" he cried, sitting up suddenly then checking his movements to make sure he wasn't acting any way threatening towards her. There were some things worse than murder. A real male should never imagine some things.

"Why'd you think I wanted to?" he exclaimed in shock. Where had this come from? He was no beast.

"It's not unheard of for a male to take his pleasure when he desires it," she murmured, though she was blushing. Perhaps it was from embarrassment. Perhaps it was relief at speaking of unmentionable things. Perhaps it was seeing his surprise.

"Why would I even want you like that?" he cried protesting his innocence and trying desperately to reassure her. Mostly though, he was caught off guard and unsure which words to use. Luckily, this wasn't a terribly unfamiliar feeling.

. . .

"You were doing so well," she said, taking complete offence because it suited her. It was easier to lash out than admit that she'd judged him harshly.

"You know what I meant there. You know I didn't mean it like that."

"Because I'm not the beautiful Lillium," she reminded him and cursed herself inwardly. He'd lied perfectly about preferring her to the other females. It was a wonderful lie to put some matters to rest. It was probably best not to drag up that disaster.

"You are far more beautiful, and I was just angry. Besides, she's with Wynn now anyway." He didn't understand females. They twisted everything he said. It wasn't fair.

"Wynn is quite the male," sighed Lea dreamily, and Erroh tasted the bitterness of being second choice. Well played, my dear. He felt the need to apologise yet again, or else smash his head against the nearest tree. Either would be a sufficient end to the night. There was a fine looking trunk a few feet away. He could get a good concussion from that one.

"If I could have returned after the first test I would have," she said. It sounded like an apology.

Erroh poked the flames with a stick; a few delicious sparks took flight in the rising smoke. They were lost in the dark sky above; he watched them for a moment and then spoke from his heart.

He began by admitting how unprepared he was for a life walking with another when he'd first walked into the city and why he had answered the questions in the way that he had. To her credit, she never interrupted, and she never blinked away in shame. Even when he told her of his sorrow when the lights went out, and he was left alone to weep and bleed. She never stopped staring into his eyes as he spoke, and when he had finished his tale of woe, the weight of relief was quickly replaced by embarrassment when she remained mute. So with a shrug, he turned from her, crawled into bed, and pulled his blanket over his head. Tomorrow would be better, he pledged. Sleep immediately began to take him.

She didn't move for a time. Instead, she thought upon his words, and she knew most to be true. She listened to the living night and desperately tried not to miss the hum of her home. No, it wasn't her home anymore. Her home was with her man. Her mate. Her Erroh. Cursed as such a life with him might be.

The most beautiful girl in the world glided silently over to the only male she had ever wanted and stirred him gently from sleep by leaning in closer and kissing his forehead tenderly. Just the once. She took his head in her delicate bruised and marked arms and hugged him. She should have broken the Cull's rules for such an embrace. She should have held him in the darkness when he was convinced the world hated him. For once, the uttering of a word didn't ruin the moment. She released the hug delicately and slipped back to her bed. Erroh slowly drifted away into sleep, a grimace no longer etched upon his face.

The absent gods knew something terrible was coming. Not just in the wind but a storm nonetheless. They could see the tempest of blood and blades that could kill them both. They could see that each step brought them closer to the very eye. The gods were silent as the Alphalines slept, for they knew they were fated to a beautiful day before a tragic night.

20

ROUTINES

Waking up was never the best part of Erroh's day, but he still woke at first light every bleary-eyed morning nonetheless. It was all part of his routine, and he liked routines—they kept him alive. A light mist floated through the green trees around him, dissipating in the dawn's early rays of warmth. He blinked a few times and yawned lazily while stretching out. All part of his routine, and she was messing with it already. She wasn't actually doing anything in particular but that didn't really matter. She was awake and fixing her hair across from him and his morning was ruined.

"Any food left?" she asked without looking back.

"We ate the last of it last night." He could smell her fresh perfume.

"It was a good meal," she admitted, tying the dark strands up in a ponytail. She wore it well. She wore everything well. He wrapped his cloak up and stuffed it into his pack. Her own pack was sealed and sitting by the tree. Her damaged armour already strapped tightly across her chest. He took out his unreliable map and ran his finger towards the stain. It didn't look any more promising than the day before, but she didn't need to know that. They were heading south, that was enough for now. He boiled a little water with the last embers of the fire and poured them both a steaming cup of cofe. She grimaced once more at the taste but with nothing else for sustenance, she finished the cup. She did however decline a refill. With their hearts beginning to beat a little quicker, they strapped up and began their walk.

The road was difficult. Few wanderers had passed through enough to make a path and only years of walking allowed Erroh's keen eye to spot the easiest route to take. Lea studied him and quickly learned that a slight break in the trees was enough to keep their progress steady. She also remembered that following the splashes of sunlight through the canopy above their heads were fine waypoints as they marched deeper and deeper into the eternal green. Aye there were obstacles, cutting briars and thick underbrush, and she did notice Erroh's wariness of fallen logs but still, they made better time than expected. The world wasn't entirely covered in these trees; there was as much open plain as green where they were headed. She also knew there was a thousand miles of snow to be walked at the end of their journey, but snow was not something she was entirely unfamiliar with.

She fell in step beside Erroh where the path opened up enough for two. "I have missed this. I've seen nothing but stone in too long a time."

"Your steps are lighter now," he said and it was no lie. She avoided snapping most twigs and not every loose stone was kicked loudly through the undergrowth. A few more days and she would be just as silent as when her masters taught her the path years before. By late afternoon, their path reaped rewards and a familiar wet music played in their ears. It was a wonderful ballad of water rushing north.

"You can drink as much as you want now," he said smiling when they reached the edge of the flowing river. He scanned the far side of the bank. Wild bushes and ancient drooping trees clustered together all the way along its edge. A slight wind jostled the green leaves making it challenging to track any hidden foe. He'd learned swiftly on his travels that any water source be treated with suspicion. He moved quietly drawing his sword. Beside him, Lea was bolder, and he approved. Gracefully stepping along a long fallen log, she crept out over the water to the far side, her eyes hunting, her face flushed with excitement and fear. She hid herself among the undergrowth. It was only her perfume in the wind which would give her away. He smiled to himself at her instincts. He had not suggested she do anything of the sort. She was merely demonstrating her prowess. She was more a predator than she portrayed herself to be after all. Her masters had taught her well. He moved to the nearest bend in the river and waited. His eyes moved along further up and saw no sign of brigand, beast, or brute. After a time she appeared opposite, weapon sheathed and a content look upon her face. He bowed and began refilling his canteen.

Their canteen.

It called to him, so he answered. In full dress, he dropped into the water. The clear flow was soothing and cool. Its hushed lazy song soothing as it continued its journey to meet up with the Great Mother somewhere beyond. He waded slowly into the middle of the river where it reached up to his waist. Its firm current begged him to come join its long journey back North, but he resisted. Instead, he took to the task of scrubbing the filth of a hundred miles walked from his clothes. It was a difficult task with little more than soap and a wire brush. She appeared at the edge beside him and sat down letting her legs drop into the flow.

"How are they feeling?" he asked of her bruised and blistered feet as he slid his shirt off and began scrubbing. The garment had once been dark black but the road and wear had turned it charcoal grey. Shame really, it was a nice shirt.

"They hurt." She lifted each one in turn from the water and dropping them back down again. He was no great judge of feet but they were fine enough, he supposed.

"I remember the pain," he said wading across and throwing the shirt to dry in the blazing sun. He started to undo the belt in his trousers then stopped himself once he realised the problem with this routine.

She watched him, and she was far more disappointed than she expected when he stopped removing his trousers. There was nothing wrong with being curious was there? She kicked her feet in the water casually, and silently willed him to stop looking at her. He did have the right idea though. She could feel the sun warmer, this close to the cool water.

"I'm going to go bathe a little further upriver," he said turning his back and striding slowly against the current. He disappeared behind the bend leaving her to remove her own shirt and then after a moment's thought, her trousers too. It felt terrifying and exciting. Stimulating and liberating.

She didn't know exactly what happened because she always thought of herself as a good swimmer. She never imagined herself the clichéd drowning damsel in need of rescue but that's precisely what she became. She dropped into the river and immediately lost balance. She stumbled forward and sank down under. The sudden shock paralysed her. The sweeping water gripped her in its embrace and refused to let go. Pulling, dragging, and strangling the last breath from her chest. The dull noise of the world filled each ear and the cacophony of her struggles terrified her as her squeals became nothing more than the bubbling calls of the dying. She pushed forward and tried to raise her head above the current. Beautiful daylight appeared in her vision all too briefly followed by the crashing horrific world of drowning. Her feet struck painfully against rocks and her screaming mouth filled with water. Her lungs tightened and the world turned black and yet somehow she knew she was crying.

Then Erroh was beside her. She felt his sturdy arms grab hold. His strength matched her involuntarily thrashing limbs, but she couldn't stop herself kicking and punching wildly at him regardless. Until he struck out at her with a clenched fist beneath her chin and the shock brought her back to the world of normality. He took hold again, and she let him. He held her in close, and she stopped struggling completely. She tried to flee from the river, the panic surging back, but he held her above the water, and he never let go and pulled her to shore.

"You drown really loudly," he said, gently slipping away from her claw like grip. It was here that he dropped the guise of the stereotypical hero. He took a moment to enjoy the view of the half-drowned damsel wearing next to nothing shivering pathetically by the water's edge. After a few breaths, he pulled his eyes from her body and tightly fitting garments and sat up on the bank. "Don't think about it too long, Lea," he said as if nearly dying was a simple event out in the wastes. "You can be the one to save me from drowning the next time," he said making room for her beside him.

"Thank you." She smiled a smile only for him. He nodded casually but inside his heart melted.

A little.

————

While her clothing dried out in the afternoon sun, Lea sat and watched him carelessly assemble the pieces of his bow and string it up. Observing such a mighty weapon being put together brought calmness, but the awful thoughts of suffocating water quickly returned when he left the bow against a tree, and dropped the sparring blades at her feet and began stretching.

"Come on then," he muttered and tapped the tips against his chest. She didn't bother to stretch properly, stepped up to him timidly, and was immediately made to pay. He leapt forward and struck fiercely. She blocked but his power drove her backwards and a second blow sent her crumbling to the floor like a rag doll. She said nothing. Instead, she got to her feet and waited for his next barrage. A few breaths later, she was lying in the long grass along the river edge nursing the beginnings of a fine new bruise across her cheek. He spun away and spat at the ground irritably.

"You were better last night," he said reaching out to help her. She rolled away from his hand. "Maybe it's just hunger. Maybe with a full stomach you'll move a little better. Maybe if I hunt us a little meal you will recover some of your grace." He gestured to the bow against the tree. "Or maybe it's just too much for a female to spar every day," he said, dropping his sword to his side. Anger flared inside her, but she caught the biting retort before it left her lips. All thoughts of drowning and rivers were lost for the moment.

"I'll do better," she growled, changing her stance again and waiting for the next assault. When she did meet it, she countered two strikes before a delicate sweeping kick sent her flying once more.

When the dust had settled, and she nursed her pride and a few bruises, he did something unexpected. It was a simple gesture that brought a smile to her face. He handed her the bow and quiver and led her through the treeline into a clearing. The bow was sturdy and reassuringly heavy and in a life lived well among priceless objects of Samara she'd never seen any piece as remarkable. The body was carved from dark oak and the faded finish was smooth to the touch. She ran her finger up and down its curve and plucked delicately at the cord as they walked. She was in love with the piece but played it coy.

"I think it's strung a little tight," she said.

"Loosen it so." He passed across the key and taking their packs and dropping them in the shade where he took a seat to watch. She adjusted the weapon for a few moments before testing the draw. All it needed was a coat of varnish and some unconditional love. There weren't many arrows to waste. Not that she would.

She let the arrow fly. The string whipped back and snapped against her forearm, the usual pain shot through her arm, but she hissed it away without thought as she always did. She and Lillium had spent much of their lives hidden away in a dark dungeon hitting straw targets in everlasting competition. They'd been sisters in arms, trying to best each other to the point of mastery. Lea was the finer shot. Lillium would argue differently.

The arrow embedded itself in a tree trunk.

She took out another arrow and pulling back, released a second.

The arrow hit an inch from the first.

"Impressive," he said nonchalantly. It was an incredible shot. He reached out and snatched the bow from her.

"Watch this." She frowned as he took the joy from the moment. Erroh pulled the string back, thought of pigeons and let loose. The arrow shot wide of the target. A few feet wide of his target in fact. It lodged in a defenceless patch of wild flowers. It definitely killed one.

Fuk you, wild flowers.

He dropped his head dramatically and handed the bow straight back to her.

"You should keep this."

"To keep?" she asked in surprise, in disbelief, and in excitement.

"Aye, as a gift."

She squeaked. He was sure she squeaked. It was a nice sound. Her smile was a wonderful spectacle to behold as well. As was her little jump in the air. It was a fine bow. It was fine when she fired it. He had owned it since he was a child and treated it as nothing more than a tool, but she saw it as something grander. She was welcome to it.

———

As the sun set on another day he prepared a little fire. She watched him make the spit and tend to the little flame. He did so effortlessly, and she committed his technique to memory as best she could. He gave the impression that a wild storm or torrential downpour would be little challenge to him. Perhaps that was why he had few worries about marching through the snow. When the time came, she would be happy to offer suggestions. She prepared the four birds, stripping the feathers and then the viscera. It made her dizzy and her appetite was lost for a time but soon enough that gnawing hunger stirred once more. She speared each piece and set them to cook only to hear the swords dropped beside her again.

A second sparring session in one day?

"Come on, beo," he said, stretching. "It's time to prove my prowess to you again."

She tried harder and he was made to pay for it.

———

They sat opposite each other by the fire again and despite the searing pain he chewed heartily, for his hunger was ravenous after the day. Though he'd struck at her in sparring, she'd still caught his ribs badly once more, but he dared not show weakness lest she go even harder at him or worse go easier. She attacked her own dinner with the same vigour, deriving as much pleasure as she could from each bite. The fury in her eyes from hunting and combat was fading and now she ate in honour of the kill. Drenched in sweat from the sparring she looked incredible. More than that, she looked far more at ease than before.

"You beat the pulp out of me," she said tearing at a leg.

"A few lucky blows," he replied. It had been a fine melee altogether and good for shaking off lingering thoughts of drowning.

"No, you were faster."

"Sorry," he said, looking at the fresh bruises along both her arms. Who knew what discolours lay under her blouse.

He chewed his food guiltily. She had obviously trained with highly skilled teachers but years under Magnus and his watchful cruel eye had driven Erroh further. Was it far enough to challenge his master? Perhaps not yet.

"Why do you want me to be so good anyway?" she asked.

"So you can be elite."

"I don't need to be. I have you to keep me safe," she said mocking him.

"Well then, I need to practise to keep you safe."

"You certainly need practice with the bow," she said glancing at her new gift with unabridged love.

"You sound like my father."

"He sounds wise." She laughed, finishing the piece of meat and tossing the bones into the fire. She had christened the weapon "Baby." She was in love with Baby. Not Erroh. Not yet. "No one has ever given me a gift," she said. "Thank you." She squeezed his hand, and let it go just as quickly.

"What about your family?" he asked in mild surprise. Thoughts of lavish gifts Lexi had received from their parents came to mind: silken and gold and embossed with jewels. All he'd received were weapons, broken bones, and suggestions how best to rule the world should the time ever come. In truth, he was happier with his lot.

"Fuk my family," she spat, thinking darkly of her clan. He was her clan now. She looked at the bow again and her mood improved.

"Where are they from?" he asked.

"A little south of here, where the green meets the white," she replied. The meal had been going so well. The further south he travelled, the less Magnus had been welcome. In truth, the Southern Faction had suffered most under his march. Her father's estate lay above the border of the south. Magnus was still considered a tyrant and a coward at her family table. It would be interesting times if Erroh sat down to a meal with her father and brothers.

He nodded thoughtfully. He even smiled.

"When you meet Magnus, you can decide which stories are true," he said.

"Agreed."

It was the worst type of night. The air was sultry and dry, with the heat from the day appearing to be trapped by the heavy-laden branches all around them. So for the second time, he dropped into the water. He would admit that bathing was somewhat of an obsession with him, but cleanliness was only part of it. Body odour and hunting was the other.

"I promise I won't try anything if you want to cool down," he called over to her.

"I'm fine right here," Lea said from her seat at the bank. She dipped her hands in and splashed water into her hair. She would face water again; she just wouldn't befriend it yet. Maybe tomorrow.

He swam over and wedged himself gently against a patch of reeds beside her.

She examined the bruising on her arms, her legs, and even her fingers. "Why did we have to spar twice today?"

"I just want you to be as capable as me in case I die," he said.

"Please don't die."

"I'll do my best,"

"Do better than that."

"I'll try."

He climbed from the water and sat beside her.

"I'm right here in case you get into trouble." He nodded towards the dark pool. She pleaded with her eyes, and he almost melted, but that was not how things could be out here. If she let fear overcome her now, she may never swim again. She needed to find her daring, the same daring that would serve her well out here in the wastes, and keep her alive with or without him. Hopefully with him. He didn't want to die either. Not for a while.

She slid carefully into the dark water, the fear dissipated with the cooling pleasure, and she let her head go underneath.

"It's cool in here," she said when she resurfaced, bobbing gently in front of him. Her hands waved gently in the dark water keeping her afloat. Once again, she proved herself with a simple display of courage. He wondered just how courageous she was, then he wondered about himself. His stomach turned and shivers ran up his spine as though someone had stepped upon his grave.

21

THE STAIN

"I prefer to walk anyway!" he snapped at the mare. It seemed to agree and walked off on its own merry way. He dropped his shoulders and hated the beast a little more. From atop her own mount Lea stared with undisguised glee. He sighed loudly. The horse made an annoying nickering noise and began eating some long grass. He wanted to curse it. So he did. Loudly.

"We could share my mount if you can't catch your own," she called over from her perch. He repeated her words in a mocking tone under his breath, which delighted her immensely. "She doesn't like you," said Lea, patting her own newly acquired horse. She knew the skill well and took great enjoyment in seeing her mate flounder spectacularly in a simple task. His skill making the mount's harness was dubious at best, but it was his ineptitude in trapping his chosen mount, which surprised her most. She considered offering a few suggestions on both fronts as he was always willing to share his teachings at every moment but instead she held her tongue. It was too funny. And so was mocking him.

"Aye, but she'll get to like me," he replied, desperately grasping the looped rope in his hands; waiting for the moment to snare the animal. She was magnificent. Black and grand was certainly pleasing to the eye, but her legs won his heart. They were thick, muscular and built for speed. Moreover, there was fight in her. "In time, she'll get to adore and love me," he added through gritted teeth. It hadn't taken too long to track a herd of wild horses out in the great northern plains but herding their choice of mounts into a dead end was the trickier part. Lea had little problem, but Erroh was in his second hour.

"Just like our love," he mocked and side-stepped the beast and sent her cantering back towards an enclave of briars and shrubs. She whinnied disapprovingly but by now was becoming accustomed to his presence. She chewed some grass for a moment but kept an eye on Erroh as he stepped carefully near her once more.

"Oh, yes, my dear Erroh, poets and bards will write great tales of the love we have for each other." She brought her mount forward by gently kicking her feet in the stirrups of rope. It hesitated, but she patted it a second time. Their maiden ride had been fierce and swift. The chestnut horse fought her every inch of the way but now, at rest and back where they'd begun, she was serving a new master while Erroh was still trying to introduce himself.

"There are other horses, Erroh. You can take this one, and I'll just get another one that doesn't have such good taste in males."

He hissed her suggestion away.

"I want this one." Erroh neared the beast and finally slipped the loop around its head. He stepped closer and patted it. No problem. He rubbed the sweat from his brow. A long few hours chase but worth it. In truth, he hated horses and they hated him back. He would much prefer to continue walking but if he wanted to reach Conlon by season's end, it was wise to ride a horse at least some stretch of the way. He brought the rope up and around her and secured it tightly, patting the beast as he did, and with a heave, struggled onto the startled horse and immediately fought its erratic protests. It kicked and neighed, and he grunted and cursed in reply, but eventually the horse settled enough that he could run some of the fire from its will. No easy task. He kicked the animal forward and it took off like the wind.

Lea had almost expected him to be thrown, if only from his inadequate tack, but miraculously the knots held and the rope tightened. A petty part of her was disappointed. He charged the beast down along the water's edge, his pack bouncing with each powerful stride. She urged her horse after him, not just keeping pace but also challenging him further. They raced the sun across the sky with barely a rest and the miles disappeared under them.

Elise had instructed him well enough not to push too much lest he injure or even kill the beast mid stride, so when he felt the weariness in her run, he brought the animal to a stop. The sun was already beginning to set. The sky was a beautiful crimson and blue. The night would be clear with a sweetness to the air, and they'd covered many miles: a fine day.

With less cover from trees, they sheltered themselves

from biting winds behind a mound of moss-covered boulders. Exhaustion and new pain from the day's ride made them weary and after a reluctant sparring session, they nestled down under the stars with salted quail and muted conversation.

She finished her fine meal, leaned back, looked up at the twinkling sky, and silently began counting. It wasn't long before her breathing became a little louder, and he knew she had fallen asleep. He sat and watched the shifting logs burn in the little flames. He thought about her laughing and it warmed him more than the fire ever could. He lay down and fell into troubled sleep. His dreams were of the town.

———

Days and nights passed in a blur of movement and repetition. They became companions of the road and any feelings of affection hid behind silent hours of riding and the call of sleep. They lived safe routines. Every morning, they shared a pot of cofe beneath the rich blue sky, and then they continued their race further and further south. Where the land opened up they ran their mounts fiercely and swiftly, and where clusters of woodland filled the landscape they eased the beasts through precarious trails leaving fresh paths in their wake. Twice a day they fought with swords in each hand. He even accepted instruction from her on how to use the bow, but she was the true master and every morning she would slip away silently and hunt. All beasts would cower in the shadow of the diminutive huntress. She never failed to make a kill. They spoke just enough that silence was never awkward but exhaustion became their other companion and more often than not one of them would drop off while the teaching of the fine arts of cards was in full flow or before the debate between archery and swordplay was completed. The sun still kept burning their skin but more and more there came the taste of bitter cold in the air, particularly at night.

There were moments when she looked at him differently, and she felt stirrings of what might eventually occur between them. These moments were fleeting, they made her blush, and they were welcome.

He enjoyed her perfume, her wit, and her victorious smile every time she hit a stinging blow in combat. Was this love? No. It was affection but it was a good start.

She nearly kissed him once before he ruined everything. It happened after they reached their first destination at the stain on the map.

———

There was no settlement, it was a stain, and Erroh was crestfallen. So much for procuring a more reliable map, eating a fine meal, and sleeping in a straw bed without the worry of the turning of the wind. So much for a wonderful night in a welcoming tavern, testing their wits with a few hands of gambling. So much for many other futile hopes.

"What now, beo?" she asked, taking the map from him. He'd watched the heavy clouds forming all day and with darkness closing in, he'd still taken a chance that the stain would be sanctuary. He cursed his eagerness and foolishness. The land was far too barren to house a settlement yet he'd ignored the signs and led them miles from the cover of forests, miles from their river, and now they stood with nothing more than long grass and a few miserable looking trees scattered here and there as shelter. A wiser young Alpha would have made camp ten miles back and sat out the oncoming storm. The horses shuffled, feeling a change in air pressure. The thunder rolled a few miles away doing its best to catch up. He pulled at some grass bitterly. Grass didn't burn.

"It's going to be a long night," he said miserably and dropped to the ground. She passed the map back, and he almost stamped it into the ground. Instead, he returned it to his pack where it couldn't do any more damage. It was his own fault, but he was desperate to blame anybody but himself. Maybe the innkeeper, fuk him.

"If we leave now, we might find a bit of shelter," she suggested as the first flash of lightning struck. She started counting to herself.

"Night will fall within the hour," he hissed.

There was no grand cluster of trees to hide from the coming wind and rain but they did have light to find a beech tree with a trunk big enough to rest against but small enough not to attract any stray bolt of lightning. The thunder though was not a beast to be easily countered and as they settled in under the sparsely covered branches, a great roar erupted all around them, loud enough to make the Alphalines jump, and for both mounts to break free from their restraints and bolt off into the darkness. He cursed inwardly at the strains involved in recapturing the mounts, but he said nothing. The sky lit up, and he briefly saw the fear in her face. She could probably see his. He tried to find the comforting words but no sound came. All that came was another terrifying roar and another flash of light. The storm did not intend to blow out so Erroh held up his cloak and gestured to the most beautiful girl in the world. He invited her to climb into his bed, and she said yes.

The rain had a taste of the south to it. The downpour turned to a frozen, steady rainstorm and it dashed itself against them mercilessly as they attempted cover. He had been in such predicaments before but the sensation of a girl holding tightly against his chest was something different. Her hair quickly soaked through, and she shivered against him just like at the river. With every gust of wind, a fresh wave of frozen water battered them. It was a good cloak and it had always served him well on nights like this but it could not cover them both. He adjusted and pulled it gently over her freezing face. She nestled her head against his chest, curled up, and hugged him a little tighter. Another wave of rain soaked him through. He dug his own head into the wet grass and waited for the shaking in his body to stop. This was his penance for such a foolish action.

"There are finer ways to fight off freezing to death," he whispered through gritted teeth. The thunder shook the world and some lightning struck the ground far away. He couldn't stop himself from jumping slightly.

"You actually think we're going to freeze to death?"

"Probably not, but you have to admire my attempt at trying to seduce you." He laughed and listened as thunder roared a mile above them.

"You nearly succeeded, my love," she mocked and recoiled immediately at her words. She shouldn't have called him that.

"Oh, I have not yet begun to charm you," he replied, and she started to laugh. It was a delightful sound considering the circumstances. She hadn't blamed him once though she had good reason to. He was eternally grateful that she held her tongue. Pretty tongue that it was, he imagined.

"I look forward to your attempts," she cooed, feigning seductiveness. He smiled despite the pain in his head (the pain one can only achieve when using freezing wet grass as a pillow). He shifted his position, which was harder with her wrapped tightly around him. Not that he minded. Her weight was comforting and her warmth spread through him. Her perfume wafted up and touched his senses and if it wasn't for the mound of stinging ice where he usually kept his thoughts, he could easily fall into a deep slumber.

"I said that I look forward to your attempts," she repeated playfully and tore him from his imaginings. Evidently, Lea was not done playing just yet. Silly pretty Alphaline, don't tempt me any more than I already am.

"I think I've done enough wooing, for tonight," he answered as arrogantly as he could.

She raised her head. She was close enough to kiss.

"Oh, have you now?"

"With barely any skill I've taken the most beautiful girl to my bed and left her begging for seduction." The thunder suddenly returned above them, and he jumped bravely.

"I wouldn't say I'm begging," she whispered playfully. "Although my blouse is very constricting." She tugged gently at her shirt. She was closer. Closer than ever before. It was harder not to kiss her. He could feel the warmth of her breath; she held it.

She loved this play. Play was wonderfully dangerous and play was better than focusing on the cold. She heard him sigh as another wave of unrelenting water splashed against his beautiful face. The world felt still, and she knew she was falling in love with him. It had started as a delicate stumble, which had grown into something more these past few weeks. More than that, she believed he too felt strongly for her. They belonged to each other, and she knew she was safe in his arms, safe enough that tormenting him with mischievous innuendos was harmless and fun. Unless he took it too seriously. Part of her thought that might be a great deal of fun.

. . .

"If your clothes are bothering you, please feel free to remove yourself of their burden," Erroh whispered, closing his eyes against the next wave of water. A few droplets began to gather at his collar and slid down his neck. "I'm sure you are pleasing enough without them."

"You've watched me in enough rivers to know I'm more than just pleasing," she countered.

He managed to look both brazen and embarrassed at the same time. He was a man of many talents. "I haven't even seen all of you but give me time."

"Aye, you will see all I have to offer," she agreed.

He touched her hair with a freezing hand. She turned with it and looked into his eyes. Raindrops fell against her delicate cheeks as they smiled for him. He was doing a fine job charming her. He stroked her hair, and she shivered from his touch. It might have been the rain. She waited for him to lean in and claim his prize, and she wanted her prize too. She wanted to lean towards him, kiss him, and never stop.

He suddenly turned away from her.

"I'm such an idiot," he said with a sigh, shaking loose droplets from his hair as he did. All fun aside, he was cold and wet. "I'm sorry for all of this." He let his hand slip through her hair one more time before pulling away. He took a breath, counted a few times in his head, and thanked his luck that he hadn't messed everything up again. She had him under her spell and one lustful moment could have jeopardised many weeks of hard-earned trust. Their kiss would come in time but there was little sense in rushing matters. He knew little of the ways of females, but he certainly knew she wasn't ready yet.

. . .

Oh Erroh. Idiot. She accepted his apology with bemusement and laid her head back on his chest. She twisted her body and rested her leg across his own before pulling some of the cloak over his head at the expense of her own comfort. A devastating and kind manoeuvre which left a cool chill along her side. He didn't stop her, as the relief was immediate. She hugged in closer and somewhere above, the storm began to move off. He began to relax and soon fell into a light sleep. This light sleep lasted the night and for the first time since the dead town, he did not suffer bad dreams.

———

When dawn arrived, everything was different. It was different because Lea was not up and ready for the day. Her tiny frame held him firmly as though prey pinned to the ground by a snare. Her thigh still strewn across his lap completed her netting. He dared to stroke her hair once more. In her sleep, she smiled at his touch, so he chanced touching her perfect cheek. A few loose strands of perfect black hair lay carelessly across it. He pushed them aside. Aye, a perfect cheek. She was perfect. Everything was perfect. He was falling for her.

Whoa there little cub, whispered the gods in his mind.

Was he in love? Surely not. It was all in his mind. It had to be. Besides, it was a stupid word. A better word would be fondness. Aye, he had a fondness for the most beautiful girl in the world. Maybe it was affection with a little desire thrown in as well. That sounded right. It couldn't be love. He was merely following his instincts. He began counting again but it didn't help. Love would come with kisses and gifts in a safer time in better lands. For now, love was likely to tear their precarious companionship apart. Had emotion and desire to have a fine night with her not driven them to this dismal place? Was there room in the wastes for young love? No, there wasn't. Love clouded judgement and that was too dangerous. It was easier when they were on bad terms. He would ignore his natural urge. No problem at all. He would be vigilant until they returned home and it would be fine. It would all work out. Another few months was all he had to endure. She stirred and opened her perfect eyes and smiled, and his resolve was tested immediately.

22

I'VE MADE A HUGE MISTAKE

They left the city of "stain" and continued across the plains once again. She took the lead and drove her recaptured mount forward. Erroh kept pace. For hours, they pushed forward with a light drizzle following their every move. It was nothing like the deluge from the night before but it still left a thin layer of cold dampness upon their clothing. It felt as though with every mile they travelled, the sky darkened and the season changed a little more. They met up with the river and continued on south as if the detour had never taken place, as if nothing had happened at all.

Lea noticed the tracks first, but Erroh halted their ride. He did so at a spot by the water where the divots and broken branches were plentiful. He dropped from his mount and muttered a curse under his breath. He dug his fingers into the mud and cursed a few more times.

She could see the signs too.

"A massive group made camp here," he muttered to himself. His eyes danced anxiously across the grass and mud, searching for something, anything.

"It looks as though it was quite a long time ago," she warned and rested her hand on his shoulder.

"Aye," he agreed bitterly and pushed her hand away irritably. What did she know about tracking anyway? There were plenty of hoof marks but the closer he looked across the clearing the more imprints of infantry boots appeared as well. If it was the killers, they were capable of moving quicker than two steeds over open land. No army could march that swiftly.

"Perhaps it isn't the killers." She could see the agony in his face. She'd heard his cries countless times while sleeping to know what haunted him.

"Perhaps not," he said. Her casual words irritated him though he couldn't understand why. He wanted to be alone, to catch a breath, and work through his memories. When he finally looked up, Lea was already midway through her stretching routine, her wooden swords standing erect in the soft muddy ground. Potential killers or no, it was afternoon and there was training to be had.

She had loved her night with him but dared not say a word come the humid dawn. She had tasted briefly what her future could be like with him, and she had found it sweet. She had seen the love in his eyes desperately fighting the inevitability. Her childish beliefs suggested as much and though her own emotions were stirred, she still took her wooden swords in her hand to batter him down. Love was love but their exchange of violence was divine, like duelling gods in the tales of acolytes. He was the wild son of Magnus and Elise, and she was simply Lea the unloved of Samara, but she would be more.

"I'm ready," she called from across the invisible sparring ring, and she could see the distraction on his face as he nodded feebly. She didn't hesitate. She charged forward striking viciously. These last few weeks had hardened her but since his recovery she was yet to beat him. That day would come. Erroh countered and grazed her cheek as he did.

"Sorry," he muttered and attempted to finish her off, but she spun away easily. His movement was an education in war, and she was an ample student. She spent many a quiet hour swaying easily in the saddle dissecting their bouts. It was a fine waste of daylight trying to understand her own ability as much as he did his own. Her gruelling lessons in the city had only taken her so far. The dances she shared with her mate were something else entirely. They were incredible, and she strived to be incredible as well. In fact, she strived to better him. On fleeting occasions, she could sense where the attack was coming from, as though the world slowed and she was gifted generous time to manoeuvre. In the blink of an eye, such ethereal moments were lost to her, while she knew that Erroh was ever present in that world. Nevertheless, all of that would change. This she knew as truth, as true as the feelings she was developing for him.

Erroh didn't have the heart for the fight today. His mind was askew with thoughts of dead towns, eerily familiar tracks and foolish pledges, but despite this, he attacked with shattering violence for it was a given that he should win. They clashed again and again until she countered a weak strike with a hefty kick to the shin. It was hardly a devastating blow but it irritated him nonetheless.

"Sorry." Grinning, she kicked him once more before laughing gleefully and leaping away from retaliation. To add further insult to injury she spun both her blades gracelessly. "You're not so tough, son of Magnus," she mocked, her beautiful eyes wide open, alive and dazzling. His eyes fell to the path again and fury struck him.

He rubbed his shin. "I'm tougher than you'll ever be, woman." This rebuke delighted Lea, and she charged back towards her man, eager to hurt him.

His mother had once suggested that all Alphas were unable to let the world pass them by without interfering. They could only live their life and actions without restraint. They could not walk, they must stride. They could not whisper, they could only speak. They wouldn't let matters rest; they could only act and sometimes not for the best. The fire in their blood stirred by a lifetime of rigorous training under brutal masters caused extremes in behaviour, and in Erroh's defence, his mother was correct.

Both Alphas moved around the campsite. Lea was a constant motion of grace, her face impassive, her body perfectly balanced with each strike. She felt as though she were on the precipice of divinity as everything slowed around her and the world took an extra breath just for her.

Erroh was a tempest. He was ferocious, unpredictable, and devastating, his usual calm torn away in his own wake. He was laboured in every motion, blinding anger stealing his flow and each missed strike adding to his fury.

"I think we should follow the tracks for as long as they head south," he growled suddenly, revealing his thoughts while retreating away from her onslaught. He spat in the dirt and muttered a curse under his breath. He wanted to tell her everything that troubled him, but he was not capable. He was but a little angry cub being stung by an oblivious goddess, so he did what instinct suggested. His retreat brought him closer to the edge of the river. He glanced sideways briefly as she hunted him down and for a moment forgot the anger.

"I trust you." She grinned and battered him to the edge of the water. It was a melancholic grey reflecting the dreary clouds above them. The drizzle falling upon them matched the mood of the river, and he lured his beloved in.

She saw the opening; he parried a hit and slipped back. His balance went, and he crashed into the water beneath. His feet held firm though, and he did not fall as though expecting it. She hesitated and withdrew her attack. After so many weeks of sparring, she stood above him victoriously. A delighted smile upon her face she prepared to finish him. A little rap across his knuckles would finish the job and add a little smugness to her victory. She might follow through with a satisfying crack to his face. That would be enough. They would laugh about it later.

Then he did something unexpected.

Fuk it, but he was quick. She tried to swing, but Erroh leapt from the water, and she could only watch helplessly as he fell upon her. His powerful arms surrounding her in an embrace, for that is what lovers did until they gained enough nerve to kiss.

Face to face, closer than ever she felt his lips graze her own. There was no malice in his eyes. Just deep concentration and deeper sadness, and she could never break free of his hold. Why would she ever want to? And then Lea felt the sudden force of pressure across her perfect chest. One last wistful look into eyes before the world changed. She was weightless and then she was flying and his eyes were with her own. They were all she could see because the rest of the world was moving too quickly. The clouds were below her, and she was floating in his hold. She broke from his gaze and glanced skywards. She found it puzzling that the river was already up there and it was rushing up to meet her. He never let go of her. This was what made it worse.

They collapsed headfirst into the water. Only luck and hopeful judgement on his part prevented either of them from being knocked out. He pinned her to the bottom of the river. His slightly larger frame too much to break free. He held his breath while she lost the last of her air in one terrified scream. Fighting under his terrible weight and unyielding grapple, she lost both her weapons and tried desperately to break free. The noise of drowning was the same as before. Her screaming his name to relent and her drowning muffled pleading that she was beaten only magnified it.

Suddenly he released her from the hold and pulled her head above water before dragging her to the edge of the river where she stood in the waist high water and cried at him for a few desperate moments. In all that time, Erroh said nothing. He simply fished in the water and recovered her weapons. She refused to meet his eyes. Slowly she climbed out of the river and sat in the grass shivering. Her face grave and pale.

"Are you alright, beo?" he said, climbing out and tossing the weapons vaguely in the direction of her rucksack. His head was drooped in shame. Regret now evident, but she didn't care. She knew why he did it. She knew he was teaching her a cruel lesson. She knew he was teaching her the brutality he was capable of, the toughness he possessed. Now she understood the pain he had endured under Magnus's teachings. She thought she had the upper hand in their battle, but she'd never had a chance.

"Don't call me that ever," she hissed, before leaning over the edge of the bank and throwing up.

They left the camp in silence; following the old tracks as

their new guide. She rode like a girl with a broken spirit because he didn't have the strength of character to keep his emotions in line.

———

A few hours later when the silent guilt first began to engulf him, he slowed his mount to walk alongside her. "You were amazing in that fight. You nearly had me." She looked across in disgust. Her eyes were bloodshot from silent tears. She kicked her mount gently and taking the hint, it broke into a canter.

Why, Erroh, why did you do it? he thought. It was because of the tracks. Though it didn't make sense, he instinctively knew. They were tracking the beasts who slaughtered innocents and those same voices inside his mind silently nodded in agreement. He wondered when it would be a good time to start making it up to her.

When they could afford to ride no further, Lea suggested they make camp. They were her first words since their fight. He took his time preparing the fire, so he could form engaging words while she brushed her hair and took out the weapons. When the first spark took hold, she began her stretches and showed the true depth of will she possessed.

She walked to the invisible ring and raised her sword in challenge. "Come break my heart again." A few breaths later, she found herself on the ground bleeding from her beautiful lip. She brushed off any of his attempts to help her up.

———

His dreams were of drowning, pulled down by the little boy and his heavy armour. Erroh tried to kick free from the icy grip so he could exact revenge on those who committed the evil act. He tried to tell the clawing creature of his intentions but the child kept reaching for him regardless, dragging him deeper into the murky depths.

Lea awoke from her slumber by his thrashing and whimpering. She looked over at her beo. No, she didn't mean to call him that. She meant to say her mate. Instinctively she reached over to touch his forehead and calm his terrors as she did most nights, but instead drew her hand back as if burned. It was nearly dawn anyway. The bitter air was freezing and her stomach groaned so she grabbed Baby and swiftly disappeared into the wilds leaving him to his nightmares. She had already begun preparing and salting the freshly killed meals when he roused himself from his restless sleep.

"We need to get you some new arrows," he said, looking at the weather worn bolts as he dressed himself and chewed on the meal left for him.

She nodded.

He offered some cofe that she'd freshly brewed. "Do you want some?" She nodded again and drank the black poison.

"I still have some coins from Samara, we can get some at the next town," he proposed, drinking his own black ambrosia and wishing again that he had some milk.

She nodded a final time; kicked some dirt over the dying embers of the hidden fire and began to pack up. He took that as a sign it was time to leave. The silence they first shared as they departed Spark City had returned, and this fresh silence was worse. By the second day, he gave up trying to talk with her altogether, instead allowing the tracks to occupy his thoughts and hoping time would grant him a little grace. How long had it taken Magnus to earn Erroh's forgiveness when he had pushed his son too far? Had Magnus ever been so cruel? Had his infamous father ever betrayed his trust like he had Lea's? He had learned more about himself in that foolish moment than in two years of walking the road alone, and it was a lesson neither wanted to learn again. He was sorry. Fuk it. He was sorry but there were no words to offer her.

———

Three wet days after his terrible act, the tracks took an unexpected turn. "We're somewhere here," he said, running his finger along the map's rough sketch of a river. His fingers shook, and she immediately saw it too. Felt it too. There was an indentation on the parchment just east. A marking too pronounced to be mistaken for anything else. Regardless, he still asked her in the vain hope that he was mistaken.

"What do you think?"

"I don't think it's a stain," she said, looking again at the disturbance in the ground. It was easy to imagine a scout discovering the settlement and the charge that followed. Part of her still wanted to believe they followed wandering nomads. The same part that believed in love, hope and honeyed breads. It was "a few days' ride at most," he muttered, as if requesting permission to pursue. She nodded as if allowing recklessness. Would he take up his blade and charge headlong into raging battle like the legend of Magnus the butcher? Or hide and observe like an outcast in the wild. She had never shed another man's blood and a cold fear ran through her, cold like a river that, once flooded, could never be contained again.

"If we find more than we can handle, hide yourself in the green." He scratched his arm subconsciously, and she didn't like that distant tone.

"You meant to say, "we hide," didn't you?"

"Aye, that's exactly what I meant to say," he said looking away towards the river, towards the tracks where they veered away into the green of the wastes.

"Don't let it come to that, Erroh."

————

They were a lot closer to the town than they thought. By the following morning they stood side by side under cover of trees along the quiet town's outskirts, their beasts left to graze a mile behind. They were hunters now but what exactly they hunted was in the knowledge of the gods.

Lea notched an arrow and followed Erroh, all the while ignoring the temptation to shoot him. Maybe she could shoot him just a little bit, she mused. Nothing fatal. Perhaps his rear. It would certainly be a new approach to understanding him. Growing up she had loved to challenge herself with puzzles and riddles. She loved the eventual unlocking of answers to receive a treasured resolution. She thought she had begun to crack the enigma that was Erroh, but the passion was leaving her bit by bit. Now there was only a simple desire to understand him as her companion of the road and father to their future children. There was no great secret to unlock and it was foolish to hold on to childish thoughts of great love. Her father was cruel, and he was a killer. It was his nature. She wondered had her parents believed themselves in love in the first days of their coupling as well. She knew she should have been thinking of the silent town in front of them, but her thoughts were miles behind at the river. When he saved her and when he had brutalised her. She would never forget the fury in his eyes and oh, that betrayal of trust. She knew she would never look upon him the way Mea looked upon Jeroen. She knew she had made the wrong choice in the Cull.

It felt eerily familiar creeping around the perimeter of a suspiciously quiet settlement searching for any signs of life. The town was nothing more than a handful of two story buildings, worn, aged, and tended with love; a few paths of damp mud leading up to an old mill with patches of various crops planted throughout. A little nothing place, in the middle of nowhere and an oasis to any passing traveller. This charming town felt inviting and were it not for the two large messages painted sloppily upon one of the tavern's wall, Erroh and Lea would have immediately felt welcome.

"The tainted flee from the flame."

"Uden The Woodin Man sees all."

Both Alphas finished the circle and sat in cover. There was no crimson river of blood, no scorch marks, nor any pile of horrible ash to be found. No females had burned here; there had been no attack. Erroh quietly thanked the gods. It wasn't a prayer, merely a nod of gratitude. The flapping of long dried clothing in the early morning wind was the only sound that reached their ears. It sounded like complete isolation. The town was abandoned. He sat and watched the world for movement. She sat behind him clutching Baby tightly. There was plenty of light left in the day and the town was going nowhere.

Her heart beat louder than normal. A wild unsteady rhythm and her stomach churned bile. His hands shook a little, he flexed them a few times, and they became still. Her eyes fought anxious tears while his eyes blinked sparingly, darting from shack to shack, and corner-to-corner looking for movement. Despite the clear day, there was a bite in the air. The world was still, and she had something important to tell Erroh, so she decided to say it. "I've been thinking about us," she whispered and heard him sigh loudly.

It would be testament to the type of man he was, in the reaction he gave. Not that she really cared anymore. "I know you'll take me to bed," she whispered, but there was a terrible sadness she couldn't conceal, the type of sadness of a girl who'd had her hopes crushed unexpectedly. "I know it's part of what our communion is."

"Do we need to talk about this right now?" he whispered back just as his eye caught the movement of a small patch of dense thicket along the outskirts. He held his breath. Just the wind gusting. A small brown cat strolled down by one of the side streets. At the corner of the mill, it stopped and licked its paw for a little while. It seemed perfectly at ease. Erroh took this as a good omen.

"I won't resist you. When you call upon me, I will lie with you. I will moan and do as you please, and I will offer no last kiss."

"Aye," he replied.

The cat stretched leisurely, hopped up on a barrel, and sprawled out, and Erroh began to relax. The Riders had certainly been through this way but it was unlikely there was a den of ambushing murderers lying in wait.

"Know this, Erroh. I will never take a moment's pleasure from your touch." Her whisper sounded more like a curse.

He opened his mouth to speak but fell silent. He dropped his head in shame and counted a few times in his head. "I'm going to announce myself to the village. If anyone comes attacking, put an arrow between their eyes." He crept away from her damning words.

23

NOMI

Her name was Nomi, and she was popular with her people, so popular she was rarely left wanting, despite her failings. Perhaps it was her knotted blonde hair and her kind smile which earned her favour. Her voluptuous chest and appealing walk probably didn't hurt that much either. She was delicate and graceful but anyone who knew her knew of her strength. Such things were desired among her pack. She was no more than two decades old yet she felt far older. Maybe it was just this morning's march which made her feel so worn. In truth, she thought it more likely it was the previous night's activities: her duties in wartime, so to speak.

She walked with a slight limp along the riverbank beneath the shade of tall trees. Her shoulders slumped as she dragged her awkward war hammer behind her. In most warriors' hands, it would be a brutish, brutal weapon for easy bludgeoning, but in her calloused hands, she wielded it gracefully enough. She kicked a stone into the water and sighed loudly. She liked walking alone without the weight of animal fur and leather weighing her down. It allowed her to think of deeper things like her god and her faith and the loss of those she cared for. Easier to allow a few tears to be shed in the silence of these woods, than in the arms of a caring man right after furrowing.

"Too warm," she whispered and wondered if any of her comrades would hear. It was unlikely; she was at least a mile from the rest of the finger. It was just little old Nomi on her little trek, scouting the river's way for the rest to follow. No, not alone. Oren wasn't too far away, she imagined. She rubbed her belly and thought about the previous night. Oren was a big man with thick muscular arms and powerful hands, which favoured gripping her rear as he thrust himself into her. Perhaps her rear was another reason she was so popular. Allowing him and any others their additional fun with unnecessary appendages was hardly the behaviour of a good little southern girl but still, it was all about duty and attaining the eye of a strong buck. How many times had Oren alone taken her to bed this march? One might say more than enough. She rubbed her belly once more and cursed its emptiness before sitting down along the river's edge.

"Too warm." She began to undress. There was barely a breeze and her body was covered in a thin layer of sweat, grime and his touch. It didn't really matter but perhaps if another came to her bed this night, they may prefer a cleaner flavour of bed mate. So she would bathe to please them until she had no further need. Needs and duties were a fine thing, even if she was becoming a little tired of the tedium of repetition.

She dipped her feet into the water and its warmth was still a pleasant surprise. The flow took her, and she pulled her blouse free and left it at her side. She heard the breaking of branches behind her and continued to undress. Of course, her nakedness was bound to bring Oren running for a grope. It was inappropriate to lie with a man two nights in a row. His seed was weak unless given enough time. Still though, Oren was their leader and who was she to say no? Oren wasn't the worst. She just wanted a little Nomi-time was all.

She slipped her dress free of her shapely thighs, honed by marching, before dropping her club in some long grass and diving into the chest high water. Thoughts of home filled her mind as the water rushed past her ears. She fought the pull and glided as though she were a lutefish spawned for tepid temperatures. She exhaled slowly, kicked herself into an easy stroke, and surged forward swiftly. She couldn't swim like this back home. The frozen rivers were for quick bathing expeditions alone.

"Warm," she cried deliriously, rising for air before meeting the gaze of three young men emerging from the cover of the undergrowth. Her solitary morning was ruined by the sudden threat. Three outsiders with leering eyes. Enjoying her.

This was bad.

It was worse than that.

The current caught her, but she stood up out of the water. Her breasts shimmered in the blazing sun, but she took little notice of their staring from their place a dozen feet or so away. She took a breath and swallowed the fright. Three strange brutes dressed in foreign clothing with foreign faces and foreign tongues. Tongues she imagined that would like to lick the wet from her skin.

Oren would never allow that and neither would she.

One of them stepped forward. His hair was red and his skin was freckled and pale. Like the rest, he carried a hunting pole, and he chuckled at her making no effort to conceal herself. He called to her. Each incomprehensible word laced with humour and pleasantness but Nomi could only think that he spoke too loud, yet she dared not sway closer, to hear him clearer above the purr of the river's flow. She looked to the evergreen beyond and wondered was Oren near? He'd ridden on ahead along a barely used path while she had followed the route of the water. If he could hear them, he would kill them without a moment's hesitation. That was his way in wartime and in truth, if they aimed to do her any misdeeds, it was fair.

"You leave me." It was both a threat and plea. They smiled. One of them bowed and their eyes did not blink. Their clothing was not worn like any group of wandering nomads she knew of. They were darned and cared for. Clean and new. These men were from a nearby village she imagined, and fresh fears stirred inside her. A few mantras played upon her lips, but she remained still. This was no time to be thinking of her god. This was time to be questioning her god, just as her sister had. Fear was replaced by deep sorrow for the swiftest moments, and she pushed it away along with her sacrilege, like a good little southern girl. In her god, she trusted.

"Leave me now," she hissed desperately, as one of them with long brown hair and matching beard, lanced some of her garments with his hunting pole and walked along the riverbank. He held them out over the water and waved them enticingly in front of her. He suggested something in his crude barbaric language and beckoned the naked girl come to his call and recover her decency.

Laughter.

They were too loud, and she feared for them and for herself. If they attacked her now, there was little she could do. If she could reach her club, she could fend them off but not for long. She was no great warrior. She couldn't even become set with child. She swam towards the edge and reached for the treasure but skilfully, as if teasing a biting cub, he whipped the garments from her reach, and she stumbled in the current.

More laughter.

She cursed their jests and despite herself reached for the garment a second time with the same result.

"Tainted curs!" she screamed and swam from her clothing towards her club.

They cheered and enjoyed her complete shame as she leapt out of the water into the long grass. She grabbed the club and raised it menacingly and to her surprise, they took a step back. The third man was far younger than his two companions were, and he grabbed the arm of the clothes bearer. He offered a few kind sounding nothings and the clothes were thrown to her feet.

She made no move; instead, she listened to the forest and the gentle crashing beyond. Oren had heard.

"Too loud." They failed to understand. The youngest hunter smiled and bowed, as did the red-headed man. They spoke loudly, and Nomi could discern their apologetic tones. After a while, they even drew their eyes from her naked skin.

Very popular in wartime.

"Run," she hissed and they smiled.

She swung her club weakly and they leapt away. "Run from here." Still they smiled and added further apologies to their gibberish, and the crashing suddenly grew loud and they finally noticed it and Nomi wanted to scream.

Oren charged through a break in the trees upon his warhorse further up along the river. He roared and raced down towards the three men who now swiftly learned their folly. They spread out and walked towards the charging Oren holding their arms up in a display of contrition and peace making. "It was just a little fun. You are a lucky man. She will likely grant you many heirs."

If that's what they called out to the rushing man, he didn't understand them. It wouldn't have made a difference anyway. Oren pulled a long sword from his waist and still the fools had no idea that there would simply be no discussion. In the last terrible moments of the redheaded man's life, he screamed desperately as the horse suddenly swerved his way and ran him down. She heard the heavy crunching and knew they were all doomed.

She had tried.

So she did what she should have done when first she'd picked up her club. She charged towards the closest of the shocked brutes and swung the club against the back of his head. It was a hollow crack and the man fell to his knees as if in prayer. He croaked, and she fought the urge to throw up. This was how it was. She struck him again as Oren leapt from his horse and crashed down upon the last foreigner, stabbing the blade into flesh as he did. They struggled for a few breaths, but soon enough the body went still. She stepped behind the man praying as the life left his body and struck him fiercely, and he collapsed in the grass.

"Again," Oren called, and she nodded before striking again. His failing body shuddered, and she struck again ending his life. Once more and his head became little more than mush and hair. The grisly task was done.

"Silly Nomi," Oren said shaking his head though he was not angry. He recovered her clothes and sniggered to himself at her nakedness.

"That desperate for a child you lure three of the enemy?" He pulled a dagger from his waist before slitting the throat of the crawling redheaded man as though it was a small thing. Her blood-covered hands were shaking, and she noticed the dead man's blood was all over her. To kill was a terrible thing, but to die was probably worse. To give birth was the saving grace. It was duty, for this was war, as their god had decreed.

"I need to wash again," she muttered.

24

CATHBAR

Erroh walked tentatively, each step far louder than he would have hoped. His eyes never left the window in the nearest two story building. That's exactly where he would wait in an ambush. He hoped Lea thought the same way. They'd discussed tactics many times, over food and cofe in the good old days when she thought more of him as a mate, but in such a short time how much had she taken in? Could he trust that she would not hesitate to save his life? He shook that thought immediately. Of course he could trust her. She was a better person than he, and her stinging words laced with gentle desolation showed her true strength of character. If only he was capable of finding words that could soothe her hurt.

Deep down she knew he would not take advantage just yet. He would wait at least a week and then climb atop her. She would stare into his eyes and let him and that would be that. She wouldn't be afraid any more. Why not flee back to Samara, she asked herself for the umpteenth time? It was a fine question with probably a damning response. This life out here in the wastes with her brute was a better one than the lonely grey walls of Samara. Besides, she was stronger than her mother was. She would learn to control him if needs be.

This was no male's world.

Any half-decent tracker would see the confusion of the cavalry in the muddy ground. Deeply indented hoofmarks had circled the outskirts, while heavy boots had marched right through the centre of the village without stopping. The temptation to leave a message behind was just too much to bear it would appear. He signalled Lea to follow, and she did so in silence.

They went from building to building with blades raised but there was little to suggest recent occupancy. The smell of spoilt food was in every home. They moved quietly, two skulking apparitions stalking each room with lonely efficiency. The residents had simply packed up and left. Perhaps it was a plague or sudden mass hysteria. Perhaps they learned of a roving army nearing, and attempted to reach the city. Perhaps Erroh and Lea had simply missed them, as they passed, no more than a valley apart. For whatever reason they left, there was now an entire town to play in, with maps to locate and trinkets to claim. They could continue tracking the Riders tomorrow. Tonight they could relax a little and besides, he had been given permission to take a female against her will for his evening's entertainment. May as well take her in a comfortable room.

———

Erroh's new armour was bulkier than his old piece but the
metal was tough, with each plate hidden underneath the
leather covering. He thought about offering the piece to Lea
but it was a little heavy and it wouldn't bring out her eyes. He
sat in the upper level of the first old building: the fine ambush
spot he had identified earlier, should any unwanted bandits
come knocking. He could smell the musty odour of damp and
many years of occupants but it felt as though this had been a
happy place. In the bedroom where he sat, the walls were
adorned with decorations, the drawers neatly filled with
simple garments of toil and a little side room beyond held a
child's bed with walls painted in bright pink. Aye, this had
been a happy home before it was abandoned. Glancing out
through a curtain covering the little gap, he watched the
wind's invisible hand carry rain around the settlement. Each
powerful gust sent wave after wave of icy cold water crashing
wonderfully against their shelter but the warmth within
remained. It was almost enough to shake the terrible feeling
he had about this town. Instead of dwelling on such things, he
continued stirring the stew. He was no fan of stew but there
were plenty of vegetables at close hand and they both needed
a break from flame-cooked meat. If only for a few nights. He
added salt. He didn't taste it first; it just needed salt. He
tapped at the cork of the unopened bottle of sine and inhaled.
The foolish previous owner had believed that stashing the
bottle in a bag of potatoes would protect it. The foolish
previous owner had not planned on trying to deceive Erroh, a
true alcohol hunter. Her footsteps on the stairs below
suddenly grabbed his attention. The creaks on the stairs were
slow and methodical as if taken by a lamb led to slaughter.
The whistle of the gusting wind played a calming song and
hearing the melody he added another log before leaning back
in an oversized brown couch. The thickly stuffed piece was

impossibly comfortable and unfathomably old. Strange that some things like this survived the fires while great metal beasts were burned to charcoal. It was also strange to feel so comfortable on a night like this. Lea walked into the room and dropped the new arrows in the corner beside Baby. Her hair was sopping wet after being caught in the beginnings of the downpour.

"We're not sparring tonight are we?" she asked, looking out at the storm.

Aye, my dear, but not with swords.

He shook his head.

Darkness began to spread out across the land. The fire under which the cauldron hung was warming up the room nicely. "I think we can take one night off," he said, adding some more salt.

Watching the rain, she both felt relief and nausea. She took a freshly liberated blanket and hung it across the window blocking out any stray gusts daring to venture inside. She removed her armour and tossed it by the bed. It was a big bed, suitable for two. She sat down by the fire and let its soothing warmth dry her off. She tasted the brew and added a little salt.

"Those painted words are unsettling," she said.

He nodded in agreement.

"They didn't even stop to ransack this place," she said.

He nodded in agreement.

"An open town with fine plunder and no resistance," she said.

"They just kept on moving through," he said after a few breaths. He ate his stew and stared vacantly as though the weight of the Four Factions of the world were on his shoulders. It was strange that there were still moments when she forgot the depths of his cruelty. She resisted the urge to ask him what his thoughts were.

His mind was awash with discouraging notions. He was a better man than she believed. He was sure of it, but he was tragically inept when it came to sentiment. He had been wrong, and he knew that now. She had to see that on his face. Wasn't that enough?

She sniffed unpleasantly as he filled her glass. She met his eyes but mercifully said nothing.

He thought about what she had said at the edge of the town, and he felt ashamed. He thought about her screams as he trapped her under the water. She was right not to trust him. His father had probably faced the same difficulties. Possibly more, but he was not his father. He clinked her glass and said the wrong thing again. Humour was all that he had.

"You'll need that for later," he joked, gesturing to the bed.

She nodded and poured the contents down her throat and grimaced in silent defiance. Her face was pale, but she was beautiful, and she needed to be put out of her misery. He reached out and ran his fingers through her long black hair. She did not shudder or recoil from his touch. He leaned down onto the floor where she sat and stared into her beautiful dark eyes and whispered his words into her ear. It was such a lovely ear. "I want you so much, my beo."

She tensed but nodded her head slowly.

"I promise you," he whispered holding her nervous face in both his hands. She looked petrified. "I'm not going to touch you." She looked a little less terrified.

· · ·

He smiled, and she hated him.

"I give you my word, Lea, that I'll never take you to my bed, until you want me,"

"And if I never want you?"

He shrugged and lay down beside her in the warmth of the fire. "In all my life I've only made one oath. Now I make another. I will never hurt you again." She almost believed him. Almost, but not quite.

"What happened at the river was shameful. I was not myself, though it was no excuse. It was the behaviour of a scared cub with no idea how to control his emotions. I'm so very sorry, my beo," he said.

She wished he wouldn't call her that.

"It's easy to say that now, Erroh." Her previous fear and melancholy was replaced with growing confidence and perhaps careful anger. "Stop calling me that as well," she added and spoke a little more.

She spoke of his betrayal in the river, his act of cruelty, and he accepted her condemnation of his honour without argument. When she recalled the horrors, he forced himself not to look away in shame and when she asked why he did it, he told her.

He spoke once more of the horrors of the town and left nothing out. He relived the grisly discoveries and the nightmares and then he spoke of the wandering bandits. Tears rolled down his cheeks as he did. Not just for sadness but for the release of his last few demons. Her gentle sparring of words had driven the cruellest act from him. A terrible attempt at displaying the true extent of what his father had put him through. However, Magnus was older, wiser, and a little more vicious, but he was a better teacher. She looked at him, through him and accepted his apology but was loathe to forgive or forget. Then he told her he had never expected to fall in love with her.

She hadn't expected that.

She hadn't said anything and the only sound in the room was the gentle crackle of the warm fire and the calling wail of the rainstorm.

"You said you'd only made one oath before. What was it?" she asked after a time, her thoughts spinning anew, yet more settled than before.

"Vengeance for the boy."

"It's a good oath," she said after a moment's pause.

"And my second oath?" he asked.

"That's a good oath too," she whispered.

A stray gust of wind blew at the blanket; a few isolated raindrops crossed the threshold. Lea could not help but hug her arms tightly and move closer to the fire. "It would have been a little awkward under your cloak tonight," she said, listening to the gentle tapping of the rain hitting the old slate above them. "Good oaths," she repeated to herself. "So we are hunting them?"

"The Riders?"

"You're going to kill them all?" she asked.

"I'm going to kill them all," he said with steel in his voice. He could never know how great a lie that was to become though.

"Are you training me to be a killer?" she asked.

"Aye, but I have little intention of putting you in harm's way." He could never know how great a lie that was to become either.

"Except in rivers?" she muttered. He nodded pitifully and it meant little. Fuk him, she wasn't ready to let things rest as they were just yet.

"Are we still heading to Conlon?" she asked. Were they still not the Primary's royal messengers?

He nodded. "If the tracks are just innocent travellers, we'll ride through to Conlon and then on home."

"And your oath of vengeance?"

"Can wait until I have spoken with Magnus."

"It wouldn't be a bad idea to have a small army to call upon," she admitted, and they both smiled.

Erroh stood and stripped off his clothes, leaving one garment to cover his decency. He dropped onto the bed and stretched out wonderfully. She noticed he had left a deliberate space in the straw for her if she felt inclined. Instead, she listened to the rain a little longer and sipped on her beverage. After a long enough time that he was sleeping, she quietly removed most of her own clothes and climbed into the straw beside him. He stirred slightly and instinctively draped the blanket over her before rolling away from her. Nice touch Erroh. She had been tempted to seek rest in another room or building but if there was a chance of reconciliation, she would have to offer some neutral ground. She loathed him but his words had been genuine, which was something. Her own father would never have offered anything as powerful as an oath to anyone. Her mate had surprised her once again. He stirred a few times and moaned a few sobs in his sleep. She turned her back from him and hugged the warm blanket and sleep soon found her.

———

When Lea woke first, she felt completely disorientated. She also felt warm and safe. Her head was nestled against his chest again while he was in a deep, peaceful sleep. Somehow, through obviously no fault of her own, her body had become intertwined with his in a lovers' embrace, and she noticed that not all of his body parts were completely at rest either. She slipped away from him as gently as she could. After a stolen glance at his lap, she covered the blanket back over him and climbed out of the bed. Not yet, she thought to herself. She wasn't ready to forgive him after one night of smooth talking.

It was well past dawn but the sky was doing its best to convince the world otherwise. The rain never let up. She stuck her head out through the window and let the fresh breeze brush up against her face. She didn't realise how much she'd missed the comforts of a roof, a bed, and the suggestion of civilisation. She wanted more than anything else in the world to have one more day in the silent town. She brewed some cofe, walked down to the street, and darted across to the wooden building opposite where she fed some apples to the horses in the stables and brushed them down. She closed her eyes and thought of a life with Erroh in such a place, and she wasn't sure how she felt.

"Another day would be fine," he agreed when she broached the subject. He looked as though he would agree with anything she suggested.

They took great pleasure in rummaging through each shack for a second time. It was a fine waste to the breezy damp morning. He left some little bags of pieces he found for the next traveller, much to her dismay, while focusing on more practical things, like heavy leather boots for the south, a new cloak for her and sturdier saddles for a smoother ride. She squeaked louder than usual when she found a large supply of differently salted and spiced meats in a locked larder. He loved the unabashed excited sounds of someone who wasn't used to receiving gifts or scavenging treasures as she smashed the lock with a sturdy kick and discovered her spoils within.

Erroh didn't know what to do with himself as the day passed on. It felt strange to do nothing except watch and wait for the sky to clear. The last time he had such a stillness had been by the rock. She on the other hand was at ease walking around as if it was their own little village and her wanderings brought her to the tilled patches on the outskirts of the town where she discovered a new interest, digging her soft fingers through the water logged fields tending to crops. Aye, her predecessors had done the mule's work but as she dug, pulled, and examined the fresh vegetables a wonderful sense of peace overcame her. Thoughts of a possible future living this way returned to her mind, and she allowed the illusion to warm her. There were worse things than a farm with a mate and cubs.

They practised with their weapons in the centre of the little town. She fought with renewed vigour and took fewer hits than ever before. Erroh held nothing back, and she relished the fresh challenge. She matched his terrific speed in certain moments. They were like ominous apparitions, their bodies moving as blurs. They attacked as if frenzied and while she had improved her skill, she still couldn't match his mind for battle. Thinking like a beast bred for war would only come in time, but she knew herself capable. They clashed with each other for hours, ignoring the thunderous downpour that drenched them through to their bones, lost in the forgiving beauty of passion. When they called a truce both Alphas collapsed in the mud and panted until words could be spoken.

.   .   .

"A good fight," she said between breaths.

He spit some blood from his lip. "One of the finest."

She didn't know why she desperately wanted to savour these moments but every breath she took with him that day she tried to burn into her memory.

He never believed in gut feelings or omens yet still, there was something in the air. It felt as though absent gods whispered terrible warnings in his mind, and every time he saw a hoof print in the ground, he felt it more.

———

The following morning they shared some toasted honey bread. She wore a little smile on her face, and he thought it suited her wonderfully. They also shared banal conversation of unimportant matters and it felt good. Overall, it was a fine morning preparing for the road. Lea triple checked the meats and vegetables until she was satisfied with the supplies. As the first of the early afternoon drizzle began to fall, they climbed onto their massive beasts and with a little regret departed the desolate town. He did not bother taking a final look at the warning. The sinister words were already committed to memory. The town of Cathbar had been good to them when they needed it most.

25

HEATHER AND SKYROAD

They followed the tracks south for a few more weeks fighting rainfall almost every day. Making rough cover and stripping twigs of damp bark took up most of their evenings. They made slow progress but they loved every rain sodden moment. Each night they would recline on opposite sides of the fire and discuss their separate worlds. She explained the politics of the city and its prejudicial rule. He admitted to suffering pressure from growing up in the household of Magnus and Elise. He offered his views on great battles from the Faction Wars while she challenged him with the history she had learned. She spoke of her life before Samara. He spoke of the road. They shared all that they knew and once more, they began to cherish each other's company. When the shattered moon had moved a little further across the clear sky, they would answer the call of weariness and lay down to sleep comfortably apart. Their sparring became more intense. Erroh put it down to desire to do many beautiful and sordid things to her body. She added her own brand of intensity herself. Maybe she was feeling it too. Each session lasted longer and longer until one of them would eventually yield, purely from exhaustion. Countless dreary mornings Erroh would find Lea's beautiful body wrapped around his own. Some nights his low whimpers drew her to him, other nights, she just wanted his warmth and a respite from the raging winds and raindrops on her face. She never said anything as she stretched and climbed out from under his blankets and neither did he. He was true to his word and behaved like a perfect little Alpha, and he was made to work hard for her forgiveness. Her trust would eventually return, but he never chased it. They had all the time in the world and there were worse ways to waste a life away.

That is, until they found the slaughtered remains of the inhabitants of Cathbar.

The dreary sky must have known of the massacres below for no sun could pierce the veneer of cloud blanketing the sky. There was no sunlight to offer levity and they stood on top of a heather covered hill in silence. The all-consuming wildflower had left the landscape a wild purple and grey. Lea let a clump fall silently from her hand without notice but the smell was still prevalent in her nose. It had always reminded her of her childhood but all she could see were the dead now. The heather would bring new memories.

There was no Rider to be seen for miles but they had been here. Erroh roused himself from the shock first. He steered his horse down the slope towards the ruined convoy. She hesitated, and he didn't blame her. After a few moments, she followed down through the ocean of colour. Her mind grasped the images and stored them for a lifetime of nightmares ahead, however long that might be.

They never had a chance. The amount of dried and hardened bloodstains in the trampled grass told them as much. If there had been losses suffered by the mysterious riders, the fallen were taken with them while the victims remained behind, forgotten, and spread out across the land.

There was no smell of decay. There was only heather. Erroh felt the nauseous turn of his stomach, and he fought the urge to throw up. He would do that later. Beside him the miserable spectre that was Lea walked by aimlessly. She let go of the reins and allowed her horse to wander and graze oblivious to the horrors in the grass it fed on. The attack had occurred some time ago; they still lay where they had been felled, like broken logs ruined by the harsh elements.

"Go tend to the horses, Lea." He could deal with this. More than that, he would make her believe that he could deal with this.

"You're not going through this alone again."

He didn't argue. He wanted to, but he had no words.

The massacre had been quick, savage, and efficient. The weak that had taken flight had not escaped the flames after all. They had merely prolonged the chase. Uden The Woodin Man had claimed his next victims.

Who the fuk was this demon?

What powers did he have that traversal across the world took him so little time?

Erroh ran his quivering fingers through his black hair and tried to stop his head from falling off. The six carts were untouched save for a few boxes gracelessly removed to locate any hidden stowaways and there was a large scorch mark in the ground where the brutes had completed their barbaric ritual.

"There's little we can learn here," Erroh growled as if strength in tone was something to build upon. He found a spot and cursed the absent gods for allowing this misery. It was as good as any place out here, and he searched deep within him for the will to begin the wretched task. It was his only repayment for their hospitality. They'd slept in their beds, eaten their food, drank their liquor while every one of their absent hosts lay out here rotting. "We'll honour them," he said, and her pale face nodded in agreement.

It was much the same as before, and he attacked the grisly task with the same grim efficiency. The elements had begun the process already but the earth would do the rest. She dug with him. The grave was no more than twenty feet each way and a few feet deep. Admittedly, it was an easier task with his mate at his side though he'd wish no such horrors on any person. For the rest of the day they dug in silence until the grave was big enough to hold all the lost souls. The real horrors began as night fell around them. Dragging a corpse apiece into the grave with the stench of sweet heather in their noses was a torment that stole their voices and their breaths. Searching for each body with a torch in their hand became a miserable game of hunt-and-hide.

It was the body of the young girl which broke Lea finally. The little one had not come of age nor would she ever. This was what had saved her from the fiery grave. Her body lay further away from the rest of the carts. Fear must have given her wings, and she had run far. The little one had taken a bolt in the back of the head and died before she dropped. Her hair had been red, her shirt had been pink, and Lea fell to her knees and wailed openly. Erroh watched on in silence wary of adding to the lament. After a time, he went to her and placed his grubby hand across her shoulder. There was a grave to finish. She took his hand and squeezed it.

"It's a good oath," she whispered.

The gods granted them a beautiful dawn and a clear sky

above. Sleep called but neither wanted to rest. She looked back at the mound, at the scorch marks in the earth and the world felt all too real. She felt helpless and small. She looked at her strong mate beside her as he led his horse away from the desolation, and she understood his pain. It was now her oath too.

———

Miles beyond the blood soaked basin the two Alphas made camp. Off the beaten track, they took shelter among some fruit laden trees, though neither had the taste for food. Erroh lay down under his cloak and closed his weary eyes. Just a few hours' sleep and off again to ride further from the memories.

She slid in beside him. "Please don't say anything. I can't take any jest or wit to ease the tension," she said, closing her eyes.

"As you wish, beo."

For a few days after they buried the bodies, Lea struggled with their mindless trek. The going was easier, but she was laboured in everything she said and did. The only time she came alive was in the fighting. Like a rabid beast, she attacked with little regard for her own welfare. She was amazing and pushed him further than anyone had before, apart from Magnus. Eventually she locked the thoughts away and began to find her beautiful smile once again, which was a good thing because the trail went completely cold at the foot of one of the great structures of the ancients.

The skyroad was more than a simple stone road. It was ugly, enormous and a terribly unnerving thing to gaze upon. As if by the hand of the absent gods, it rose steeply into the air almost as high as Samara's walls and probably older. He felt dizzy looking upon it. It was manmade but not of this time. They followed the steep sloping path into the sky. With monstrous supports every thousand feet or so, it was no surprise the beast remained sturdy under the relentless assault of the wind. From there they could see the land spread out for miles. Only patches of open waterlogged glades broke the constant view of green and it was humbling. The skyroad led south, beyond the horizon.

"I've heard of such things," she called above the growing roar in their ears.

"It's a road across the sky," he replied wrapping his cloak tighter around him to fight the chill.

"We'll make good time," she called again, tapping the quiver at her waist absently. Her hunting eyes little more than thin slits.

The trail disappeared altogether atop the skyroad. Even the most skilled tracker would struggle to track on stone. Every ten miles or so a side-road led back down to the ground and disappeared into nothing out in the wastes. More than that, where the vibrant green met ancient grey there were numerous clefts and footprints spoiling any tracking. Still they tried, but after countless journeys up and down and numerous hours lost in the process, their hopes faded and after a dozen failures; they gave up completely.

"It's nobody's fault," she muttered, pulling her mount's reins harshly as they returned to the peak. The beast snorted in reply.

"Maybe if we choose a likely path and gamble," he suggested but they both knew the cause was lost. Lea took his free hand and kissed it gently.

"I want to kill them all too. And when we find them we

will," she said before releasing him and climbing atop her mount. In that crushing moment, she knew she could never be a typical female, eager to spawn little cubs and rear them well. She was no Mea, content with her life on a farm. She believed she'd wanted it all her misguided life. She had even tasted such a thing in Cathbar, briefly, but finding the dead had finally woken her from her stupor and now a terrifying truth had landed upon her like an executioner's axe. No longer did she wonder why Erroh was the only man for her. She could sense his rage and it matched her own. She was drawn to him like no one before and there was love, it grew every day but there would be no happily ever after. They were not destined for a long life. They would die by steel but before she stepped into the darkness, there would be blood on her hands as well. And whenever they took to hunting these brutes, she would be by his side. She would follow him to the end of the world. Even against his wishes.

———

They'd long since passed the unreliable map's boundaries and travelled countless miles over many days along the skyroad before the signs of age began to appear on the monstrosity. Stone chunks missing from the waist high parapet on each side of the road became frequent and soon enough terrifying holes appeared on the path revealing dense woodland far below them. The road came to an abrupt end where one of the supports had collapsed, leaving a gap over a deep river. In the distance, the construct stood segmented and fractured as if this one break had begun its great downfall like a keystone in a bridge. It was no longer impressive. Instead, it was the same as every other ancient structure burned in the fires throughout the world. A worn road lay at this last exit, which they took.

It followed the river south, so with heavy hearts they kicked their mounts forward and returned to their inglorious mission as messengers for the Primary.

———

She needed levity and surprisingly, in the river, she found some. In the darkness and with a little trepidation she dropped into the water and floated over towards him allowing the gentle current to tug slightly at her and bring her closer. He didn't seem to notice as he scrubbed at his clothing with the soap. He cared about bathing a little too much. He'd said it was about hunting, but she suspected it was something else. He would tell her when he needed to, she supposed.

"I won't pull you under," he jested without looking up. She bobbed in the water opposite him, watching his hands as they attacked the garment. There was something oddly relaxing about it. Something in the back of her mind, like little electric sparks.

"I trust you," she cooed.

He threw his shirt ashore and then a realisation struck him, and he pointed to the riverbank where all his clothing lay in the damp grass, in dire need of the campfire warmth.

"We usually bathe in private. You caught me unawares," he mumbled.

She started to laugh.

"I finally caught you off guard," she mocked, splashing some water in his face and finding this terrifically amusing.

The moment was contagious.

"I am beaten," he replied laughing. The release couldn't be held and their joint laughter echoed far into the green. Such a wonderful sound after so many bitter days chasing ghosts was uplifting.

.   .   .

"May I recover my clothing, Mydame?" he asked finally when he'd caught his breath. He eyed a low hanging branch drooping over the water and formed a plan involving reaching up and snapping it free to cover his dignity. The danger was in the leap from the water.

Her face darkened but the smile never left her beautiful eyes. "Mydame?" she mocked swimming to the bank where his clothes lay and pulling herself up onto its grassy edge.

"So I'm an ignorant old wench then?" He didn't like that mocking tone. Not one little bit.

"You're amazing and incredible. The finest of all females in the world," he cried in mock panic though still watching warily as she reached for his defenceless clothing.

"Finer than Lillium?"

"She has a fine chest but yeah, probably."

She tossed them into the air. It was a good throw. She must have checked the wind and everything because they landed a great distance away in a shrub.

"Whoops."

He suddenly became aware just how very cold the water was. He needed to explain just how cold the water had become.

She dropped back into the river and swam in an arc away from the bank to give him a clear route to recover his garments. Her eyes were mocking and suggestive. He was her amusement for the evening and after everything he'd done, she was fully entitled to a little retribution.

"It's very cold," he said and despite everything, he was enjoying the teasing. It was a fine distraction from serious things. It was a reminder how newly mated couples should behave and play while walking the road. He climbed out revealing only his rear for her enjoyment. He thought it a fine ploy on his part, but he hadn't taken a step before her sudden scream of terror shattered the serenity of the night. It was primal and his urge to save her overpowered him. His instincts took hold and his thoughts raced. A sudden strong current? Bandits? In terror, he spun around and was halfway into the water before he caught her smile and realised her ploy. Well played my beo. You nasty witch.

"I'm okay now," she informed him without meeting his eyes because her attention was elsewhere, and he felt like he was in the Cull all over again.

"Thank you very much," she said, still not looking up at him.

He picked up his damp clothing and covered some of his pride. "I deserved this didn't I?"

To her delight, the fresh night air was not cold at all.

"You may take your petty revenge. All you have to do is ask," she joked tugging gently at her shirt. She felt that wonderful desire overcome her somewhat. They had travelled so far, and he was hers to command. A few stolen glances on both their part was perfectly acceptable. Nothing wrong with a little bit of play.

"You are radiant. I'll put on a fire for when you finish, my love." He bowed grandly before retreating back towards the camp in search of his warm cloak leaving her to float alone in the water playing his words in her mind and committing wonderful sights to memory.

Aye, he was her love too.

26

THE HISTORY OF THE WORLD
ACCORDING TO A GOAT

The path they took opened up and traces of other people began to appear. Tilled fields, felled lumber and fenced off livestock replaced the lonely wilderness. When they spotted a sign at a crossroads saying "Keri" five miles east they both directed their mounts down the new path, keen for a break from the monotony of the road.

Soulful, wailing notes from pipes filled the valleys. As sad as the instruments sounded, the tune they played was upbeat and the closer they neared, other instruments accompanying could be heard. The familiar song would play all the way through and then begin all over again.

They passed through a few more fields with crops, vibrant, plentiful, and ready for harvest, and Erroh's hesitation began to wane. They spotted the first living souls in months working one of the fields. It was a father and his young son. They seemed at peace with their labour and offered easy waves as the Alphas passed. They walked their mounts the last of the way. The music filled the air as hooves and feet left the dry earth of the road and touched upon cobbled stone of civilisation.

The town of Keri was ancient and impressive. It won him over from the first sight of the tall towers, turning windmill and clusters of neatly thatched roofs. There were great mountains reaching into the sky all around the settlement. It was a natural protecting wall of stone concealing the town from the world. If it hadn't been for the signpost and the pipes, they may easily have passed by. A roaring river flowed through Keri's heart. Each bank was alive with colour from the end of season's bloom. The buildings were remnants of the ancients. There was no decay to be seen, only whitewashed walls, glimmering windowpanes and neatly trimmed gardens. He looked back up at the enclosing mountain range. The fires had not penetrated this town's defences. No war had ever been fought in her streets. This town had hidden from history. He loved it already.

"Here for the festival?" an old farmer asked, leaning against a wooden fence with a tin of paint in his hand and a few brushes strapped to his waist. It was a long fence. He was well prepared. He wiped his hand on his shirt and offered it to them both.

"Aye, we are indeed," replied Erroh.

"You have no idea what I'm talking about do you, young man?" laughed the old man, and Erroh shook his head. After the last few days of bitter cold atop the sky road, the warm sun was pleasant upon their faces. It almost felt like the beginning of a summer season instead of the end.

"This is Keri and sure 'tis the festival of the Puk. It's near two decades old now. Nothing but an excuse for food, drink and a few fights in truth." As he spoke he massaged his worn knuckles. Painting was apparently hard on the knuckles.

"Sounds perfect," said Erroh, looking down the road towards the tightly clustered buildings. He'd never heard of such a thing but it sounded like this festival was everything he'd been missing in his life.

"There are quite a few inns, but I doubt there are rooms this late in the season," the old man suggested. He shook his wrinkled head slowly and ran his fingers through his snow-white hair. "Very late in the season."

"I sense a proposal," replied Lea, smiling her most Alphaline goddess smile.

The old man could only but smile. "The name is Holt, and I have lovely stables."

He led them up behind his house to a large barn and its straw filled loft. They cut a fine deal for the night but with few coins on hand, Erroh agreed to leave their mounts as collateral until he could acquire some additional funds. He filled his front pockets with helpful playing cards just in case the game at the table was competitive and open to a stranger with his own set of cards. Holt returned to his painting while Erroh and Lea walked into Keri, excited to taste the hospitality the town had to offer.

Wooden stalls were set up, just like in the market district of Spark, in the town centre. People haggled, laughed, and enjoyed the festivities. Music blared loudly from a little stage where five dancing musicians played their parts loosely. A few eager revellers clapped and sang the accompanying words fuelled on by pints of clear ale served at a stall by a large and boisterous barkeep outside a beautifully preserved inn. Erroh looked skyward. The shadows of the mountains were both unnerving and comforting. The founder of this town had chosen wisely. While the world struggled, this town had flourished. Were it not for seeing the skyroad in all its glory he never would have believed such a thing possible.

He wondered were there other such untouched settlements out in uncharted regions of the world.

The innkeeper's laugh pulled Erroh from his thoughts. He practically threw a free mug of ale to both of the Alphas who received them gratefully.

"To the Puk!" he roared, raising a mug of his own. "The king of the travellers." He drank down heartily. Before they could thank him, he had already turned to a wild-looking young man eagerly waiting a refill.

"You've already had six, Emir." He laughed as he poured the slightly swaying Emir his seventh. Behind the innkeeper stood his wife, shaking her head in mild disapproval and pouring drinks where needed. Some customers would offer a shiny piece that she pocketed quickly before her overly generous husband could refuse payment. All around them was merriment, and Lea linked her arm in his as they walked through the crowds. At the centre of the square stood a huge bronze bell supported by two large wooden posts. Erroh tried to read the carvings in the metal but the language was archaic, the numbers resembled no date he recognised. He could have spent the afternoon gazing at things of quaint beauty in this place, enjoying some rest and forgetting about miserable things, but there were words of the road he needed to share. The massacre of the townspeople of Cathbar had occurred only a few hundred miles away. The leader of Keri would need to know.

———

His name was Jeremiah. He was small, stocky and an immaculately shaved holy man. Lea was beginning to think of him as a holy idiot. It wasn't religion she had issue with; she had studied a few written forms of religion as a young cub but found little to interest her. He was an idiot because he was not listening to her mate. Watching Erroh's control in the face of such delicate stubbornness, she now discerned that her mate had the patience of a saint. She smiled to herself for her wit but offered nothing else to the conversation. It was difficult to argue with any zealot at the best of times. There was little to know of the gods, absent or not as any books or capsules on religion were rarer to find than anything else. Beliefs were just another part of the lost history of the human race and its slow declination into extinction and its slow redemption thereafter. She was a little indifferent to these matters. If there were absent gods waiting in the wings above them, she assumed they would return whenever they felt like it. Perhaps there would be trumpets.

"I don't think you understand the seriousness of this threat," Erroh repeated. Lea had taken a seat behind him on the ledge of a great window where she seemed content looking down at the revelry far below while he continued to argue. The Holy Mayor's office was similar to the rest of the town in being ancient but meticulously maintained. It had pale white walls, supported by dark brown beams with only an oak desk and a few padded chairs that passed for decoration. Upon Jeremiah's desk lay a little wooden stick that resembled a basic sword. It was only the size of a fist but Jeremiah touched it absent-mindedly every few moments when speaking. The holy man ruled the town of Keri with a satin grasp. He was a gentleman, and he was a gentle man. He carried the perfect emotions on his seasoned face whenever Erroh recited each horrific incident, but he was not interested in thorough answers or further investigation.

"It is tragic, young cub, but there is little to fear in Keri. This great town can withstand any attack."

Lea was bored. Everyone below in the square seemed to be having a great time. She felt stimulated to be around the energies of people again, and she was eager to spend some time with Erroh away from war and death and bad decisions. She wanted that constant crease on his forehead to disappear for a little while. He was prettier that way. She had a plan, a simple plan.

"This town would fall in a day to anything more than fifty swords," muttered Erroh.

"I'm sure it would take a little more than that, my wandering friend," replied Jeremiah.

Erroh played his first ace of the day.

"We're Alphas."

The holy man tilted his head and nodded in agreement. "I thought as much and it changes little. The report is appreciated and noted. We'll keep our scouts on alert." He spoke as if dealing with children. Then he smiled a politician's smile and gently insisted that Dia's whispers travelled as far as this hidden place. He assured them he knew of barbaric attacks, but she had ensured him this town was under no threat. He even suggested that two young Alphas would recognise its strength soon enough.

He wasn't a bad man, thought Lea. Just a fuken idiot.

"Now would you kindly go enjoy the Puk?" he insisted, rising from his chair. Lea hopped from her ledge silently and laid a calming hand on her mate's shoulder. She wanted to hit some sense into Jeremiah too but this man's priorities lay in the clouds with the festival. They had tried. Perhaps he was right.

Perhaps everything would be all right.

Perhaps there wasn't an army marching upon this doomed town, whispered the absent gods in her mind.

"As you wish," she said and led her mate from the office down the wooden steps to lose themselves in the crowd. It took only a moment to attain fresh mugs of ale. After receiving the blessings from the barkeeper, they decided to investigate the great and apparently famous festival of the Puk.

"Nothing more to be said or done," she said pulling him through the crowd. He thought about giving the holy man his full title but dismissed the thought immediately. Magnus's name commanded little respect in this part of the world and would unlikely have helped his cause. Now, if he'd been trying to intimidate the older man, it was something else entirely.

———

Keri was a fighting town and proud of it. Whenever many of its inhabitants weren't grinding out a living in the fields, rearing beasts or hunting the lands, they honed their skills for battle. It was common for settlements to develop their own customs and traditions out in the wastes and Keri took their love of violence to godly levels. In their words and in their actions there was a fervent love for all manner of weapons and warfare. It should have unsettled Erroh but instead it was oddly comforting. It almost felt like home. Swordplay was a religion among these wonderfully naïve peasants and had Erroh displayed his prowess, he could have been their god. As it was, he was content to walk with his mate arm in arm to view the most important sermon of this festival, the grand contests of blade and bow.

The event took place on the outskirts of the town where two sides of the mountain met. The battlefield was lush and green with festive buntings and flags commemorating mock battle and harmless glory. Lea was drawn to the freshly painted archers' targets, while Erroh was impressed with the largest sparring ring, floored in wood chippings, that he had ever seen. Proud young men full of boasts and heckles marched around like caged beasts while females portrayed a little more poise, simply warming up and preparing themselves for combat. Erroh and Lea sat beneath the steep valley wall watching the competitors prepare excitedly. All around them children played with sparring swords, screaming, laughing, and scoring killing blows. Their parents bunched together, discussed odds on each potential fighter, making whispered wagers from tips they'd received. As per tradition, last year's champion would not be present to defend her title. Such a rule left the door open for another town favourite to reclaim his prize, but a few strangers had entered the competition this year so all bets were off.

"You should enter, my beo," she suggested giddily.

He smiled and shook his head. "I prefer to be here with my beo."

"There's money to be made." She took his hand in hers.

"I could win this too easily. Cards are more of a challenge," he said taking note of the slope running across the mock battlefield. Whoever held the higher ground would have the upper hand, he found himself thinking. No, he shook the tactics from his head. It was time to relax.

She started to laugh at him.

"Of course, you could win this easily," she said.

"You could win this too, Lea. You are fierce. If there was a war, you'd bring far more to the fight than little old me. Most days you match me with the blade and there's also the bow." She started to laugh again but his eyes were serious. She spent a moment enjoying the compliment and another moment thinking of its merit.

"You wouldn't win as easily as me though. You are a female after all," he said laughing, and she tugged his hair sharply. "Perhaps you could win us a night's lodgings." He pointed to the painted targets. She smiled and shrugged but made no move to leave. She was happy here in the shade with her mate.

The winner of the first duel was quick but carried his blade too low. He left himself open with every attack yet the crowd never noticed. The man was skilled but it was crude and ungainly and any true swordsman could take his head off in moments.

"Watch her shoulders as she strikes," whispered Erroh of the next bout between an older lady and a young man.

"The cub hasn't noticed yet," Lea added.

"Neither has the crowd." The older female sent her junior flying.

"That poser would slit his own throat if he tried that with a real sword," she whispered watching the next round of competitors.

"He doesn't know what to do with his free hand," Erroh added as the flashy combatant broke through his opponent's guard and struck a killing blow. The crowd roared in approval while the Alphas merely applauded politely.

And so the afternoon went on, watching the fierce competition between brave but inexperienced warriors, and they loved every relaxing moment of it. When she sat against him and her warmth sent cool shivers down his spine he thought of no greater peace than this. Her perfume was intoxicating, and he tried not to take deep breaths. In all this time, he still couldn't decipher its aroma, and she would not say. She teased him by leaning across and placing her delicate fingers on his thigh and whispering seductively in his ear. "You're prettier than all these men."

"I aim to please," he replied pompously, but inside his heart began to beat faster. He wasn't quite used to compliments.

"Aye, you do, and sometimes you please me," she giggled before looking at her drink as if it had betrayed her trust. "I'm not that easy to mount after a few drinks." She shook her mug absently. It was time for a refill.

"I'm aware, my beo. I'll have to get you more drunk," he said, watching the next participant warm up. He was a burly monster of a man with a red shaggy beard who appeared drunk. More than that, he looked familiar, but Erroh couldn't place him.

"I like you calling me that," she said.

The monster was a force, and he attacked relentlessly, ignoring any blows he received until his far smaller opponent collapsed in a useless battered heap. "I am the Quig!" he roared much to the approval of the crowd.

"Well done, the Quig," called a tall female standing near them. She was a few years older than both Alphas with long brown hair and a hardened face, but she was regal and curiously beautiful with piercing serious eyes and a confident stance. She muttered a curse looking at the ruined man on the ground and spun away as if looking at any further violence was too much to bear.

Someone passed "the Quig" an ale, which he ignored until he had pulled the trampled man to his feet. With that feat accomplished, he passed the drink to the vanquished and patted him affectionately on the back. Some people called him Quig. His actual name was Quigley. "Next year, Emir," he said, and Erroh immediately warmed to the monster of a man.

The semiconscious man accepted the beverage gratefully and with assistance from his best friend was propped up against a tree to enjoy the rest of the festivities. His lip was pouring blood but it would not get in the way of his drink. Erroh respected his determination. He raised his glass to Emir who returned the toast with a bow. Emir then spotted Lea and smiled the most attractive, blood soaked smile he could muster. She returned the gesture and returned her eyes to the fighting. He was already a distant memory.

"This is a nice town, Lea," Erroh said quietly and upon noticing her empty mug poured half the contents into hers.

"Perhaps it won't burn like the others," she whispered. Perhaps the holy man had good reason to be so confident. This was no little settlement in the middle of the wastes. This was no fleeing caravan of immigrants. For all their flaws in the competition, there were many who could wield a blade. There were fewer things fiercer than men and women protecting their homes.

They watched the rest of the fights merrily and fitted in with the rest of the locals. They cheered where necessary and booed unsporting conduct. The gorgeous young winner of the entire tournament was cheered on deafeningly by the masses. He had danced around the Quig easily enough. Leaping in and scoring blow after blow despite the bigger man's infectious laughter after receiving each strike.

Erroh thought this was tremendous, as did Lea.

The laughing giant eventually fell to his knees and waved his arms in defeat. The crack of the wooden sword across his face from the swift swordsman was a cheap but acceptable blow and it sent Quigley to the ground. The victor with extravagant blonde hair raised his sword and most of the crowd roared in appreciation. Emir ceased his drinking for a brief moment to boo and shout ridiculous profanities. A few others joined him. The big man pulled himself to his feet as a young girl with blonde hair and tightly fitting clothing presented him with a new mug of bubbling white ale. A few people chanted his name, and both Lea and Erroh joined in while the new champion of Keri, Stefan, did a lap of honour around the sparring circle, roaring to the many gods of war above. A few female supporters surrounded him and escorted him away for the ceremony. The champion of Keri would pay for few drinks tonight.

"Well fought," murmured Erroh offhandedly as the procession passed by. The champion nodded and made to walk on until he caught sight of some fresh game in the form of Lea. He stepped through his admirers, and in truth stepped a little closer than needed, to shine a dazzling smile in her direction. She returned the expression.

"May I ask your name, little miss?"

"Lea, sir," she replied in a high-pitched tone Erroh suspected was flirtation, a tone she'd never used with him, he also noted.

"Gracious that was a fine victory," she added enjoying his attempt at charming her. He had a sharp chin and blazing blue eyes. She liked the agitation on Erroh's face at the champion's advances.

"Aye, it was." He kissed her hand in his most agile move of the day. "I am Stefan. Champion of Keri and elite," he glanced at Erroh and, unimpressed with what he saw, smiled at his quarry and gave her his most disarming wink. Erroh got the sudden urge to knock the silver-tongued charmer out cold. He began to count in his head.

"You're Elite? Wow, you must be an Alpha," Lea squeaked excitedly.

"I'm no Alpha, my dear. I'm so much more."

"I'm sure you are, Champion," she agreed, dropping the smile a little.

"We'll be sure to meet later," called Stefan, fighting the

pull of his many devotees every step of the way to the stage in the centre of town.

"Oh, aye," replied Lea, sniggering to herself at some joke only she was privy to.

Quig finished his ale and checked his whisker-covered face for blood. He was still pretty. The girl attending to him certainly seemed to think so. Emir left his safe haven by the tree and commiserated with the bigger man. They laughed and displayed war wounds as only best friends could, while the crowd cleared from the arena through the gap in the valley walls down towards the revelries in the centre of town.

Erroh raised his mug to both. "Hard luck, gentlemen."

"It wasn't our year," said the big man clinking glasses.

"It might have been if we'd been sober," said Emir shrugging. "Wouldn't have been as much fun though," he added.

"I'm the Quig, and this drunken wretch is Emir," he said, beckoning the two Alphas to join them. "And this beautiful lass is Lara," he said of the maiden bearing gifts of ale.

"I am Erroh, and this is Lea. We're wanderers from the road." It seemed reasonable enough, and Lea couldn't help notice a gentleness in Erroh's voice and his usual confident stance was less dominant.

"He'll never shut up about this," hissed Emir, staring ahead at the champion walking with his followers.

"I tried my best," the Quig said shrugging.

Lara took his arm in hers and once he didn't fight the advance, took hold as though she would never let go. "You did great." They were an unlikely couple to most onlookers.

"You should have just leaned on him," Emir pointed out.

"I hate that pompous fuker." Erroh laughed at this and liked the drunken fool.

"I didn't want to kill him. Sure 'tis Puk," Quig said before punching Emir lightly on the shoulder. The gesture almost sent the smaller man flying.

"Friendly game of cards later?" asked Erroh.

"Aye," said the big man. "I have plans for the now though." He allowed the female to lead him towards a side street away from the walking crowd.

"You have to watch the show, Quig," warned Emir but any person knew that look all too well. The big man was tired after his day drinking and fighting. It was obviously time for a few hours' "sleep".

"What's the show?" asked Lea. Her voice was high-pitched and laced with fragility. Perfect.

"It's the reason for this festival," said Emir, only too happy to answer her question.

"It's their own version," called the giant disappearing down the side street.

"It's less fun to watch without Quig cursing all the way through, and I probably have a few idiots with runny noses banging down my door. It was nice to meet you both," Emir said before wandering off through the crowd towards the only badly maintained building in the entire town.

"You really thought it a fine fight?" muttered Erroh as they made their way back towards the centre of town where the stage was now empty of musicians. Perhaps they had retreated to catch their breath and work on a new number.

"I thought he was a fine champion," she replied, enjoying his prying. "He had a fine look to him too."

Silence.

"I wonder what else he's a champion of?" she teased.
More silence.

She turned to him to kiss him on the cheek and to tell him she was playing but there was a tremendous ruckus as the grand champion of Keri was led on to the stage. He raised his victorious fist in the air and the Holy Mayor presented him with a rapier of gold. Its pommel decorated with emeralds. It caught the light and sparkled as he swung it theatrically to the enthralled crowd before bowing once more and clearing the stage.

"Shiny," whispered Lea dreamily and nudged Erroh's ribs. "You could have won me that and it may have earned you more than a kiss on the cheek."

"A sword like that is not fit for battle. No great warrior has ever been struck down with a golden blade," he said and regretted his decision not to enter. And just what did "more than a kiss on the cheek", suggest anyway?

The show was a comedy. Worse than that, it was an historic comedy. The four actors took to the stage in saggy regal gowns. They were both grand and playfully eccentric. Each of the men represented the kings of the different factions. Their outfits were matching but for each a different colour. White for the snows of the south. Yellow for the dead lands of the far west. Blue for the clear sky in the north. The emerald green king of the east faced heckling, and he gestured crudely to the audience, while at the side of the stage the Holy Mayor read from a theatrically long scroll in a comical voice, much to everyone's amusement.

"The history of the Puk that would be king," he pronounced loudly.

It was splendid pantomime, it was entertainment, and

Erroh's mood began to turn sour as all four kings danced around with swords, clashing and proclaiming themselves true leader of the world. They fought, fell, and laughed in their ridiculously coloured clothing and the crowd kept shouting for the northern king to win. Most, but not all.

Eventually the stage became still and a female with a burning torch jumped onto the stage screaming, "End the cycle!" and all four kings shuddered and yelped before dropping to their knees.

"They agreed to meet in the city under protection of the Primary," continued Jeremiah as a stunning female clad in barely anything entered onto the old creaking stage.

"The whore Elise was present, however, and she was to choose a king."

The crowd whooped and booed and screamed and drank.

The girl posed suggestively at each of the four kings.

"I'm not sure this historical recreation is entirely accurate," whispered Erroh.

Lea was silent though she was certain her mother-in-law did not dress nor act in such a way.

"I will choose," giggled the whore as each king dropped to a knee like before and promised her the world.

"Who will I mount?" she said.

"Who will I mount next?" she asked the crowd. They screamed their own particular political views. A drunken member of the audience nudged Erroh in the back in a "this is the best performance ever," gesture. Erroh smiled in agreement, but his eyes told something else. Regardless, the drunken man was appeased and returned to ogling the near-naked female on the stage who appeared to have made a very important decision.

"Perhaps I will take them all at once as are our ways," Elise decided and many agreed.

"But the Puk showed up with a fine set of horns!" roared the holy man suddenly and a man wearing a goats head and a beige shirt jumped onto the stage with an impossibly long theatrical blade and attacked the emerald king who fell with a whimper.

"Fuk you, Magnus!" shouted another drunken spectator. Holding his sword in one hand, Magnus mounted Elise to the mock horror of the remaining kings, the holy man, and most of the crowd. The three remaining kings danced around howling their disgust until the "Puk" ceased his act and the stage went silent. Released from his grip, the girl fell at his feet and began to worship him.

Fuk this town.

"The Puk felt bad for he had done little to ease the tensions between the kings," Jeremiah continued in a hushed voice. The crowd agreed and the mayor raised his hands for silence. "He met each king in turn to right the wrongs of his actions."

"I am not of these lands. I am but a savage. I will embrace the three remaining and war no more," declared the Puk before comically sneaking to the first king and putting his arm around his neck in a warm embrace. The second hand produced a little dagger and struck down the figure in blue. He repeated the process to the rest of the men laughing loudly as he did. Some of the crowd roared in anger but all could agree that this year's production was the best one in years. Elise stood behind Magnus and whispered in his ear while feeding him grass. He nodded and agreed with whatever she proposed.

"I decree," announced the character of Magnus, "that no king shall rule this land ever again. The world will be ruled by one man and that man will be me."

Jeremiah silenced the mob and prepared for the great finish.

"But thank God that the Primary saved us all from the Puk."

The female with the torch arrived back on the stage. Behind her stood two men in painted wolf masks. Their outfits were snug and as dark as night. She waved the torch in the goat's face, and Magnus and Elise cowered in fear.

"The city will rule fairly!" screamed the Primary.

"We will vote for the leader of the Spark or the Wolves will tear your pelt," she decreed and the wolf made tearing pelt gestures. Magnus jumped up and down in exaggerated rage. The crowd booed, cheered, and drank even more.

Lea took his fist in her hands and led him through the crowd.

"You don't need to see this, my love."

27

ACE OF QUEENS

L ea struggled to keep up his pace. His heavy boots echoed loudly as they marched through row after row of identical homesteads of thatched roofs, wooden arches and freshly painted walls. He turned up a little side lane to escape the throngs of sweaty bodies taking delight in his tainted heritage, and cool air came rushing down from the mountain striking his face. He thought once more how well this town was hidden from the world. He kept walking until he met the river where the sounds of revelry were lost in the rush as it passed. A man could be sucked along in its current and never come ashore, he mused. She said nothing and just tugged gently at his hand.

"Is that what you believe too?" he snarled, thinking of the show.

"Are you okay, my beo?" she replied.

"My father is no betrayer."

"Aye."

"My mother deserves far more respect than that," he snarled.

"Yes, she does." Lea placed her arms around his neck and pulled him in close.

"I'm sorry I snapped at you," he whispered loud enough to hear above the flow.

"We speak a different legend in the city," she said.

"Thank you," he said and left the riverbank to find the nearest tavern willing to gift up his payment for stay in the grand shithole of Keri.

"It was a terrible performance anyway," she suddenly quipped and spat into the water dramatically.

"I love you," he said shaking his head before turning away, and she froze mid-step. He said love. It was a strange little word with enormous ramifications. Her heart skipped a beat.

"I love you too," she said in reply after only a wonderful moment's hesitation. The beautiful words carrying weakly in the wind were lost to him as he turned the corner and the sound of the festivities grew once more.

What Cull?

What river?

———

As night drew in, the cool breeze of the mountain range turned to an icy gust. Rain fell upon the impeccable weavings of straw and cascaded like a thousand miniature waterfalls all around the empty town square. It was a terrible night to be out under the stars but inside "The Sickle, Star and Hammer," the weather was just perfect and the sweet alcohol was alarmingly inexpensive. It was Erroh's kind of place. The musicians had moved their little troupe into the corner of the large room. Thankfully, the actors were nowhere to be seen. The two-storied tavern was the biggest in the town with rich

woollen carpets adorning its polished wooden floor in all
places but the dancefloor. There were no empty frames to
sing at in this dwelling for there were colourful paintings of
tropical locations and fantastic landscapes hung neatly on all
walls. Stained tables with deep cracks and deeper tales were
filled with emptying tankards, flickering candles and huddled
elbows and the pattering of rain outside was lost in the
crackle of the raging fire burning in the corner where Erroh
and Lea sat playing cards. In truth, Erroh was playing cards,
and Lea was losing at cards. She was good at it too.

The scruffy Emir sat nearest Erroh and attacked his pint of ale
with the same relish as he did with a sword. Drinking was a
skill he was better suited to though. His hands shook
constantly. Perhaps this was because there were a countless
number of deaths he was responsible for. He did not think of
himself a good man even though he was. He was good
looking despite his unkempt appearance. He had a wicked
sense of humour but hid his smile behind a miserable grimace
of wretchedness, bitterness, and intelligence. He'd seen the
city and lived there for a time though such a life had left his
heart broken and untrusting. He did not like his hometown
either, though there were enough reasons to stay. Most of
them were at this very table. He looked at his shaking hands
and willed them to stop. He imagined cutting into flesh with
precision, and his hands became still.

To his right sat the tall figure of Aireys. She was pretty and
only a handful of years older than Lea but many considered
her a little old to be unwed in this town. It wasn't that she had
refused all thoughts of marriage. She just never found a man

that could hold her interest for longer than a night. In truth, it was more that the man she had always loved showed very little interest in seeing her for even one night. She was quick with her wit and quicker to show a kindness to those in need. Some whispered that she was the greatest fighter the town had ever produced and that was why she was destined to rule in the next elections. She was popular with all who engaged her but only Quig and Emir knew her best. Especially Emir.

Quig shuffled his cards across from Erroh and grinned to himself. There was something in the air tonight. He eyed his two closest friends and once more resisted the urge to say anything more. Instead, he gestured for another round and placed a bet. He was doomed to lose but it was a small matter. Every moment played was a gift. Quig's farm was a few miles west of the town beyond the roaring river. It had nice grassland with a healthy herd of cows and fields of wheat. Perhaps such a farm was why many females sought his hide for marriage despite his lineage. He was a consequence of the Faction Wars. He'd never known his blood family but his first memories were of older brothers and a wandering clan. He remembered loud roars of thunder, charging horses, smoke, and ruin and screaming. Then he remembered the wilds for a while until an elderly farmer and his wife found him and swiftly took him in. He'd had a wonderful childhood until inevitable age turned on his adopted parents, and though it was already the sixth season without either of them, he still missed them every day. He did not think himself an ample swordsman or fighter of any sort. In fact, despite his great muscles and fierce stare, he was gentle, kinder, and a great deal smarter than most people believed. He did not crave conflict like most Keri residents and found himself happiest out in the fields with scythe in hand reaping his work.

"No, Lea, don't raise again!" cried Erroh. Lea raised the pot and Emir laughed. Quig matched the bet and upon revealing his last card, took the winnings with a chuckle. Pretty girl, terrible card player.

Above them in a private section, the champion of Keri stirred another outburst of applause as he raised the golden sword in the air to his entourage.

"That sword is so pretty," joked Lea.

"I hate that fuker so much," spat Emir.

"Most of us do," agreed Quig.

Aireys said nothing. She took the cards and dealt a fresh hand. They all passed on the first round of betting apart from Lea who raised to nobody. Nevertheless, she did it with a delightful grin. Erroh sighed and added to her bet. The hidden cards remained unused. It was less sport when the company was so grand. Besides, through fair means he'd earned more than enough to pay for their lodgings as it was. He kept them safely in his breast pocket while the rest were for his beloved to squander with careless play. The smile on her face was worth it.

"All in," squeaked Lea.

"Call, my dear," laughed Quig matching her bet.

"Fold," she replied after a moment, and Erroh's head dropped to the table.

"More please," whispered Lea, and Erroh dutifully split his own meagre stack and pushed it across the table.

"Lara. Can we get a bottle?" called Quig above the noise of the room. The barmaid nodded and dared a quick smile in return. She dropped her current order and quickly went about choosing a fine bottle of sine much to the irritation of her previous customer. She was new to the skill of waiting upon drunkards but in the darker days ahead, she would improve.

"She's a fine little thing. Hold on to her," suggested Aireys wryly.

"Wonderful for overcoming a tragic loss no doubt, and she brings booze. I think you should marry her," muttered Emir.

Quig shrugged and eyed his friends carefully. "Last thing I'll ever do is take advice from either one of you. Especially in affairs of the heart."

"What does that mean?" asked Emir, slurring his words.

Aireys said nothing. Her thoughts were elsewhere. To be precise they were in a place where precarious plans were born.

Lara appeared at the table with her finest choice of sine and a few glasses. With the skill of a girl who was fearful that her parents, who were also her employers, might see her misstep, she took payment swiftly and gifted her beloved Quig a delicate kiss, before disappearing back into the crowd to address aggrieved patrons of delays and such. Something about the festival made people act impulsively; it was something enchanting. Maybe it was something in the water. Probably the alcohol.

"It looks like love," mocked Aireys as she dealt out the new hands.

"Better me than him," laughed Quig, nodding towards the grand champion who was currently pushing away one of his followers with the pointed end of his prize. This caused more of his comrades to cheer loudly than ever.

"I'll drink to that," declared Emir, and with glass in hand drank to that.

The band kicked in with the same song they had heard

upon arriving. Erroh found himself singing along to the tale of a wronged prisoner who wouldn't give ground regardless of the beatings he received at the hands of his jailers. His mother had taught him the song many years ago. Wars came and went in all regions but the great songs were universal. One of the musicians sang the words and by the fourth line, most of the crowd were singing along. It was enough to raise any spirits. It was a grand call to arms.

Lea would happily admit that her reckless play was creating a very healthy and stable economy at the table. She didn't lose every hand she played but it felt as much. Not that she minded in the slightest as it was her debut as a card player, and she loved every loosely betted second of it. He merely liked the sport of it and tonight he was playing his finest just to keep her in the game. Such thoughtfulness was not lost on her. She loved cards, and she loved being in love. As the night drew late Lea spoke words of the road. Words involving abandoned towns and graves among a valley of heather. She'd earned the right to tell the story, and Erroh only added a few points to her tale of caution. If the mayor of Keri was disinterested in dangers, they would spread the word at the source, but to their joint surprise, their new companions shared the same ignorance. Keri would remain untroubled. Growing up hidden beneath the mountains left a certain complacency that was only attained when living in a time of peace. Their new friends were sympathetic but resolute in their words and knowing it was futile to argue any further Lea excused herself and shared a few hushed words with Lara before disappearing upstairs to one of the many available guest rooms with her bag. When she re-emerged a little time later, she silenced the entire room.

. . .

"A goddess," whispered Emir suddenly and covered his mouth for speaking out of turn. He tried not to leer at the figure standing above them at the top of the stairs, but he couldn't help himself. He was but a lowerline and she, well she was something else entirely.

"Wow," gasped Quig and dared a wink at Erroh who had not seen her yet.

The band finished the last note of a ballad. There was no applause or drunken heckles as a stillness filled the room. Those who saw her first fell silent and the silence was infectious. It spread out through the aisles. A few females stared in mild disapproval but even they begrudgingly admitted that she was a sight, and she looked like she belonged in the city.

Lea wore her yellow dress of silk, and she wore it well. Erroh turned in his seat and immediately thanked the gods she had insisted she keep such an extravagant garment on that sunny day at the city a lifetime ago. The band began a delicate melody in time with each step she took as though they were hired in her honour, and Erroh's heart skipped a beat of his own. She looked more like the Lea of the Spark than the incredible wanderer of the road he knew so well, but this was no terrible thing. Her lips were a richer red than ever, her smile was for him and him alone, and Erroh smiled in return. Her hair was expertly pinned and tied up without a strand out of place, he found himself running his hands through his own scruffy locks, and he felt underdressed for a night of cards, laughter, and drunkenness.

The world seemed to hold its breath as two sets of Alphaline eyes met each other and the Puk's magic took hold.

If she realised the silent stir she had caused, she never let on as her graceful feet touched the bottom step and glided across the room towards Erroh. Every reveller parted way for her and when she took her seat at the table, the room finally took a breath and returned to their merriment. The moment had passed.

He dared to kiss her cheek. A fine manoeuvre after such lengths she had gone through to present herself. Her wonderful perfume stirred his senses, and he desperately wanted to take her in his arms and beg release from his oath. "You look incredible," he whispered. Words didn't do her justice, so he stared at her for a little longer.

"Maybe I'll meet a nice young farmer boy in here," she said mischievously, but her eyes were wide open and only for him.

"Or maybe a nice young doctor," said Emir shrugging before dealing the next hand. Aireys reached across and punched his shoulder. Enough to bruise. Enough to remind him of his place in the world. Enough to make herself feel better.

"You keep with those comments Emir and our new friend Erroh is likely to take umbrage," Quig said sniggering.

"We're all friends here," laughed Erroh and tore his eyes away from his goddess as she opened the betting feebly. Staying out until dawn to win a few meagre hands was looking less appealing than before.

From across the room the blonde figure of Stefan the grand champion of Keri sat in silence as his friends and fans celebrated all around him. He couldn't take his eyes off the beauty in the yellow gown of silk. He thought she was even more alluring than Aireys. What was her name again? It was a small matter, as was charming her away from the little skut of a companion lucky enough to have her eye. Charm her for a night and let her limp home to her forgiving and grateful lover come the morning. He liked to think it was a kindness helping a young couple through troubled waters and when he felt like it, he was capable of stirring a fine brew of trouble. What didn't kill could only make stronger. This didn't make him a bad person. It just made him a man and as a man, women were so very enthralling. He glanced at the table and the many females smiling, laughing and playing up to him. He knew they saw him as little more than a prize and that was fine by him at least for now. Perhaps he would know love someday. His eyes flickered to Aireys. She was different to most but all she ever caused him was annoyance and pain. Love hurt, so they said. Ha, he had little interest in things like that but if Aireys came and sat at his table again, he would gladly pay for the meal. If for no more reason than seeing Emir's pathetic face. The girl in yellow laughed at something stupid her companion said, and he wondered just how long it would take to remove her clothing.

Lea reached across and claimed her third winnings of the night. She sipped her sine carefully and found herself swaying with the music as the next hand was dealt. She thought the couples on the dance floor seemed to be having so much fun, but Erroh would be disinclined to embarrass himself. She couldn't dance either but sometimes that didn't matter. She looked at her losing hand, added a few more pieces to the bet, and felt just fine about herself as someone matched it. She caught a glance of herself in the far mirror and smiled. His reaction pleased her greatly. Aye, out on the road every time she caught him gazing lustfully at her in her finest armour with muddy blotches across her face she smiled, but sometimes it was nice to remember what it felt like to be delicate, graceful and feminine. Dancing would be magnificent but to sit and feel wanted was more than enough. Then he surprised her.

"May I have this dance, my beo?" Erroh asked, and she leapt from her seat as he took her hand and led her through the crowd out onto the polished wood of the dance floor.

They weren't terribly skilled in the art of dancing but after a few loose steps, they stopped noticing the stares. They spun gracelessly and fought many stumbles all the while laughing and gazing lovingly into each other's eyes. Eventually when they felt as if they'd sparred for hours without respite Erroh kissed her hand gently and turned to lead her back to their seats where Emir stepped forward and took her hand.

"I wish to steal Lea's heart." He'd have asked Aireys, but she was likely to break him in half were he to suggest it, let alone step on her toes. That said perhaps after dancing with Lea, Aireys might warm to such a suggestion. It was a simple plan and Stefan ruined it because Stefan ruined nearly everything for Emir. Some might argue it was the other way round though. They weren't long into their own clumsy manoeuvre before the champion of Keri walked from his balcony down to the dance floor.

Emir laughed as he attempted another twirl, which ended with him careening into another dancer. Lea laughed with him and for the briefest moment Emir forgot about his bitterness for the world. Then he felt a hand on his shoulder. It was a forceful, sweaty grip and it stole away the good cheer.

"It's my turn with this ravishing beauty," Stefan said

smoothly and pushed the drunken healer to the side. Emir muttered a curse and his hand fell to an empty mug at a nearby table. Around them, Stefan's comrades took to the floor with their own partners.

"Fuk off, Stefan," growled Emir.

"Watch your silver tongue my friend or I'll cut it out with my gold." Stefan grabbed Lea's arm firmly enough to stop her fleeing the dance floor.

Erroh hopped off his chair to rescue his damsel when Aireys stopped him.

"The champion is permitted to dance with anyone he chooses. Best you sit this one out, hero."

"He would be wise to handle her with more grace," warned Erroh knowing that Aireys was right. He was supposed to be a simple wanderer of the road and not a fierce Alphaline protecting his mate.

"I would imagine she is the type of female who can handle herself. Besides, it's only a dance," Quig said, though he watched Emir for signs of trouble. There was no need as the dejected figure of the drunken healer returned to the table leaving the empty glass behind.

"If it's your right to claim a dance then who am I to argue?" Lea said. She thought him attractive enough but his hair was too neat and sleek, his features were too sharp, and his eyes were a little cruel. He was a boy pretending to be a man. She glanced at Erroh and smirked. Erroh was a real man, though he did his best to behave as anything but. It was only a dance, and it would be fun to tease him about it later.

"I shall lead you, my dear," Stefan whispered. The music

began, and he pulled her a little too close. Holding her hand tightly he took her waist and swayed across the room as if she was nothing but a little waif in his hands. Admittedly, he could dance well enough that she found herself gliding across the floor answering each move with his subtle suggestion. A turn, a step, and a pirouette he moved her gracefully. The music rose, and he pulled her tighter as lovers did. What's more, she allowed him.

"Is this dance nearly over?" Erroh asked nobody in particular at the table.

"Not for a while. We could play a hand," said Aireys.

"He seems to be enjoying her," said Emir, ever the man to stir a brew of trouble. Aireys looked to the gods.

"Are there any other 'entitlements'?" Erroh asked. His fingers were shaking and his mind was preparing for war.

Emir was happy to answer. "Well the dance thing you know already. I'm sure there are other nasty things. He is the grand champion."

"Free drinks," said Quig, glaring at his best friend.

"That's about it," said Aireys, ever the calming politician.

"Look at the leer on his face. I wouldn't like my wife in his arms," muttered Emir helpfully.

After spinning her, Stefan suddenly dragged the goddess back to him and leaned in for a kiss, but she slipped away from his grasp before he had the opportunity. She smiled slyly as she did and Stefan wanted her even more.

"I look forward to getting to know you a little better," he said and took her hand. It was calloused and firm and somehow, this made her more enthralling.

"You will know me for this dance only," she replied playfully.

"Then may I take you someplace else to dance?" he said and kissed her hand.

"That's appalling behaviour," slurred a very drunken Emir shaking his head. He was having a fine time tormenting his new friend.

Quig leaned forward.

"So tell me, Emir. How would you feel if he still danced with Aireys like that?" he asked, ever the witty fuker. Aireys punched Quig in the arm. It was a fine strike, hard enough to silence the great oaf before he said more and ruined everything. The big man grinned sheepishly. The damage was done and in truth, somebody had to say something some time.

"What does that mean?" Emir hissed though his face was a little red. Maybe it was the drink.

"This dance is over, champion," Lea said as the last note rung out and the crowd applauded and called for the next.

"So will we continue this dance somewhere else?" He swiftly reached down and grabbed her rear and pulled her against him grinning. A fine technique used by a moron whose understanding of females was grossly overrated.

She struck him across the face fiercely. The crack echoed across the room and the shocked champion released his grip and stepped back in bewilderment. Pretty lady had quite a sting. He tried to laugh it off, but she slipped away from the dancefloor leaving him to face his friends' shocked expressions. Bewilderment turned to fury. How dare she embarrass him this way?

. . .

Erroh's mind was calm. It was quite simple. He was going to kill him. He leapt from his seat swiftly but was intercepted by Lea before he reached the dance floor. She placed her hands across his chest and shook her head. "This is not the place to lose your temper, my beo. It's only you who gets to take me home tonight," she said pulling him back towards the table.

"Very well. Keep the whore then!" shouted Stefan, laughing, and the room took sudden notice. Curious eyes from all corners of the room watched as events took shape. Wonderful and violent events no doubt. There was danger in the air. It wouldn't be Puk without a bit of danger.

One, two, three thought Erroh in his mind.

"The price to lie with her is far too steep anyway," Stefan added taking delight in the audience.

Four, five, six.

"There wasn't nearly enough meat to grab on to!" he shouted loud enough that the entire tavern fell silent for the second and last time that evening. His friends sniggered. A few nodded in agreement.

Seven, eight, nine.

"Do what you must, Erroh," whispered Lea. Her face was red. Her hand squeezed his tightly. She was right to be angry. Her rear was a thing of beauty.

Ten, eleven, ah fuk him.

Erroh released himself from her hold and wobbled drunkenly back to the dance floor looking about as threatening as a pigeon. Stefan sensing little danger grinned and swatted away the lazy left fist thrown his way. "Ha," he managed to cry out triumphantly, before the real strike, a furious right jab, sent him flying backwards.

Then the real drama of the night began.

28

GOOD NIGHT AT THE SICKLE

S tefan was pulled to his feet by his friends. His eyes were dazed and his face was a ruin of blood, mucus, and tears. They held him steady until he regained balance. It was only a slight concussion. Emir and Quig swiftly appeared at Erroh's side as the crowd of Stefan's followers surrounded them. Quig dared any to strike out next with a dangerous glare while Emir helped matters by laughing obnoxiously at Stefan's wounds. Erroh pulled out the tooth embedded between two of his knuckles and rolled it in his fingers. He thought about giving it back to him. Throwing it away seemed like a terribly rude thing to do.

"I'll kill you and your stupid whore!" roared the champion, spitting blood and wiping his eyes to clear the dizziness. Erroh dropped the tooth on the floor as both groups exchanged verbal blows.

"Calm down, Stefan, you were out of line," warned Quig and stepped in between both factions with his arms raised to calm the storm.

"He was attacked without provocation!" one female shrieked.

"Give us a smile," jested Emir. Someone shouted at him to shut his mouth. It may have been Aireys as she too stepped into the crowd to avoid a fight.

More exchanges were thrown back and forth until a fine golden blade appeared in the hands of the champion and the crowd separated immediately. Aireys pulled Emir to the side away from pointy objects lest he stir even more. Lea stayed with Erroh. Her heart was racing, and she watched the champion raise his golden blade menacingly. Without taking his eyes off the golden sword, Erroh gently eased her back to the safety of one of the tables. "This is a small matter." If he was scared, he showed nothing. Perhaps a blade in his face was a regular occurrence in taverns.

Only Quig stepped forward. "You need to catch yourself right fuken now, Stefan," he warned, keeping his massive frame between the two aggressors. He didn't need to.

Erroh skipped away from Stefan towards the massive burning hearth in the corner. A fine technique if one was suffering the cold of the changing season. He knew he needed to be careful. If he took a misstep, he was likely to kill the pompous fool.

The bloodied champion spat some blood from his mouth and charged past Quig. He swung his golden sword, but Erroh sidestepped and ducked away with ease. He retreated to the edge of the fireplace and reached for his weapon of choice. It was the first thing he could think of and under the circumstances; he thought he did quite well. Quig tried one last attempt at reasoning for peace but before he could get between them, Lea touched his arm.

"It's going to be fine," she said, and she was right.

Erroh held out a long black poker in front of him and took up a defensive stance. He knew he looked ridiculous, the nervous laughing from the crowd reassured him, but it didn't bother him in the slightest. "Surely you don't want to ruin that pretty blade," he said letting the glowing tip float in front of the grand champion's face. His right hand felt a little naked without a second sword. He found this quite interesting.

"Blood wipes away easily enough?" Stefan hissed.

"From a blade perhaps, though not from your hands," Erroh said, and Stefan hesitated until a few dissenting voices braying for blood rekindled his anger.

The crowd roared as if in the tournament, but there was little cheer as both men faced each other in a bizarre duel. Most called for peace and a drink, others called for vengeance and the others screamed for the Regulators to come and end this madness. Bar fights were always a sign of a good night at "the Sickle," but blades were a different thing entirely.

The champion attacked, and Erroh just blocked his efforts. His body smooth in motion despite the danger. The champion attacked for a second time and again Erroh just swiped each strike away as if he were suffering the irritation of a child poking at him with a stick. He didn't intend to embarrass Stefan so much. It just happened that way. He never countered any attack at all. Any loose strike on skin was likely to leave terrible scarring and nasty as Stefan was, he didn't deserve such a fate for doing little more than being a drunken brute with wandering hands. In truth, Lea's rear was quite the impressive thing. Who wouldn't be tempted?

Soon enough the crowd's fears turned to humour, as it became all too apparent that even with a poker, this mysterious wanderer surpassed their champion. It was here that the first mentions of the Alphalines were whispered.

When drunken fatigue began to get the better of Stefan, Erroh parried a laboured strike, grabbed his wrist, and drove the blade into the shiny wooden surface at their feet.

"Enough!" Erroh roared grabbing his collar and bending

his arm into a hold. Stefan struggled and screamed under the powerful clutch. He fought the pain for an impressive three breaths before yielding. Erroh released him and stepped away.

Without warning, Stefan grabbed his sword and struck viciously. He struck with the speed that had earned him the victory that day, and he struck a killing blow.

When the Regulators questioned him the following morning, he was quick to point out that he had been attacked first. His assault was justified. It was to protect his honour. There were a great many witnesses. He was grand champion.

The crowd screamed in horror, but Erroh swatted away the attack nonchalantly. He followed through with a powerful downwards strike of his own in the dead centre of the freshly tempered blade. He thought about Tye as the weapon broke in half. It was a shame. It would have made a lovely decoration in any homestead. Now it would make two. To finish he elbowed Stefan in the ribs and the vanquished man fell to his knees. The broken piece fell to the ground loudly beside him. The metallic ringing it created resonated throughout the room and fell silent like most of the onlookers.

Who was this fierce warrior?

Was he an Alpha?

He didn't appear to breathe fire.

"This fight is over," he declared, holding the glowing sword near Stefan's face. The champion finally took the hint and dropped the remains of his trophy. People converged on both warriors and heated words were traded once more. Fists and fingers were raised and pointed accusingly and fresh new tempers began to rise. Complete strangers stood beside Erroh as if he were a family friend. Many local arguments between neighbours took the opportunity to resurface. Age-old disagreements about land and money and possibly perspective mates, reared their ugly heads and Emir was happiest of all among the mayhem. "Enough of this childish shit," Quig ordered. It was a mildly threatening and terrifying call for peace and it was enough to lower the tension in the room but the atmosphere remained volatile.

Erroh and Lea slipped away from the dancefloor. Nice town, best not to overstay the welcome.

"Okay. We all just need to calm down," said Emir taking the diplomatic torch from Quig. He walked between each irate drunkard, and without prejudice patted each one on the back and smiled his warmest smile. He wore a "No need to fight, drinking is so much better" expression on his face.

Quig eyed his small friend warily. It was not like him to be the arbitrator. Emir reached Stefan and placed both of his hands on his shoulders. The kind gesture took Stefan off guard completely. It must have been something in the air. The festival of the Puk working its magic.

"We're good. We are all good here," cooed the drunken ambassador of harmony. His warm smile beamed from ear to ear. Aireys wondered when best to suggest walking him home. It was time to do stupid things.

Lea grabbed her bag and followed Erroh towards the door. He didn't take her hand, and she sensed a fight brewing.

"Let me take a look at that, Stefan," said the healer to his patient. He began shooing the champion's comrades away. "It's fine. I'll fix him right up." Emir gestured over to his closest friend. Quig wasn't just good to have as a friend he was also terrific in a fistfight.

"Can you give me a hand over here?" Emir asked and the

crowd relaxed and separated. Stefan hated Emir, but he still allowed the healer's delicate hands to inspect the gap in his mouth.

"Aye, that's bad," he muttered holding Stefan's face in his hands tenderly before grabbing an empty glass mug from a nearby table. People knew of his unorthodox healing techniques. They thought him wretched and a drunkard but they also knew his skill as a healer was unsurpassed if not somewhat peculiar. They thought it impressive that Emir treated Stefan's wounds despite their many years of feuding. It all began when they were in their youth and Stefan had been quite the bully. And Emir? Well, Emir had been the smallest target before he left for Samara.

Emir swung the glass ferociously. Some people heard him laugh as it connected with the back of Stefan's head and the entire room exploded like the glass. Stefan collapsed on the hard dance floor, and Quig allowed his friend to take one punch in the face before he stepped in and joined the melee. Thus began a wonderful flood of violence. From every table at least one patron ran to the dance floor swinging fists. It didn't really matter who they punched as long as they gave more than they got. Hitting someone they suffered a genuine grievance with was a bonus, and besides, it wouldn't be a festival without a memorable skirmish anyway. The large innkeeper sighed from behind the bar and made mental note of who broke what. His wife took actual note on a thin slit of parchment while their daughter Lara watched on proudly as her man decimated all who stood before him.

Erroh grabbed the bottle of sine. They were already at the door before three men, finally sent Quig through their playing table. He climbed to his feet and immediately threw himself back into the fray. Neither Erroh nor Lea looked back and nobody noticed the two Alphas slip out of the door into the streaming rain.

She missed the warmth of the room immediately. Within a few moments, both of them were soaked through. The weather didn't help his mood, and he stormed off into the downpour, ignoring the rumbles of complete devastation behind him.

"I think you broke the town," she said struggling to match his pace in such an outfit with matching shoes. He popped the cork and drank deeply before handing it to her.

"I lost my temper, and I overreacted."

"You were standing up for my honour, so does it matter?" she said as they walked over the bridge and the flowing river underneath. The wind blew through them and overwhelmed any sounds of violence behind.

"It matters to me, Lea. We should have sat and played cards and laughed and drank and strolled home without causing any type of stir!" he snapped, looking at her and her dress.

"Does it matter?"

"People learn of our bloodline and every fool will come looking to challenge. Even you," he said and shook his head as if she didn't understand. As if she was a foolish girl from the city, without any clue of the road. He scratched his arm suddenly.

"I'm proud to be an Alphaline!" she snapped.

"Mated to the son of the betrayer Magnus and the whore Elise?"

So that was it.

"I'm proud to be mated to you, Erroh."

He laughed humourlessly.

"You certainly didn't give that impression on the dance

floor with that thug," he said and increased his pace for effect.

It was her time to laugh. Foolish beautiful Erroh, he just hadn't a clue about females.

"It was only a dance."

"It was not only a dance."

"Well, it was to me."

Silence.

They walked for a little time until she took his arm and squeezed against him. He pulled away because that's what foolish young Alphalines did when they were angry at the world and needed to blame someone so they chose their beo.

"I'm sorry. I shouldn't have played along with Stefan. It was just some fun," she said.

"You loved the attention."

"I love the attention I get from every man!" she snapped back and drew away from him. She'd almost forgotten what it was like being at odds with him. Silly boy.

"I could have killed him," he warned.

"Now that would have been an overreaction," she said.

They walked without saying another word until they finally arrived back at the house of Holt, which at this late hour was shrouded in darkness but for two sheltered lanterns burning at the gate entrance. It was here that he stopped to say his piece and to do so in private lest his voice carry and wake their temporary landlord.

"You shouldn't have worn that dress," he hissed and regretted it immediately. She was crestfallen, but he couldn't help himself. "What did you think would happen?"

"I thought it might be nice. I was wrong," she said coldly. Her perfume drifted into his nose. He thought of the effort she'd made, and he ignored the guilt. He knew he was being unfair.

"Learn from your mistakes." All around them, the rain poured down. He offered her the bottle.

"You are needlessly cruel," she whispered. In the dim glow of a light, he could see the tears forming. She was about to ruin the paint around her lovely eyes.

"I keep us alive!" he snapped and pushed her away. It was just a little push. So he could turn away dramatically, storm off, and turn in for the night.

"Don't ever touch me again like that!" she shouted and pushed him right back. "You're vile. Just like your parents. Just like history suggests." She knew she had gone too far even though he probably deserved it.

"That's not how history should have been written," he said. What colour she could see drained from his face. A low blow, she mused.

"I didn't mean that about the dress. I'm sorry," he said and left her at the gate.

She was sorry too.

"I liked it when you hit him," she said stopping him at the barn door. It was her attempt at an apology.

"You hit him first."

"You finished the job," she countered and dared a smile. There was barely any light to see but there was enough to see how thoroughly soaked through she was. He thought it best to get her inside, and out of the stunning yellow dress with matching shoes.

"We work well together," he said shrugging.

"Maybe we should become mates." She stroked his chin.

"My parents would never approve, you're not nearly enough of a whore or barbarian," he said and leant his hands upon her waist. She was warm.

"Oh, give me time, my love," she said and gazed into his eyes.

Stop talking, Erroh. Kiss the girl, you fool.

"So you do love me?" he whispered.

"I've loved you longer than you'll ever know you moron."

Their lips met.

Finally.

He pulled her tightly, and she let him. They fell through the barn door without breaking their embrace and crashed against the wall. They did not part; they did not breathe, they just gave themselves to each other. It was perfect. She conquered his mouth passionately, and he countered with all he had. It was the greatest moment of his life. It was the greatest moment of her life too. She pushed herself against his body to experience all of him. His hands moved around her body, and she wilted under his touch. She thought of his oath.

"It won't be tonight," she said suddenly.

"As you wish, Lea," he gasped before she set upon him once more.

———

He lay on his back in the soft dry hay in the loft. The hanging light above gave the dimly lit room a warm feel. The rain was beginning to clear as the night moved on towards morning. He wore only an undergarment, but he covered himself in a blanket. Lea emerged from behind the cloak she'd used as a curtain hanging from one of the barn's old beams. She was radiant in her nightgown, and he craved her dearly. His heart skipped a beat as she crawled under the blankets next to him and ran her cold fingers across his chest.

"You're very subtle in what you want, my love," she whispered, allowing her hand to move a little further down before kissing his neck.

He smiled awkwardly. Sorry about that.

"It will not be tonight," she reminded him, and he nodded in agreement, as he touched her chest delicately. She did not resist. Instead, she bit her lower lip and smiled.

"We should sleep soon," she suggested before climbing atop him, pinning him wonderfully, and meeting his lips once more.

"A few more kisses before sleep," he whispered and met her challenge with equal vigour.

29

ALL THE TIME IN THE WORLD

The first rays of a virgin dawn shone through an open gap overlooking the courtyard. The early morning amber sky suggested a stunning day ahead. The world shimmered after the rain. There was a fresh taste to the world and there was something in the air.

Erroh and Lea were oblivious to the natural beauties of the world. They still hadn't slept. She lay across his body and her warmth stirred him in many wonderful ways. He looked into her eyes and kissed her for the thousandth time since the night before. He was proud of his behaviour. He held her beautiful face in his hands and brushing her long black hair from her eyes, thanked the gods for good fortune. Such fervent kisses and delicate, exploratory caressing was enough to drive any man deliriously insane. He wanted more though. He wanted it all. He wanted her all. Then again, there was no need to rush for there was plenty of time for both of them to become closer. This night had merely been a wonderful beginning but they had all the time in the world.

After paying their debt for the night, the Alphas saddled up their mounts and departed Keri. There was little movement in the late morning sun. The town was having a sleep-in ahead of the final night of the festival and as much as they would have enjoyed a few hours' sleep, they thought it best to leave before questions with authorities' about Stefan's assault were brought to light. They were justified but still, some settlements had their own peculiar laws. With barely any sleep and the taste of a hangover in their mouths, they still found themselves in good cheer. Though neither said it, they both were looking forward to camping down for the night and continuing where they left off. She sipped from her canteen. It made the drilling pain in her head tolerable, but she didn't mind too much. She couldn't stop smiling and neither could he. They left the town of Keri through the gap in the mountain down a slope and out into the clustered forest beyond. They followed the river south like always.

When she laughed, he thought it one of the prettiest sounds. He laughed too and continued with the story. "The entire night I just kept slapping the exact same ace of queens down on the table time and time again."

"How did he not realise you were cheating earlier?" she cried.

"We may have been a little tipsy."

"I'm surprised he didn't kill you," she said between gasping breaths.

They had been riding all day through broken woodland. His mount "Highwind" was agitated. Erroh could sense its displeasure at their leisurely pace. Calm yourself silly beast. It's a beautiful evening, the land is opening up, and we will return to full pace come the morning.

"When I slapped the same card down three games in a row the massive brute finally drew his sword," he sniggered. "It was a fine blade too," he added. Trying and failing to remember any further details about the drunken card player.

"Yet, somehow you survived," she gushed wiping the tears from her dark, tired eyes.

"I happily exchanged monetary reparations with many apologies, and he saw sense. As big as Quig he was. Looked like him as well."

"You'll always find a way to talk your way out of anything," she jested, but her voice trailed off as a flicker of movement caught her eye in the distance. She wasn't quite sure what it was, through the thick briars and undergrowth.

"I can convince anybody to my way of thought, given enough time," he said.

"You convinced me, beo," she said and met his eyes. She wanted to kiss him.

"It's a good story," she said returning her eyes to the way ahead.

"I should work on some new stories. Maybe you'll show up in some too."

"Make me taller."

There was another flash of movement up ahead moving swiftly to the left. Perhaps it was boar. She grabbed her bow and notched an arrow straight away. Her horse whinnied, and Erroh finally noticed that all around them an eerie silence had fallen. It wasn't the silence of a beautiful goddess upon a stairwell nor the appearance of a decorative sword in the hands of a drunken fool. Something was out there.

Maybe it was a boar.

She held her breath and the taut cord. Her prey was

human. Her prey was not alone. Suddenly they heard a familiar and menacing hissing sound and a crossbow bolt embedded itself in a tree between the two Alphas. A second shot went through Erroh's calf and pinned him to the horse's side.

She heard him scream, and she froze.

Another bolt passed over her head and lost itself in the wilderness somewhere. The world was slowing down, and she was frozen. Highwind bolted, and Erroh cried out for her.

She was too scared to move, and he was gone.

A figure appeared in a gap in the trees atop a great war horse. The animal was magnificent. It was built for marching, battles and cold lands like the south. Monstrous and intimidating and it wouldn't stand a chance in a race against her own mount. The Rider was reloading a crossbow, and he wasn't doing it with any great haste either. He didn't realise his magnificent beast had wandered straight into her firing line.

Take the fuken shot while you still can, a voice whispered in her ear.

The Rider wore heavy leather and steel armour with a thick layer of animal fur underneath. His crude steel helmet covered only his head. Behind him, other Riders were charging. Was it a scouting party or the entire army? She looked past their charge and got an answer and her body went cold. The world went still. She thought of the little girl. She thought of Erroh. She held her breath and put the arrow right through the Rider's head. The only sound was the clink of the steel tip against the back of the helmet. He managed a final grunt as his limp body drooped and slumped over on his horse. The crossbow made more noise falling from his dead hands. His horse continued to walk forward slowly. She was a killer now, just like Erroh.

Another projectile flew past her ear. She heard the air screaming as it did and it roused the survivalist in her. It was only a breath since Erroh's panic-stricken mount had bolted, and she spun her own horse around and raced off in pursuit.

Highwind refused to break from her gallop. She vaulted through each and every obstacle in her path and tore the ground away with each powerful stroke, and Erroh was helpless. He pulled his foot loose and the animal cried in fresh pain. The bolt hadn't gone deep and only a small stream of blood trickled from the wound. She would heal easily enough, whenever she stopped running. He stared at the object that protruded from both sides of his boot. It hung and bled him dry as if he were nothing more than an archer's dummy but at least he would be a harder target to hit at this pace. He tried desperately to form coherent thoughts but most sense had abandoned him to the pain shooting up his leg. His eyes stung from tears and his lungs were raw from wailing for Lea to follow. He pulled desperately at the horse and felt a little give but Highwind was not ready to yield. For a few breaths more, they raced before he felt her resolve weaken a little. Branches and loose briars whipped and tore at his face but still he fought the animal until they broke through some heavy coverings out into an open meadow with waist high wild grass. It was here in the lazy evening sunset that she finally slowed and relinquished her control to her master. Behind him Lea emerged through the treeline, unharmed but for a few scrapes across her face. She'd never looked more beautiful. He would always remember how she looked in that moment before everything in the world turned to tragedy.

"Which way?" she screamed.

From beyond the treeline, he could hear the brutes atop

their bigger warring animals. He felt naked out in the open as Lea raced towards him, but he waited for her. He would not leave her behind again. What sounded like the felling of a hundred trees filled the air as their attackers drew nearer, and Erroh's mind raced.

What if this little dell was already surrounded?

What if there was a fatal arrow already notched?

What if he this was his last breath?

What if it was hers?

What route would bring them through this terror?

His eyes followed the river that would eventually lead them back to Keri through heavy undergrowth.

Their second route led back into the deep of the green. It was a fine place to lose themselves but a finer place to meet an ambush.

The third choice was an open pathway between two sets of treelines. It was the most obvious route for the pursuers to take as there was little cover but their mounts could charge as swiftly as the wind and speed was a fine advantage.

His mind was awash with plans. None of which were simple and none of which could work.

She pulled up beside him and reached for the arrow straight away. Their eyes met for a moment. Before he could give permission, the arrow was wrenched free and dropped into the grass beneath them. He let free a shriek and bit into the reins in his hands. Take the pain, a voice in his mind said. It may have been the echo of his father's teachings or it may have been the absent gods revealing themselves to him a little more each day. Behind them, the rumble of killers crashing through the woodland grew ever nearer, and he took the silent voice's advice. Take the pain for now and worry about the bleeding a little later.

"I killed one," she said in a voice she didn't recognise as

her own. Perhaps that was how it would be now that she'd drawn blood. Her eyes fell upon his foot and hatred overcame the terror and shock.

"We race the wind!" he roared and drove his beast out through the dell down along the narrow slit of green between the trees. He dared not look either side lest he see an inescapable ambush. He kept his eyes on the route ahead and willed his mount to carry them from harm's way. Soon enough the sound of their pursuers was lost to the delicious rush of wind and with a mile or so of clear path ahead a wonderful hope filled him. It was the right call, and she charged with him a few feet behind, her cries of encouragement to her charging mount matched his own. They raced the wind and lost.

He never heard the arrow and how could he?

It was from close range and that's what made the deadly projectile so devastating. They'd had the greatest intentions to fix her armour but there had been all the time in the world for such things. He heard her cry out. A screech of terror and wet agony that was terrifying like thunder. He looked behind and saw her leaning forward in her saddle. The reins had fallen from her hands. They danced and bounced majestically under each stride from the beast. Her hair was loose. It was beautiful and then he saw the arrow in her back. A trickle of blood came out of her mouth from biting down so hard on her lips, but she didn't scream. She held it in. She was so brave. He belonged to her, and he was supposed to protect her. She slipped from the horse's back, and he couldn't stop her falling. Her body was broken. She tried to break her fall with her hands but instead collapsed in a ruined heap in the dry grass. The arrow broke as she tumbled, and he leapt from his own mount to help her. He could see the little piece of splintered wood jutting out from a little hole below her shoulder blade. It was deep. Far too deep.

The Rider emerged from the bushes a few feet away still carrying his crossbow. He roared some unrecognisable language and reached for another arrow. Erroh saw tears streaming down her cheeks and her eyes blinked rapidly with every laboured breath she took. She was dying. He was no healer, but he could feel it and the absent gods? Well he couldn't feel them now at all.

A little further back Lea's vanquisher atop his warhorse casually began to reload. Without thinking, Erroh screamed and charged the brute furiously. He pulled Mercy from his back as he did and waited for the bolt to end his life. Unexpectedly, the Rider met the challenge. He dropped his crossbow, pulled an axe from his belt, and charged down on his prey. Perhaps it was honour among killers or pride in death that he relinquished his advantage, but he would never have a chance to regret it.

He attacked from high, but Erroh blocked with such fierceness that he knocked him from his saddle wherein Erroh pinned his axe wielding wrist with a foot and struck at his chest once, twice and then a third time. His sword cut through leather, steel, and flesh. When the Rider's howls fell silent and his body fell still, Erroh pulled his sword free and returned to his fallen mate. If there were other attackers, he would meet their attack in a similar way, but if these were her last moments, he would spend them holding her.

She looked up into his eyes and saw he was crying. "It really hurts, Erroh," she said faintly.

"We need to get you back to the town," he whispered and wiped the blood from her mouth. She was prettier that way.

"I don't want to move, Erroh. Just hold me for a moment."

There was a steady little flow of blood coming from her wound. She would likely be dead long before they made it back to the town but if he removed the arrow piece, she could bleed herself dry in a few painful breaths. He didn't have time to think and neither did Lea so he did the cruellest thing imaginable, and he did it selfishly.

"I have to get you up," he whispered.

"I cannot ride," she pleaded.

"You have to try."

"I'll never make it back. You have to leave me behind." She was so brave, and his heart was breaking.

"I love you," he whispered and ripped a piece of his shirt.

"I love you too." A silent tear slipped from her eye.

"I'm sorry," he said wrapping the cloth around the protruding piece of wood. Please let it stem the flow. She moaned in agony and it tore him up inside. It tore her up a lot more though. How could such a small insignificant piece of wood do such horror?

His clothes were damp. In fact, they were ruined. They were soaked in her blood. He wanted to burn them and wash himself clean but instead he wrapped a second tourniquet around his foot and embraced her before lifting her from the grass. She cried out loudly as he placed her broken body back onto the horse. He did so as gently as he could. It wasn't gentle at all. He cut the reins and using the rope, wrapped her wrists to the saddle tightly. "Hold on, my love," he whispered and meant it in many ways. He took the remainder of the rope and attached it to his own mount. He pulled himself gingerly on top of his own mount and slid his injured foot painfully into the saddle.

"It's them, Erroh. I saw them. Don't lead them back to the town," she begged weakly, and he heard the terrible sound again. A sound he'd heard once before all alone beside a rock.

Something akin to the sound of a thousand terrible things crashing through the undergrowth searching for a kill. He hissed his mounts to swiftness and they obeyed. Charging forward they escaped the noise and their attackers, but Erroh felt no relief this time. His race was only beginning.

He kept her dying wish as best he could. He drove both mounts through the undergrowth as night drew in and left a difficult set of tracks to follow. He knew every moment was precious, but he took rockier ground where possible. It was in the river many miles from where she was felled that he knew their scent had been lost. He led both horses through the cold water. Walking the beasts slowly across the uneven surface of the riverbed was harder than the most painful of sprints. Night was upon them and still there were so many miles left to walk. He allowed both beasts a precious few moments to drink from the cool water and regain some of their lost stamina. He walked them for a half mile upstream until he came upon a path that would easily conceal their tracks at first glance. If the Riders discovered the town, it would be through no fault of their own. He had done what she asked. He could do no more.

He kept his eyes on the way ahead in the dark light. He told himself that it was because he was wary of tripping and injuring his foot further but the truth was he was scared to look at her for very long. She hadn't spoken a word in hours. Her moans of pain were growing weaker and weaker and her delicate face was deathly pale. Her features were stretched and tight. So much blood lost, and she so very small.

"Not too far," he said quietly, pulling Highwind up the bank followed by Lea's proud mount "Shera." He patted the horse gently and willed her to stay strong for the final hour.

"One more time for Lea, my ladies." He kicked off and raced one last time. He could sense her slipping away into the darkness with each bump in the ground, each dragging pull of the cold wind and each exhausted mile taken. He felt the tears, streaming back down his face. Like a river that would never stop flowing. Like each lonely hill climbed, like the land which never seemed to end; there was still so far to go.

He knew he was running the horses into the ground. On some level of understanding, they felt her pain, and he loved them both a little for it. Around midnight he looked back and still she took breath. Cruelly enough he began to believe she was going to make it, but he soon lost that belief.

The road worsened as he neared the town, and she made no noise at all, despite Shera bouncing her broken body roughly as she tackled both uneven terrain and exhaustion. He dared a glance and his heart dropped seeing the outline of her listless body sagged across the saddle. Nothing held her but the ropes.

Brave Erroh, too cowardly to hold her in his arms and ease her passing into the night. She had looked so beautiful in yellow. He groaned but kept the race going and his mind turned to prayer, unworthy as his absent gods were. He begged them to take his life instead of hers. He cursed them and challenged, but his words were empty like his beliefs. "Fuk you!" he snarled at the end of the one-way conversation until the gods answered with a fresh downpour. Droplets struck his eyes blinding any vision he had, but the horses never faltered. They charged along the river, and he trusted them to take them the last leg of the journey. His fingers bled where he held the reins and his body shook from the cold, but that may have been shock. His mind was awash with sorrow and hate. His foot was a dull numbness ready to strike him down. For the briefest of moments, he considered giving up. Bringing the horses to a stop and taking her in his shivering arms and saying goodbye. Like he should have, many hours earlier before dragging her through so much torment just in the grim hope that she could be saved. He considered this, but he was a coward and never stopped the charge until they passed through a deep cluster of trees and met a familiar slope and a gap between the valleys. It was the most stunning sight he had ever seen, but he never let his mount slow. They raced through the opening, down past the first few houses before crossing the largest bridge and almost killing a few tipsy merry goers along the way. The noises of the horse's hooves on the cobblestone brought little relief, for he knew she had died a few hours back, but he was unable to stop. He had a race to complete. He had nothing else in the world, but he had that. He reached the centre of town and fell from the saddle in front of Emir's office. His screams for help were not silenced even as his face crashed into the cold wet stone. He could taste blood in his mouth but all that mattered were his wild calls for the wretched drunken healer. He tried to rise but his injured foot was still stuck to the saddle, and he thought how ridiculous he must look. He tried to free it but its numbness made it difficult. The world began to spin as running footsteps echoed all around him. There were a few shouts, curses, and hysteric arguments as a crowd gathered. He could hear the heavy panting of the mounts, and he screamed for Emir once more. He finally freed his leg, it fell painfully onto the ground, and he screamed as numbness made way to horrific agony. Some desperate hands helped him with the monumental task of climbing to his feet. Beside him, dark figures were tending to his mate. He reached out and touched her hand.

It was as cold as ice.

He collapsed and wailed to the absent gods for failing her. He pledged to seek out each one and slit their throats. The hands reached for him again and with no will to fight, he was hoisted from the cold and wet ground. Tears streamed from his eyes freely as he was carried like surplus lumber from a mill, ready for burning. So many voices but one familiar voice shouted out above the many. It was from a man he had met a lifetime ago. A man he had befriended.

"Let Emir see to her!" Quig roared and the crowd parted.

"Get them inside!" shouted another less familiar voice.

Erroh moaned miserably. He could have kissed her until she passed into the darkness, but he'd tortured her instead. Someone kicked the office door in, and Erroh was carried towards it. Another lit a candle, and he was brought into a cold room where he was dropped onto a hard surface waist high. He wondered absently how serious his own injuries were. Did he care if he'd join her in the darkness this night? Somewhere outside where rain still fell and races were lost, he heard some fresh bouts of shouting. They placed her gently on a long stone slab a few feet across from him, and he reached out to touch his beautiful mate. She looked just like a porcelain doll his mother had kept in her study. It had looked beautiful, perfect, and fragile.

"Who broke my fuken door?" shouted Emir stepping through the shattered doorway. Emergency or no, it was not right to break a healer's door. "Oh fuk," he whispered, seeing his patients for the first time. His head was spinning from the drink. This wasn't actually a problem. "Everyone, get the fuk out of this room now." This was his battlefield, and he was a general.

"Not you," the healer muttered to some unknown girl.

"Or you," he hissed at Quig who stood over Erroh looking troubled.

The sounds of conversation began to disappear outside in

the cold wet night, and Erroh felt a great exhaustion overcome him. He tried to lift his head but all strength deserted him.

"Go see if Erroh will be a distraction to me while I deal with Lea," All authority now lost from his voice.

"He looks fairly fuked," suggested the big man helpfully.

"Lea's barely breathing over here," muttered Emir. "She's in a lot worse shape than him, though," he added as if it was her own fault. It was not. It was Erroh's for failing her.

"Sorry, Lea," Emir muttered as he ripped the armour free. Lea's groan was almost inaudible but it was there. The healer slapped his cheeks sharply and shook his head to rouse himself. He inhaled a few deep breaths and the youngest ever master healer of Samara got to work earning his next pint of ale.

The girl was not yet lost to the night.

30

TALES FROM THE SPARK

1 24th Solstice 217 Spark City

That bitch Roja staked her claim on him as soon as she heard his line. Did I actually think she would pass up the opportunity? If she doesn't find a suitable mate in the son of Magnus then I don't think she ever will. She'll end up as Primary, just like her grandmother. Dia is dressing her for the position either way. Son of Magnus and granddaughter of Dia? It's quite the formidable partnership. I really don't want to think about that. His name is Erow or Eeero or something like that. He is remarkable. Lust at first sight? He is beautiful with his perfect jaw, blazing eyes, and adorable nose. Aye, that's right; he does have a nice nose. Ha, all the girls thought him incredibly pleasing to the eye. Maybe it was the manner in which he tore the Black Guards apart that caused such a stir around the chambers. We shouldn't have found it as arousing as we did but well, we did. Perhaps that's what swayed that red-headed bitch's mind. Of course, where there's a Roja, there's always her little witch friend Silvia following behind. Oh, to be a higher-lined female in this city. Just to have a voice that carried some favour. Thank the gods for my Lilli. As you know dear journal, she is highest line and I owe her so much. I'll forgive all the bets she owes me, for there are many. She's the reason I might have a chance with him. She'll challenge if Roja chooses him first and take the wrath, which comes with it. I can't challenge for that is not how things are. It would be in bad taste to challenge. It would be a terrible shame on my name and all that biased shit. We've all heard stories of Dia's actions when things don't go her way (when some of her females forget their place in the city). I will state my intentions after Lillium and the shame will be less severe. It is precarious at best but I will trust destiny to steer the Cull in my favour. Aye my dear journal, I know how naïve this all sounds and it is, but what choice do I have? Lilli has been mocking me all day since he entered the arena. She said I was glowing in the dark. She said it's "love at first sight, except he didn't see you." She was looking at him just as much as I was though and why wouldn't she? He's handsome and have I mentioned his nose? Joking aside, my Lillium is the truest friend a lower-lined Alphaline could have. We have decided that both of us must be ruthless to throw Roja off the scent. Lillium despises the south, and she despises Magnus, so I'd imagine she'd find it easy to attack Erroh. He will understand eventually when I'm wrapped up in his strong arms. I'm writing like a little cub. It was only the first meeting. It's the thrill of the Cull. He might turn out to be a weak-willed warrior with nothing but blood and war on his mind but still there's something about him. I love his walk. I'm excited and terrified about the whole event. I don't think it's hit me yet. Roja has competed in a few already. For such a tramp, she's quite fussy. As lowest line, I'm to lead the Cull. They say it's to create a fairer battleground between the lines but I've never heard of any victorious female who led a Cull. I know I should be jealous and worried that Lillium warms to him when we battle wits tomorrow but I trust her. Ha, she prefers the tall ones anyway. He's pretty and small just like me. I want him so I will make him mine. It is a simple plan.

125th **Solstice 217 Spark City**

Well, that could have gone a lot better. In fact, it was a disaster. He was drinking before we started. Do I need to say anything more? Is it any wonder nobody chose him? I'm not supposed to say anything of what occurs but it's late and my head is spinning from the glasses of magma Lillium has been serving all evening. He hurt me. Let's leave it at that. Okay, I'll elaborate slightly. He delayed accepting me and it was so humiliating. Lillium has been trying to comfort me all evening. I think she's mixing me another drink right now. She's searched for the words all night but what can she possibly say? "Oh, don't worry you're obviously his fourth choice, so hang in there." She had always intended to drop out after the first day, but she says she will battle wits with him once more. Perhaps she just doesn't want Roja getting him without a fight. I didn't press the matter. Fuk it. Is it wrong that I still like him? Perhaps I'm in denial or else I'm just a little too much like mother. I'm hiding in my room as I write this. Silvia told all who would listen of my shame and I'm the butt of every jest now. You would think it would take more than that to make me cry so pitifully. Rumours spread that Silvia would replace me as leader but if I walk away now, I'll never live the humiliation down. I am really drunk now. Lilli, if you've stolen these pages to read, I love you for helping me through all of this, even if you've no skill with a bow.

.   .   .

He did better today but it is all for nothing because
terrible things happened and I am to blame. He answered
everything honestly and we tore him apart for it. I joined in
too. It felt good and now as I write here I feel all the worse
for my behaviour. The Primary shared uneasy words with
Roja before the Cull. She wanted her to walk him through
testing the other Alpha males but Roja refused outright. I've
never seen anybody turn down the Primary's wishes but if
anybody can it is Roja. At this point, I wonder and worry why
she hasn't pulled out from this choosing? Perhaps it's her
blind devotion to Magnus or her allegiance to that little witch
Alexis. Ah, I'm being a little unfair to the girl. I barely know
her. Why blame her for Roja's sins? In truth, I'm angry at the
entire world tonight, dear journal. Let us forget the terrible
showing of the questions and focus on his testing of the
Alphas. I swear to the absent gods it was only one fight he
was to endure. He'll blame me and how could he not? We sat
near each other, and he shared his meal. Forget his perfect
nose for a moment. It is his eyes, which are most beautiful. I
could see a spark in them. He said sorry after I shouted at
him. He fuked up the apology but it's a small matter seeing as
I lied to him to get him to fight. "Silly Lea," I hear you say,
dear journal, and you are correct, but I honestly did it to
protect him. Who knew what recompense our petty Primary
may have fashioned had he refused? I'm such an idiot and to
my detriment, I fear I have lost him forever. He was amazing
in ill-fitting armour, and he never had a chance. I could hear
the crack of his rib from the rafters. Instead of allowing him
to attend a healer, Dia had him fight all three. I was not
allowed to see him between each bout either. Why did that
wonderful fool keep fighting? I think it likely his hatred for
all of us spurred him on, and as they tore him apart; my heart

broke (and my chances lost). I'm writing this with tears in my eyes. He was so brave. All three Alphas won the day and will have their suitors, Wynn more so than most. He is gorgeous and Lilli has put herself forward. She wept when she told me she was stepping away from Erroh. I imagine they were tears of relief. Sadly, Roja still maintains an interest. If she chooses Erroh, I don't care. I'll challenge and risk my honour and hope he picks me in return. We will be given an opportunity to address him and I will tell him of all my feelings. Surely, he wouldn't reject me if he knew the truth. Please Roja. Don't be in the Cull tomorrow.

If he is not chosen, I will declare myself.

127th **Solstice 217 Spark City**

He wasn't able to attend today. I pray he'll be there tomorrow. Roja and Silvia didn't seem to care a great deal. They spent the day drinking with a couple of young Wolves in a tavern. I heard them returning with only one of them a little time ago. I expect they've made a man out of him by now. Maybe between the shared groans and writhing mass of naked bodies they'll find true love this very night. Speaking of love. Lillium fell asleep talking about Wynn. She said he couldn't keep his eyes off her. This appealed to her greatly. I would imagine it is the nicest feeling. She very nearly chose him outright after one day but after the debacle with Erroh, I think she'll wait another day. I wish I had entitlements like her. Little things like a decent room without a breeze, a choice of fruits at meals and oh yes, the right to choose the man of my dreams without putting my name to shame. Lea, line of Wiiden and Amelia. It's hardly a title of great renown. Lillium is beside me, and she won't wake up. I'll just move her as far over the bed as possible and try get some sleep. I can only imagine the look on Wynn or Erroh's face if they were present. Two fine females to share a bed. It would certainly make for interesting conversation the following day. I'm sure Roja would agree.

128th Solstice 217 Spark City

He said he wanted Lilli the most. Well I'm sorry, Erroh, she has chosen Wynn, so that fuken ship has sailed. When I told Lillium what he said, her face dropped, and she cried. Then I started to cry. I can't believe how much I've cried because of that cur. Yet I still want him. Where's your pride, girl? I am my mother's daughter, and I will be alone forever. When the city and no mate want me, I will walk the wastes like some of the elder females have. I'll do it in my favourite yellow dress. I need another drink. I blame that stupid whore Silvia. I think I would have died a happier girl if that idiot had not asked such a ridiculous question. At least one thing I'm certain of is that neither girl really likes him. They enjoy their life here far too much. I heard there was some disagreement between them. It was about the young Wolf they took back to Silvia's room. Could just be more rumour though and they certainly wouldn't tell me. I don't care really. I only care about what a disaster everything is. Why did he say it? Why? Why? Why? It is no small matter. No small matter at all. I hate this Cull. I hate it so fuken much and I will claim victory. They asked to see his body and it was broken. I don't know how he was even standing. He looked right through me. Tomorrow I choose him no matter the cost. My stomach turned when I wrote that. This is all real. What if I'm wrong??? Of course, I'm wrong. I'm so scared and I think I'm going to throw up. The words are dancing. Why am I still writing this? I will face the wrath of Roja but the Cull has gone on too long. I've earned the right by now. It'll work out.

He broke my heart again. I just stared at the page for a few moments. I don't know what else to say. He was horrible today and drunk. Roja and Silvia both have stepped from the choosing. He's mine if I so choose but I need to think on matters tonight. I need some sage advice one last time from Lilli. She leaves early tomorrow with her perfect mate Wynn. They already kissed when they walked along the river. I foresee many children soon. She met with Erroh and was taken with him. She kept telling me how lovely he is outside the choosing. She talked more about him than Wynn. She fought his fight so much and I don't know what to do. We're having our final ever game as maidens in a little while. I can't believe she's leaving. She is taking everything in her stride. I will leave too with Erroh. Oh god. Mated with Erroh. I've heard his lands are beautiful. As long as we don't have to go south, I don't mind. I never want to walk south ever again. I never want to set foot in my father's stronghold ever again either. No, we will walk east and fall in love. Or fall apart. This is so scary. I've wanted this for so many years. We all have. Well most of us. Maybe we are meant to be together. Maybe we aren't. Maybe our love will soar like eagles in the sky, or else our hearts will be shattered in a hail of arrows. I'm so scared.

I am Lea mated with Erroh, Line of Magnus. I am mated for life and I am terrified beyond belief. Erroh looked confused and equally terrified. We must be perfect for each other after all. His fingers shook when we committed our signatures to the register. He couldn't look me in the eyes. I'm not surprised. We're going to meet for the first time later. I can't believe both Lillium and I are mated and leaving. Well, she's already left and all I have left is Erroh. My Erroh. That sounds weird to say aloud. Let alone write. Roja was really strange. She hugged me and congratulated me. She seemed genuine, grateful even. I don't know. It was nice. She still mocked me a couple of times but there was little malice in it. Have I mentioned how terrified I am? I'm really fuken terrified. I still haven't finished packing yet. I'm not sure I'm ready for all of this. That's a lie. I *know* I'm not ready for any of this but I'll be hopeful. Goodbye Samara, The City of Light. The first Spark since the new world and all that shit. You have fed, bedded, educated, and frustrated me. If I don't concentrate on all the pessimism, I feel exhilaration thinking of the future. My future. Our future. Walking hand in hand out in the wastes. I know we'll work through our problems. I'm looking forward to properly hunting again. It's been far too long. I should be ashamed of myself. I can't remember half the lessons for the road. It'll all come back to me. Until it does, my mate for life will look after me. For better or worse, we belong to each other.

I am Lea, mated to Erroh. May the gods help us.

31

REMEMBERED

The new door was a little heavy for the rickety old frame and it shook the whole building when it caught the wind and slammed itself shut. He looked out the window at the rain. It was certainly the season for it. The rain would eventually cause rust to form on the door. That would solve his problem. He missed his old door. It had been quite efficient at its job. Had the ever-obliging idiots waited a few seconds more he could have staggered through the rain with key in drunken hand. With the benefit of hindsight, he shouldn't have taken so long finishing that last drink.

Emir sat upon his wooden stool and sighed loudly as he flicked to the next page. Lea had such beautiful penmanship apart from the more drunken passages. He knew it was an invasion of privacy but it didn't discourage him from reading it. It never occurred to him to feel bad about it either. Their courtship was a riveting read. Besides, it was a perk to his job, as he would never accept any additional payment to his weekly town wage for doing what came naturally to him. Lea tried to shift positions again. She grumbled and complained a few times in her stupor. He tore his eyes away from the journal to watch her closely. The restraints around her small wrists were cutting into her pale skin again but at least there were the first signs of a healthy blood flow in her body. She lay on her stomach, but her face rested in a silk pillow, it was the only comfort he could safely offer her. Her fever had broken and come dawn she would be through the worst of it. She shifted and caused the fine strands of rope to tighten. He wondered if she were capable of breaking the ropes that held her safely in place. He smiled away the superstition. She was strong. Stronger than most, but she was no godlike creature to be feared. He knew most tales of Alphas were just legend.

They were human. They were just a bit better at it.

Beside her Erroh stirred. He was stooped in his seat with his head resting against hers. He'd never left her side this last week. Things had obviously improved between them after the Cull. Emir slipped the journal back into her bag. The perfect crime. He thought again of their unique kind. Erroh had barely groaned as he'd dug into the wound and cleaned it. Alphas were known for a higher pain threshold. It wasn't intrinsic in their genealogy. It was dedicated training, and he must have faced some brutal training. The son of Magnus. The actual son. It was hard to swallow so he chewed on it a little more and still could barely contain his awe. He sipped his cofe and grimaced at the taste. It was bitter, cold, and lacking any character. He reached across his desk and poured some clear liquid into the mug. Much better.

"I'll take a glass," whispered Erroh, breaking from his vigil. He stretched his aching body and stifled a cough trying not to disturb her. Her colour had improved. He offered a prayer up to the gods. *You weren't able to kill her. I have less need to spill your divine blood.* He felt warmer believing in something other than himself, even if he hated whatever it was.

"Cofe or sine?"

"Both," Erroh said yawning. He took the mug from the doctor and drained the contents with great skill. He watched the little wisp of air escape the mouth of his mate. The old white tiles that covered the room reminded him of cleanliness. Her eyes were closed, and he suddenly worried that she wasn't warm enough. The little fire in the corner of the room suggested decoration over practicality. Any heat seemed to disappear long before it reached either of them. He adjusted the blanket to cover an exposed shoulder. Her skin was still hot but Emir was confident that she was recovering well and if that's what the healer believed, that was good enough for him. Emir had his trust. He remembered watching the drunk healer working his fingers deep in her wound. He remembered his calm determination as he battled the darkness for her life as if it was no matter at all. As if an artist searching for inspiration his scalpel cut and tore until what remained was a masterpiece.

"I have seen far worse," the artist of blood had muttered that terrible night.

"Her body looks broken," Erroh had said.

"Some bodies take more breaking than others," Emir had muttered, many breaths later.

"And some a little less," Erroh had said.

"I've seen a man take four arrows and still live," the artist of blood had said as the first rays of dawn lit up the room and warmed their faces.

"That cannot be true. That would be the actions of gods," Erroh had said.

Emir had looked up from Lea's broken form and peered curiously at Erroh. "Aye, gods."

. . .

Erroh ran his fingers along one of her binds and willed her pain to strike him down instead. He marvelled once more at her bravery and wondered would he be capable of such courage when facing death? He stroked her long black hair and doubted himself for a few breaths.

"I'll stoke up the fire before I leave," whispered Emir, stretching the fine stretch of a man who'd enjoyed an evening reading matters that he had no right to be privy to.

"She'll be alright?" Erroh asked.

"She's a tough girl."

"What if I need to get you?"

"I'll be with Aireys all night, so I won't be too far away," Emir said and held his hand out to pat the back of the ferocious Alpha. Emir had no skill at reassuring people. Especially fire breathing Alphas. Still, Erroh was a good soul. He went against his instincts and patted him on the back. Son of Magnus. Fuk.

"Thank you," muttered Erroh. He would not believe she was through the worst, until she opened her eyes and spoke clearly. Whatever magical remedy Emir had used on her had taken away some of the pain and most of her sobriety.

"I'll be at the Sickle for a time. I'll tell Jeremiah you're asleep and not to be disturbed." The mayor had taken it as an affront that guests were accosted while theoretically still in Keri territory, and was unyielding in his pursuit of finding their attackers, not even considering the thought that it would be safer for the town to draw as little attention to itself as possible.

"I appreciate it," Erroh whispered.

"He'll get the full story eventually, though," warned Emir.

"The longer it takes the harder it will be to track the Riders and less chance the Regulators will leave fresh tracks back here," said Erroh moving his fingers back to her hair and running a few strands gently through his raw fingers.

"You're going to spend the night sitting beside her aren't you?" Emir said stoking the flames with a poker. The fresh heat surged out but was quickly lost in the chill. It was a small matter. The embers were soothing to stare upon.

"Aireys and I may stop by before we retire for the night," Emir said and caught his own smile swiftly. He was still getting used to the idea of Aireys being more than just a friend. There must have been something in the air that night. Aireys had pulled him from the melee after flooring his attacker with a deceivingly vicious left hook. That sudden show of delicious violence was likely what won his drunken heart. Looking up at the girl a full foot taller in heels, Emir had to admit there never appeared to be a more unlikely partnership yet it mattered little to her. She had led him from the tavern, through the rain in unusual silence and tended to his minor injuries in her house. The opportunity to leave just never seemed to arise. The night continued, fuelled by a fresh bottle of wine and witty conversation. Listening to the rain against the roof in a cosy room decorated in paintings he'd never felt more at ease. He spoke of bitter things, which made her laugh and shake her head as though his cynicism was a simple veneer to cover his true feelings. A stained easel stood proudly in the corner, and she roused him from his wretchedness by talking passionately about her painting. He had never wanted to leave, and she had not asked him to. Offering him a bed in the spare bedroom, she took him by the hand and led him upstairs where fighting disappointment that the night had ended, Emir thanked her with a kiss that dear friends often shared. It had been a fine kiss just wide of the cheek. Perhaps closer to the lips. In truth, upon the lips. When he hesitated in pulling away he knew things were about to become awkward. When he felt her tongue, he knew things were about to become very interesting. Removing each other's clothes had felt like the natural thing to do. After many hours of breath-taking furrowing, he had expected the gentle push off in the blazing sunny morning and a few silences at the card table the following night. He had not expected a magnificent breakfast and certainly not the lunch she dropped in later at his surgery while he stitched up another subdued citizen. She had seemed a little embarrassed and unsure what else to do, holding the basket with far too many delicacies. He had never seen her lost for words so he had kissed her and asked if she would meet in the evening. This pleased her greatly. Then Lea and her arrow slowed down their progress somewhat.

"You're certain she'll be fine?" Erroh asked one last time for safety.

Emir buttoned up his jacket and opened up his brand new, annoying door. They hadn't even painted it yet.

"She'll be fine. If you won't join us for an evening's entertainment at least try to get some rest," he suggested before disappearing out into the night. The wind caught the door and slammed itself shut causing the building to shake and Lea to wake with a start.

She jerked against the white holding binds. "It's alright, my beo," he whispered stroking her hair as she fought the blur of painkilling syrup. He knelt down so she could meet his eyes.

"Erroh?" she croaked in an unrecognisable voice. She tried to move her arms again and discovered her legs were also bound. Her eyes began to clear, and Erroh finally began to relax. No fever left at all.

"The binds are to keep you still, while sleeping," he whispered and lay his hand on hers.

"They really hurt."

"If you hurt yourself again, Emir will kill me," he said and began to unwrap the restraints. She lifted herself up onto her elbows and then suddenly whipped her arms in to cover her exposed breasts. Erroh diverted his eyes though he grinned. She was far more alert than she had been for days.

She sat up gingerly, held a sheet against her skin, and draped her magnificent legs down the slab.

"I don't remember very much," she said in that same croaky voice. He passed her a glass of water, which she took and sipped slowly. She did everything slowly. She looked so delicate and exposed. Her frame looked like it would shatter under any strain. She was so beautiful.

"Anything stronger?" she joked, coughing the rawness from her voice while blinking the sleep and weariness from her eyes.

"Now you're talking like me," he whispered and resisted the urge to tear her stitching with a passionate hug.

"I really must be badly injured so," she smiled reaching out and tugging weakly at his hair.

"Seeing as you're awake now, I thought I would finally take all the pleasure of your body."

"Well you've certainly prepared my outfit for such a disappointing experience," she said before exhaling deeply, and Erroh could see the pain in her face.

"My Alphaline hero," she whispered, and he fell silent.

How could he tell her that his heart was broken at the thought of her in such a state? How could he say he would forgo his oath and live a safe life with her and her alone?

How could he put all his love for her into simple words and expect them to mean a fraction of what he truly felt? How could he tell her he only saved her because he couldn't be without her?

He couldn't.

"You're good at catching dinner, so it seemed like a waste," he whispered, and she laughed as if this was exactly what she expected him to say.

A few white candles flickered as they burned away the last remnants of the dark. Erroh thought about the deadly race to get her to safety, and he suddenly wanted to reach out and take hold of her, but he knew she would snap in two if he did. As if to reaffirm his worry, she coughed weakly.

"I feel like shit," she said sipping the water and wiping her mouth.

"You've certainly looked better," he said lightly before taking a shallow breath and exhaling slowly. He took her hand and kissed it. Too close my dear. Let's never come this close to doom ever again.

"My head is spinning. I think I'll lie back down," she said quietly, gently pushing some of her hair behind her ear and still somehow managing to be stunning this close to death.

"I have to tie you back down."

"I'll be fine. Let Emir be mad at me." She lay down in the bedding of stone and thin blanket. A bed fit for a queen. "This beats the cold mud," she muttered as he propped her up with a pillow.

"Will you climb up and hold me until I fall asleep?" she asked drowsily.

"As you wish," he said and, ignoring discomfort, held her broken form.

"I thought you were going to leave me to die on the road."

He hushed her to silence. Silly female. As if he would

ever leave her behind again.

"You should have," she added nuzzling against his shoulder. She kissed his neck and relaxed her head on his arm.

"But I'm glad you didn't," she sighed dreamily.

"I'll never leave you, Lea."

"So I'm stuck with you?" she asked as her eyes opened and closed battling sleep.

"Aye, you're stuck with me for the now."

"I'll keep you until the morning at least. For now you make a grand pillow," she said.

"There are worse fates," he whispered.

"You should go play some cards," she whispered weakly.

"I won't leave you," he reminded her but sleep had already taken hold.

Summoning all the skills acquired over the tough years on the road, Erroh released himself from her loving embrace without waking her. He stepped onto the ceramic floor and tested the strain on his own stitches. Satisfied it was going to hurt for a while he sat by the fire and thought dark thoughts, for that is what a young Alphaline was inclined to do after blood has been spilled. It was a justified kill on his part but more than that, he imagined Magnus grinning. His father had declared that whenever Erroh mated for life he would sacrifice everything for her. At the time, Erroh had argued such a thing was a weakness in his character. Magnus had laughed heartily, and Erroh had felt like a little cub. Fair enough, Dad. All this love for a girl he had known only a handful of months. Not even mentioning that he still hadn't tasted the true gifts she had to offer as well. That too would likely make Magnus laugh. His arm began to itch, so he took his ragged shirt off and placed it neatly beside his stool. He reached over and retrieved Vengeance from its scabbard. He watched the twinkling reflections of the burning amber in the razor sharp blade. It was beautiful.

He placed the sword carefully against the old blackened steel grate, leaving the tip to play in the flames. He tried to remind himself that his victim had merited such a fate but guilt was difficult to be rid of. He'd relished vanquishing the man but what madness had made him charge him down without seeking cover? What type of person had such a bloodlust? Magnus? Elise? Was this how it started? Was this the first step to becoming a warmongering legend like his father? He wasn't his father. For one thing, he lacked the same brilliant mind for war. When Magnus's army marched, the entire world held its breath. When Erroh marched, it was more like a shuffle. He could be no legend. He could be no king.

Erroh checked the blade. It was the hissing of burning steel, which he hated the most. Not to mention the bubbling of skin. Oh, he hated that as well. The tip trembled in front of his eyes. He hated this process but in a way, he loved it. Some fiends needed to be remembered. He glanced over to make sure she was asleep for this part of the ritual. She would find her own way to handle the taking of a life.

He would see to it.

Picking the spot to tattoo himself he took a deep breath and hesitated. The tip wavered precariously over the carefully chosen spot. He could feel its sharp heat. He wondered how many lives had this Rider taken? How many females had fallen in the flames? He released his breath and slowly took the blade away. Somehow, the men before who had fallen to Erroh's steady hand were better than this brute.

Some enemies did not deserve to be remembered.

32

HUNTING THE DEVIL

"This rain will be the death of me," muttered Quig, buttoning up his grey long-coat and tightening the scarf around his neck. Erroh sat on top of the wall alongside and chewed his apple. This was not rain. This was just low cloud. Lea sat under a branch of a tree enjoying her first day of freedom since her injury. Emir had cut off her medicine a few days before, insisting that nothing good would come from additional dosages and now that the last of the headaches, chills, and grinding muscle pains of withdrawal had ceased its assault, she was ready to face the world once more, albeit in the rain.

"I think Erroh could offer a few pointers," suggested Emir facing Quig in the sparring circle. He held a wooden sword in his hand and a shield in the other. Lea's attack had stripped them of the belief that their town was safe and though such a revelation brought little reassurance, holding a blade somehow made it easier. Wooden or not.

"I'm only good with a poker," said Erroh slicing another piece of apple with a little knife. He offered a piece to Lea and then to Aireys who watched intently as her boys battered each other senseless. She wore a lazy contented grin on her face despite the heavy feeling in the air.

"I'll take any instruction from a poker-waving wanderer at the moment," the healer suggested.

They heard the gentle clipping of three sets of horseshoes on cobblestone and instead of offering a witty retort, Erroh cursed instead. A fine curse with the right amount of profanity and crudeness and just loud enough that Jeremiah atop his steed could hear it as well. Erroh understood that the Holy Mayor was attempting to procure justice but every day his insistent prying increased. Erroh's suggestion to "leave things as they lay," hadn't been acknowledged, let alone discussed. So every day with all the good intentions that would likely see the town burned to the ground, he sent out his loyal Regulators to scour the land in search of their accosters. However, not before a few "further enquiries," in the hope of learning any details which would help, no matter how insignificant they may be. Erroh's skill in deception had increased with each bout of practice. Today was no different.

"You don't appear to be interested in retribution, do you, my friends?" the Holy Mayor asked pleasantly, though his exasperated eyes focused upon Lea. Emir had protected her behind the cold walls of his office but now, in the open air, she was fresh blood for questioning. She looked away and found a piece of bark to be incredibly interested in. It was brown.

Erroh spat an apple pip away. "It was a hunting accident, sir." It was the third time he'd suggested such a thing, and he knew Jeremiah saw through the lie.

"Perhaps it would be best not to go hunting the devil, lest you find him," said Emir in fluent holy speak. On occasion he'd read some of Jeremiah's book as well.

"The devil is everywhere," replied Jeremiah, preparing a sermon in his mind.

"Yet your sheep can't seem to find him. Nor should they try," interrupted Quig. Emir laughed louder than was necessary. His eyes challenged the mayor. Perhaps it was the affection for Aireys or perhaps it was his distaste of anything involving leadership.

"The Primary does not share your fears. So why should you?" the Holy Mayor asked.

It was Aireys who spoke and her words were cutting. "You think the Primary is all knowing? You think her all compassionate? You think this town matters to her a thousand miles from her city gates? You think this town could survive any attack? You think we could defend ourselves if any brutes lay siege upon us? Your Regulators will lead doom to us all. You have lost your head, Mayor," she said angrily, each question louder than the last, and he offered nothing more but a weak smile. He looked to the heavens and ordered his three men to ride out into the wastes, and in beaten silence he turned his own beast around and returned home to seek guidance in prayer.

"Is it really all as bad as we fear?" Quig asked tugging at his beard absently as the Mayor disappeared.

"I think we're all going to die. Especially me," Emir said feigning a grin. Nobody disagreed. He tossed Erroh a sparring sword. His eyes were pleading even if his manner was casual while Aireys's eyes narrowed to slits. Though nobody had brazenly come out and said anything, after the disagreement with Stefan, it was apparent Alphas now walked among them. Some said they could survive a brace of arrows. Others said at least double that. A small number decided that they bled like everyone else. Aireys wished to see just how skilled their kind were.

"If you start losing, just kick him in the leg," Lea suggested helpfully, and Erroh shot her a betrayed glance. After stretching a few times he grabbed a second sword and did his flashy spinning technique thing with both blades.

"Well that's terrifying," muttered Emir. Nobody disagreed either.

Both Quig and Emir took turns being knocked to the wet ground but what impressed Erroh most was how eagerly they returned to battle. In Emir's case, it was to save face in front of his lady and for Quig it was the sheer challenge of it. He even laughed a few times as he was tripped and sent flying while trying to kick at Erroh's injured leg. Though he wasn't built for grace, he was certainly built for power. Quig's massive frame was capable of crushing the life out of him if Erroh let him get too close. There were certainly worse opponents, and Erroh soon found himself enjoying the skirmishes.

Lea marvelled at Erroh's fierce speed and wondered how far she had come, that she could face his ferociousness and hold her own. Her shoulder ached but the exhibition took her mind off it. Her fingers twitched and her eyes counted combinations, and she saw the fight slower than the world turned, and she craved to be part of the violence something fierce. A strange thought occurred to her: that she was turning into a warmonger like her mate. Like her father. Like almost every other Alpha, scribed for greatness in the annals of Samara. She thought about the sound of a wet arrow hitting the back of a helmet, and she wondered if she had come too far?

. . .

"We could always leave the town and find a sanctuary?" suggested Emir, holding up his hand while he got his breath back.

Quig took the opportunity to grab some water and regret his current life choices. He didn't hate Emir's suggestion. "I hear the weather is nice in the Spark." He'd always wanted to travel the road like so many wanderers. Perhaps search for his lost lineage. It was a fool's thought. He would likely never leave Keri.

"Is there any stronghold closer?" asked Lea.

"Nothing as secure as a town filled with so many aspiring soldiers. Myself included," said Aireys. It was easy to read the desolation on her face. She was a fine fighter, but she was no hardened warrior. "Maybe we could hold out with a proper defence," she added trying to rise above the mood.

"We could hammer our fists on the gates of the Spark and demand entry," Emir said unperturbed that the Primary would not allow them entrance into her little kingdom.

"You would be hammering quite a time, but the Spark is the better of suggestions. Especially if Lea was with you," Erroh said, ignoring the glare from his beloved. Where he went, she went. Had he forgotten already?

"Why so?" asked Quig curiously.

Because she's an Alpha like you?

"She knows the city quite well," Erroh said.

Aye, an Alpha so.

"So we should convince our brothers and sisters to flee this town?" asked Quig.

"There is still the matter of the second town we came upon who tried to flee and were chased down, slaughtered and burned to nothing," said Lea.

"Are all you Alphalines so negative all the time?" asked Quig.

Silence.

Erroh shrugged. "You should see what we're like when we're left alone in the dark."

"Or thrown into rivers," added Lea. Their eyes met and they smiled.

"None of this is fair," said Emir and picked up his sword. They were damned to hell either way.

"Then again, the Riders may simply never discover this place," Erroh said tossing a sword to Aireys and beckoning all three to face him.

Emir attacked first. Emir always attacked first. It was as if he couldn't help himself. Quig would charge from behind the smaller man and swing wide powerful blows. Erroh would sidestep both men and withdraw from their attacks, leaving no opening in his guard for the graceful Aireys to take advantage of. Her form surpassed both Quig and Emir together. She struck relentlessly and viciously like any respectable killer and danced away. She was worthy of the title of grand champion but even she couldn't penetrate Erroh's defence. As he repeatedly blocked, parried and countered he heard his father's whispered suggestions in his mind and followed them unquestioningly. Any warrior could be talented at attacking, but in defence against numerous foes was where he excelled. He was an Alpha with two masters though. His second blade served as his shield and it served him as Jeroen gently insisted it would, and despite so many blades spinning and stabbing, he effortlessly stepped through the carnage delivering blow after killing blow to his opponents without breaking his guard. He was built for war but more than that, he was built to survive war.

Lea saw a crimson patch of blood from broken stitching around his foot yet still he moved as if it were a stroll in a lush meadow. If he was in pain, he showed nothing to his opponents. He was serene within devastation, and she craved to stand with him.

A few hours later, they parted ways drenched in sweat and mud. For Quig it was to tend to his fields. For Emir and Aireys it was to seek victory in another sort of battle while Erroh took Lea by the hand to the outskirts of Keri.

There was one more wound.

They rested for a time at the bottom of one of the great valley walls before carefully climbing to the top of the natural fortification. The sun was beginning to set and the land was still. Evergreen trees and withering shrubbery lined the top and they found a smooth log to sit. The wind caught her hair, and he stroked her arm tenderly as they gazed over the edge to the rest of the wastes below them. It was a fine view at least fifty or sixty feet high to the sloping ground below and at least four or five times that to the dark forest below.

"Do you think an arrow could reach the forest with that strong arm of yours?" he asked.

"I could do it against the wind," she said quietly and hugged herself subconsciously.

"Oh, I know that, but with your shoulder as it is now."

"Emir would be furious," she said, and he laughed.

"It was a good kill," he said suddenly. She said nothing, but he heard her breath cut itself short. She took one of his hands in hers and failed miserably in trying to find the words.

"It's a lovely view," she finally managed.

"A good spot alright. It's a fine thing we're both here to witness it."

"Thanks to you, beo," she said. Her lips trembled a little and her face drained itself of any colour. Perhaps he should have waited a day or two more.

"He deserved it," she said coldly, pushing herself away from him. She got to her feet and stepped a little closer to the edge.

"He did," replied Erroh.

"He did," she repeated to herself. Her hair danced wildly in the wind's invisible hold. Each gust willed her to fall from the great height, but her balance kept her steady. She remembered the blank look in the Rider's eyes as the arrow sent him into the darkness forever. She was a killer, and he deserved it. They all did. She stepped back from the edge and threw up in a defenceless little bush.

"There's a lot of death coming, isn't there?" she said wiping the bile from her mouth.

He nodded.

"It'll never get any easier killing. Sometimes, I struggle to walk with the weight," he said quietly. She collapsed in his arms and sobbed quietly.

After a time when her eyes ran dry and the wind cut through even the warmest of embraces she stroked his face. "Next time I won't hesitate."

———

All lanterns were extinguished and after last calls, drunken patrons made their merry way home. Some battered and bruised. Some in the arms of their new-found lovers. Some alone, thanks to some new dental work. As the hour of the witch approached, the whole of Keri found itself still and peaceful like the rest of the natural wastes.

One flame remained fighting the good fight against the darkness however. An ancient grey candle gave off just enough light to see in a dark room with barely any decorations. Inside Jeremiah read the thin pages of his book. His nervous thumb struggled to turn each page though he knew most passages by heart. A glass of red wine with an empty bottle stood at his desk. He paced back and forth but couldn't shake the terrible thoughts from his mind. The wine was taking a little edge off but not enough to offer any relief. He had a plan to finish the bottle and move onto the next. It was all in the God's name. He took to his knees again and whispered words to the heavens above. He did not expect an answer, what type of god could be expected to answer every prayer anyway?

What type of man would need that?

He prayed for himself.

He checked the window again and peered out into the lonely night. It was late. It was well past late, and his Regulators still hadn't returned.

33

REID

E very afternoon they met in the town centre and waited for Aireys. As head of Keri council, she frequently fought the good fight with Jeremiah over town matters but it was a struggle to convince him of the new threat the town now faced. With face flushed and knuckles white, she would leave his office and vent her frustrations with wooden blade and shield. She struggled to compete with Erroh but their daily skirmishes swiftly caught the attention of the town's inhabitants and such a spectacle brought fine political aspirations. She lost every fight, but she never gave in. It was the makings of a fine mayor and of a legend too.

When the Regulators finally did return, Erroh, Lea and Quig were sitting at a bench below the political office waiting for her. To amuse themselves they argued with Emir over the significant value of salt to the world. Quig had suggested it was one of the more colourful ways to evoke an infuriated overreaction from the diminutive healer, and he had not been wrong. The town was enjoying a blue sky without a cloud and there was a suggestion that this season's warmth would drag on for longer before the wet months took hold. There

were worse places to be and there were worse arguments to
be had.

"You're not listening. It's not just for making food taste
better," the healer said.

"But you will admit that it adds to a stew," suggested Lea.

Emir shook his head. "It does, but that's not my point."

"See now, I don't like salt in my stew. I like pepper," said
Quig raising one hand. He thought it a fine gesture to
accentuate his point.

"Though both do make a fine combination," Erroh
pointed out.

Two dishevelled figures upon horses rode by them in
mute silence. Their heads were bowed and their clothes were
muddied and worn. Perhaps had there been three riders, the
friends may have taken greater notice.

"Pepper is far more important than salt in a good stew and
it also makes you sneeze which is wonderful as well," said
Quig licking his lips and thoroughly enjoying the torment of
his friend.

"It's true, salt doesn't make you sneeze at all,"
agreed Lea.

Emir suddenly realised the rise they'd earned. "Oh fuk off
the lot of you." After a moment, he laughed too.

"I knew a man who liked to put sugar into his stew,"
Erroh said after a thoughtful pause.

"Sugar is fine for a stew but finer for a cup of tea. No
need for salt in tea, that's just madness," said Lea.

"Fine, I won't keep going on about the incredible
medicinal and indeed practical uses of salt any more but let it
be known that I hate you all," muttered Emir laughing.

The two figures dropped from their mounts. Both wore

grim expressions and made no eye contact with any passers-by. A cloud of despondency hung above them. They tied their horses to a post across from the mayor's office, walked up the wooden steps, and entered the doorway without invitation. After a time Aireys appeared but it wasn't to engage in friendly combat. It was to request the presence of Erroh to discuss worrying events.

———

"Please, Fabien, tell the tale again for the Alpha," asked Aireys softly.

Erroh noticed the haggard man's hands. They shook dreadfully as he gripped the glass of wine. His companion leant against the far wall. He too shared the same shocked and exhausted expression. His glass was already empty and Jeremiah was preparing a refill. Fabien took a deep breath and began to recite the tale that would likely lead to all their deaths.

"We followed the river for a day and picked up a few tracks," he whispered. "It was Reid's idea to stay out longer." His voice rose and broke at the mention of the third Regulator. Jeremiah refilled his drink. It was all he could do.

"On the third day following the tracks, we discovered at least a thousand brutes readying themselves for war."

"And plenty of cavalry," said the second man from behind them. His eyes were vacant. A few drops of wine rolled down his chin, but he didn't care to notice. Most knew him as Hale.

"They were camped along the river," Fabien continued. "Reid wanted to know if they would favour any peace," he whispered and took a breath. Jeremiah's skin had taken an ashen look. He watched both Regulators for sign of any top ups. It seemed incredibly important that they have full glasses. If nothing else, he would manage that. "He had his arms raised and carried no sword as he approached, and they just grabbed him and slit his fuken throat."

Silence.

"Flung him into the river as if nothing had happened," Hale said, and Jeremiah opened another bottle.

"We could only watch," muttered Fabien. His composure broke, and he wept tears for his fallen friend.

"May the lord have mercy on his beautiful soul," said Jeremiah and wiped a tear of his own. He would cry aloud when nobody was there to watch.

"We watched them in secret for two days," said Hale.

"They move slowly and only follow the river," Fabien said. He held his hand over his eyes and sniffed pitifully.

"That river?" asked Erroh, looking out the window at the great raging beast that flowed right through the town.

Both Regulators nodded and cold shivers ran up Erroh's spine.

"This town will fall," growled Erroh. Anger flowed through him. He gripped one of his wooden sparring blades as though it was steel, and silently cursed the unknown army and then himself. He'd begun to fall for this town's charm and naivety. He'd almost believed the walls would conceal them all.

"That's why I called you in here, Alpha," said Aireys. He thought it was strange not calling him by his name twice.

"You're trained to think like a conqueror," she said and dared not meet his eyes. If she was insulting him, apparently she didn't want to see.

"I'm just a man," Erroh said, watching the river flow through the edge of the valley.

"You are more than that," she challenged.

Like the Alpha that he was, he shrugged weakly. If they

wanted him to meet this army and defeat them, they were grossly overestimating an Alphaline's ability. Was Aireys aware he couldn't actually breathe fire?

In truth though, he had thought like a conqueror. He had never stopped formulating plans since he had arrived. Intricate plans. Simple plans. All of the plans. It would all depend on the people of the town. It would also depend on himself and Lea. Deep down fearful thoughts reminded him that this was not his land; this was not his fight.

He wondered what his father would think.

"How long do we have before they land on us?" Aireys asked.

"Three or four days at most," said Fabien. His head began to shake. This debriefing needed to end soon. They looked to the Alpha in the room for an answer.

"You know my feelings, Aireys. The people need to be told. Only then can you make decisions," Erroh said before bowing and leaving the office. After a few moments, Aireys followed behind him leaving the holy man to tend to his flock. He had no comforting words to offer, but he knew he had a third bottle somewhere.

———

Word of the urgent town meeting spread like wildfire. Rumours abounded of a large force marching on Keri. When Lea and Erroh entered the square, the densely gathered people quickly parted for them right up to the stage. In times of war, those who were fearful turned to the strongest warriors. Apparently, it was good to be the king. Standing on the wooden platform was Jeremiah, Aireys, and one other Regulator, a tall warrior in a long brown coat and a receding hairline that belied his age. His eyes scanned anxiously at all around him but his demeanour remained calm and relaxed. A man used to keeping things to himself.

Jeremiah addressed the crowd first. He retold the incidents of the past few days with more truth than Erroh expected. He added little honey to his words and allowed the fear to show in his face. When someone interrupted him with roars of how Keri was "a fighting town," a few brave warriors cheered their enthusiasm for a resistance. They were passionately unyielding. They were courageously hopeful. And they were gloriously foolish. The town had never fallen. It never would. Could it? More voices joined in and jokes were thrown around gleefully. How quickly their fallen comrade was forgotten. Jeremiah reeled them back in desperately. He did something Erroh didn't expect, or want.

He confirmed rumours of other towns and the slaughter of defenders who stood their ground and the slaughter of the ones who tried to run. When the crowd fell to an eerie silence, he pointed to Erroh and Lea and confirmed their pedigree. Lea dipped her head in embarrassment while Erroh stared straight ahead as though he was playing cards. Only his left hand making a fist offered any suggestion that he was angry. Aye, many suspected seeing his ability in the sparring ring but still, fuk the mayor for confirming it. Fleeing under the cover of darkness just became that little bit harder.

"We are caught between two actions!" roared Aireys, eying the mayor. It would appear she thought revealing their lineage was an underhanded tactic as well. "Do we wait for their attack and hope we can hold them? Or do we leave for a sanctuary?" she asked and many voices replied for they had never tasted the horror of real battle. They cried out that Keri was a town of fighters and forbade talk of cowardice. Keri was their home and it would not fall. All they needed was alcohol and blades. Walls and grit. Fire and arrows. Perhaps a gate? Roars became camaraderie and crude jests elicited laughter and shallow bravery at the expense of the unknown foes. It was here that Aireys and Jeremiah finally found common ground. They met each other's eyes and acceptance reached them both. They were both vying for control of a town brimming with idiots. For a breath, Aireys could almost see the world through the eyes of Emir. It was like the fuken festival all over again.

And then Erroh climbed up on stage and started to talk.

They hung on his every word as he stripped them of their delusions. He was a lion and they were nothing more than little lost lambs. None of them realised just how lost they were.

"With a dozen Alphas fighting by your side, this town will fall and any attempting to hold will fall with it," he said loudly, and his words echoed around the square. "If we attempt to flee, we will be tracked down and slaughtered by their cavalry long before we reach sanctuary. Our one chance is for a few warriors to hold this town for as long as possible. To halt their pursuit. If only for a day." He took a breath and looked around. He needed to be careful with his next few words.

"For those who choose to stay there will be no salvation. But some must stay behind."

His feet creaked on the wooden boards underneath, and he wondered would it shatter under his weight. It would be a fine sight for those in need of inspiring sights. An Alpha with flailing arms collapsing in a grand heap of soon to be firewood.

Firewood.

They took it in and digested it slowly among themselves.

He wondered how Magnus would have fared speaking to such a crowd. Far better no doubt. He was not his father and there were horrific decisions to be made. He wasn't sure he was up to the task.

He glanced across at the two most powerful people in the town and realised his opinion was valued far higher than any others. He felt dizzy looking out over the hopeful faces staring up at him. *Save us Alphaline, save us from the bad men with the swords.* For a sheltered town of fighters who spent their entire year dreaming of innocuous glory in the arena they knew a real warrior when they saw one. Erroh could see their fear under the roars and bravado.

"Better that some survive when the dust is settled and the last fire has gone out." He stepped back to let the crowd know he was finished. How did actors perform like this all the time?

"Thank you," said Aireys from beside him. She watched the crowd struggle with his difficult words. There were no more jests and this was probably a good thing. "I will be the first to throw in my sword," she said loudly. She could have been voted in as mayor in that very moment.

"Do it for your loved ones," she called out, desperately trying to control the emotion in her voice. Somehow, it made her more courageous, and many people dropped their heads in shame. She knew she was going to die. She faced it like only a legend could. No one stepped forward with her.

"Why don't we hide out in the wastes and just let them pass on through?" a voice cried from the gathering.

"And what if they did not simply pass through? How long could we last without dying of hunger? The wastes are vast but too difficult to conceal so many. No, we form a convoy in no longer than two days and take to the road as one," she said though her face was grave. She had expected one or two to join with her but silence had greeted her. Well, that was fine. She would stand alone and slow them down by taking longer to burn than most.

Lea stepped forward and reached up to Erroh. If their lives came to nothing more than giving the people of this town an extra day's advantage, then it was a life lived well. She wasn't just scared, she was petrified, but there was also an unsettling ripple of anger stirring in her. She could see the lust for vengeance in Erroh's eyes. He wanted to stay, fight, and kill as many of them as possible. She knew this because she wanted it too. There were always grand dreams of a great revenge but in a world this size, all they could ever be were two warriors useful in battle. This town had taken them in at their most vulnerable and they would never get a greater opportunity to make a difference to so many.

"This town has been good to us, my brave, warmongering Erroh," she said, and he nodded grimly. He suspected the town was going to need someone to lead them in battle. He suspected they would turn to him for all decisions. He suspected their strength would rely on his nerve. Despite everything, he made another of those oaths. It was a good one as well. As death approached, he would show no fear. Walking the road he'd always accepted that death could be just a few breaths anyway. At least now, the uncertainty was gone. Such grim thoughts hurt his head. It could lead a mind to madness.

That could be useful in battle.

"I aim to kill many of those fukers!" he roared.

The crowd suddenly cheered him as though he'd spit fire. They chanted his name, and he found it pleasing. Why not enjoy a little acclaim? He wondered if any actually believed they would live through the days ahead.

They did.

With Erroh and Lea's names added to the list of defenders, other voices declared themselves for war. Erroh watched on in silence as they recklessly threw their lives away. That wasn't to say he didn't love each warrior who raised their swords and delivered their names into the first regiment of Keri though. They were now his brothers.

They were loud and brash and cheered on by those with better sense. Moreover, they believed in themselves. They would become heroes, attain the finest mates, and spawn many adoring cubs. They would have epic stories to tell and medals to display. They would face this unknown foe with the gods at their back and the Alphas at their side and they would know victory. They would save this falling town.

They were wrong and they would all be dead very soon but every single one of them would show heroism before they were slain.

———

The night never ended, or at least it felt as much. Torches were gathered and handed out to any man or female who had need of them. To the gods above, the valley must have looked like a million sparks were spitting out from the town centre's fiery glow. As important as gathering some fighters, preparing to move an entire town towards a safe haven a thousand miles away was a different beast entirely.

Discovering who could lead the town towards salvation

should have rested on the mayor, but he would not be moved. He had sins to atone for. He confided in Aireys that he would face the horde alone under the comfort of a white flag. He would seek a peaceful resolution when they neared their territory but until that terrible moment arrived; they both put competitiveness aside and discovered they made a formidable force. They rallied the town and whipped them into a frenzy of activity. They challenged their neighbours to work harder than ever before in their lives. Their great operation's hub was situated in the cobblestone ground of the town's centre, where all around them busy villagers ran through the streets with various missions to complete. They attacked whatever tasks they were given fervently. Hale and Fabien were resupplied and sent out on one final mission to track the ever nearing forces while the rest of Jeremiah's dozen Regulators were dispatched to all surrounding farmsteads with word of many terrible things. Those who joined the resistance were welcome. Those who helped were thanked. Those who refused to leave their homes would never have their stories told. The hours passed swiftly as though time had cruelly hastened and betrayed them when it was needed most.

Erroh and Lea walked through the town hand in hand observing the operations. Her grasp was reassuring and it felt right. He felt guilty not labouring with the rest, but he had other things on his mind. It wasn't just planning their defences, for he already had most of that figured out already. What mattered now was ensuring Lea's survival. If her injuries were still crippling, he could have insisted she leave with the convoy but as it was, she was a force to wield in battle. His father would be so proud of his warmongering thinking. Had Magnus ever thought about denying Elise a place in the battlefield? Probably but his mother was an elite warrior and on occasion the turning force in a battle. Lea was nowhere near her level and he; well he would never be half the legend his father was. He suddenly wished his father was here but Lea's hand squeezed him and that was enough. He brought it up to his lips and kissed it tenderly.

In truth, the town behaved admirably. Erroh expected the grumblings of revolt to rear its ugly head in dissent but there wasn't a whisper. Perhaps Emir's proud proclamation that he would fight for Keri had swayed people's discord. If the wretched healer was ready to die, who were they to show derision? It felt wrong to deny him the opportunity though.

Preparing for war was far easier than preparing the convoy. A few dozen carts were rolled into the town centre where hasty inspections were carried out. Those that passed scrutiny were lined up and prepared for hauling. The rest were broken down at Erroh's request. There were no valuables allowed to be stored upon the carts with every man, child and woman only allowed to carry one pack upon their back and nothing more. Trinkets and treasures would be waiting for them when they returned. The miller worked tirelessly with his apprentices to fill bag after bag of grain and though each cart began to fill up with small sacks, there simply wouldn't be enough for so many for very long.

"What a miserable fate, to escape this attack and still die out in the wastes from starvation," Erroh said, as the last sack was loaded.

"Ah, it's a small matter. If they don't find enough to hunt, they will just arrive in Samara that little bit thinner," Lea said. "Worry of better things."

.   .   .

It was no longer Keri. It was an ever-moving machine of preparation. They were heartbroken, tear eyed and desolate but they never stopped. The years of over-confidence were stripped away and all that remained was survival. A few hours before dawn the torches began to flicker out as their bearers' energies were spent. A few were tossed aside as some sneaked a little sleep anywhere they could. Erroh wanted to join them. He wanted to close his eyes and curl up in a ball on some soft straw. He wanted to listen to her breathing change as she lay beside him. He was supposed to have the rest of his life to enjoy those moments. They were supposed to have a long happy life filled with those moments. He let out a loud yawn. She did as well.

The smarter move on their part was saddling up on fresh mounts and sneaking back to Spark City with news of attackers. They owed no debt to the people, apart from saving her life and taking them in and asking for nothing in turn of course. They never even begged him to bring his steel to the table. Lesser drowning men would have grasped at anything. Lesser men would have dragged him down.

Erroh turned to his mate.

"We're going to need a lot of arrows."

34

WE'RE ALL GOING TO DIE

E rroh stood below the two great natural walls of the valley and muttered a few warnings to the absent gods. It was here at the gap in the landscape where the battle for Keri would take place. He walked through the parting from river edge to valley wall a few times wondering if further inspiration would strike him. It's what any decent leader would do.

Leader.

His heart began to beat rapidly at the thought. This doomed leadership had been thrust upon him without discussion, and he had agreed without much hesitation.

No small matter at all.

No small amount of pressure either.

"Take a breath, my love," Lea said from behind him.

"Breathing is an underrated gift," he said.

"Perhaps we should take as many as we can for now," she said. She was so brave, and he needed to be strong like her and hide his terror.

He took a breath.

The deep river meandered and split the land in two parts

at the entrance of the valley leading into the town. One side
thinned out as the river bent, leaving only a foot or so of
traversable land before touching a wall of impenetrable rock
straight up. With a few archers sitting atop, no fool would
dare attack from this side. The other side however would be
quite the enticing target for attackers, and it was here that all
the fighting would take place. Erroh walked the gap again
counting approximately forty feet wide. A smart young cub
could cause some ruin to invaders with the right tactics before
their defences were overrun. Magnus had always said he
expected great things from his son. He had made him believe
that he could surpass his own accomplishments if given the
opportunity. Now Erroh would repay that debt of confidence
or shatter under its weight. He sighed. Holding a little town
was no great tale to be told. It was no conquering the Savage
Isles. It was no conquering the Four Factions.

He pointed to the ledge where Lea had faced her demons.
"Can you climb up there with Baby?" She scrambled up the
steep rock face quickly and stood atop the crevice, waiting
for further instruction. Erroh walked down the slope towards
the tree line separating the town from the wastes. It was a
couple hundred feet of beautiful, open grassland. The
clustered trees at the bottom offered a fine staging point for
any attack but it was all uphill after that, and the warriors of
Keri would make it a treacherous climb every fuken step of
the way. Erroh would ensure that. He pointed to a thin tree
trunk a few feet to his right. A moment later, an arrow
embedded itself in the hard wood. He nodded approvingly.
There was a strong wind and the arrow still hit its target. It
was quite a distance. A few seconds later, another hit the tree
a few inches below the first. A third and final arrow struck an
innocent tree a foot to his left, causing him to jump. She
raised her hand and waved, a mischievous smile on her face.

It made him feel better. This battle would need a few leaders, and she would be one.

———

Emir shouldn't have been in the tavern where a meeting of the future generals of this doomed battle were taking place, but there was no place else he'd rather be. He listened as the leader of the Regulators, Cass, introduced himself to the Alphaline, Erroh. He wondered if the quiet man with the receding hairline and unsettling stillness resented the young cub marching in and accepting leadership. It didn't really matter, they would all be dead soon enough. He stifled a curse and turned his attention to Erroh as he addressed the small group of warriors and revealed his plans. They were simple. They would build a sturdy blockade across the gap to the water's edge and stake the land to stop the cavalry charge. With arrows, oil, flame, and swords, there was to be great violence in the days ahead. He however, was to be denied a chance to stand and die with his friends. He topped up his ale before retreating to his solitary table to listen. He had put his name forward with thirty others. It should have been his right to stand firm with bandages, stitching, and every medical trick he could perform under the heat of battle. His skill could save lives; his skill could help hold the town for longer. He wanted to be with Aireys and Quig in their last moments. He didn't want to be alone. When those two weren't around, he always felt alone and now Aireys had ordered he be alone for the rest of his life. She had banished him to walk with the convoy for the safety of the city.

He drank back and spluttered as his mouth overfilled and the ale spilt down his shirt. It wasn't fair. He cursed loudly, causing a few faces to turn around in irritation. He glared back at the dead men who judged him silently. There's nothing to see here you curs, apart from a wretched healer too good for war and death. Go listen to the plans to devastate the invaders. A few feet away Aireys looked and tried to catch his eye. He eyed his reassuring ale instead. How could she do this to him?

"How many times have you made the trip, my love?" Aireys asked him once again, stroking the stubble on his chin. She already knew the answer. He knew this.

"Five times."

"We need you to lead them," she said, as a tear flowed down her cheek onto the pillow they shared.

"There are others that have been to the Spark," he pleaded.

She shook her head sadly and kissed him hoping to end this sorrowful conversation. How many years had she dreamed of him in her arms? Far too many wasted. He pushed away slightly, only slightly.

"They need your guidance. They need someone who knows the city. Someone wretched enough to do whatever is needed," she said firmly. "Wretched and beautiful."

"I want to be with you on the battlefield," he whimpered back, his own silent tears rolling down his cheeks.

"I want you to live," she argued.

"I don't want you to die," he whispered.

Erroh's plan was received well, probably, because of the violence it entailed. The mountain range was too severe for Riders to navigate. A skilled climber could eventually scale the great height but where Lea and her choice of archers were stationed, there was little chance of any brute making it to the summit alive. If the Riders were unable to penetrate the defences along the slope, it would take them a day's hard ride to enter from any other direction, and even then, they would need a detailed map just to find the defiant town. If all went to plan, the town might gift two days to the escapees. This would be enough for them to reach the skyroad.

Placing Lea along the ledge was both his shrewdest and trickiest manoeuvre of the day. Her ability with the bow would cause absolute devastation but more than that when they were overrun, he demanded she flee across the top of the valley and lose herself in the forest and peaks beyond. Away from eager listeners, she argued, begged, and threatened the leader of Keri for another station, but he was resolute until she eventually gave in. Her heart broke at the thought of not being at his side at the end. Walking into the darkness hand in hand was something she could have faced.

———

In the final hours before the convoy departed, when sleep and cheer were forgotten, Erroh assembled the feeble army of Keri in the hope of lifting their spirits. A harsh, bitter wind blew through the gap in the valley, and it looked as though rain was in the air. Watching their loved ones prepare to leave was causing whispered doubts to spread through their ranks. Among the group of anxious men were Aireys and Lea, who sat side by side at the foundations of the new wall in a bond of sisterhood. They looked as nervous as the rest but more than that, they looked as nervous as Erroh felt. He closed his eyes and thought about the Rider who struck down his mate while ignoring the growing silence all around him. He remembered slaughtering the brute, and he held that wonderful bloodlust close to his beating heart before opening his eyes and facing his downcast audience. He spoke his mind and nobody interrupted him for he spoke loudly with just the right amount of madness to his tones.

His father would have approved.

"In the next few days I'm going to die," he said and let each word sink in.

"We're all going to die brutally."

Silence.

"Every one of us will step into the darkness, and no one will cheer our names or sing our sacrifice, for this is an insignificant little town."

Heavy hearted silence.

"We will never know if our loved ones make sanctuary or if these beasts that tear our bodies apart will ever be stopped."

A few looked around at each other.

"We will all be dead," he said.

The collective audience appeared to agree.

"We will not die heroically. We will die to keep a few hundred alive, nothing more."

As he spoke, he met the eyes of each man. He could see the impact his cruel words were having on their faces but it was a better thing to face horrifying thoughts among comrades in the light of day, than alone in the dark recesses of the mind. If they bit down hard and chewed, they could eventually swallow. His father had told him that the finest warriors accepted death long before battle. A man with hope for survival was more likely to cherish the gift of life and more willing to do anything to prolong his life: flee his brothers in arms, or sacrifice the line.

"You will all die unless you leave with the rest today."

He caught a few nervous glances look back towards the town behind them.

"And you will be valuable to them. They will need warriors for the journey. You will not be showing any cowardice. Any who want to leave, leave now and live good lives."

He waited a moment and corrected himself.

"Live great lives."

Stefan stood up and looked around. His head dropped, and he muttered how sorry he was before leaving the gap and disappearing across a little wooden bridge and into one of the narrow side streets. Erroh didn't blink but inside he regretted the loss of his skills. Another brave soul stood up and followed and then two more quickly followed. Fewer walked away than he had expected. He knew the ones that stayed had a greater chance of holding their nerve and the line. It would be all about holding the last line.

"They were the smarter ones," he jested when the last sound of footsteps were lost in the wind. A few laughs accompanied his attempted wit, and he nodded in approval. He met each man's eyes and sized them up. They were weathered by fear or age and dressed in loosely tailored armour with inadequate blades strapped to their waists. They were inspiring. He had no flames of hope to offer, but he could add a little spark. It was time to reward the brave ones with the truth.

"My name is Erroh, and I am the son of Magnus."

He glanced to Lea hopefully and then back at the awestruck men. He drew the sword of his father to add credence to his claim. It felt lighter in his grip. He stabbed the blade deep into the grassy ground and stood back for all to see the crest of the Puk horns.

"Some of you might recognise this,"

It wasn't even his father's favourite blade. Nor his favoured weapon of choice, but the crest was both feared and revered throughout the world. A few recognised the sword immediately. He heard someone mention "Mercy from the Savage Isles."

It was a sword fit for a king.

In truth and in war, it was Magnus any wise soldier wanted fighting at their back, regardless of affiliation. And now from nothing, they had been gifted his apprentice. They'd all seen his ability in sparring. Only a warmonger would choose to stay and fight with strangers and only a champion could rise to leader of that line. When he spoke, it was hard not to listen. They would stand with the great son and kill as many as they could, because he told them to.

"We will not scream as they strike us down. We will not cry out as we bleed until empty and we will not flee when our comrades fall in front of our eyes. I lied to you, brothers. We will not be forgotten when we step into the darkness. Every single man who fights and dies beside Magnus's son will be remembered. There will be songs of bravery for each of you."

He paused and eyed them once more. They hung on his every word for they had nothing else.

"I give you my word. Our deaths will raise the great man from his slumber. Magnus will march once more, and in the end, every single barbarian who attacks this town will perish a just and terrible death!" he roared before dropping to one knee in front of his comrades.

In his mind, it was a speech worthy of his father. Perhaps his father would have cursed more.

There was no outburst of camaraderie, no outlandish cheering, and wild jests directed at their vanquishers. There was just stony silence. Maybe their prejudice against Magnus had blinded them. Maybe their ignorance ran deeper than a mocking festival. Maybe he had said too much or indeed too little. Maybe he had said the wrong thing. He normally said the wrong thing. This time he just about got it right.

One warrior took a knee and bowed in reply. Another beside him followed suit. One by one, they dropped to their knee and offered complete fealty. A few warriors lanced the ground with their own swords. No words were offered but the feeling was shared. They would be as good a warrior as their leader. They would do as he did.

"We have a lot of work to do before the storm arrives," he said grinning.

———

Four barrels was enough. It had to be enough. That said, Erroh wasn't familiar with the combustibility of lantern oil so he counted the barrels again. There were definitely four barrels standing side by side. He hoped it would be enough. He and Quig rolled one barrel each of the thick black liquid down the slope towards the clustered tree line where Lea had struck the arrows. Villagers not tasking themselves with the great evacuation collected thin slivers of tinder and placed them along the slope but the truly gruelling part of their preparation was placing sharpened stakes as tall as themselves into the ground from valley wall to water's edge right down the slope. The stakes were wide enough for any man to slip through but it would nullify any cavalry charge. At least for a time. Precious time. This battle was never about winning. It was about time.

"This will warm their hearts eh?" laughed the big man dipping a paintbrush into the opened lid and lathering the side of a tree. After a few clumsy strokes, they moved onto the next. Drips of dark fluid trickled down the trunk and rested on the roots like a black cancerous river dying the bark a terminal sickly colour. Both men spent the afternoon coating trees while the rest laboured with the massive spikes. By nightfall, the delightfully named "slope of death" was complete.

———

Emir sat opposite Jeremiah and Aireys as the citizens of Keri wept their sorrowful goodbyes. It was near dawn, he was exhausted, bitter, and what they asked of him was bullshit.

"This is bullshit, Aireys, there's no way I'll do it!" he shouted. How could he be the mayor proxy?

Jeremiah said nothing. He was pale and looked like he hadn't slept in a long time. Relinquishing his title was the last order the Holy Mayor wanted to ever make, as it allowed Aireys the opportunity to just reach out and grasp it, but she had little intention of claiming such things. Instead, she was choosing to die.

"We trust you to do it, and it's only temporary," she said and Jeremiah nodded. She placed her beautiful calloused hands on each of his cheeks. That usually worked.

"If it's only temporary?" They'd been working at him for over an hour. He looked into her beautiful eyes and knew these were the last words they would speak. She loved her people more than she loved herself. More than she even loved him.

"You care for them until we meet again," she lied.

It was a beautiful lie.

Erroh couldn't face the sadness any longer. Lea had returned home to their loft a little time earlier to bathe and sleep and without her at his side, he felt his spirit drop, seeing families' tears as brave warriors said goodbye. He walked home and instead of climbing in to bed, washed the aroma of oil and sweat from his exhausted body in the well by their barn. Holt had packed up and left but the thoughts of taking his quarters left a bitter taste in his mouth. The barn would suit them just fine for the now. When he'd scraped most of the grime and pollutants from the day's exertions away, Erroh stepped into the barn as quietly as possible. He could smell her perfume from below, and he inhaled deeply.

"Please tell me that that's you, Erroh," a voice from above called down.

"It's Stefan, coming to claim his prize," laughed Erroh donning his undergarments.

"Oh, great. I had hoped you would visit before you left. We have a little time before my smelly mate gets here."

"I'll only need a few moments. I'm grand champion."

Erroh hopped up onto the ladder a little clumsily. His breath smelled of alcohol after accepting a few toasts to the health of line of Magnus. He climbed the ladder and took a moment to appreciate the new lighting she had decorated the room with. The candles were lit in little glass jars in each corner. They flickered and swayed and danced like they were enchanted. He knew how they felt.

She was sitting upright, leaning forward with her knees pressing into the soft straw. She let the sheets slip down slowly, past her shoulders and then to her exposed breasts. After a few breaths, when she was satisfied that he had taken in enough of her upper half, she let the sheets fall away revealing the rest of her incredible body. She smiled suggestively and waited for him to come and claim his prize.

She was the most beautiful creature in the world, and he wanted to take her. He wanted to rip his one garment off and pull her body as close to his as possible. And get even closer. He stepped towards her and said the wrong thing.

"Lea, I can't."

Her face turned from excitement to puzzlement, to surprise to sadness and finally embarrassment.

At least she wasn't angry.

"What do you mean?" she cried suddenly aware of how naked she was. This was supposed to be a divine moment shared between them both. Was he ruining everything again?

He was.

"I want to," he said, stepping forward and reaching out for her. "But I can't."

She crossed her arms to cover her breasts and swiftly reached down for the sheet to recover what dignity she could. She had almost forgotten how shit he could make her feel sometimes. Almost but not quite. Maybe she should have kissed him a few times first? Tonight was supposed to be unforgettable. Now this moment was unforgettable. Thoughts of Lillium flashed in her mind. Had Lillium ever been this embarrassed when she took her mate to bed? She missed her friend. She wished she wasn't naked. Her shoulder was a little sore. She didn't want Erroh to die. Life wasn't fair at all.

"I'm sorry," she said dejectedly and frowned at the voice of a girl she didn't recognise at all.

"No, Lea, I'm sorry," He sat down beside the partially veiled goddess. Her perfume teased his senses and his head was spinning, just sitting beside her. A part of his mind was tearing down his walls of resolve. He knew he was being a fool, even more so than normal. Take the goddess, a little voice ordered him. Take her in every way imaginable and achieve as much pleasure with her as you possibly can. The little voice kept going. He wanted to pleasure her, he really did. He ignored the voice.

Then he gave his second speech of the day.

"I haven't been good enough to you, I've hurt you and put you in this danger," he whispered and raised his hands up to quiet her protestations. "I need to say this, beo," he said gently, and she nodded resentfully and let him continue.

"When I fall, give me your word that you flee no matter what else occurs."

She didn't reply. She just held the sheets around her, but her eyes suggested that this wasn't the time to speak about such things.

"When they kill me, promise me that you'll live on." He reached out to touch her cheek. It was warm.

She closed her eyes taking in his touch but said nothing.

"You deserve a proper chance at happiness," he whispered gently. He brushed his fingers through her shimmering black hair. She didn't want to melt under his touch but it was Erroh's touch. Fuk you and your touch Erroh.

"You deserve a chance at happiness with someone else."

She opened her eyes and whipped his hand away.

"No," she hissed loudly. "You're my mate," she said pushing at him aggressively.

"And I am thankful to the gods you chose me," he said accepting the shove.

"Fuk you, Erroh." How could he?

"If I do one thing right by you, it will be this," he said getting up and sitting as far away from her as possible. "If our mating remains without all gifts shared, you become a far more appealing choice of mate."

"You said you would never hurt me, Erroh," she said weeping and hating herself for it.

"I love you with all my heart, Lea. I'm sorry."

"I love you with all my heart too, Erroh, and I'll stay alive for you, but I pledge I will never love another after you!" she snapped. She knew his expression. She had seen it a few times, and she knew he would not be moved. Even if it was breaking her heart. Even if it was breaking his own.

They sat in the candle light and feared for each other as a harsh wind battered at the barn wall. Eventually she sat down beside him. Their situation was too horrible to stay annoyed at him for too long. Admittedly, she could see his ridiculous thinking. Countless men had wanted after her in the city and certainly, there had been wonderful charming moments when temptation had nearly swayed her judgement, but all who had tried had failed to get what her mate was rejecting outright. No pretty boy or handsome man had been of real interest to her until the day she had seen her Erroh. She had known in that moment that he belonged to her, even if he did absolutely everything imaginable to fuk it all up.

Despite their difficult beginnings and all the tears, the last few months had been all she hoped her life would be. This was who she was now. She knew he was going to die and it terrified her, but she would be strong, like he was strong for the town. If he wanted her story to continue, while his reached its conclusion, then so be it. She would hold back the tears when he fell, and she would honour his request.

After a time, they lost the need to argue. They lay beside each other in the warm straw and listened to the howling wind outside. She was covered by the bed sheet, but he could still make out wonderful shapes under the thin veneer. She nestled into his shoulder and listened to his heartbeat for a time. He leaned in and kissed her on the lips. She accepted and kissed him back passionately.

"Just a few kisses," he said between breaths.

"If you insist, my love," she said letting the sheet drop below her waist again. She pulled gently and playfully at the solitary clothing that guarded her prize. "There are other things we can do that in theory don't fully count," she whispered before biting his ear gently.

His resolve was shattered as he dared a gentle exploratory touch of her skin. Every part of her form was perfect. She reacted with pleasure from his touch and he from hers as she finally stripped his clothing free. Lost in her eyes and her taste, he was intrigued by just how far the term "in theory" was going to take them.

35

THE CHAMPION OF KERI

E rroh stood and watched them hard at work. If it was heavy and bulky, it was useful for the blockade. A few wooden stakes had been buried deep into the muddy ground to hold everything in place and it did the trick. The blockade became a chaotic wall of barrels, furniture, carts, and sacks more than fifteen foot high. Along the top, they hammered countless rows of thick timber planks and draped thick carpets atop leaving a grand walkway. It was easier than expected with an entire town to call upon for materials. He felt relaxed and his eyes turned to watch the clouds overhead. He didn't mind the sharp bracing wind but a heavy downpour would ruin his entire day. He let no such worry show on his face though for today he enjoyed the quiet and a weakness in the knees. He sipped at his cofe and walked down the slope towards the tree line tipping his hands against every brutal spike lining the riverbed along the way, beautiful wooden beasts protruding from the ground like vicious godly fingers. They reassured him with their ugly presence. He tested the bark at the treeline and began painting a fresh coat. After a while, Quig and Aireys joined him. They offered few words, and Erroh didn't push. They were missing those closest to him. There was nothing to be said and still plenty to be done.

Jeremiah spent all day offering prayers up to the gods and sharpening blades. He was covering himself on both counts. He jested at the idea of Keri delivering a little taste of "hell" to their enemy before sending them there. Erroh didn't understand his old religious term but it was a grand word to say aloud. As the last day ended and the shattered moon reared its head, the heroes of Keri were ready to face the oncoming hoard. At midnight, the first watch climbed out along the top of the blockade with torch in hand. The duo walked the wall and whispered anxiously with each other, careful not to trip or wake those around them. They knew there would be no attack as no Regulator had returned heralding their doom, but their general had required a watch, so they watched the night and wondered how many miles the town had already travelled. It was the only thing to stave off the despair. Few slept soundly the first night. Most warriors kept constant vigil along the gap and counted the hours. Their gaze never travelled far from the tree line while high above the small garrison of Lea's archers sat between both ledges of the valley wall peering out across the land. A few other sentries were posted on the far side of town where there was no blockade. They kept an eye on the road to ensure no foe crept up and slit their throats while sleeping. Dark thoughts entered every man and woman's mind of the battle to come, but few spoke such fears aloud and while every hour gained was a blessing from the absent gods, this great wait was enough to strike the first blows of madness.

The first night passed.

Then the next day.

And the day after that.

By the fourth morning, Erroh's hands no longer shook.

He had no more adrenaline to spare. His mind was clear of thoughts except for the treeline and the hours' passing. Looking at the tired faces of his brothers, he could see many of them were as single minded as he but others were restless, as the uneasy quiet took hold and took over. War was war, but desolation was another thing. Another day or two of this delay and dissenting voices would begin as whispers. Whispers to words, to rational, and then to retreat. Aye, they would have a point, but even if a week passed and they all fled the wall, whatever army marching towards them would catch the town's scent and easily track them down. No, it was best to wait here and give the fukers a bruise or two while they had the chance. He wondered would he still feel this way a few days from now.

What would his father do?

He climbed down from the ramparts and walked down the slope of death over the clumps of straw and strips of kindling, avoiding the spikes as best he could. He could feel the eyes upon him, but he did not look back. He reached the bottom of the volatile slope and faced the dark woods beyond. Somewhere beyond the enemy neared and they weren't going to hurry themselves despite the welcome the town was planning.

"What the fuk is taking you so long?" he roared suddenly and far back at the blockade, he heard some laughter. Excellent. That would stave off the darkness for another few hours at least.

———

He only referred to each man as "warrior" and they appeared to appreciate it. He hadn't learned everyone's name so it worked out well. The aroma of so many bodies close together along the line reminded Erroh of the camp of his father's army, and it felt homely. Walking along the top of the barricade was precarious but it soon became second nature. He did his own sentry duty in the hope of leading by example. Most of his brothers were older but as Erroh grew more into the role of general, his voice became deeper, older, as though going through a young cub's change all over again. He no longer simply spoke. He snarled, roared and barked orders, observations and jests and they listened, obeyed, and laughed. It was better to appear in control than give in to temptation to grab the nearest soldier and scream in his face "I haven't a real clue about what I'm doing." He doubted that would go down well with morale. Instead, he donned his warrior's skin and worked towards becoming the warmonger they so badly wanted.

Every morning after they released their sweet embrace for perhaps the last time, Lea would take her place to watch over the world. When they witnessed her ability with her bow, her standing increased tenfold. They never assumed there would be two elite warriors to fight by their side. It wasn't enough to warrant a false dawn that a victory could be attained; they frequently reminded themselves of their ominous future. They mock sparred and practised techniques, and Erroh wondered how well they might have fared with a few hundred of these desperate men to call upon. As it was they were worthy to be called Rangers, and his father would have gladly accepted any into his outfit. These proud warriors deserved more from the world than they were going to receive, and he hinted as much to the gods who he didn't believe in.

. . .

The Quig recovered his sense of humour and with it his popularity. In an inspired moment, he set a wager that he would kill more than any other before he was felled himself. Lea of course had been first to accept the challenge, she mused that her only real competition would be the flashing blades of Aireys. Soon enough the warriors threw their own predictions into the ring and all of a sudden, the fear of not killing enough before stepping from the world became a serious topic between the warriors. Some bets on who would die with fewest kills were made and nobody wanted the odds on that. When Quig appeared atop the barricade with a massive battle scythe and a fresh boast about becoming the new champion of Keri, the warriors nearly lost the run of themselves. The antique weapon's blade stretched out longer than any sword, and hung as nothing more than a decoration in his parents' household. When wielded by massive powerful arms, devastation would follow in its wake. Erroh made a show of arguing that it wasn't a fair bet anymore. His argument that "it wouldn't be fair to their attackers either" was well received by his army. Magnus had told him of the strong bond between fighters at the worst of times and it struck back the clanging of the madness.

———

The depression returned when the two bedraggled figures of Fabien and Hale appeared from the wastes. They had word of the attackers and the defenders began to light a few fires.

Jeremiah pleaded with each man to stay, but they'd lost any taste for war when their friend was butchered in front of their eyes. They shared the look of terrified mounts that were readying themselves to bolt, and Erroh dismissed them from duty lest their misery infect the rest. They briefed what they could, took on a few provisions, and departed the town within the hour. They never looked back and nobody saw them off on their journey. Their eyes were on the bottom of the slope.

The additional intelligence didn't really help morale. They simply confirmed well over a thousand on foot and at least a hundred Riders. It was fivefold the tracks Erroh and Lea had followed for so many weeks. Were they hiring mercenaries and bandits? What type of lunatic would command an army of outcastes and rogues anyway? Erroh's heart sank at this fresh intelligence but when speaking with his warriors, he feigned delight that there was simply "more blood to spill." With the alternative to Erroh's merriment being complete and utter panic, the warriors joined in with his humour. Fresh bets were made. Lea was now considered the dark horse.

He leapt from atop the massive barricade once more and stepped through the long spikes towards the tree line. On a spike at the bottom of the slope of doom, he hung a crudely painted sign. He wrapped the sign with rope and secured it tightly. The words "Welcome" would be the first thing the brutes saw when they charged in. The warriors thought this was the greatest act ever. Even in death, the town of Keri would remain courteous. When one had nothing else, it was still nice to keep some values.

———

Erroh and Lea had taken a bedroom to themselves near the town centre and every morning they woke wrapped in each other's arms, free from the constraints of clothing. "Don't change out of that outfit, my love," he said watching her naked form as she slipped out of the warm bed sheets in search of her passionately strewn garments.

"Am I to be an interesting tactic to shock the enemy," she laughed posing in mock seduction.

"It will raise morale too, my beo," he said yawning as he looked out the window at the clear morning sky. A fine day to die, he mused. She turned back to swipe at his brazenness but the first shouts of alarm distracted her. They grew in number and so too did another sound. A low groan which he recognised from a long time ago near a rock. Their eyes met, and he fought the dread. He thought her stunning and wanted more time with her. Enough time to grow old together. She was terrified and beautiful, and he leapt from the sheets as she struggled to dress herself.

"One more kiss," he said embracing her.

"There isn't time," she cried and kissed him regardless. He thought she was shaking but it was his own body.

"Remember what you promised me," he said and released her. He composed himself and donned his warrior's skin and then his clothes and then his armour. It was time for bravado and brutality. He imagined his fears and eternal doubts locked away in a cage, never to be freed again. Only Lea was allowed to see his hands shake or hear his heart skip beats, while everyone else would see a brute with a taste for savagery, just like his father.

———

They walked in silence down towards the gap. He had so much to say but no words came. Eventually they parted ways. She climbed up the mountain, and he took his place on the peak of their fortification.

He passed a makeshift table with a few plates of dried salted meat for the warriors to chew on. Though he had little desire, he took a piece and chewed heartily as he climbed out on top. The dry salty flavour turned in his sick stomach, but he forced the food down. It was better to have reserves of energy if the fighting was relentless. Besides, there was nothing worse than being stabbed in the stomach when you're already hungry. He licked his lips and a dismal thought occurred to him. Such a piece of meat was a terrible last meal.

"I really would love some boar," he muttered taking hold of a jutting wooden piece of debris and leaning out over the edge. All to earn a slightly better view of the approaching army through the deep green and to appear as calm and collected as his warriors needed.

"I'll ask the lads to hold off attacking while we get you some, sir," Quig jested from behind him. Beside him, Aireys dressed in her combat armour laughed heartily.

Erroh smiled dangerously. "Ah, no need. We've been waiting long enough as it is." His voice travelled across the blockade. He heard jests and a few bouts of laughter, and Erroh thought that as long as Quig stayed alive there would be few problems with morale. It was the little things.

"Nobody leaves this barricade until Lea makes the signal," he reminded them as he pulled himself back to solid ground. The constant rumble was still growing but still too far into the woods to be seen. Jeremiah walked past them and knelt towards the sound. He held a white sheet of cloth on a small wooden pole. The holy man would not be swayed in search for peace, and Erroh thought his nerve was impressive. He was dressed in full black, and he carried no blade. Perhaps he was deadly with his little flag.

"They will kill you," said Erroh.

"Aye, that seems probable, my good friend."

"So why bother try?"

"Because I have to try for every man here," he replied.

Erroh tried to hide his frustration. "Do you expect your god to keep you safe?" Every man was worth his weight in ranks this thin, and he was certain Jeremiah was needlessly throwing away his life.

"I expect my god has little control over the next period of my life but I'm sure he watches with interest. He knows I do this to avoid bloodshed," replied Jeremiah, wiping away a bead of sweat that was rolling down his face. He took a breath and his face turned a little paler as though he knew the futility of his action. "I hope to die well. I hope my lord is waiting for me in the darkness with a candle and a nice bottle of wine."

It wasn't a bead of sweat, it was a tear.

"I will ask the absent gods to send on a second bottle," said Aireys gently as she watched the first flickers of movement through the trees.

They heard heavy hooves breaking through canopy and leathered boots marching over uneven ground but most of all they heard the heavy roll of large wooden wheels rumbling towards them.

"I will save a seat for you in the darkness beyond," said Jeremiah smiling. He patted Erroh on the back and sighed. "But send them all to hell if I do not return." He slipped down the barricade.

———

Lea could see everything. Like little scurrying creatures wild with a scent they scrambled through the forest. The land was brushed aside collectively, and she tasted fear on her tongue.

There were so many.

She ground her teeth and shifted a little closer to the edge. She could feel the warmth from the flaming metal barrel as its flame thrashed madly against the sharp wind. "Not yet," she whispered and watched them draw closer. Though she was fearful, she took heart in their appearance. Aye, they were terrifying in barbaric armour of animal skin and fur with terrifying banners of black and red, but it was evident these killers' favoured close quarters over long distance warfare. She had feared facing a garrison of longbow archers but those few with quivers along their waists carried crude crossbows on their backs. She smiled to herself and ran her finger along Baby's grip. She and her boys would rain great devastation upon them before they found their range. At the rear of the approaching convoy massive carts rolled, pulled by a half dozen mounts. As the leading army drew to a halt behind the thick cover of the trees, the massive carts were rolled to a stop near an opening in the woods along the river's edge and the world swiftly fell silent as a stillness fell over their foe.

She looked down at the pathetic numbers that would stand against this ocean of black, and she felt proud to stand with them. She eyed her anxious little group of comrades sitting rigidly beside her and across the gap, and she suddenly thought about her older brothers. What would they think of her in this moment? What would they think of her mate? Her line would not die along with her today but it was a small comfort. It probably shouldn't have been.

Jeremiah walked slowly down through the long spikes and over the uneven ground carrying the large white flag of peace. He stopped and waited half way down the slope at the last line of spikes where Lea had suggested he be safe from a stray arrow. The flag fell to his side and blew gently in the wind. He stood motionless but for his lips which whispered comforting nothings, to himself and perhaps to something above. His mind was calm and his face was serene; he would have no fear. There was no movement. There were barely any whispers from the trees but there were sets of eyes and they watched and waited.

Lea thought of them as little ants, needing to be burned away. She watched a runner no older than a cub charge back through the undergrowth with word of a lone figure with a flag. She followed his route through the woods until he emerged down by the river where she lost sight of him amid the chaotic unloading of a marching army. Somewhere among the unpacking of tents and supplies and the herding of travelling beasts the unseen generals were briefed on their path ahead. The world held its breath and time seemed to slow to an agonising crawl and the holy man waited for movement.

Eventually after a few hours, there was movement.

Three figures with raised swords broke from the green. Behind them followed two heavyset mounts with Riders atop.

Erroh held his breath and hoped. He may even have prayed. He wasn't alone among the many silent whisperings from all standing atop the barricade of Keri.

"Nobody is to attack regardless of what happens," he hissed.

The Rider began a charge on the holy man. He heard the Quig on his right mutter something under his breath. To his left Aireys stared coldly in acceptance. The rest of the line watched on in silence and then in horror.

The Rider pulled his axe free and completed his charge. The holy man accepted his own demise like a leader should. He did not recoil as the large beast filled his last ever vision. The axe screamed in the air as the killer swung and hit its mark across the holy man's neck. Jeremiah's last thought were of a candle in the darkness, a few more steps, and then a fine vintage.

The blade struck and embedded itself in bone, muscle, and flesh. The body fell to its knees, supported by the grip from the Rider. With a grunt, the killer placed his foot on the dead man's shoulders and pulled the battle-axe free. He swung again and cut Jeremiah's head free. As both parts fell messily onto the ground, the killer began to roar in triumph.

As far as mental assaults go, this was devastation and it winded every warrior behind the blockade. In one fell swoop, every man doubted themselves and each other. Erroh felt no differently as a few warriors fell to their knees in anguish. The killer roared crude undistinguishable words, but Erroh suspected taunts. Someone needed to shut that fuker up.

"That was savage," whispered Quig weakly. He gripped his weapon but stood proudly. He too could see the terrible effect on morale.

"Nobody is to do anything!" Erroh shouted.

Nobody did anything. They just listened to the taunting war cries and lamented their comrade.

Then somebody did something.

Erroh dropped the few feet onto the ground below. He didn't let himself think. He just did it. It was in his blood.

He sprinted alone down through the battlements. A lone figure dressed in black with flowing cloak trailing out behind him as if he was just out for a run, looking for a fight. His warriors needed to see something incredible. They needed to see him in all his Alphaline glory. They needed the line of Magnus to lead them. He heard himself roar an impressive challenge of his own, as he pulled Vengeance and Mercy from their scabbards. It was five armed combatants against one little cub?

The odds were hardly fair.

. . .

The killer watched curiously as the solitary young man came running towards him screaming his little head off. He grabbed hold of the reins in one hand, in the other gripped the bloodied axe, and met the advance. The order was to kill the one with the flag and no more. The full attack would begin with the horns, as was the way, but The Woodin Man would approve of this reckless challenge. He would see it all, and he would reward those that pleased him.

Running.

All Erroh could hear was the racing wind in his ear as he picked up speed. That and the manic war cry he let loose. A few feet from his quarry, he suddenly changed direction from the rider's right to his left. In a blur, he slipped under the first cavalry spikes and leapt at the taller foe on his weaker side with Vengeance raised. The Rider struggled with the choice of swinging from the wrong angle, or swapping his hand holding the axe. It was no consolation that whatever decision he made would have been wrong. There was a dull wet sound as the sword was thrust in and swiftly drawn away, and Erroh continued his run without breaking stride. The Rider grabbed out weakly on instinct before slumping back in the saddle. After a breath he fell and by the time his corpse hit the ground, Erroh was already beneath the second Rider deflecting a careless strike and knocking him from his perch. The winded brute tried to rise, but Erroh fell upon him and stabbed violently through his chest. His leather armour was easy enough to penetrate. It was lined with fur for the cold but not for a vengeful general. Turning and twisting the blade in the wound, he tormented the brute until his anguished shrieks echoed loudly against the valley walls and suddenly fell silent.

The three remaining attackers moved in around him. They roared in that strange foreign tongue, and Erroh withdrew from his victim with both blades raised. The two armies watched as they attempted to surround him. Two brutes attacked from either side while the third attacked from behind, but Erroh spun with both blades and met every stroke as if it were no small matter at all.

"So that's why he twirls his blades when he fights," said Quig in a low tone. A cold reassuring thought occurred to the big man. In all the skirmishes they'd shared, Erroh had never come close to revealing his full ability. What delicious ruination was he capable of inflicting?

He put on a show for that is what they needed to see. His comrades needed confidence, and his enemy needed a cause for concern. He spun his wrists in magnificent, frightening arcs and parried blow after blow while allowing himself to draw only thin slits of blood from each of his attackers. Let them know their folly and let them know their doom long before their felling. Let every one of them see the consequence for spilling Keri blood.

They relied on rudimentary strength and speed to attain victory and they never had a chance. When he realised the show had lasted as long as needed, he ended it swiftly. He invited an attack with the suggestion of a break in his guard and when the closest took up the offer, Erroh swiped away the attack and rammed "Mercy" through her neck. She seemed frustrated with herself as she fell to the ground holding her throat. The female's long hair fell from her helmet, and Erroh stepped back in shock. She gasped for air and tried to stop the bleeding with her gloves, and Erroh struck her again.

She was as old as his mother was, and he had killed her. It was the greatest crime in the Four Factions.

What would the Primary have to say about that?

He swallowed the shock and met the blow of the brute at his right. He ripped the man's sword from his glove and plunged his blade deep leaving one more attacker to make a show of. The flow of war surged through him and a frenzy took hold. He was Alpha, and he was unstoppable. He wondered if the few days' wait had indeed driven him to a madness. He grasped that madness because fuk it, what else was he going to do?

"Come on!" he roared in a voice he didn't recognise. He didn't recognise the laugh that followed either, but he felt just grand about both. As if some historic jest had just been delivered in a tavern surrounded by his closest friends, he roared manically and the eyes in the trees blinked a few times and continued staring. This was not usual at all. His laughing echoed loudly, and he waited for the final fighter to make his move, and when he did, it was poetry in motion.

The brute charged, and Erroh blocked with his right and spinning with the momentum, swung with all the strength in his left across his enemy's neck. The steel cut through cleanly and by chance, his second sword caught the liberated head before it fell to the ground.

The legend of Erroh had its first sonnet.

He raised the bleeding head of the brute to Jeremiah somewhere above in the heavens. The blood dripped down the blade and onto his fingers. He wiped it across his forehead and only then realised he was still laughing hysterically. Underneath all the horror and the madness of battle, deep down where nobody could see, Erroh could still smell the faint aroma of Lea, and he held her close to his mind as he put on the show. He dropped the sword, freed the head with his foot before giving it a satisfying kick down the slope, and sheathed his swords slowly before turning his back from the entire army and walking back up the slope. He fell silent and climbed back up through the ramparts accepting little help from his brothers.

36

IN THE SHADOW OF A GIANT

"Jeremiah was a good man. We should aim to die with as much bravery," he said meeting many eyes of his stunned Warriors. They waited for one more rousing speech, but there was little to be said. He had spoken with his blades and the enemy were still reeling from his voice. He popped the lid on a nearby barrel full of water and poured a ladle full over his face and hands. Around him, his Warriors returned to their positions. Nothing more to see here, friends. Back to work.

"Are you okay?" whispered Quig.

"Just want to wash this shit off my face," Erroh replied, scrubbing some of the blood from his skin. There was some under his fingernails. He should have cut them sooner.

The Quig patted him on the back roughly. "That was incredible. Probably as good as me."

"I put you in the lead with five," Aireys said.

"It'll give them a few things to think about at least," said Cass watching the sky, the men, and the ramparts, anywhere but out among the spikes where his friend still lay.

"Would be fine if they believed there was a whole flock

of Alphas hiding back here," Erroh said shaking the water away. He wasn't clean. He'd never be again.

"I wonder when they'll surrender?" wondered Quig. He blinked away his worry and resumed the mantle of legend he would become.

"If it were me, I would send a small number on foot to test our armour," suggested Cass. They agreed with silent nods. It was early evening before the attack came.

———

Lea had arrows everywhere. At least two dozen were lanced in the ground in easy reach waiting patiently for her wrath. She held another twenty in a quiver on her back, nestled in between her two short swords. Many more quivers rested against a log behind her. Along the top, her boys were equally supplied. If nothing else, this was a town stocked for a siege. All these deadly projectiles lovingly created for faux honour in the tournament would now fulfil their true potential. She counted the arrows in front of her and decided that if every one of them were unleashed in anger, it was a life well spent. She would step into the darkness with revenge on her lips and boldness in her heart. She spotted the attack.

The brute sprinted out from the protection of the trees. He roared menacingly, carrying a sword and shield in both his hands. He led the war cries. A thunderous roar imbued with pride, hatred, and bile. A second figure swiftly followed and then a third carrying one of the black and red banners. He waved it wildly and many more emerged from behind the line of green. They broke from three separate parts but all towards the same destination. They carried no crossbows and charged up without any type of discipline, spreading out through the spikes in one manic charge. She counted over fifty in the first wave. She notched an arrow and waited. Her mind was awash with terror, hate, and doubt. She thought of the fallen town of Cathbar, of the burnings and then she thought of her first victim and dread took hold. What if she froze again? Countless eyes from below the ramparts and across the gap waited for her lead. She looked down for Erroh, but he wasn't watching her like the rest. He watched the attackers and his weapons weren't even drawn. He'd counted the numbers too, and he was waiting for the mayhem.

He would not need to fight.

He trusted her to lead.

Twenty feet from the barricade she led. The cur kept running for a few seconds with an arrow in his neck before collapsing in a heap near the bottom of the wall. She offered the kill up to the little girl buried in a grave she would never see again. Then she notched another arrow and let it loose on another invader. He died instantly as Baby sent the arrow through his unprotected forehead. This was easier than hitting quail. Around her, the archers rained down as many arrows as they could. While lacking the years of intense training from exquisite masters and drunken tournaments, they still managed carnage with their own lessons learned. As the screams of the injured and dying filled the air, each archer showed more daring. They were cold and they were calculated because that was how their Alphaline sister behaved and they showed no prejudice. All who charged died. The battle was over before it ever really begun. The last brute to fall was struck by seven arrows. A costly expense but the arguments over who claimed the kill were priceless. All that remained were the moaning few at the bottom who had not fully perished. Erroh raised his hand and the archers withdrew.

. . .

"A kill is a kill," Erroh suggested coldly, and a few warriors led by Quig dropped down and set upon the defenceless brutes with grim efficiency. They took to killing better than most normal people and it was a fine thing indeed. Erroh heard a Warrior scream out "three" in delight as he struck down his third victim bleeding profusely from a couple arrows in his back. It seemed to lift the rest into their own frenzy. Nobody wanted to come last in this contest.

The assault was annihilated with at least fifty aggressors dead at the hands of the defenders. They were fifty souls that would never smile, laugh, cry, or hurt ever again. It didn't matter that they deserved to die. He glanced up at the dark clouds above as night drew closer, and he wondered that they might indeed survive the first day after all. It was one more day to breathe, one more day to kiss her, and one more day for the convoy to get further away. It had been nothing more than an exploratory assault, but he still took heart as the sun went down and no second attack came.

———

It was a terrible task, but he dared not let such grotesque endeavours take the fire from his warriors. That said, Aireys and Quig had insisted that they aid him. On three, they gripped each body and flung them over the wall of spikes into the raging water. They did it in silence and took turns casting nervous glances down towards the woods. Most bodies floated away while the heavier armoured ones were likely dragged along the river's bed by the strong current.

"I'd prefer a funeral pyre to a watery grave," muttered Aireys as they climbed back over the wall.

———

The invading army lit fires far back from the woods and settled in for the night. In Keri, the mood was lighter than anyone could have hoped. Erroh allowed himself a smile, receiving the many pats on the back while walking the line across the top of the barricade. No lives lost in the first skirmish. If only Jeremiah could take heart from such a feat. There would be deaths come dawn but they had earned a day for the town, so nothing else mattered.

Around midnight Lea appeared from her perch, a goddess sent by the gods, as spoils for a task well done. She touched his neck tenderly and placed her forehead to his. While a few Warriors kept first watch, the remaining men sat and ate heartily. Quig led the revelry with his boasting. His scythe had "tasted the blood of lesser men and hungered for more."

"After we were finished with them they could barely fight back," argued Lea, much to the joy of her archers.

"A few still had fight left in them," he argued before proclaiming that he would not clean his blade because "red brought out his eyes."

Then the tallying up of the dead began and according to the numbers given, ninety-seven attackers in all were felled in the assault. Quig demanded a recount and even though they laughed and mocked, all the pain was evident upon each man's face. They struggled with the horrors of what had occurred earlier but they found comfort in each other's company. They found comfort knowing they were among brothers. They found comfort knowing they would not die alone. They found comfort laughing in the face of darkness.

———

In all the carousing, one solitary figure in his long cloak sat on top of the barrier. It was not his watch, but he wanted to be there. He ran his fingers through his thinning hair. It was the years of worry catching up with him. Keeping it short seemed to stem the decline somewhat. He took a few short breaths and signalled the archers above him.

"I'm taking a quick walk," he whispered and slid down the barricade in near silence. Forgetting his issue with hair loss for the time being, Cass crept down the slope through the spikes.

The stroll seemed to take an eternity, and he had never been more scared in his life. It was the head of Jeremiah he found first and after a bitter search in the near darkness, he found the rest of him. He wrapped the head in the white flag of peace and placed it upon the body's chest. Ignoring the revulsion, he began dragging his friend back home. It took him longer than he thought. He took a break half way up and regretted the added weight of his armour. Perhaps many things in the world would have been different had he not worn it for this distasteful task. He leaned against a spike, caught his breath, and as he did, caught some movement near the spikes of the riverbank. It was a long dark shape and it was crawling up towards the ramparts. The Regulator sat and watched in bewilderment. The form was small and feminine in appearance. She was gathering intelligence. Even though she was unarmed and wore no armour, a cold thought occurred to him. She simply had to die for this was war.

He had watched the Alpha cut a female down without hesitation or remorse and some of the bodies at the bottom of the slope had been female so why did he alone struggle? Was this another sign that he was even less of a man than he thought? He stepped on a twig, and she flinched. He could see her long matted blonde hair, and he could see his blade in the moonlight. This felt wrong.

She may have been beautiful, but he couldn't tell.

. . .

Cass collapsed at the bottom of the wall on the side of Keri. A kind hand reached out and offered water, which he took gratefully and drank between precious deep breaths. Quig oversaw the recovery of Jeremiah and they pulled him back to familiar territory. Cass tried to wash the blood away. He was covered in her. She had not died after the first strike and instead of peacefully slipping into the darkness, she had raged against the inevitable. Like a wild beast, she had struck at her killer with a dagger. Were it not for his armour he would have bled out long before he could make it back. Now her final strikes had left nothing but a few scrapes. The final blow had left the little sharp blade embedded uselessly in his chest plate. He had killed a female. He hoped it would be his last.

"I have another to add to my tally."

———

Erroh yawned and stretched his arms out wide. It was a harder task to achieve with his mate asleep across his chest. They were near the battlements in the closest patch of soft ground. He had woken up in worse places. He watched her wake to the cruel world they both faced. She blinked her beautiful eyes a few times and then smiled warmly as they met his. The moment could not last as realisation struck her, and he had no words to offer. In an instant though, she hid the fear and kissed his forehead.

"I like you," she whispered.

"I like you too."

He had a bad feeling about today. It was early and there were plenty of hours to assault the town. Some of his warriors were going to die in the hours ahead.

He was right.

One of the archers spotted a large group of Riders taking to their mounts and riding out into the wastes to find a break in the mountain range. The ground vibrated ominously until the last of the brutes disappeared, and Erroh put worrying thoughts from his mind. The nearest route through was a thin pass, well over a day's hard ride through unforgiving terrain. Even then, it was quite possible to miss. Had he not made a few wrong turns in his life? It was a small matter. Even if the Riders did make it through, Keri would probably have fallen long before. Regardless, he sent Cass and another Regulator to watch the pass and returned to the blockade to wait and watch the forest and the sky for movement and a turn of the weather. He closed his eyes and donned the warrior's skin. He unsheathed Vengeance and Mercy from behind his back and began to practice a variation on the form Jeroen had taught him months ago in a different life. He had come so far in such a short time. Eyes along the line watched the show with interest, and he was eager to impress. He caught a glimpse of Lea up above as he spun, and he marvelled how much she pushed him on with her own ability. He imagined Magnus would be proud but not at all impressed.

When his father was his age he had already invented the great weapons known as "The Clieve," had gone on to conquer the two islands of his birth and was already eyeing the Four Factions for himself. They were fine deeds indeed. Defending Keri would barely be a footnote in Magnus's great legacy but deep down, Erroh knew his father would approve greatly of his actions. Magnus would have stood and bled with these brave Warriors as well. The only difference being, he would have found a way to survive the oncoming storm.

Once again, he wished he was here with him now. Just to say goodbye and perhaps ask if there was any way he could avoid dying.

It was the little things.

He completed his routine and sheathed his blades as a runner brought steaming cofe for the Warriors along the top.

"There are worse ways to start our last day," said Quig loudly before blowing the steaming cup to a likeable temperature.

"It won't be our last day today, my friend," said Erroh and almost believed himself.

"Either way, I plan to better your score," the big man declared, sparking last moments of heated wagers.

"And how will you feel beating an Alpha but losing to a girl?" said Aireys, climbing up beside her companions. She sat at the edge of the blockade, rested her sword against her thigh, and sipped a cofe of her own.

"I see no girl, I only see Aireys," Quig jested.

"Emir thought I was a fine enough girl," Aireys quipped back swiftly though her face dropped at the mention of their absent friend. She looked away in an attempt to compose herself.

Quig squeezed her shoulder. "He thought you the finest girl that ever lived."

"I hope he finds someone far better than me to warm his heart and someone even bigger than you to protect him from himself," she said quietly.

From the trees, there began the stirrings of movement and lamenting thoughts of friends were swiftly forgotten. The morning's serenity exploded as the daunting and foreboding sound of battle horns suddenly filled the valley.

37

THE TALE OF THE BRIGAND

The noise reverberated through the valley down into the souls of every listener. It was a cacophony of dread whose first few notes caused more disheartenment to the warriors than the death of Jeremiah. This type of warfare couldn't be attacked with a pointed stick. All they could do was prepare for the inevitable assault.

Erroh took two long strips of cloth and began wrapping Mercy's handle tightly against his wrist and then the same with Vengeance. Who knew how slippery his grip would become in the hours ahead? Quig joined him at the summit.

"That sound rattles my bones. It makes me fear the worst," he said loud enough that only Erroh could hear.

"You should be fearful. I don't think you'll come close to besting my score," Erroh replied.

"Only the last of us to fall will ever know the outcome of this contest," Quig said.

"You could have died a rich farmer, but a forgotten one, too," said Erroh, testing the weight in his blades. The cloth would hold.

. . .

The horns played their solitary note for hours. Lea eyed the horn blowers with venom. They were disciplined and skilled. She counted at least a dozen spread out in the green. They would play for as long as their breaths allowed before one or two at most would fall away to fill their lungs without dropping the note. To the untrained ear, it was a wall of noise. Terrifying, intimidating and godlike. To one watching it was a simple regimented tactic. She knew how to silence the entire set of performers but that was their final card to play so she let the horns continue. Azel, the archer closest to her, bit his nails in irritation. It was something to do, she supposed.

Quig started to hum the beginning of a song to stave off the sound attacking his sanity. He was no talented singer, and he struggled with the tune, but anything was better than the horns. His favourite song was a fine ancient song about a man defiant, even as his jailers tortured him until he escaped. It was one of four songs he knew by heart. It seemed fitting.

"I am but a nomad, I answer to no man. Must I answer to you?" he sang and held his fingers to his ears but to no avail. *"You come any closer and I'll answer true,"* he sang louder and felt a reprieve from the desolation. The lyrics were fighting words sung for battle. He tried to remember the next verse and cursed loudly. What was it? Something about the hero slitting his jailer's throat? He moved onto the next verse instead.

"I am not done yet, not taken my last breath. I need no final meal."

"I fear no rope, no lead, or your steel," sang one of the warriors, in a voice that had sung the tale many times before. He continued and sang as if he were sitting in the Sickle surrounded by many friends and even more empty goblets. A

426

comrade to his right joined in and the next after that. As the song grew in volume, more and more warriors began to sing along. It was an ugly rendition of the song. The timing was terrible and for all their bravery few could hold many notes, but the wall of noise from every defender singing, drained the suffocating tones of the horns. Suddenly there was a spark of hope as a few beat their swords on wooden shields and drove the anthem far into the sky. The song reached its epic crescendo as the hero of the tale called all listeners to take up arms and strike out. They sang magnificently, until tragically all voices fell silent as the last lyric faded and the blaring horns returned to their ears.

It had been a nice moment, but moments pass.

Quig looked around at the dejected faces and started the first line again. Within moments, the wall of Keri had found one more wall of defence. They repeated the song over and over, taking great pleasure in the knowledge that their terrible voices reverberated down through the valley and right back towards the tree line. With a bit of luck, they were taking a little bit of the fight out of the attackers.

Finally, after the gods could take no more of the unpleasant concert, the horns trailed off. A few breaths later, the accompanying chants from Keri ceased their own performance. There would be no encore. The battlefield became a serene valley of silence in the wastes once more. A few crows between both groups pecked at the ground for nourishment, a mere appetiser, for there was a fine feast in the air. They always knew.

The brutes charged from the trees just like before in a sea of black leather, fur, and blade, surging up the slope. The ground shook as each boot charged forward, and Erroh missed the horns a little bit. The crows took flight.

Lea and her archers let loose and many fell as before but

there was no cessation to the deluge. The first dozen reached the barricade and began climbing and the world trembled under their hatred and weight. A dozen more followed behind and a dozen behind them. All lined up, awaiting their turn to kill.

The first attacker screamed in defiance and then anguish as Erroh delivered little mercy to him. His limp body fell and with its last act took a comrade down with him. It was not long before another attacker from the depthless well took his place and met the same demise.

Each brave Warrior of Keri stood atop the mound striking down at the scurrying enemy a few feet below. All who climbed met doom before reaching the summit. It was fine brutality as bloody swords from simple farmers plunged deep into skin and bone beneath them. The wilier of the attackers attempted to stand up half way and engaged in swordplay but with gravity and unstable ground at their feet, they too met similar fates.

Lea desperately tried to ignore the scurrying brutes vying for her mate's blood and kept to task as he'd asked her to. The crossbow wielders were easily cut down before they moved into range, but the curs that took to attacking the first lines of spikes were a trickier task. As they hacked with axes and hammers, she and her boys fired volley after volley down expending expensive ammunition. Eventually with only the loss of two spikes, the last demolisher was struck down and her eyes fell back to the horrors along the wall.

Erroh watched helplessly as the first of his warriors was pulled from the summit down into the moving masses below. The man screamed and tried desperately to get to his feet, striking out like a wounded animal not yet accepting its fate as prey. The impatient attackers still waiting their turn to scale the walls closed in around him stabbing and hacking. His screaming was soon ended, and he stepped into the darkness, accepting a divine glass of wine from a familiar face.

More enemy breached the line and attacked with terrifying ferocity. More blood was spilled on both sides as the warriors of Keri showed their measure. They fought valiantly but it was for nothing. To Erroh's dismay, the swell of attackers leaving the forest trickled away to nothing, leaving many hundreds more still unused. Where there had been an ocean of black and hatred, now there were pockets of space appearing in the battleground below. Not enough to suggest they could hold this wall much longer. There was just enough to finish the sacking of the town.

"There aren't enough attackers," he growled to himself as a fiend beside him slipped under a warrior's strike and leapt upon his quarry, leaving a gap in the line. The turning of the battle was already close at hand. Erroh struck his brother's killer with his sword and kicked him back over the mound where more were flooding in. He slashed out with both blades and desperately tried to stem the tide, killing and maiming viciously until another warrior leapt to his aid and helped knock the brutes back.

"Hold this line!" he roared and dared not stare to his mate far above, lest she think it time.

All along the edge, the line was struggling as more and more of the enemy reached the summit and grappled with defenders.

Not yet, Lea.

A part of the barricade collapsed a few feet down and two warriors slipped to their doom as battle hungry attackers tore them apart. The town would have fallen in that precise moment had an enraged Quig not torn into the surging brutes with battle scythe, swinging killing blows to all who met its fury. He swung his menace with thick powerful arms and caused delicious chaos among the attackers as they fled from his magnificent swipes. He was screaming numbers loudly.

Hold longer, Lea.

At the far end of the wall, the defenders were holding firm as the tall graceful figure of Aireys led the defence with sublime artistry. She sliced and tore as though attacking a fine canvas, her blade, like an artist's brush creating a masterpiece. The only sign of wear was a stream of crimson running down her side from a rogue plunging strike. It was but a scratch for a female with armour sturdy enough to be granted first prize to the grand champion of Keri. She would bleed for now and worry about such things later.

Erroh thought every warrior a hero as their great defiance was torn apart all around them. Their nerves were a steel worthy of Magnus, but inevitable defeat was closing in.

They needed one more moment.

They deserved one more moment.

He decided to take matters into his own hands. If he had taken a few breaths to rethink his action he might never have been so hasty. In his defence, it seemed like a good idea at the time. Lea would have disagreed. He sprinted towards the edge and leapt.

Falling.

He cleared the line of attackers below and landed in the mud at the bottom of the barricade. His hands spread out painfully in front of him still grasping his weapons, and he never felt more alone in the world. Time appeared to grind to a halt as the invading army took a collective breath and gazed disbelievingly at the lunatic who'd presented himself to them on a silver platter.

Erroh raised both his swords and challenged an entire army to a fight.

"That's amazing!" shouted Quig to any around him who could hear. He thought it a fine way to kill himself. The attacker that he was busy decapitating wasn't terribly moved by his words as he had other things on his mind. Aireys sprinted by him slashing at anything nasty that moved and stemmed the flow of invaders who'd breached the wall. Behind her, a few of the warriors began to strike back with renewed drive and belief buoyed on by the spectacle below them. The killers still climbing the barricade were now caught in two different minds: complete the climb or join their dying comrades below as they failed spectacularly to kill one solitary fighter.

His ankle was sore, and he felt a headache coming on. On top of that, he was tired, a great tiredness he'd never felt before. There were also about a hundred brutes staring at him. That seemed like the bigger problem.

The nearest to him woke from his daze and struck out only to meet the tip of Vengeance piercing through his throat. Erroh struck another cur down before spinning towards the edge of the riverbank and his only chance of survival. He released himself from fear and restraint and let savagery overcome him in its entirety.

With the spiked river's edge at his back, he avoided attacks from behind. Moving freely along the edge he ground his teeth as blades glanced painfully against skin and drew blood. Not enough to injure for his defence was sound, just enough to enrage him further. He was a blur of motion, and he killed mercilessly. He roared, screamed, and intimidated all who faced him but none faced him for very long. They flailed, swung, and tried to trap him in their net, but as if he were a god with an all seeing eye, he slipped from their grasp and cut them deeply as he fled. In truth, he rode his luck and was it not for the skill of his mate and her boys who rained down volley after volley of arrows; he would have fallen within moments. As it was, the enemy fell and they fell in great numbers and they feared this demon and wondered why The Woodin Man had not seen this and warned them.

Perhaps he had.

Blades filled his vision, and he waited for the defining blow to take him from the fight. It would be a fine way to step into the darkness, and Lea would take care of the next assault. The metal clashing pierced the world, and he hoped Dia could hear it all the way in Samara. Would she even care the town had fallen?

An awestruck female struck wildly at him, and he blocked ferociously, knocking her to the tinder covered ground. She held her hands up in fear and acceptance as his blades went to finish her life, but he held off the killing blow and swung wildly in a new direction instead. He didn't know why he hesitated. Maybe there was a little humanity still left in him. Maybe in his last few breaths he didn't want her death on his hands. He wondered would he ever regret the act of mercy as he lost sight of the blonde girl amid a group of venomous killers. He plunged his blade into the face of the nearest and felt a lot better about his decision. A few moments later, he had forgotten about her completely.

Sweat dripped down his forehead, though it may have been blood. He had never been so tired, yet only moments had passed since his suicidal leap. His vision darkened but his swords kept swinging. His body moving independent of his will. He struck out at someone and his blade went deep. He struggled to pull it free and slipped in the ruined bloody grass. A shadow loomed in, and he blinked his last moment away. It was an incredible shot from Lea that pierced the brute's shoulder blade allowing Erroh a moment to roll away.

It was time to retreat.

Arrows struck the ground all around him and summoning the last of his strength; he climbed to his feet and scurried back through the spikes towards the battlements. It wasn't far but each step was agony as he blocked attack after attack with reflexes he wasn't aware he still possessed. The great loneliness he'd felt dissipated when he met the unexpected counter charge from Keri's grand army. Suddenly he was no longer surrounded by murderous brutes, but his comrades attacking as one. Completely outnumbered, they sacrificed the higher ground for one desperate charge and led by the indomitable Quig and Aireys, they broke through the attackers' unprepared line, decimating all who resisted.

Renewed by the impossible thoughts of winning this battle, Erroh threw himself back into the fight with a frenzy worthy of outlandish Alphaline tales. He gored into the attackers with Quig at one side and Aireys on the other, and he felt like Magnus in his prime.

The battle suddenly turned and the brutes fell back from the wrath of a handful of brave warriors. Far too late in the battle, the sounds of horns rang out once more but this time for retreat. The warriors gave chase and cut them all down as they fled back towards the forest. They leapt over the bodies of hundreds until they reached the first line of spikes where they halted, wary of a crossbow's bolt.

Only Erroh kept up the pursuit. Overcome with adrenaline, aggression, and a grand desire to instil more fear in their enemy, he caught one last brute and dragged him to the ground a few feet from the treeline where hundreds still waited.

He could see them in the trees. He was terrified but that didn't matter at all. What mattered was sending them a final message.

"Come on!" he roared challenging the army once again before sliding Mercy's blade across his victim's throat casually. The blood erupted in a spray and though repulsed by his own actions Erroh roared laughter and held the dying man by the head as he squirmed his last few moments.

"Come on, you cowards!" he roared desperately trying to entice them to fight, and if they all came out to play, well that would be a fine thing indeed.

They did not rise to his challenge.

He let the corpse fall to the ground before disdainfully turning his back on them all and walking back up the slope, all the while laughing at their cowardice. Better to laugh than sob for his misery.

Lea wiped the sweat from her brow and discovered the remnants of tears along her cheeks. When had that happened? There were very few arrows left to call upon. There were fewer defenders as well. Twelve brave Warriors still breathing and two looked like they would never hold a blade again. It was a glorious victory but the cost was severe. They would not survive another attack. It was time to light an arrow. In the meantime, she was going to throttle the son of Magnus.

———

"How many did you fell?" asked Quig, cradling the head of the dying man. Erik tried to talk but it was becoming increasingly difficult. He coughed painfully and spat out some blood. That was a little better. He could feel himself slipping away but not quick enough. The pain was terrible, but he would not scream out. He had fought bravely by the side of so many and now he would die bravely for them. He had enjoyed the singing.

"I got eleven or twelve." He tried to move but his body wouldn't obey such an underrated task. The pain he could feel was ebbing away though.

"A fine number, Erik," said Aireys, stroking his head gently "More than me," she whispered, and he liked that.

"Where is Artur?" he said suddenly, his eyes widening with the faintest memory of his fellow Regulator, standing beside him atop the wall. He recalled a scream as both men charged back over the wall with the rest in their great counter attack. He hoped the scream hadn't been from his closest friend. Both had made an oath to be brave as the darkness called. Someone passed him a flask, and he sipped it. The sine never tasted sweeter. He summoned his strength and drank deeply and then they told him Artur had died bravely.

"He'll be dead by tonight," whispered Quig to Aireys. She nodded sadly and leaned over him. The wounds were horrible and his breathing was that of a drowning man. Not even Emir could have saved his life. She took Erik's head in her hand and kissed him gently on the lips. She thought him heroic. With her remaining free hand, she placed the sharp dagger across his throat. She knew where to cut. It was over in a couple of breaths. He didn't open his eyes, and he didn't struggle. He simply let go. She would have been eternally grateful to her own gods for such a blessing. Quig placed the peaceful man back on the grass and embraced Aireys. He held her tightly until he was sure she was not going to break.

———

Returning the bodies back over the barricade was a heartrending task and for once Erroh allowed his emotions to show. He wanted them to know he shared their grief. That he felt each one of their passing. He knew the name of each man they lay to rest, and he offered up a prayer to the absent gods he wanted to believe in. It was the first time in days he felt anywhere near normal. After the last warrior was returned, he faced his trickiest manoeuvre of the day and climbed the valley wall to face his mate.

He dismissed the archers so he could receive his reprimand in privacy, and she glared at him. They were hers to command, not his.

"How are you?" she said coldly when they disappeared from the top. If there was another attack, they would not be missed.

"I'm worn out," he said sheepishly. "How are you?"

"My arm hurts," she said. Erroh could see the strain on her face.

"Can I do anything to help, my beo?" he offered.

"I'm sure one of my boys can massage it later." Aye, she was angry with him for his little wander.

"I'm sorry, Lea."

Silence and a shrug.

She turned and watched the slope of doom. Things were afoot. She watched them all gather in the trees. Apparently, it was time to put down this brave little defence. It was an entire army against just over a dozen.

The odds were hardly fair.

The ground began to shake under the sudden charge of hundreds. They came as one massive tidal wave back up the slope and swiftly the land became a massing swell of rage. The air was filled with high piercing cries of war, and Erroh looked down helplessly at his comrades.

"Clear the wall!" he yelled. The order was unnecessary. They had all been waiting this moment. They had cleared the wall when the first attacker had emerged from the green.

The brutes kept running forward, oblivious as to why no Warrior waited for them on top of the barricade. Pride assured them that the defenders had fled. The first of many reached the barricade and began to climb, roaring triumphantly. Footholds from old wooden barrels, finely crafted furniture, and overturned carts made the climb easy enough when not having to face arrows, scythes, and sword wielding maniacs. They made good time as they neared the top.

"Take the shot, Lea," he whispered looking up at the sky. Mercifully, it had not rained the last few days, though who knew how the wind blew.

"Not yet." This was her battleground, her responsibility, and her moment. She waited a few breaths longer. The flame flickered in her eye line. Dancing frantically in the breeze, she wished it a safe journey.

"I've got this," she whispered.

She fired the flaming arrow.

38

SERENITY VALLEY

I t flew like a firefly that had come out to play long before any others. It caught the wind and it hit its mark. It struck a tree with a gentle thud and few attackers took notice. Even fewer gave it a second glance. Lea was already relighting a second arrow. She held the bow out and aimed a little higher. She let it fly and the yellow streak screamed silently into the forest and embedded itself in another tree much further back. She smiled as this one caught quicker.

She sent two more after it. Only one missed its mark, landing a little wide and ending up in a little bush, but with so many coats of burning oil applied to so many trees it didn't really matter. She turned to the slope and sent one into a spike. It soared up in flame straight away and took an astonished attacker with it. The flame took hold of his leather armour and when he tripped over some oil laced kindling trying to pat down the flames, he managed to do all the hard work for Lea in one fell swoop. The killers who had not yet entered the battlefield began to notice the rapidly growing flames all around them in bewilderment. They tried desperately to extinguish the flames but all too quickly the fires began to engulf the wood and themselves included. Perhaps had their thirst for death not blinded them, they may well have noticed the oil soaked kindling on the ground leading all the way up the slope, or the sloppily painted tree trunks stained with the volatile fluid.

The Warriors stood side by side with torches in hand and waited patiently for the attackers to cross over the summit. Caught in the frenzy of attack, the first few over the top never thought to look behind them and in truth, why would they? Victory was in touching distance. When the torches were thrown at the bottom of the rubble and the freshly oiled surface took light straight away, they began to sense a problem. Moments later, they were burning like the blockade itself.

The fire spread rapidly through the green. The first groups to flee the barricade's fire were trapped in a crush and were engulfed by the swirling flame as it followed behind. Some brutes charged the burning spikes by the riverbed but very few were able to break the wood down. Of those that did get through, many dropped into the deep waters, and drowned as their heavy armour dragged them to the bottom. Scores of attackers who managed to avoid the fire were blinded by the billowing smoke, which eventually sucked the air from them. They met their end in a deep sleep. Erroh and Lea watched it all from the finest view in the town and relished in their demise.

In the first hour alone, half of the great army perished. Those who managed to break through the burning forest and escape back to their chaotic camp licked their wounds by their tents. The smell of cooked meat filled the valley and the sky shimmered from the heat. However, there was a cost to this final desperate move. By nightfall, the cavalry spikes had burned away to nothing and though the forest and barricade still burned, the slope became a charred ashen mound resembling the fate of the ancients' world.

All that would hold the enemy's final march was the burning barricade with flames twenty feet high. They began to stock up with the last of the town's furniture near the furnace: tables, chairs, beds, and barrels. The town had been stripped clean. If the residents ever returned to live in Keri in the far future, they would struggle terribly to refurbish their homes, but it would be a golden age to be a carpenter.

The defenders watched the sky and set their weapons down. They took seats on mismatched chairs and couches, and listened as Erroh addressed them.

"When they breach the gap, all is done, my brothers," he said and the congregation agreed.

"I would like to leave," one defender muttered. His eyes were drawn, and he nursed a deep gash across his chest. He would never fight again with such an injury.

"Every one of you has earned a reprieve," said Erroh.

Quig didn't agree.

"Does anybody really think if those fukers march in here without spilling some more blood, they won't hunt us all down? Anyone who can't fight can leave, but I will not lead doom upon the rest of the town. Fuk this, I'm staying."

"And I will be with you, brother," Erroh said and left them to make peace with his mate while the rest began discussing the score.

———

"Are you done, Lea?" Erroh hissed holding his cheek.

She slapped him a third time. "Not yet."

He took a step back, just out of range. She stepped forward and delivered a fine crack across his cheek.

"I did what needed to be done," he said, aware that leading her down the side street away from eager ears was a futile gesture as they were making more than enough noise for the rest at the fire to hear. He'd hoped for a few heated exchanges and then a few embraces after. Maybe a last kiss? She wasn't ready to forgive heroism. Sometimes Alphalines just didn't play well together.

She prodded her finger in his chest. "It would have been a stupid death. You searched for glory like your father." He'd desired warmth and reassurance and instead received chastening. Was spitting bile how she wanted to spend her last few hours with him?

"I did what was needed." He pushed her away before spinning around and marching off. She didn't follow.

He thought about climbing up to watch the burning forest but the fear that she would appear was too great so he headed back to the closest thing he called a home. In a dark empty kitchen, he recovered some dried salted meats and some bread. Lighting a near dead candle, he ate heartily but still left her a portion, muttering a few curses as he sliced the meat. In the lowlight, a weariness struck him like never before. His body craved straw and cotton sheets but the cold ground with a few blankets was all he had. Still, he was asleep in a few breaths.

"So this is where you hid yourself," Lea said. She sat with her legs crossed beside him, the solitary hanging candle lighting the little plate of cold food in front of her. He didn't reply as feigning sleep seemed the smarter move. She sighed loudly, and he heard the sounds of eating. He wanted to end the argument and take her in his exhausted arms to kiss, love, and sleep with, but he was still a vengeful little Alpha who had been shouted at a little unfairly. He'd turned the battle. How could she criticise him for that?

Women.

"Oh just wake up, Erroh," she muttered, finishing the last mouthful. He was asleep on his back, and she could tell from his breathing that he was pretending. She slipped her leg across him and sat down on his lap. She loved him so much that it hurt. Life was so unfair.

"Wake up, idiot."

You're my idiot, and I need you.

"I think you've put on weight," he whispered as she leaned over him and let her long hair brush his face. He felt stirrings immediately.

"I forgive you," she said gently.

"Will you get off me now?"

"No,"

She leaned in and kissed him delicately on his lips.

"I forgive you too," he said.

"You were amazing today," she said gently. The candle flickered as it neared the end of its life. He thought she looked magnificent in its dying silhouette.

"I thought you disapproved."

"I was proud as you tore through them. It was the thing of legends. If I survive all of this, I aim to spread word of your heroism." She touched his chest.

She kissed him again, biting his lower lip slightly.

"I was terrified," he admitted.

"So was I," she said and her face turned serious. "I will never become mated with another man. I wish to be known as only Erroh's mate for life. It's a title which will serve me better than another man." She held his gaze, and he could tell that she wouldn't be swayed on this matter. He wanted to argue that she was so young and many seasons of life were still ahead of her and that she deserved happiness, but he held his tongue.

"As you wish, my beo," he said stroking her face.

"Thank you, my Erroh."

The hanging candle hissed and the room fell to darkness, and he decided to reveal his own plan. "If you die though and I survive, I'm going to kill Wynn, mate with Lillium, and keep Roja as my concubine."

She tugged at something delicate, and he yelped in reply.

"I think you could choose a finer concubine," she hissed, but he could hear her smile hidden among the words.

"Besides I don't think you could beat Wynn, not to mention that he's far prettier," she informed him. "In fact, in this light, perhaps you could pretend you're him for a little while?" She began straddling him gently.

"I love you, Lea," laughed Erroh, gripping her tightly.

"Shush, Wynn wouldn't say that," she said, as he lifted her off him and pinned her down in one smooth motion. She couldn't help but be further aroused. As he kissed her, she thought of him staring down an entire army and them blinking first. Her Erroh, nobody else's. Deep down where her naivety lay with childish hopes and dreams, she believed that if any man could survive the final attack it would be her Erroh. She would keep her oath and flee, and she would survive for him. She would do her part and expect him to do his.

―――――

The following day Erroh sat on a comfortable couch near the flames chewing on some freshly barbecued steak. He was not alone.

"I've craved some barbecue since we cooked the bastards yesterday," muttered Quig and then realised he had spoken aloud. He sat against a timber barrel stained with old wine holding a slab of charcoaled steak. It was burned to a crisp on the outside and crimson right through. "I suppose that makes me a cannibal," he admitted guiltily and wiped some juices from his beard.

Aireys started to laugh.

"I did as well," she said biting into her own steak fiercely. She took another of the honeyed onions and tore a few strips free. A few of the Warriors with them began to snigger in agreement.

"So the smell of our burning enemies brought a great hunger upon us all? That's some fine savagery right there, brothers," Quig said.

"Magnus would approve," Erroh said and the sniggers turned to giddy laughter.

"War has changed us. It's probably better that we all die soon," he said laughing.

"You sure this is the last of our stocks and definitely not some poor fool's leg?" Aireys asked their chef.

Erroh laughed and bit into his meal while Quig eyed his meat suspiciously. Lea reached over to take it from him, and he snatched it away from her grasp. "My leg," he hissed as if a hound with a bone. A leg bone.

"Cannibalism is underrated," Cass said, letting a smile creep slowly across his lips. He was sitting among the Warriors on a patch of soft grass enjoying his homecoming. The Riders hadn't located the break in the valley after all and they had returned to dispirited comrades nursing burns and

444

heartache. Aye, when the fire went out they would charge but that was tomorrow and tomorrow was another day for the convoy to escape. He accepted another slab of still burning steak from the archer Azel.

"You're a fine chef, Azel," Cass said.

"I aim to please, friend," said the chef winking at the Regulator and lancing a few more pieces of meat onto a skewer and putting them against the flames.

Their great defence was at an end so they ate the last of the supplies and drank whatever alcohol they could find as if it were the last night of their lives. The mood around the bonfire was boisterous with a dignified sense of acceptance. The work they had been charged with was to hold and delay. They had succeeded beyond their wildest dreams.

"Any regrets?" Quig asked Erroh.

"I wish I could forget what pigeon meat tastes like," he said drinking from a bottle of wine. A bitter red, but after the last few days it was ambrosia.

Someone muttered, "They were good in a pie", and Erroh grimaced. He'd take their word for it. In truth, he regretted the obvious things such as his probable death and fear for Lea but, as with most young Alphalines who took to the road to find themselves and an eventual mate, there was nothing left unsaid or done. There were no regrets for the life he had chosen. He passed the bottle to a warrior on his right.

"Well I wish I was mated to an Alpha that was better in a fight," said Lea, leaning against her man. Many Warriors nodded in mock agreement. Jests were made at their general's expense and laughs were boisterous. Far away, the rumble of thunder began to roll. A sleeping giant was rising from its slumber.

"Sounds like a storm is coming," Aireys said gently.

"There's enough of a storm already here," muttered a Warrior.

"It can pass right by," said another.

"If the rains come at least we'll be clean," growled Quig.

"I regret that Erroh didn't wash more," said Lea and everyone laughed.

"I regret not hitching a lift with the convoy," muttered Erroh enjoying the banter. All that was needed was a deck of cards. Maybe he would hop down to the enemy camp and ask them if they had a spare pack on hand.

They spent the last night eating and drinking their spoils of survival. They could hear the thunder miles away but refused to let it sully the cheer. The closest the mood came to dropping was when Lea declared she had killed most with the flames and Quig announcing, "Had I not been saving Erroh, I could have killed at least twenty more." Voices were raised as the numbers were called out and final bets were made. Before the night came to a close Aireys stood up and said what needed to be said. She silenced everyone and dipped her head in the direction of the two Alphalines who had led them.

"Thank you," she said, careful not to let her voice break.

"You were worth standing with," said Lea bowing in return. Erroh and Lea slipped away before the last drink was finished and lay together with armour and weapons at close hand in their little kitchen. The floor was hard but they only knew comfort while holding each other tightly. They fell asleep beside each other one final time.

39

DYING EMBERS

It was the first few hours of morning when the heavy clouds descended and with them came the end. It started as an innocent little bit of drizzle hissing lightly as it came in contact with the weakening flames but soon enough in a dreadful peaceful hiss, the heavens opened up and the heavy downpour covered the world. The Warriors of Keri faced each other one last time. It had been an honour.

The Riders took to their saddles.

Quig and Cass rolled the last of the carts straight through the muddy, glowing mound. They drove them as far into the dying embers as they could as the deluge turned to a tempest. The first Rider led his beast over the slippery mound and crashed into their territory. Ash the colour of death flew and the last few sparks of defence were extinguished. Aireys reacted first and leaping wildly took the attacker's head off with a fine swing of her blade but the mount continued its frantic run. It crossed the cobbled bridge and into the town square long before anyone else and stopped by a trough to take a drink. The headless Rider remained atop still holding the reins.

High above Lea watched them swarm around the defenders. She screamed as her friends formed up into a pack of cornered animals and met each attack with valiant acceptance. More and more Riders charged clumsily over the barricade breaking a pathway for the soldiers to follow. The final piece of good fortune was that each Rider continued their charge down to the town in the hope of catching fresh game instead of running down the last few defenders at the wall. Infantry followed behind them and surged through. Erroh was fierce, heroic and surrounded. He swung his blades furiously in the last few moments of his life, and she screamed to the absent gods for him and fired down at the enemy and then Aireys was gone.

Aireys plunged her blade deep into the chest of an attacker but as the cur fell backwards, he took her weapon with him as a final gesture of hate. She scrambled for it, breaking their last line before a stray glove reached out and gripped onto her armour. She managed to let out a little shriek of contempt before it pulled her into the masses where they fell upon her aggressively.

Quig followed Aireys. Emir would have wanted him to be beside her, when she died. The big man leapt forward, slashed with his great weapon, and cleared a space almost immediately. His mind was reeling with sorrow, hate, and the counting of numbers. He had never thought himself a killer or warrior but now he aimed for first place. He swung again and roared like the true champion that he was, and raised his tally.

Cass and the last of the warriors leapt into the path of the swarm to take out as many as they could. The Regulator took a small dagger to the chest and as he collapsed backwards into the raging black water, pulled two of the killers with him. The unforgiving current took all three. Those with him were met by the final charge on Keri and were sent into the darkness beyond. They never screamed out.

Lea roared at her archers as brutes began to scramble up the valley edge towards them. Their time was done. On both sides, they swiftly disappeared into the cover of the thick foliage while she waited a few more breaths to take out a killer bearing down on her mate. Behind her, the noise of scrambling brutes grew close. She unsheathed her swords.

The nearest brute thought she was an easy enough kill. He raised his blade and charged while the two others searched for the cursed archers. In a blur, she slipped under his strike, and he felt a horrible tearing pain across his belly. He dropped his sword trying to stop the contents of his intestines from spilling out, but it was a futile final task.

She leapt forward, whipped her blade across the second assailant's throat, and left him to die by the first. The final attacker managed to strike once before she countered and sent both her blades right through his chest. He was dead long before she pulled them free and returned them to their scabbards. She notched her final arrow and leaned over to watch the last moments of Keri. She took a breath and fired.

Quig was swinging when the first crossbow bolt struck his chest. He roared and swung again sending another into the darkness. Another arrow pierced his leg, and he stumbled. He swung regardless of balance, howled with pain, and then triumph, as he took his victim. None could near his mighty scythe until a Rider charged down on him and lanced his great heart with a long pike. He never screamed out for mercy. He just closed his eyes and never opened them again.

Erroh tried to make it to the big man, but a thousand hands grabbed him. They gripped his wrists and his blades were torn from his grip. They punched and kicked until he fell to the ground in a ruin. They moved in with killing intent and, in the wet cold ground and all alone, Erroh thought of Lea in her yellow dress, and then everything went dark.

She watched Erroh go down under the rushing horde, and she fell to her knees and never wanted to rise again. She thought about praying to absent gods, but she doubted there was any god nearby to enjoy such misery. She almost turned to despair but instead her hand reached out and took hold of her pack. It was time to move, a voice in her head reminded her. She knew which route to take, where the cover of trees were at their thickest. She heard the fresh sound of brutes below, attacking the climb, and she left her perch and vanished into the safety of the forest.

———

Darkness.

Pain.

Awake.

He hung outstretched from the back of one of the large carts. His wrists in thick rope, his body bowed to kneel in the wet mud. They thought him no longer a threat. He blinked his eyes and tried to clear his vision but the sky was dark. How long had he slept? All around him was good cheer, and Erroh threw up on himself. He could see many tents lined around the camp, some with small fires burning outside. Children in groups of all ages walked freely through the crowd, as it gathered around the massive unlit pyre in the centre of the camp. Their triumphant mood after the magnificent victory over thirty or so warriors was evident, as they laughed and joked in the ugly barbaric language. There was more to see but his eyes never left the great stacks of firewood. They had found Lea. They had probably taken her when the beasts had overrun the town, and he had not been there to protect her. He struggled in his restraints.

Aireys was barely conscious from the loss of blood and the numerous blows to the head. It was a small mercy. Her long hair was matted and dyed red from her wounds and her eyes were glazed over. Her vanquishers carried her along, and she never tried to thrash for all fight had left her.

Her fate was sealed unless he could do something. He struggled harder and felt a little bit of give in the rope around his right wrist. His muscles screamed in protest, but he persevered, tugging fiercely until he slipped in the muddy ground and fell against the cart's frame with a dull thud. Sharp pains shot up his arms into his back and nearly made him pass out. He had lost far too many friends today. He would not lose another. He climbed to his unsteady feet and began again.

They strapped each of her thin muscular arms to the wooden pyre, while a tall brute with a long beard and cruel features addressed the crowd. Erroh twisted his wrists and pulled his right hand as hard as he could. The crowd began to laugh at some joke made at Aireys's expense, and he hated them more. How dare they laugh at such a heroic warrior? They would know his wrath. With a violent jerk, he freed his right and immediately went to work on his left wrist. In his haste, he never noticed a soldier come up behind him and catch him squarely on the jaw with a fierce punch. He cried out and his attacker shouted nonsensically in his face before striking him a second time to deter any further thoughts of escape.

They lit the fire.

With the last of his will, Erroh suddenly grabbed the brute by the throat and squeezed. He screamed to Aireys so she might see his final gift. He dug his fingers deeply through skin into muscle, and he pulled. He screamed her name again and wrenched the killer's throat free. The man spluttered and fell to his knees. Streams of warm liquid sprayed wildly, and Erroh screamed for Aireys a third time.

She couldn't see properly. She remembered rain and fighting but everything now was a blur. The only resounding thought she could grasp was that she was going to die. Her only regrets were not dying beside her friends and only telling Emir she loved him once. The straps around her wrists were all that kept her from collapsing. The wound along her side was deep and with every moment, she was slipping from this life. It was a fine life, and she had lived it well. All of them had. The fires began to burn around her, and she felt the presence of Quig and it reassured her.

He was waiting.

Suddenly she heard her name called out from near, and she tried to open her eyes through the flame and the draw to sleep. She would not scream. Her name was called again, and she looked away from the darkness back to the world of sorrow. She looked beyond the roaring animals that were enjoying her demise and saw Erroh.

He was still killing.

She held onto that thought. It kept her warm. She raised her head and closed her eyes as the flames took hold. She would show them how a brave Warrior of Keri stepped into the darkness. The pain intensified. Her clothes took light and there was no more air to breath. She was terrified but held her scream. Then she heard the familiar laugh of Quig and the clinking of glasses. She heard a whisper that it was her bet, and she stepped into the darkness assisted by the arrow from some sympathetic killer that had seen more than enough. Nobody seemed to notice the arrow as her limp body fell forward and burned away silently into ash.

40

TOO MANY RATS IN THE NEST

It was a shithole, and even that description was lending it quite a kindness. On one hand, it was a rather large tavern with good light and a decent location, but there was no escaping the fact that it was indeed a shithole. Wrek wasn't entirely certain why he was seated in this particular shithole or indeed, why Sigi seemed so eager to have a drink with him here, but he had his suspicions. He didn't care about grand plans; he only wanted the drink. Preferably not in a place like this though.

A drunk did have some standards.

"It could be the new Rat's Nest," said Sigi stirring the warm brown liquid in front of him. It may have been soup. He tasted a bit and grimaced, and Wrek felt a headache coming on. After a moment, the headache continued talking.

"There's a great opportunity here. If we play our cards right, we can own this city," Sigi said excitedly and Wrek offered a weak smile. A lesser man may have lost heart after the attack on the tavern, but Sigi had shrugged it off. He had simply made bigger plans. Wrek followed the sine, and the barrels of sine were carted off to the city of Samara where the duo of nomads swiftly began to make a little noise among the stalls of the market. Not to mention an absolute fortune. Who knew higher yield sine was in such demand anyway? As word spread of two scruffy merchants selling bottled ambrosia at criminally low prices, customers flocked to them, and the market became Sigi's to command.

And where did Wrek the drunken bouncer fit in with this divine distilling endeavour?

Well, he was the muscle when disgruntled tavern owners came calling about his aggressive strategy for undercutting their prices. They brought convincing arguments laced with a few shiny pieces, other times proposing illustrious partnerships but mostly they brought sharp sticks, but it never mattered. Like a hound, Sigi would point and Wrek would ravage. It wasn't much in a way of a living but Wrek never complained. Soon it became known that neither were to be played with. However, it wasn't just brutality that earned Wrek his place at Sigi's side. It was Wrek's uncanny ability to move with good graces among the Black Guard. As the gates closed to wanderers and those seeking refuge, the barrels of freshly brewed sine were never halted on their midnight treks from the wastes. But as the funds rose and the barrels were drained exponentially, Sigi got fresh ideas and Wrek, well, Wrek wasn't going to argue as long as he was needed.

Wrek decided to feign interest. "Do go on."

"I spoke with some interesting people in the market. A couple who can move freely through the gates and they have a fine place for us to use." Sigi's eyes darted around the room as he spoke as though he was committing the first act of treason against the Primary herself.

Wrek just massaged his knuckles. Yesterday's dispute had split open a little bit of his skin. Maybe it had been from the day before.

"You want to move the distillery closer?" the behemoth asked.

"Aye. So the trips you make will only take a day each way now."

"Can they be trusted?" Wrek asked sipping his white ale. It was terrible. Just like this shithole of a bar. Just like this rotting city with its locked gates. Every day more and more unfortunates were turned away. Every day more and more shacks were erected down along the walls of the Spark. They could all smell war in the wind, and so flocked to the one light in the darkness. He pitied them but there was nothing he could do. The Primary had spoken and her word was law. He shrugged and thought about the freedom of salt mines. He missed the salt mines.

Sigi smiled confidently. "Of course, they can be trusted."

"Would it not be easier to just set up a distillery inside the city and avoid the nightmare of the gates altogether?" Wrek asked.

"If people knew the location of my distillery, I doubt I'd be alive for very long. No, that will come in time. When I can afford more swords," Sigi said eying the décor with as much distaste as Wrek did.

"You underestimate the cover of protection I provide," Wrek said sniffing, in truth, a little hurt that Sigi thought him unequal to the task.

"You underestimate your talents. You're far more than a bruiser. People around here respect you, my friend."

Wrek didn't believe him for a moment. "Aye, for my violence but it's a small matter. Who are these reliable people?"

"They have a farm not far from here. Secluded from the world," Sigi whispered.

Behind them, a few men entered the bar loudly. They

were already drunk and the sun had not yet set. They roared for the smoothest ale, as they had "a mighty thirst." They wore their muddy work clothes and spoke loudly. The old innkeeper behind the bar nodded and began pouring. His hands were covered in spots and his grey hair was thinning. He was jaded and they were annoying and Wrek hated them.

"We spoke of buying a tavern in the city, so what about this place?" Sigi asked, and Wrek noticed the excitement in his voice.

"It's an absolute shithole and likely to waste a season's coin on new interiors alone," he whispered.

"It's a roof over our heads when the rain comes." argued Sigi.

"I don't mind the rain."

Sigi looked downbeat, but his eyes were sharp. "Will you trust me?"

"Of course I trust you."

"Excellent," Sigi said brightening up immediately. Wrek suspected his opinion didn't matter at all. He was no skilled distiller, and he was no accomplished entrepreneur. Sigi was the rising star in the city. He was the man with ambitious plans and Wrek was hanging on for the ride.

"You bought this place already didn't you?"

"Aye, we did."

Wrek sighed and took notice of two pretty little things enter the shithole inn, a redhead and a blonde. They were in heated conversation of matters he imagined to be of the manly variety. This was hardly the place for them to find potential mates or indeed garner the right breed of suitor. They took a seat at the far end of the bar and waited to be served. One of the drunken workers stood up from his stool and walked unsteadily towards them before bowing pompously towards his chosen object of desire. She just smiled and waited for him to go away. Wrek's knuckles turned a little white. The lout grabbed a chair without seeking any invitation and barked over at the bored bartender "Two fine glasses for these fine females."

"How's the ale?" asked Sigi, gaining Wrek's attention.

"It's mostly yellow water with some mud at the bottom," Wrek hissed and eyed the little line of sediment in a nice mound at the bottom of his glass. It was ale but it was badly brewed. There was movement at the far table as the other three louts, no doubt buoyed on by their comrade's daring, descended upon the two females, surrounding them with slurred boasts, bitter odours, and boorish leering.

Sigi tapped Wrek's glass. "That's not going to sell at all. I could brew some myself, but I'm no master at ale. It's so much work and waste for such a little profit." He scrunched up his face in worry.

"Maybe we just don't serve it in glasses," he muttered, under his breath.

After a moment, he thought this idea grand and Wrek sighed again.

"So we fix this shithole up, increase the flow of sine, and earn a fortune to retire on?" Wrek asked cracking his knuckles. He caught the female with the red hair swatting away an exploratory hand from her leg before it moved further up her matching red dress. The hand returned with an attempted charming grin though it made no further move. Resting on the leg was fine wasn't it? Point made. They'd only just met after all.

Sigi leaned forward and whispered. "There is something in the wind, my friend, and someone with the right mind can have it all. This tavern is simply the next step," he said in a strange tone.

Wrek nodded and stood. If this tavern failed, it was a

small matter. He would support Sigi's endeavours. If they ended up without a piece in their pockets, they could always find a decent shack at the edge of the city wall and grubby though they may be, he'd spoken with a few refugees and found them fine enough people. Moreover, if the tavern made money, well that was grand as well.

"You look after the alcohol, and I'll make sure the clientele are of the highest standard in here." Wrek removed a strap of leather from his pocket and wrapped it tightly around his hand.

"Have they paid for all their drinks yet?" he shouted to the barman. The man nodded that they had indeed.

"Ah good!" he roared and began the process of immediately improving the quality of patrons that were welcome in "The Rat's Nest."

41

THE SLOW MARCH INTO MADNESS

The miles. Oh the miles. The terrible miles.

The chain around his waist clinked loudly as they walked and it was a constant reminder that he would be their pet until he died. The Hero of Keri was no more. They marched south, and Erroh marched with them. Any joy at seeing the Riders return empty handed after their two day Hunt to ensnare runaways had now dissipated. Any relief at marching south towards the snowy mountains instead of north towards the great sky road was now a distant memory. He told himself that operating the great defence was the right decision but what if he'd been wrong? What if they could have fled when the fires were first lit? What if they could have lived? No, he already knew the answers and though they should have made him feel better, they didn't.

He felt the pull of the chain as it rose into the air from its iron peg at the back of the cart. Maybe he should drop to the ground and allow the cart pull him along? He felt the edge rubbing his raw skin as the chain grew taut, and he hurried his pace. Amazing how the presence of incessant pain turned a brave warrior into a subservient hound.

He had tried to walk with his head held high but as the miles were marched, he found it drop by degree. Now he stared at the ground for most of his day. The long convoy of killers travelled the same route the river took and they only ever marched south. When the water veered off on its own merry course, they trekked onwards while Riders searched for the next river going their way. When they camped, Erroh was able to rest his aching body and get a few hours' sleep but it was never enough. The days in which no fresh flowing rivers could be found were the worst. His heart would sink when the first of the torches along the carts were lit. There would be no sleeping on any of these nights. As fatigue set in, Erroh would spend hours trying to keep his feet from tripping up in the low light. A few Riders held out torches for the soldiers but few torchbearers came anywhere near him. They knew his threat still. They remembered the manic demon.

By the seventh day, black and purple marks had formed where the chain rubbed against his skin. By the second week, every tug from the chain after he took a misstep was enough to make him cry out.

Feeding time broke up the monotony. On the first day when he still had fight in him, they brought a plate with steaming meat. The brute was alone and offered the meat cautiously. He muttered gibberish, and Erroh feigned stupidity. The fiend stepped closer and pointed at the food, it may have been boar. Erroh leapt like a frenzied beast and charged him to the ground. Unfortunately, his comrades came to his aid swiftly enough, though Erroh suspected he broke his nose. They beat him unconscious for his crime. When a second brute arrived the next day with another piece of steaming meat, he attacked again. On the third day a female appeared.

He saw through the ruse immediately. She was beautiful

and similar in age. She had long flowing blonde locks and a kind smile that suggested both warmth and wantonness. They had chosen the finest alluring bitch of them all, and Erroh found her arousing. Though she spoke that same brutish tongue, she whispered deliciously of the marvels of meats she had procured for him and only him, and when she sat down next to him, it was difficult to ignore the many fine shapes to her. He took the food she offered for a man's will could only sustain so much. It was unsettling how much glee there was in her deceiving eyes as he gorged himself upon the greasy pieces. In truth, he'd never eaten a finer meal. She smiled wonderfully when he swallowed the last mouthful and touched his arm as if finishing a meal was to be congratulated. She pointed to herself and said a word he didn't understand. She laughed and squeezed his shoulder. It was pleasant to be touched tenderly. He struck her fiercely in the face, and she collapsed on the ground unconscious. He ignored the guilt as a little trickle of blood flowed from her nostril. She did not deliver any more meals to him after that.

It was a child they sent next and with him a bitter clear broth with a few chunks of vegetables for sustenance. The child was a handful of seasons in age, and he knew no fear. At first light and at sunset he would deliver meals, and Erroh allowed him safe passage. The most pain he could inflict upon the child was a few half-hearted growls and aggressive facial expressions but after a few days, he dropped even those needless attempts. He simply accepted the food and ate.

Mish liked to talk so Mish talked and the cage hound would listen. Every day, if Mish felt like it, Mish would regale the cage hound with tales of things he thought ever so interesting. Things like the Hunt's great war and the battles ahead and

Uden The Woodin Man and silly cage hound couldn't understand a word of it. The cage hound had a great honour ahead of him but never seemed grateful or said thank you. Instead, he made stupid noises when he opened his mouth so Mish would keep talking but that was okay because Mish had nobody else to talk with. Actually, he had a few hundred people to talk to but few listened apart from Nomi. Nomi was kinder than everyone else was. When he was old enough, she would be his first. He informed her of this, and she laughed loudly and said she would be honoured but that he should be mindful not to settle for a flawed female like herself. Mish wondered if she wanted the cage hound for herself for a night. She had been charged to take care of the cage hound when no one else would, but he'd struck her down. She still insisted the cage hound be cared for anyway. She obviously wanted him fit for Uden The Woodin Man.

The child couldn't shut up. He kept talking as if nothing else in the world mattered. Longer and longer, he stayed with Erroh every day, and his head reeled trying to understand the incomprehensible words. There was something almost familiar, but he suspected that was just his own mind slipping away into madness. Occasionally a few words would stick in his head, but he would only repeat them aloud when alone away from eager ears in the cold nights. Instead, he just sat and ate his meal and waited until the young one grew wary of one-sided conversation. The boy was an enigma: he never seemed to take a breath in between sentences. It was a skill that all children possessed.

———

The days all melded into one great nightmare. He felt as if he had walked a thousand miles at least but who knew? The chain continued to hurt more each hazy day and his body became weaker. He wondered was he ready to tally up his final score as all time champion of Keri? He had done his part in this unknown war. Who would lament a beaten warrior if he found himself a sharp rock to run down his wrists anyway? He felt his resolve lessen with each sunset. He felt the darkness engulf him in despair, but he kept on walking as if he had a choice.

Countless days of torment struggled on.

They became weeks.

He missed the old Erroh. The Erroh that had died on the battlefield of Keri with the bravest men. He swiftly learned that the shell that remained was too nervous to gamble his small stash of chips on one great bet. He thought he had known loneliness walking the road. He'd embraced that loneliness. But without her warmth beside him, he felt a loneliness of the soul. The ache for her was more pain than any metal chain could ever inflict and soon enough he repelled the memory of her completely, preferring the pain of his miserable fate to the tragedy of what he'd lost.

Then he began to die.

While his captors were dressed in their thick leather outfits lined with fur, he still wore the clothing from his last day as a free man. Every night he huddled up into a ball and tried not to freeze. He felt a deep chill in his bones that could never shift even come dawn and the walking which followed.

The further south they walked the whiter the great mountain peaks became. They caught no scent of settlements and mercifully enough he took no part in any further massacres. Erroh liked to believe they spotted a few towns along the way but him and his Warriors had taken some of their fight. Thoughts like that warmed him until the bitter wind stole that pleasure.

He started to cough when the first snow began to fall. It was gentle at first with soft little flakes dropping lazily from the sky and melting harmlessly in his hair. He remembered his mother had told him during a lesson why snow fell, why it was cold, and why it could kill. They'd discussed the matter in front of a small warm fire in her own study. He would have given anything to hold the tepid mug of tea he had let sit too long. He was never going to see her again. Never hear her dismissive tones when his father annoyed her. He would never hear her laugh at inappropriate moments, and he would never hear her heavy cough which wiped her out in the wetter seasons. He soon stopped thinking of Elise.

———

Erroh recognised the curse words first; they were easier to pick up because they were the words used by his captors most. Perhaps had the little annoying child who named himself Mish spoken a little slower, he might have picked up the ugly language a little quicker. As it was, after a few weeks he had learned a few bits and pieces. He still couldn't decipher most of what was said to him but one repeated sentence was that the "brute of oak" was to be revered, and he would soon meet this man or something along those lines. Was this the fabled Woodin Man? He thought the child referred to a testing of blood, but Erroh could never be sure. The child rarely repeated words slowly enough for Erroh to decipher. On the coldest night, the child appeared with a heavy blanket.

"*Something* Nomee," the child said.

"*Something* cold *something*," he added.

Erroh shrugged and the child sighed.

"*Something* dog of cage," Mish suggested and threw the blanket at Erroh before disappearing off into the night.

He soon learned that they were southerners but their language was a bastardisation of many tribes' dialects, as if all the warring tribes of the south came together and somehow pulped sayings and terminology into a crude language. Erroh tried and struggled with the grammar but at least it was something to do as he gave in to despair a mile at a time. There seemed to be no mating of lovers in this army and this too perplexed Erroh a great deal. They were no army of chastity however as many females were with child and at least a dozen youngsters of different ages ran freely through their camp. These southern brutes did not believe in one for life at all. They believed in procreation. Some females took a different male to bed every night. Furrowing was as normal as sharing a meal for survival.

The girl came to him one evening. She had the smell of alcohol on her breath and a slight stumble to her walk. She was fearful and sat down a few feet away. He clenched his fist but made no move to strike so she sat in closer. She stared into his eyes and whispered something incomprehensible. It was loneliness, which stopped him from telling her to fuk off in her native tongue. She looked him up and down a few times and again, whispered gentle words that were lost in the wind. Her beauty was natural and wild. Her eyes were terrified and innocent. None of his captors took any notice of them. He wondered was she sent to test his resolve? Perhaps if he throttled her for a second time it would send the right message but in truth, he didn't want to strike out. He was tired of the world, and she was something different. Without warning, she leaned in far too closely and inhaled deeply. She frowned again and muttered a curse. She wasn't happy with this at all. He could tell. Erroh was wise in the ways of unhappy female expressions since he had met Lea. He needed his mate so much. Where was she? Was she safe? He put the thoughts of her away as quickly as they appeared. He was never going to see her ever again. He was dead to her now. The female said something crude, and he grasped her meaning easily enough. She looked across to the water and back to Erroh encouragingly. She waited for him to realise what she was trying to explain. He told her to fuk off in her language. She stood up and strolled back to the nearest campfire where she sprawled out in front of the warmth. A few other figures huddled in close to the flames and they cracked a few jests at her expense. She didn't appear too troubled with this at all. After a time she took the hand of a tall brute with a strong jaw and brought him to her tent not far from where he lay in the cold. She glanced at Erroh briefly and closed the flaps. After a short period, he heard the low groan of a male and then the accompanying cry of a female wrapped up in the act.

"I wonder how many more miles to go?" he asked the wind as his eyes grew heavy from tiredness, and he started to drift from awareness. The absent gods knew but they weren't in any mood to reply.

42
___

THE HUNT

They called themselves "The Hunt," or at least that's what he gathered from the unintentionally helpful child. The Hunt were the "fingers" of Uden The Woodin Man and apparently, Uden The Woodin Man could "see all". He hadn't a clue what any of it meant.

Every day Mish would give a fine sermon of the world from his innocent point of view. Sometimes it was the same piece of zealot drivel while other times it was some new piece of lore. Sometimes what Erroh understood was both ridiculous and humorous from the mouth of one so young, but other times it was horrific, and Erroh did all not to scream into the face of the young boy.

"All tainted life must die, and the givers of tainted life must be burned to ash. Just like the Arth did in the ancient times. When the last fire is burned out and the last false god has met his end at the hand of Uden, the new world is ours," Mish said in the same matter of fact tones he saved for almost every point he made.

Erroh nodded and the child continued.

Mish pointed to Erroh knowingly. "You burn in fires."

468

Fuk you, Mish. "I untainted, I not burn," he added, pointing to his chest.

"I'm going burn?" asked Erroh, and the child thought his pronunciation hilarious. He laughed for a few breaths and fell silent.

"Soon," the child said coldly.

———

Since she pointed out his smell, he couldn't but notice it. As the Hunt unloaded themselves for the night, he stripped to his undergarments and slid into the water. It was a truly miserable undertaking with the chain around his waist. A few others had taken the plunge all along the freezing river and took little notice as he scrubbed at himself with his dirty fingers. When his body could take no more he climbed back out and met the blonde staring at him by the edge of the cart. She held a plate of vegetables and meats and offered them to him as he used his blanket as a towel.

"You please me," she said in her tongue. She tilted her head sideways, and he felt like prey.

"I like look at you," she said simply. She was beautiful, Erroh's hand formed a fist, and she smiled uneasily. "Washed for Nomi?"

"For Erroh." Erroh pointed to his chest.

She thought for a moment.

"Ah, Forerro," she said wonderfully and pointed to her chest. She had a wonderful chest.

"My name Nomi."

He actually laughed. He didn't know such a thing was possible but it happened. He neared the precipice between laughter and tears, but he never fell over. If he cried in that moment, he might never stop. She leaned in far too closely again and smelled him and shrugged. It felt unfamiliar and uncomfortable. Like the first time Lea had ever been close to him. Only with Lea, he had not felt such a desire to kill her. Although he had nearly drowned her a little while later.

"Get warm, Forerro."

She lit a fire near him and bade him join her in its warm glow. Despite himself, he sat near her and enjoyed the respite from the cutting wind. Her hair was luminescent in the flames. It waved delicately in the breeze, and he wished to sway with it. She could easily have been a radiant female from the Spark. She was probably about as trustworthy too. She slid some loose strands behind her ears, and he knew she was trying to charm him. Fuk off, whore, he wanted to scream but in truth, he needed something more than walking the road in chains. He knew she was the enemy. He suspected she was ordered to give up her body for the cause, but he would never take her to his bed. He only wanted his mate for those particular acts. Well, that wasn't entirely accurate. He was male and ever since he was young he had wanted to bed every female with a nice walk and a shapely figure, but he would stay true to Lea for he had nothing else. He said nothing and lay back down in the dirt.

He had honour and that was something Nomi admired above most other things. Honour was once a common trait among her people or so she'd heard. She found him enthralling but perhaps that was just the debt she owed to him. She thought of it as a debt of mercy. She liked that her people feared him. They whispered that he brought great fire from nothing. They were foolish superstitions. Still though, it was rare that any of her people felt any fear. It's what they needed she suspected. Honour, fear and a little taste of mercy. If any of her people dared to walk near him now though, they would see how weak he had become. Perhaps that was why he hadn't struck her a second time. Few men ever dared to lay a hand upon her lest they face her wrath, yet this one had. And now? Now he appeared to be a little more compliant to her approaches. She desired a child and maybe only the lunatic who'd faced an army was powerful enough to give her one. No man's seed had taken so far and of those who accepted her into their bed did it for pleasure alone. She felt older than she was and though she disagreed with most of her people's fanatical beliefs, her duty to mother a child for the Hunt's war effort was her only wish in her insignificant life. She watched him in the firelight for a little time until he fell asleep wherein she stole away back to her own tent alone.

Nomi replaced the child in attending him. Erroh saw right through their ruse, but he didn't retaliate. He was simply too tired, miserable, and beaten to do anything but smile weakly when she sat down next to him at the end of each day. They had weakened him through the innocence of a child and now they were intent on corrupting him with desires for a goddess. No, she was no goddess. His mate was a goddess. Nomi was something else entirely and as she quietly set alight a fire, he would shuffle closer without hesitation and devour whatever foods she gifted him. He became tame. He became lost.

Both figures sat on opposite sides of a tiny fire. Above them, the shattered moon lit up the land and it almost felt like the road. She offered a swig of some potent brew, which he took without hesitation. It burned him and infused him and it held a coughing fit at bay. She muttered something about the night sky above, and he remembered momentarily the feel of freedom.

"Count the stars," he said in his own tongue. He said it to feel normal again.

"Kont thee stairs," she repeated watching him intently.

He tried to ignore the hopeful expression. Why did she try to win his favour anyway? Why couldn't she just be like the rest of the Hunt? Cruel savages he could kill. He wondered could he even kill Nomi.

"Count. The. Stars." He pointed to the shimmering dots a few miles above them. He began counting in his own language, she quickly caught on, counting in her own language with him, and after a while she began to repeat in his tongue, until he closed his eyes and leaned back against the wheel of the cart, listening to her broken attempts. He found it oddly soothing. Something in the way she pronounced certain words. He felt himself drifting away under her spell as tingling shivers ran up his spine into his head. Then he felt something else. Her lips suddenly pressed against his own. They were silken and glorious. For an entire breath, he forgot where he was. For a few precious moments more, he forgot all the misery in her force, as she tasted him. He felt no guilt. His mate was lost to him forever, and he knew this cough was going to develop into something sinister. A cough never led to good things. He knew from experience. Her tongue touched his, and he closed his eyes tighter. He felt he could kiss her forever or at least be kissed by her forever. He knew he could take her right here in the cold and still he felt no guilt. It was only natural. He felt the first stirrings of arousal and so did she. He imagined it was Lea.

"Stop, Nomi," he said suddenly in her language and pushed her away fiercely. She frowned but sat back as he asked.

"I sorry," he said. She had tasted like his old life. He tried to look at anything in the world apart from her eyes as she tilted her head in puzzlement.

It's not you; it's me.

She tried to say words but shrugged her shoulders. He wondered was it embarrassment. Instead of pushing the matter, she disappeared away and left him to his misery, guilt, and potent bottle of brew but before he could reach for it and salvage some of the night a tall brute stepped over him, the same soldier who lit the flames of Aireys's pyre. He took a few steps towards Erroh and waited for the attack. Instead, Erroh reached weakly for the bottle and the brute kicked it away. A dull ember of rage surged through Erroh like a delicate stream and it quickly trickled away as wrath gave way to sadness, and he sat back towards the fire. He stared into the night sky and began counting the stars once again. Before he closed his eyes and tried to sleep, he whispered a little prayer. "I love you, Lea."

———

The following evening Nomi returned at the usual time and lit a fire.

"You speak our words well," she said quietly looking around the camp lest someone hear.

"I speak some," he said in a terrible accent. She was impressed nonetheless.

"Turning into us slowly," she said smiling at her own jest.

"Never!" he spat.

She stoked the fire and thought on his venom for a little while. She wondered why he refused her. She knew she was attractive. Maybe he wanted other men. That would be very bad. They would kill him outright. "Why did you stop last night?" she asked feigning indifference.

He tried to form the words right in his head. "Sharlikt, for one life," he whispered.

She looked confused trying to understand his attempt. He said it again.

"You love," she said after a few awkwardly thoughtful breaths.

"One person for all life. Love," he said, and Nomi was terribly confused but also thrilled at discussing such a topic. All of this was new to her. He spoke of a different world entirely. "Why one for life?"

Good question.

"For big love," he said and seemed pleased with himself.

She thought on this impracticality. Wouldn't it be a little boring to wake up beside the same face every day? That said, with Erroh it would take quite a long time before she tired of him. "Are you happy?" she asked, and Erroh raised his chain and an eyebrow.

"Happy with big love with one person," she said quickly, and her face reddened. He looked out into the darkness beyond the ever-constant snow-covered forests and steep mountains, and she could see true sorrow in his face. She suddenly felt the urge to embrace him.

"I miss her."

Nomi lay in her makeshift cot but couldn't sleep. She found herself turning, twisting, and quickly tiring of every position she settled in. For so long she had always thought in black and white. Things were or they were not. As a child, she was told certain things, and she believed without question, but as she had grown older, dark questions about the Arth and the Hunt had entered her mind. She knew she wasn't alone in her thinking. She thought about those closest to her and bit back the tears. She never spoke out of matters herself. Was it because she still believed in Uden and his cause? Or was she just scared to die? She thought about Erroh. She thought about him in her bed. In her. What's more, afterwards she would let him hold her in his arms for a time. That would be nice.

Her mind spun.

If he gave her a child, would it be tainted like the father? And was she tainted for thinking these thoughts? These matters were not simply black and white. She turned over and peeked out the flap at the prisoner. She thought about his rejection and felt the sting afresh. He turned down her approaches because he was thinking of one female far away. In truth, Nomi liked that thought. It brought a smile to her face. It was nicer than the truth. The truth was awful sometimes. He would never see his "one for life" ever again. These black thoughts hurt Nomi deeply. He didn't deserve to die. None of those poor fools holding that town deserved to die. She had killed one of them. It had been an easy shot. Nobody had even noticed. The girl had simply stopped moving as the flames had overcome her, and she had returned the crossbow back to the armoury while most drunkenly revelled in their pathetic victory.

She sat back in bed and tried not to think of him anymore. She closed her eyes, nestled into her cot, and imagined a world where one for life was enough and swiftly she fell asleep.

———

The chain pulled at Erroh painfully, and he stumbled forward. His chest felt like a tight fist and each breath he took was exhausting. He wrapped her cloak around him and it offered a little reprieve but in truth, the march was choking the life out of him. He couldn't shake the ominous feeling. He knew he was to meet their false god Uden, but he didn't believe he would survive another week at this rate.

"It's not a good cough," she said from beside him, no more than a foot away. She had taken to walking with him these days, and he didn't mind the company. What would Lea think?

"Still be fit to die," he said grimly and coughed a few more times until the cart jerked him again.

"Don't want Erroh to die."

The snow struck as evening hit. The land darkened and the harshest wind Erroh had ever felt tore down the mountains through their convoy. With the gale came a terrible blizzard. All around him, his captors swiftly brought the convoy near to the treeline and began preparations for the storm ahead. He looked for her, but she was nowhere to be seen. The snow whipped his face painfully and soon enough a wall of white was all he could see. His mind raced at the thought of attempting an escape but it was the raving thoughts of a cub nearing his end. If he somehow managed to break heavy iron and lose himself in the blizzard, he wouldn't last an hour. With no better cover at his disposal, he huddled in against the wheel and waited for the storm to pass by. His hands became numb, and he found himself unable to close them into a fist. So cold. He felt his chest tighten as he gasped for air and then he collapsed. Too cold for anything else, he closed his eyes and wondered would the darkness be warmer.

. . .

Nomi hooked the tent sheet against the side of the cart and fought her hair as it waved madly in the gusts, blinding and stinging her. He lay motionless below her, and she screamed for him, but he did not stir. She dug some pegs into the ground and hooked the cover up over them both. It wasn't the finest tent she had ever erected but it would keep some of the snow off their heads. The break from the hazardous wind tapered greatly, and she quickly took some kindling from a cart and started to make a fire in a clear space under the cart. She cursed loudly as the flint failed to ignite the little bundle again but his shaking hand reached out, took her tools, and began to work at the little fire. The spark took hold immediately and a little flame caught the bundle of dry wood. Within moments, the little fire was warming their freezing world. She dropped a few logs down alongside the kindling and they took turns setting them to burn as night fell upon them and the storm began to ease its fury. By the time Erroh had thawed the night had cleared. Soon after that they heard the sound of footsteps.

Menacing footsteps.

"Nomi, come to my tent!" a male voice called out, and Erroh recognised it as the brute who had put to light Aireys and stolen his alcohol. The figure bent down and pulled at their tent irritably before gesturing to his own perfectly erected lodging. She sighed, shook her head, and placed a log into the fire. Her bed mate was chosen for the night.

"No tonight, Oren," she said, as though he was a pup eager for a scrap.

"You want spend time with tainted little dead man?" he sneered.

She stroked Erroh's arm. "He's my pet."

The thug growled and reached for her roughly. He pulled her out into the storm before she had a chance to scream.

"I'll show who my pet is!" he roared striking her across the face and shoving her violently to the ground.

A few other brutes looked up from their own tents, to see what the noise was. They saw Oren manhandle Nomi and figured it was on Oren's own head. She was capable enough.

Rage surged through Erroh. He jumped up from the tent and charged. Beaten for protecting him? The brute was almost twice her size. How could he? He tried to attack Oren but his body jerked viciously as the chain reached its length and held firm. For a brief moment, he was suspended in mid-air as his feet kicked out until gravity pulled him down into the snow. He roared in frustration and shock and though lying in the snow seemed like the thing to do, he struggled to his feet and embraced the hatred he thought was lost to him. He roared and tried to goad the brute to face him.

He needn't have bothered.

Nomi hated these ridiculous acts of aggression and pettiness. Oren couldn't touch Uden's offering, so he punished her instead. He'd struck her once with an open palm and sent her to the wet snow but it was the outlandish bellowing laugh, which irked her greatly. Fine leader of this finger he was. She got to her feet and tried to wipe the clumps of snow sticking to her, but her clothes were already soaked through.

This irked her most of all.

She moved with less grace than Lea but that didn't make her any less devastating. She stormed up to him and swung a frozen fist across the bridge of his nose before he realised what she was doing. There was a loud crack and then a scream and the beast stumbled under the strike. She followed up with a fierce kick to the groin, and he fell to his knees. Blood spurted from his nose, and he moaned pathetically in his brutish language that she "might have broken nose."

She hissed like a wildling hunting a crow and delivered a final strike once again to his nose. The loud crunch confirmed that yes; she had indeed broken his nose. Shattered would be a better description.

"No one's pet!" she roared as he slid cumbersomely in the slippery ground desperate to escape her. She stood over him and repeated the words until he understood and squirmed away towards the nearest campfire holding the remains of his face.

"Weak leader. Uden not see." She wiped the blood from her knuckles and walking back to Erroh. "Silly pet," she said when she saw the damage the chain had inflicted on his waist. She pushed him back into the warmth and safety of the little campsite. "Nomi make bad tent but still better here for night with Erroh," she said and stroked his arm again. He shook his head and pushed her arm away, and she laughed.

She pointed to herself, back to him, and said in the most patronising terms she could muster, "Only talking with pet."

She touched her lips. They were luscious and tempting.

She pointed to his. They were cracked and broken.

"No kissing," she said in that same patronising tone.

"No kissing," he agreed as they huddled together for survival.

43

EVERY STEP OF THE WAY

S he began to remove her clothes.

"What are you doing?" he cried in his native tongue as she wriggled out of her trousers one leg at a time. They were very good legs. She probably had no trouble walking on them. Lying on her back with the skill of a whore who removed her clothing swiftly, she removed her clothing swiftly and began rubbing her freezing legs in front of the fire. If he dared to look, he could have seen wonderful things beyond her legs but instead he turned away.

"What are you doing?" he said in her language. She wrapped a blanket around her legs and rear and began to remove her shirt.

"Soaked through," she explained as though it was no small matter. But it was a matter. She was far too close wearing far too little. He found a stain in the tent to stare at while she removed the shirt and left it drying by the flames.

"Just skin. You look. Nomi not mind."

He wanted to look more than anything else in the world but if he did, he was doomed. He was but a weakened cub.

"No," he whispered slowly.

"Erroh not think Nomi good?"

"Erroh think Nomi beautiful but no look," he said begging the gods for a reprieve. He wondered if they were enjoying the sight.

"One for life?" she asked.

"One for life," he said, and she began to wrap her blanket around her chest.

"Nomi could be one for life in Hunt," she jested tapping him on the shoulder and displaying her complete lack of nudity. See, skin all covered up.

"Nomi might find one for life in Hunt," he suggested.

"Maybe Oren," she sniggered.

"Maybe Mish when big," Erroh said, and she laughed loudly. He laughed too until he began to cough. It was a dreadful wet struggle, which made his vision darken until a desperate hack cleared the air. She pulled the tent flap open to clear the stagnant air, and he couldn't help notice the look of worry on her face.

"You are weak," she said taking his arm roughly in her calloused hands. She rolled his sleeve up and squeezed at his muscles. She shook her head disapprovingly and the reproach stung him. What did she expect after months of walking without respite?

Why did she really care anyway?

Why did he care what she thought anyway?

She fingered the freezing chain that cut into his waist and sighed. She ran her finger along the mark, and he hissed at her touch. It stung and it was wonderful. He could smell a faint odour of sweat and the road on her body, and he felt enchanted again. He could easily just reach out and tease the blanket from her body.

What did it matter if he leapt upon her anyway?

It would be nothing more but a last act of pleasure before the end?

Lea wouldn't know. Lea wouldn't need to know. What if Lea was already dead?

"You were not weak in battle," she said wistfully.

He could just pull her to him.

"You were incredible when you fought," she said in that same tone, and he took hold of her covering. "But now you are little weak pet."

He pulled gently at her blanket, and she noticed.

"You will meet Uden The Woodin man, weak as pup."

He felt stirrings and his heart beat wildly with excitement.

"And you will die and Hunt will burn world because Erroh not strong opponent," she said and squeezed his arm.

Opponent?

"Strong opponent?" Erroh asked suddenly and released his grasp on her coverings. She raised an eyebrow. Was she tempting him? Or simply playing a part? "What do you mean?" All thoughts of her body were lost beneath a wave of vengeance.

She fastened back her covering and opened the flap on her satchel and removed a little hand blade and a small little pouch of tiny potatoes. "You live because Uden need strongest opponents. Erroh special. You face army screaming. Oren choose you," she said and began cutting them up into thin slices and placing them aside. She poured a light brown liquid onto the slices of potato and kneaded each thin piece. She reached into her pack and took out a little sack of salt. If there would be no play, there was always food.

"You top line?" she asked. He didn't understand. She tried again.

"First of bloodline?" she said warily.

"Alphaline?" he said in his own tongue and her face lit up.

"Sit-e," she said pointing at him. "Spirk Sit-e?" He nodded, and she was delighted, and he wondered had he revealed a worrying secret to her.

"Oren bring Erroh Alfa-lion fight Uden. Big honour for Oren. Become general army." He finally understood why he alone was spared, and his anger grew.

"Oren already general army," he hissed in a terrible accent. In his defence, his head was spinning.

She smiled. "This not army. This one finger."

She reached for the salt.

"You need be strong to fight again like in dead town," she said.

"Did you fight?" he asked, realising he didn't want to know.

She nodded slowly and salted the oily sizzling slices. He could smell the first aromas of almost cooked flavours.

"Did you enjoy killing my friends?" he asked.

She salted the slices a second time. They looked like they needed a good coating. Her eyes met his, and she blinked first. She turned back to the meal, took the first slices from the blade, and handed the roasting pieces to Erroh. She took a few herself and began the cooking process all over again. "Did you enjoy killing my friends?" she asked, blowing at the slices.

"The Hunt are just brutes, slaughter the innocent."

"The Hunt do his work, and he sees all," she said instinctively and cursed her own conditioning.

"And all tainted burn," he growled. The child had said it enough times that he knew much of the decree of their false god.

She sat staring at the flames, watching the fresh batch of potato slices cook away.

"Who sent you here?" he asked.

"They need food for pet. Nomi make food for pet," she snapped.

He sniffed and moved a full foot away to the edge of the tent. The chain clinked loudly as he did. It was a small matter; his point was made.

"Nomi like Erroh," she muttered under her breath.

"Well Erroh not like Nomi," he hissed weakly, and if he upset her she didn't show it. She just continued cooking away. The sizzle and the breeze was enough to hide the awkward silence. Eventually, she spoke next.

"Would you killed me in battle?" she asked gently.

"Aye."

She smiled.

"Will you still strike me down, if you get chance?" she asked again, in that same tone.

He didn't hesitate "Aye."

She didn't hesitate either.

"No, Erroh like Nomi too," she whispered to the wind. She seemed so certain. He turned from her and lay down to sleep, all desire lost for the time being. He heard her place another log on the fire and then he fell asleep.

She stoked the embers to get more heat. She looked up the line where most of her comrades had already bedded down for the night. The storm had been light enough in the end. She'd lived through blizzards where no flame could survive the winds and only heavy blankets and tight cover was enough to survive the night. She knew that many people perished in those storms. Beside her Erroh coughed, and she stroked his forehead. She found her pet so endearing. His accent was atrocious, but he tried. And he would try to meet Uden in combat, and he would not survive. Her stomach turned and her infallible confidence faltered for a moment.

What if she freed him?

She shook her head immediately. There was no escaping this part of the world. Even with the proper supplies and a few mounts, they still wouldn't survive. He was too weak anyway. She knew a few of her people still followed the ancient tainted ways of nesting with just one lover. She wondered about the one who had captured Erroh's manhood, and she sighed loudly. What type of goddess must she be? As for Nomi, well Nomi had a fine enough walk. In truth Erroh was fine to look at, but were Oren or others not as equally pleasing? No Erroh had something that she couldn't quite understand. It was something in his eyes. Like a spark. She thought about his glorious rage when Oren had struck her. He would need that rage to kill.

To kill?

To kill Uden?

These were heretical thoughts. She wondered how far had she fallen? Could she come back to her world? Could she dip her fingers in blood again?

As frightened as she had been on the battlefield of the dead town, she had charged with the rest. Their blades had clashed and his power had knocked her from her feet. Falling had saved her life. She had never known fear until she looked into his beautiful eyes. He should have ended her life, but he held his swing and struck another instead. She could never forget even if he did. When Oren had ordered him captured, she knew her debt could be repaid. No potential general in Uden's army would have allowed that wild demon to face his or her god in such a fine fighting state. Uden demanded the finest warriors, and she suspected he wanted them ever so slightly hobbled. Just in case. A few months walking in chains would wipe him out and it did. Nevertheless, she had tried to help him.

Could she have done more for her pet?

Yes, she could have, but she was simply Nomi, and she was lost and scared in the "Arth that was about to burn". She lay down beside her pet, draped her blanket over him, and smoothed out the creases carefully. He didn't stir as she slid in beside him. She tried to ignore the taste of exhilaration at lying naked next to him. She knew he didn't want her. She knew he would never gift her a child, and she accepted such things. He turned, the chain rattled, and he grimaced slightly with the pain. She embraced him in her strong arms and pulled his cold body against hers. To her surprise, he hugged her tightly and whispered "Lea." It should have stung her, but instead she imagined she was this fabled Lea. Warm and sated and naked with her one for life. He stirred in his sleep and gripped her tightly, and she nearly melted. This was not going to end well at all. She tried desperately to fight the sleep as it overcame her but it was a losing battle.

His coughing woke them up. A desperate fit overcame him, and he threw her aside trying to get out of the musty tent. After a few hard fought breaths, his airways began to clear, and he collapsed beside the dead fire and waited for the dizziness to pass. Behind him, she recovered her clothes and began to dress. By the time he felt healthy she was fully clothed and already beginning to dismantle their cover for the walk ahead. Still miles to go.

———

Opponent.

Instead of standing around and waiting to be marched towards his doom, Erroh began to stretch his muscles. This hurt more than he cared for, swallowed the pain and continued regardless. He closed his eyes and worked the knots out from inactivity and by the time he had finished there was a thin layer of perspiration down his back. She had said he was weak, and she had been right. He dropped to the snowy ground and attempted a few push-ups. He lasted a dozen before the pain almost paralysed him. He had let himself go. He did a dozen more until the cry for marching was heard, and he allowed himself a brief moment to breathe before walking like their hound once more but with his head raised. Soon enough the other female in his life appeared at his side, and she was bearing a gift of a large mug of steaming green nastiness.

"For chest," she said eagerly.

"Smell bad," he said. There was a distinct smell of animal urine with a hint of honey. He shook his head warily.

"Drink," she hissed taking a mouthful herself.

Well if the girl does it.

He drank it down swiftly and held firm against the retch while she spat out her measure. It burned his stomach, but he figured anything that vile must have its health benefits.

"More later. Kill cough. Get strong. Fight well."

It sounded like a plan.

"Not long before end," she said.

"Will you walking with me every step of way?" he asked.

"Every step that I can."

44

THE WOODIN MAN

The night after the first of the snowstorms, Nomi lit a fire beside his cart and began to pitch a sturdier tent. He sat by the flames drinking his awful beverage and answered her many questions about what love meant to him. He even said his mate's name, and she took it all in. She was a good audience. She wrapped a long ribbon around his chain and the relief was immense. When sleep called, she lay back and waited for him to come join her. He said no, and she did not ask again, but when the wind began to blow, he crawled over to her and smiling her most disarming and dazzling smile, she opened up the blankets for him to join her. He lay down and felt her warmth all over. She gripped onto him and closed her eyes. He almost felt human again.

They walked together as companions for a week until signs of civilisation began to appear along their route. Campfires could be seen on clear nights as far out that they touched the horizon, and the closer they got to their home, the better the mood among the Hunt. Only Nomi was downbeat and did not join the revelry. He thought this a fine compliment.

. . .

She loved the days she had with him and the nights as well. He taught her a few words of his language. They rolled off her tongue delightfully even though he laughed loudly every time she attempted to speak aloud. She took to cursing in his language every time she slipped in the snow or nicked her finger while preparing food, and she liked those sounds most of all. He spoke of his world, and she loved every moment, imagining a life with mirth and warmth and kindness. Every morning he stood in a fighting stance with nothing more than a couple of dead branches for blades. She enjoyed watching him strike down imaginary foes. She also enjoyed watching him bathe afterwards. It was a fine payment for her care, for he never thanked her and, in truth, she never expected him to.

She stripped down each night to very little and waited for him to come to her. She would lose herself in fantasy that Erroh would succumb to desire and climb on top of her, but he never did, and she never leapt upon him. She did not know this girl Lea, but she respected her, and a strange part of her knew that if he succumbed to desire his heart would be heavy. She didn't understand why his sorrow could upset her so. Such thoughts were not black and white at all.

Only once did Erroh nearly lose his mind in her presence.

A light patch of snow had just begun to fall. They were walking along a thin beaten path between two ridges. The path was the only route through the valley. It led into a deep evergreen forest devoid of life. She smelled it first. Little more than a delicate sweet aroma of nature, which hung in her senses. He recognised it immediately though and suddenly dropped to his knees at the side of the path and began searching through some wild flowers that flourished in the freezing conditions. He was a man possessed. His hands ripped at the flowers and checked each for its match. She stood and watched anxiously, unsure of what else to do.

The cart however wouldn't stop and watch anxiously. It moved along with the rest of the Hunt. Its loud grinding roar never ceased as it drove through the deep snow. She saw the chain begin to stretch out.

"Lea's scent," he muttered scrambling through the flowers and not finding success.

The chain jerked him painfully, and he stumbled and fell. He tried to regain his footing but the cart dragged him on the slippery surface. He screamed and reached for the wild flowers but the cart was unyielding. She saw the anguish in his eyes as he fought against the inevitable, and she hurt for him.

"Can't smell her now," he cried, as the chain cut through the ribbons and pulled him along the slush-covered ground. Eventually he rose to his feet a broken man and followed, leaving Nomi standing among the flowers and the falling snow.

It was an easy decision to make because it was the right thing to do. If Lea's scent gave him respite then she would move mountains to help him. Nomi dropped to her knees and began to search for the source of the smell.

Where was this unnatural sweet smell coming from?

She dug her face into the ruined flowers and sniffed like a hound at time of the season, and she followed the scent. She touched upon roots and wondered if it was trickling sap or freshly fallen berries but to no avail. She scrambled as dementedly as her pet. Ripping, smelling, and discarding while the convoy walked on without her. The snowflakes began to seep through her hair, and she shivered, but she would not cease her search. Every time she believed she had discovered the source, it was not to be. The ground ceased its rumble as the last cart left her behind and the last walker with it and Nomi suddenly felt alone in the frozen mud and slush. Soon enough the snow began to cover up the faint smell all along the path. She cried out in frustration and hammered the ground with her fist. This was her land; she should recognise which fruit elicited such a fragrance. She cursed loudly and began to crawl along the path searching for this impossible treasure. She knew the danger of straying from the convoy when snow was falling. Already they had lost a handful of fools this march alone, but she couldn't help herself. A silence enveloped the world, as the rumbling was lost in the wind. She imagined herself lost to her convoy as well. They would discover her come the warmer season by the side of the river. She would be a frozen statue, forever beautiful. All of this for a pretty smell.

Still she dug along the side of the path for the source. She brushed some strands of hair that blew into her eyes. Wiping them away, she smelled the sweet fruit on her fingers and hope filled her. It was no growing thing at all. It was simply aroma and it emanated from a little pile of pebbles and twigs. She dug out a pouch and swiftly began filling it with the pieces. She stuffed as many as she could into the pouch and tied it up tightly before climbing to her freezing feet.

To her horror, the searching had cost her more than clean clothing. The snow had covered the path a few feet in front of her so she ran along the river until the trees clustered too tightly for a large convoy to pass through. She fought the panic admirably and lost. She considered backtracking and guessing where her comrades broke from the path, but she didn't trust herself.

"Hello!" she cried out into the silence. There wasn't even

an echo beneath the claustrophobic veneer of white. She was all but alone.

"Help me." She heard the crack of a watching beast somewhere ahead. She felt like prey. She held the little pouch of sweet smelling perfume and smelled it. She didn't know why. It was something to do while the enormity of her foolishness struck her. Further away deeper into the wall of white she heard a louder crack.

Follow the noise, her mind screamed, and she did. She ran until her chest burned and her limbs ached and finally she caught sight of a little line not yet ruined by the spiteful white. It was deep and wide and a few steps beyond she spotted footsteps. She caught their scent and then within a few hopeful breaths, the panic was over, and she was back with her people. Somehow, among them, the light snowfall appeared far less threatening. She was angry with herself. She was no child. She knew the dangers, yet helping her pet had almost caused her great harm. What type of foolhardiness was this?

Was this love?

Erroh took it in silence and opened it gently. He inhaled deeply and smiled as if he were a free man walking with his one for life through lush green forests under the glare of a warm sun and beauty of a blue sky. He gripped the pouch tightly and let the chain pull him away again. She wanted to say something but instead fell silent. She left him alone with his thoughts.

———

It was in the valley of Conlon that Erroh learned the full horrors of what was to come. Setting camp outside the city gates, the Hunt took a breath and gave thanks to Uden The

Woodin Man that they were home. Like a crushing avalanche that consumed everything Erroh fell to his knees as the truth struck him and buried him alive.

There were thousands of soldiers.

The Primary was a trusting fool and because of this, the world was doomed. How could such a thing occur under her watchful eye? The south had always been widely regarded as little more than a fractured land of glorified nomads fighting among themselves for the few fertile plains within, so Dia the Primary left them to their devices. She had only asked for allegiance and those whose voice was loudest had offered it.

Those whom Dia had trusted for decades had been liars.

Erroh looked at his jailors and recognised their armour and colours for what they were. They were no wild barbarians from the south. They were the south. Nomi had been right. Oren did not command an army. The truth was far more terrifying. The roving army that had decimated the town was but one of countless others.

He recalled Mish's words and a coldness ran up him. At the time, he'd thought it childish propaganda between barbarians of the road. He'd said a battle of the gods was coming and it would end the lives of all the tainted. A great war would be won in fire by The Woodin Man and his disciples. A war that would end all evils, for only then could the world be reborn in peace and paradise. The world had been dying for a thousand years and now with the final days at hand, the Hunt in all its magnificence would reach out as The Woodin Man's fingers and put an end to it all.

The child had liked to talk.

There were soldiers camped as far as the eye could see. They were a terrifying collection of blades, armour, and foreboding death. Nothing could stand against thirty or forty thousand strong. Not even Magnus and his meagre army. The child's insistence that Uden The Woodin Man had many fingers finally rang true. Each finger was an army. The tracks he'd followed with his mate at his side, had not been those who held him captive now. Nor were they the hidden menace that had slaughtered the town. Who knew exactly how many of these armies walked through the wastes killing as they went? What if Spark City had already fallen? How would he even know?

The following morning in the shadow of the city gates, they parted company forever. She broke her promise and kissed him again, and he allowed her. One final moment of warmth before the end, and he knew his end was at hand. She broke away, tears streamed down her cheek, and he no longer thought of her as a savage from the Hunt.

He never knew what to say at the best of times. He found the words.

"You would be fine mother," he said warmly as she stepped away into the marching Hunt slithering through the city gates leaving him, his cart, and his entourage behind.

"One love for all life," she said, pointing to the precious gift she had given him. He bowed in gratitude.

"Lea," he said softly.

Nomi smiled, gently shaking her head and pointing to her own heart.

"Erroh," she said.

The beautiful female turned her back and joined the procession.

———

Oren, still nursing his bruises, gathered his twenty chosen Riders and rode fiercely from the city and its menacing army, deep into the mountains. Erroh was allowed the luxury of a seat in his cart as it raced along with them. He sprawled out and watched the cold muddy snow disappear underneath the methodical turning of the wheels. The wind deafened him and the pace unnerved him, but he dared not let his head drop. Unlike most of the south, the route they took was upon a decent path though the view of snow-covered trees remained the same. The only significant difference was the incline to their journey.

When darkness struck they set up a small camp beneath a steep range. A Rider brought him a large bowl of dried pieces of charred meat. Erroh wondered would it be his last meal and savoured what he could. In truth, it was fine even if it needed a little salt. Though he'd done little more than sit for the day, he spread out under the cart and closed his eyes. He wrapped himself in his blanket and tried desperately not to think of Lea and indeed Nomi lying with him, reassuring him against despair. Sleep found him soon enough.

He awoke with his arms and legs bound by countless strong hands. Nomi was no longer there to protect him anymore and panic overcame him. He tried to kick out but they held him firmly as they dragged him from the cart out into the open. They stood all around him like a vicious mob, and he knew this was the end of it all. In the moonlight, he saw the blade and they pulled him out flat. All of his killers roared and jeered him, and he met the eyes of a vengeful Oren. The blade was thrust down violently, and he screamed as it went to cutting at his waist. He spat, hissed, and cursed though he couldn't feel pain beyond their grasp. He fought their hold until the hands suddenly eased and drew back and the cutting stopped, and he wondered was the act of his murder completed. Was he in shock? Had his mind protected him from the horror? He reached down to discover no wounds and met only cold naked chain. The cruel captors mocked the "prisoner and his whore" and took turns dropping pieces of shredded ribbon into the warm fire. The ribbon caught the flame and burned brightly.

On the last day, he awoke to the noise of the twenty Riders preparing for the ride. He stretched his arms and then started his routine until his eyes caught the sight of a little red strip of ribbon in a footprint of slush. Erroh dug into the mud, recovered the piece, and held it tightly. It would never serve its purpose again but it seemed dreadfully important he keep a piece of her close. One of the Riders spotted his discovery, charged over, and punched Erroh across the cheek, sending him to the ground.

"Not for pet!" he roared pulling the ribbon from Erroh's grasp and waving it in front of his eyes. They saw no threat in Erroh at all anymore.

"Want hit me?" the Rider mocked, and his companions laughed.

"Come hit me," he screamed and pushed Erroh back to the ground.

"If you want. You come take." He waved the ribbon in Erroh's face once more.

It was a fair deal.

Erroh climbed back into his carriage and wiped the blood from the ribbon, his hands, and face. It was something to do. The remaining Riders left their dead comrade behind and kept their distance as they rode out.

The path to the summit became steep, slippery, and barely wide enough for the small convoy. The four mounts pulled the cart onwards despite the treacherous conditions, and

Erroh watched as the ground disappeared beneath them as they entered the last few miles. They passed over a wild river, and Erroh imagined it began its life as little more than a trickle in the mountains above. Who knew how devastating a stream and a steep hill could become. They climbed the final mountain path in silence. There was no boisterous jesting between the Riders nor even hushed whispers. It was an eerie thing, and Erroh could see fear and reverence etched upon their faces.

Near the summit, they came upon large gates thirty feet high and painted in black. They trundled open slowly and the convoy passed through into the belly of the beast. Erroh's heart beat loudly out of time as per usual, though it was not fear of death. It was the fear of failure. He prayed to the absent gods for strength and courage but deep down he knew he was alone. They passed into the courtyard and stopped in front of an ancient stone building. It was impressive, though smaller than what he imagined a true god to reside in. The walls were painted in black, the wooden frames of the doors and sills were crimson like the banners of battle. Nothing else about The Woodin Man's stronghold suggested godliness. There was a blazing furnace for smelting in the far corner near the gate and scattered throughout the courtyard were various workbenches, tanning racks and grindstones, from which beautifully crafted weapons of every kind had been made. From giant war hammers of cold heavy steel to perfectly balanced flails and every blade ever imagined in between. They were weapons worthy of a god and they hung on each wall of the courtyard. Most of the courtyard itself was walled off but for a small section with a fine view of the frozen lands all around them. No doubt, The Woodin Man could stand and look out over his world and imagine he could see everything from here. Perhaps if he took a clumsy step, he

497

would fall a hundred feet to the river below. Could a man survive that fall? Could a god? Perhaps with the right amount of luck, nerve, and godliness, it was possible.

A short clean-shaven man in a black cloak emerged from the doors and invited Oren alone inside. The rest of his Riders sat in silence among themselves and waited. Erroh sat back against his cart and thought about the last year of his life. When he had entered the city to claim his mate, he had imagined his life turning out far differently than it did. Had he lived a fine life?

He had tried.

A few hours passed and evening had begun to take hold of the day when the door opened suddenly and Oren emerged followed swiftly behind by a giant. Each Rider fell to their knees immediately and bowed as their lord walked out among them. In truth he did look like a god. He was bigger than Magnus and just as old, but that didn't make him any less fearsome. He did not dress extravagantly despite his divinity. His boots were black, his trousers were leather, and his vest was plain and casual. His skin was tanned more than most other southerners with an overly muscular physique. He was awe inspiring and terrifying and almost familiar looking. Perhaps it was the godliness in him.

Erroh felt the fear take hold, and he stepped back absently. Then a curious thing happened. He thought about Keri. A simple thought out of nowhere. He did not think about the misery of their deaths. He thought about their magnificent stand against the inevitable. He would soon be meeting his brothers. He tried to remember what number his count was. Perhaps there was room for a dozen more. He touched the pouch he'd wrapped around his wrist with ribbon. He searched for the warrior inside him who'd faced an army. It was time for the Hero of Keri to appear one more time when all else was lost. There was no escape from this place.

This was where his story would end.

So make it a fine last chapter, whispered the absent gods in his mind.

"Who fuk are you?" Erroh shouted in their language, and The Woodin Man started to laugh.

45

THE FALL OF ERROH

"I see what you mean, Oren," said The Woodin Man in a low gravelly voice. A voice changed from an entire life of battle cries. It radiated power just like every movement of his entire body. "Remove chains," he growled slowly.

A Rider released him from his restraints and they fell loudly to the ground. The relief was instant, but Erroh showed no emotion. He just watched and waited for the attack. Or for an opening to attack. Any opening at all. The ledge overlooking the drop was looking appealing, and he wondered what it would take to convince the god to jump. Gods couldn't fly. He wondered could he reach the blades hanging along the walls. Could he actually end the war before it even began?

"You will make it to swords," growled Uden smiling.

"I will too," he added, and Erroh held his charge.

"Gemmil, get men feast," Uden said to the smaller figure in black. He returned his gaze to Erroh and gestured to the open door. "Follow me, little cub," he said before turning his back and disappearing inside. After a few cautious breaths, Erroh shrugged and followed him.

Alone at last.

Erroh followed Uden through another door into a dark chamber where shock stole his breath and words. It was a fine enough chamber in truth. The floor was covered in rugs. The wood was varnished and rich and there were just enough candles to draw the correct amount of attention to the skulls and stuffed trophies of a great many beasts that hung from three of the walls. It wasn't any of these trophies that amazed Erroh though. It was the fourth wall and the thousands of little metal capsules that were the real treasures. They covered the wall. Each slotted into a perfectly whittled hole. The holes spread right across the width of the room, from the ground to the very top of the ceiling. His head reeled at the amount of knowledge. No man or woman could ever amass such a collection in a hundred lifetimes.

Even a god would struggle.

"I like look at them too," whispered Uden from the far end of the room, the light from a great fire lit up his clean-shaven face. Stepping away Erroh could see his blazing green eyes were cold as he took his place at the head of a long mahogany table.

"More words from past, than in Samara," he whispered again and it sounded like a roar. Gemmil emerged baring two plates of steaming meats. He set them down at each ends of the table. Erroh's mouth watered but the lure of the capsules was too great. Each one had an inscription and a date. Many were older than any history he'd ever known. "I know how world came to be what is."

Erroh nodded in agreement. He didn't know why. Despite his terror, the man had an appeal.

"They speak my prophesy," Uden said.

Erroh reached for a capsule. He couldn't help himself. His

fingers touched the seal, and he gently pulled the words of a long dead race from its place of rest.

"You will not touch scripture!" roared the god in a terrible voice that seemed to shake the world. He slammed his fist loudly down on the table and the sudden eruption of rage shocked Erroh, as though he'd had horns blown in his ear for half a day. He pushed the capsule back in its place and stepped away carefully. What would he have given to spend a few days reading the little pieces of history? Perhaps when he killed the god, he could slip back after and read a few with a piping cup of hot cofe. It sounded like a plan.

"Why I here?" Erroh wore his warrior's skin well though his fingers touched the ribbon and pouch.

"I like to make tainted believe before burn," Uden said.

"If I believe, will no burn?" Erroh asked carefully.

The god laughed loudly. He was no fool, but he was a lunatic. He coughed and addressed Erroh in his native tongue. His accent was flawless because fuk him, he was a god.

"You will die after we have sated ourselves with this fine meal," he declared while pulling the skin of the chicken free and placing it aside.

"Make sure you chew thoroughly," suggested Erroh as though he was simply playing a bluffing round. "It would taste better with a few glasses of wine."

The god laughed again loudly.

"We need wine, Gemmil!" he roared. His burning green eyes flashed rage and power.

He's just a man, Erroh's mind whispered.

Gemmil entered the room and poured two glasses for each challenger. He left the bottle by the burning flames. The wine was slightly warm in the glass. The Woodin Man drank down deeply and chewed another hearty piece. Erroh didn't touch the goblet. He ate though. The meat had just the right amount of salt. He thought about asking for boar.

"You asked who I was?" the god said.

"Aye,"

"I am the south. I am the brothers of conflict under one banner. I am their god, and my wrath is infinite."

What type of answer was that?

"Can you discuss peace with Samara?" Erroh asked.

"I could, and Dia would probably believe me," Uden said and poured himself another glass. "Gemmil is a loyal man. Few from your whoring city ever come down to us frozen southerners, but when they do, Gemmil spins some fine tales of our dreadful barbaric nation to any and all bearing the messages of your queen. We don't get nearly enough guests. I pledge myself to Mydame of Spark City," he said loudly and smiled.

It suited her to believe whatever the south claimed. Nobody wanted to invade the south. Nobody wanted to face those freezing conditions. Nobody wanted to even visit.

"You are an Alpha are you not?" Uden asked.

"I am no Alpha," said Erroh. Only Nomi knew. Did she tell?

The Woodin Man stopped chewing and closed his green eyes. He swallowed his food and took a disappointed deep breath. "Lie to me again, little one, and I shall deny you the right to spill my blood."

Erroh decided not to lie anymore.

"I am of Alpha line."

"Line of?" Uden asked draining his second glass. He looked at the goblet in front of Erroh. "Drink," he ordered.

Erroh reached for the glass and sipped the warm sweet wine. He savoured the flavour and nodded his approval and thought of any way to lie without arousing any suspicion. After a moment, he shrugged. What was the harm?

"Magnus."

A flicker of emotion appeared across the gods face and swiftly disappeared.

"Does he still live?" he asked as if enquiring about an old friend.

"Aye,"

"Perhaps we'll meet someday," he said and tore into a fresh strip of beef.

"Have you been to the city?" Erroh asked, though he knew the answer already. The Woodin Man was also an Alphaline. An insane Alphaline declaring himself a god. Erroh had hoped that he would face a mindless barbarian with delusions of grandeur. Such a foe could be beaten but now he would face a master of the blade with a lifetime of experience. That was something else entirely. Erroh would put up a good fight but ultimately he knew his fate was sealed. No fine meal and sweet wine could replenish the strength he had lost while captive. Nomi had tried to prepare him. She was one of the finest people he'd ever met. So was his beloved Lea. He missed them both so much as he sat here waiting for the madman to finish his meal.

He hoped there was dessert.

The Woodin Man shook his head and smiled dangerously.

"I imagine my father will be waiting at the gates to give you the grand tour," Erroh said coldly.

"I do hope his Rangers will be waiting with him," the god said.

Everyone is going to die, Erroh thought again. Maybe he could attack him in this very room without so many watchful eyes. He looked at his plate. Maybe he could skewer him with a chicken bone. "What do you plan to do?" said Erroh.

The Woodin Man stopped ripping at his meat to laugh that croaky smug laugh. "I don't need to answer your questions, little cub."

Erroh slammed his fist down on the mahogany table. "Answer me, Alpha." His glass of wine toppled precariously and a few drops spilled across the polished surface. Erroh locked eyes with the god and refused to blink. He was a dead man either way, so he decided that insolence was the best card to play from here on.

"I like you, Erroh," he said and offered the bottle. "The words have said of what is to come. After the pain and fire there is paradise, and I will lead my people to it. The Spark is the shining beacon of decadence. Its tainted light blinds everyone but me. This started thousands of years ago, and these are the final days." He threw down the last chicken bone onto his plate.

Erroh chose his words carefully "You're a fuken lunatic," he said slowly and The Woodin Man laughed aloud once more.

"I wish you were one of my generals," Uden said shaking his head. "I'd have to rip your head off for showing such disrespect though. All gods are a little mad I suppose," he said standing up and staring at his beloved wall of scrolls. "Beautiful." He walked up behind Erroh's chair and placed his hands on Erroh's shoulders before he could react. Big, strong and fast. Wonderful.

He squeezed both of Erroh's shoulders with his powerful grip. "You tore one of my fingers apart so you're worthy to face me with a blade."

"What will be my fate when I beat you?" asked Erroh, though he was terrified.

"You may walk free," he whispered in Erroh's ear. The god pulled away and walked slowly to the wall. He ran his fingers along the line of capsules; they clicked delicately in the silence of the room. Uden closed his eyes in pleasure.

"You are no god Uden," said Erroh taking his glass of wine. "And a true feast would have included boar," he added, knowing well the second criticism would cut deep.

The god did not laugh this time.

"Every person whose life I touch is changed irrevocably." He faced Erroh and stared through him. "Can you claim as much, little one?"

"I do not claim to be a god," said Erroh. He began to feel a bout of coughing come upon him. He held his breath and waited for it to pass.

"It is time," Uden said with dreadful finality.

He led him from the chamber back out into the courtyard. It was a strange thing to know these were his last steps. And they were taken in the shadow of a terrifying madman.

"I see how fight will be," Uden said as he stepped out into the cold clear night. "Speed will serve you but it not enough," he said in the southern tongue. Erroh coughed in reply and followed the behemoth outside where night had fully fallen and the brightest lights were a dozen standing torches arranged in a large circle in the middle of the courtyard. Erroh wondered absently if such light could be seen all the way down at the bottom of the mountain range. Who would be watching at this late hour in this remote part of the world?

It was a small matter feeling this alone.

"Choose," Uden said before removing two swords hanging from the wall and checked their weight. Each silver blade was forged to perfection, untouched by battle and encrusted with dazzling blue sapphires. He swung each one casually and went through a few forms. Satisfied that they would gut the non-believer, he let each sword drop to his waist and waited at the edge of the flames. Oren and his

Riders stood outside the circle and watched on excitedly. Many chewed on meats or drank from wooden goblets. Only the best at their god's house.

He had the choice of at least a hundred weapons but none felt right in his hands. After an eternity, that was a handful of breaths to any other man, Erroh settled upon two mismatched swords. They were fine pieces but they were not anything like his own. Their weight was disproportioned or else his arms were weaker than before. He spun them in his wrists before stretching out. If the god wanted to fight, he would just have to wait a little longer.

"Die well, son of Magnus,"

"Go fuk yourself, Woodin man."

They faced each other in the circle. Erroh could hear the whispers of the many privileged Riders falling silent, and he thought about the Cull and those hidden eyes watching in excitement from behind the darkness. It was time for the sacrament of battle and another gospel given by their lord.

Goodbye Lea, I love you.

Goodbye Nomi, I owe you the world.

Erroh stood with his blades outstretched and tried desperately to calm his beating heart. Adrenaline surged through him and though his opponent stood a generous foot above him, he pledged to himself that he would at least scar the brute. It would likely be in the first few strikes, and Erroh might catch him off guard with a quick counter. It was a simple enough plan but of course, the cur made no move. He just stood placidly with each blade at his side awaiting Erroh's attack. Like a beast of prey ready to pounce on a little cub.

The Riders held their breaths. The moment was coming and everyone in the courtyard felt it.

Waiting.

What would Magnus do in this moment? He'd rip the fuker's head off and throttle the rest of the Riders with whatever limb was available. Erroh was not his father.

The tips of his blades betrayed him slightly as they shifted from their position. He thought he saw Uden smile. Bile churned in his stomach, and Erroh knew he had mere moments left. This battle would not take long. The Woodin Man finally blinked, and Erroh leapt forward.

All four blades clashed with violence and menace. Erroh going against everything his father had instructed when facing a stronger opponent, attacked relentlessly. Uden blocked and watched with emerald eyes every movement he made easily and met each strike. They thrashed back and forth in a terrifying display of skill and the Riders whooped and cheered for the fine spectacle. The mountain range echoed with each scream of hate from steel and their shadows danced in a menacing flow of beauty all along the mountain walls.

Erroh felt quicker than he thought possible as he hammered at the god with each strike. He dug into his reserves, threw everything into his strikes, and ignored the devastating fatigue, which began to grip each of his arms. Uden sensed this and struck back harder, but Erroh would not yield and, as the fight progressed, they met each other's strikes more evenly. The bigger man attempted and failed to grind him down, for having endured months in chains walking against his own will, a trivial thing such as exhaustion would not bring about Erroh's downfall.

It would be something else entirely.

They struggled for an age and Uden had to admit the little cub was the finest fighter he'd ever faced. He had assumed the clash would be over in the first few moments but the child was a wildfire. A handful of such creatures as fierce as this and any army could be defeated or indeed victorious. He wondered was he another demon sent to test him for there were many, but Uden had prevailed above them all. What if the child was of scriptures too? Such things were never realised until far too late. If he was, it was still the child's destiny to die at his godly hands this night. They locked blades and Uden pushed the little maniac back across the arena. He took a breath and realised how tired he had become. Foolish to let such a thing as breath get in the way of the kill. Perhaps this was what he had needed. A reminder of the trials he needed to face to bring his people through the fires into nirvana. He was humble to realise his shortcomings. It was the human in him. When he eventually dispatched with the child he would push himself further from this moment on. There would be difficult tests to face, in the many days ahead. Complacency had allowed his body to be ravaged by idleness.

The Riders watched in awe as their god scribed a new tale for his legacy. Some placed down their food and drink and dropped to their knees in silent worship while others watched with equal interest as the child matched the god with every blow.

Erroh was spent. All energy had left him yet somehow he still held his blades out in front of him. He wanted just one opening and then he'd be done. Sweat streamed down his forehead, and he retreated away from the bigger man.

"Come at me, god," he hissed through clenched teeth and beckoned the god smite him.

Uden struck.

He swung with all his rage and followed through with a slash that would fell any oak tree. Erroh weaved from the first but fell back awkwardly against the second. Losing balance, trying to deflect the next thrusting strikes, he fell back through the Riders and out of the ring. He crashed against one of the workbenches and collapsed amid wood pieces, metal shards, and iron tools. Uden knocked his Riders aside and fell upon the debris in search of the final attack. He leapt into the air, hacked down with two blades, and struck stone, as Erroh rolled clear.

He roared furiously as his quarry escaped and realised to his dismay that Erroh had countered as he rolled away. Somehow, the child had left a deep gash across his skin. Dismay turned to fury as he watched the blood stream from his shoulder, and he tore his shirt off. He heard his disciples curse and gasp at this unexpected turn, but he didn't care. All he cared about was the cub scrambling away.

"You think Uden bleeds like all man!" Uden shouted as the crimson drips fell to the ground below. Such a wound could greatly weaken any man given time.

"You bleed more than Erroh," Erroh hissed though he stepped backwards warily and coughed some phlegm onto the ground. Uden knew that patience would win the day, but he didn't care. He charged Erroh and struck with all he had, and he knocked one of the blades from his opponent's hand. To his dismay, the child simply changed his stance and continued on with just as much threat.

The Riders watched the actions of gods entangled in great conflict. They saw their own god unable to strike down the same terrible entity that had brought fire to them on the battlefield. A few wondered would they be rewarded or punished for delivering such a foe as an offering. Oren wondered, most of all.

They met one last time and struck at each other and neither gave ground. They were well matched, but they both knew Erroh would never stop until he died, while the god was losing too much blood. The tide turned and both knew there was something in the air. Uden stumbled and lost his sword and a moment after that was knocked to the ground.

And then tragedy occurred.

As if Erroh's body had waited until there was a reprieve in the violence, Erroh took a deep breath before attacking again and his cough took hold. His lungs tightened up, and he began to gasp. He collapsed to his knees and coughed desperately for air but none reached his aching lungs. Darkness filled his vision and Uden composed himself.

How very fortunate, the god thought.

"How very human," the god said and kicked the blade from Erroh's grasp and the crowd cheered. The loud crash of Erroh's lost sword carried in the wind as it clattered to the ground. Uden was a merciful god, and he allowed the tainted cub to catch his breath before he sent him into the darkness. It was a grand fight, and the son of Magnus deserved one last breath before the end.

It wasn't fair. All the blood spilled and it ended here over a fuken cough. He had almost touched victory. He felt the first delicious wisps of airflow into his exhausted lungs but it offered little joy. His mind was reeling towards insanity. Everything had been for nothing.

A cough.

It would make quite the story if ever told.

The pathetic son of Magnus almost saving the entire world but faltering because of a little chest cough.

It was a sick jest, and Erroh lost his mind completely.

He started to laugh as The Woodin Man neared with a blade raised. Of course, it would end like this. How could it not possibly end like this?

"You didn't see that did you?" Erroh mocked as his vanquisher stood over him. Then he coughed a few times and then he laughed a little more. A few Riders had heard of this famous laughter, though they'd never seen it for themselves. One of them had, and he thought it ominous and unnerving.

"Kill him, Uden!" Oren shouted suddenly.

"Fall silent, cub," the god said, and Erroh faced him. He did not fall silent and Uden picked him up and threw him violently through another workbench. Hammers and tongs fell all around him, and Erroh kept laughing.

"What else did you see with those pretty eyes?" Erroh shrieked hysterically.

"I see that you will die." He smashed his fist into Erroh's face to stop the laughing. Erroh just took the punch and crawled away on his hands and feet. Blood poured from his nose and mouth but still he laughed manically.

Uden tossed aside his blade and removed a great battle-axe from the wall of weapons.

"Your head will be a great treasure," he growled. He stood over Erroh and took a deep breath. Erroh stopped moving below him and let his final thoughts warm him. He looked up and stared into the eyes of his executioner. He wondered would his father avenge his death. His father would have struck this beast down, but he was not his father. The

Woodin Man took a breath and whispered gently "I will not remember you."

He wished he was in Lea's arms now. He wished he was not going to die alone on this frozen peak. He wished he could have avenged the young boy. He wished he could have lived up to the mantle of Hero of Keri. He wished he was his father. The Woodin Man began to swing the heavy axe down upon Erroh's exposed neck.

Erroh was not his father.

But he was his father's son.

With one last twist of his body, he rolled and heard the heavy thud of sharpened blade embedding itself in the ground. He didn't think. He just leapt and the god caught him in his powerful arms but stumbled backwards under the weight of them both. Erroh dug his fingers into the face of the giant and heard himself scream. A howl louder than thunder in the sky and then he realised the god screamed with him. His fingers ripped into flesh, and he gripped and pulled. Uden collapsed backwards holding his hands over a deep hole where one of his eyes used to be. His scream was godly. Erroh had to give him that.

Riders panicked and lumbered in all directions. Some to help the fallen god, while others to grab hold of Erroh who now ran free. Others just watched in reverence as different scripture was written in front of their eyes.

Erroh fell back against the courtyard wall still gripping the gelatinous blob in his hand. It would be rude to drop it. He retreated from the mayhem and his foot touched the end of his chains.

He had a plan.

A simple plan that would never work.

Still, fuk it, he was going to try.

Oren reached him first and tackled him at the ledge above

the massive drop. He cursed, struggled, and received a freshly broken nose for his troubles from Erroh's forehead. He fell to his knees squealing; Erroh wrapped the chain around his neck, and looking out over the drop, he hoped he had a terrible estimation of heights.

"Uden!" he roared and held Oren with a firm grasp on the chain. The Riders in pursuit slowed at the sight of Oren in peril. Behind them, their god moaned, wailed, and pushed away those who attempted to assist him.

With his one remaining eye, Uden watched in horror as the son of Magnus placed his eye into his mouth, bit down and swallowed. Then Erroh slipped from the ledge into nothing below.

He crashed against the cliff side with the chain wrapped around his wrist. Each time he kicked out a little and let the ripping metal slip through his grip. How many feet would it afford him? He didn't know. He hoped his weight wouldn't break the neck of Oren. A limp body without any fight would send him cascading into the nothing below.

Above him in the light, he heard the cacophony of the Woodin Man's enraged screams and of many Riders holding a suffocating Oren from death. He dropped a few more feet, the chain halted suddenly, and Erroh hung in darkness. He closed his eyes and imagined he could hear the raging waters below. Perhaps it was a blessing that there was nothing to see but blackness. The chain creaked from his weight as he swayed gently and then it started to rise. They were pulling him back up.

He took a final breath and let go. It was a good night to die.

Falling.

He did not scream. He was free. If he died, he would die a free man. It was the little things.

He crashed into the water and went straight down. The pain in his body was overwhelming. Unable to see a thing he tried desperately to rise but the current held him in its grasp. It pulled and dragged, and he was twisted upside down. The freezing water tried to strangle away all life from him, and he never imagined anything as cold as this. The first of the water he swallowed took the remaining air he had in his aching lungs, but he didn't panic, even when the river pulled him to the bottom and dragged him along like a discarded piece of wood. And like wood, he resurfaced and was dragged further along. He passed through rapids and tasted their cruelty. He heard his name screamed out and wondered why his mind deceived him so. He was tossed violently, and he could do little more than be taken with it. He struggled yet still he did not panic. Blindly he was suddenly thrashed against a massive boulder, and he felt a rib snap. A few moments later he was battered against another, yet somehow he stayed above water. He never knew how long he was at the river's mercy but in the end, when it could do no more harm, the menacing water settled and after one last painful drop, he found himself floating through a deep creek on his back looking up at the stars, and he thought how this was a fine way to die. He held his breath, for breathing hurt more than dying. He stared at the shattered moon above and wagered that Uden would know the reason for its appearance. He let its bright light shine across his face, and he began counting the stars. He heard his name again and wondered if Aireys was calling him home. Too many miles walked and now it was time to close his eyes and sleep. His body would indeed be dragged for miles. Perhaps forever.

"Tired," he whispered to the wind as he let his head slip

beneath the waters. Panic only barely struck him as he sank to the bottom. His body reeled and tried to fight, but he fought his own survival. His limbs thrashed, and he heard himself scream and then Lea was beside him.

She gripped him tightly and somehow dragged him to the riverbank. With the last of her strength, she pulled him free of the water before falling to her knees and gasping for air. How many miles had she sprinted?

He knew he was dreaming or at least hallucinating and it was beautiful. She was breathing deeply and shaking from the cold, and he thought this was beautiful too. They lay beside each other for a precious few moments catching their breaths. He reached with one shaking hand and gently caressed her cheek. She looked far more tired than he'd ever seen her, as though she'd walked a thousand miles through treacherous conditions all alone. She held her hand against his, and she closed her eyes as she felt his touch.

Lea looked down upon her shattered mate and thanked the gods. She allowed herself a few breaths to take him in. A long walk. Such a heartbreakingly long walk. Her Erroh. Only hers. She smiled warmly and pulled him to his unsteady feet. Her eyes narrowed to the only manmade light in the night. Light that could be seen for miles.

"We have to move, my beo," she whispered.

HERE ENDS THE FIRST BOOK OF THE SPARK CITY
CYCLE.
THE STORY WILL CONTINUE WITH
"THE MARCH OF MAGNUS"

Get The March of Magnus here

THANK YOU FOR READING SPARK CITY

Word-of-mouth is crucial for any author to succeed and honest reviews of my books help to bring them to the attention of other readers.

If you enjoyed the book, and have 2 minutes to spare, please leave an honest review on Amazon. Even if it's just a sentence or two it would make all the difference and would be very much appreciated.

Thank you.

GET EXCLUSIVE MATERIAL FROM ROBERT J POWER

When you join the Robert J Power Readers' Club you'll get the latest news on the Spark City and Dellerin series, free books, exclusive content and new release updates.

You'll also get a short tale exclusive to members- you can't get this anywhere else!

Conor and The Banshee
Fear the Banshee's Cry

Join at www.RobertJPower.com

ALSO BY ROBERT J POWER

The Spark City Cycle:

Spark City, Book 1

The March of Magnus, Book 2

———

The Dellerin Tales:

The Crimson Collection

The Crimson Hunters, vol I

The Crimson Hunted, vol II

The Lost Tales of Dellerin:

The Seven

ABOUT THE AUTHOR

Robert J Power is the fantasy author of the Amazon bestselling series, The Spark City Cycle and The Dellerin Tales. When not locked in a dark room with only the daunting laptop screen as a source of light, he fronts Irish rock band, Army of Ed, despite their many attempts to fire him.

Robert lives in Wicklow, Ireland with his wife Jan, two rescue dogs and a cat that detests his very existence. Before he found a career in writing, he enjoyed various occupations such as a terrible pizza chef, a video store manager (ask your grandparents), and an irresponsible camp counsellor. Thankfully, none of them stuck.

If you wish to learn of Robert's latest releases, his feelings on The Elder Scrolls, or just how many coffees he consumes a day before the palpitations kick in, visit his website at www. RobertJPower.com where you can join his reader's club. You might even receive some free goodies, hopefully some writing updates, and probably a few nonsensical ramblings.

www.RobertJPower.com

facebook.com/authorrobertjpower

twitter.com/RobertJPower

instagram.com/RobertJPower

ACKNOWLEDGMENTS

Thank you to Poll for praising and challenging me and somehow getting through the first draft with your sanity intact.

Thank you, Jill, for finding all the good in the mess of the draft after that.

Thank you to my editor, Richard, who took the tenth draft and told me to start all over again. I think that helped.

Thank you, Nine Arrow, for the incredible artwork.

Thank you, Cathbar, for reminding me to take a breath and appreciate what I'd done when it all got too much.

Thank you, Bren, for building the world with me with a few epic beats. Don't tell anybody how it all turns out.

And for the kindness of Jim who was the first warrior to fall in battle. I hope someday I become half the writer you were.

Printed in Poland
by Amazon Fulfillment
Poland Sp. z o.o., Wrocław

62708110R00312